To J

THE WITCH AND THE FAITHLESS

POLLY J. MORDANT

Polly J Mordant

Sigilhouse

Created with Vellum

For my Family

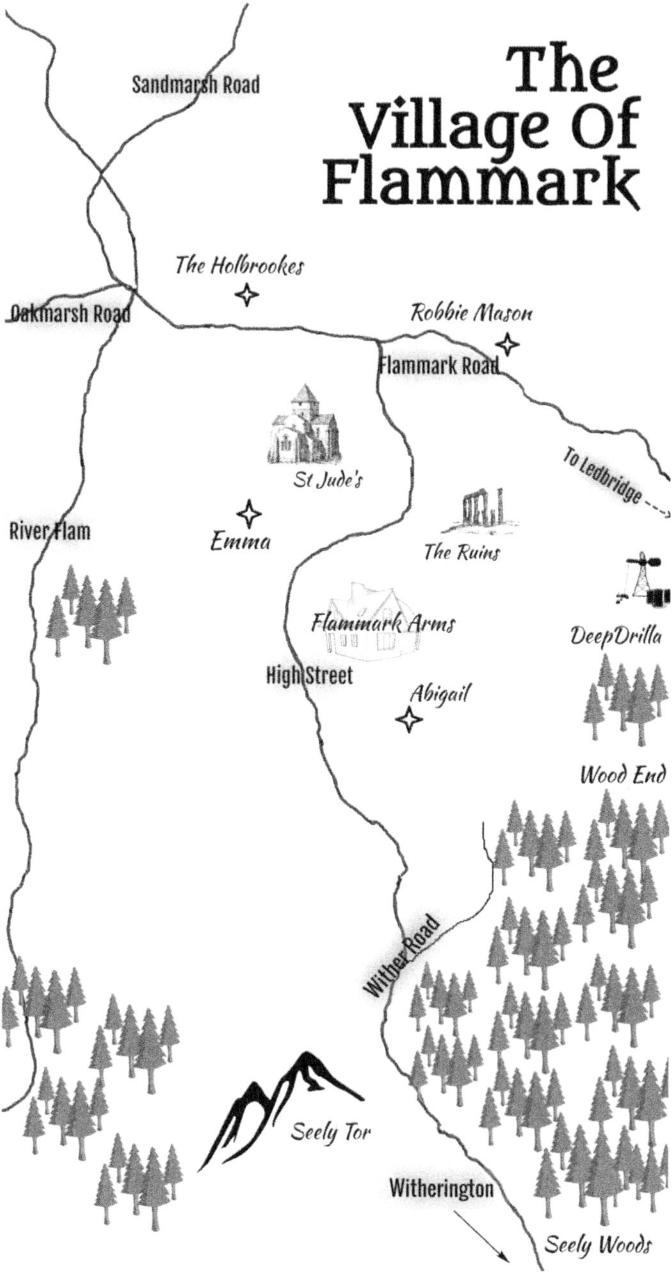

The Village Of Flammark
Sandmarsh Road
The Holbrookes
Oakmarsh Road
Robbie Mason
Flammark Road
St Jude's
To Ledbridge
Emma
River Flam
The Ruins
DeepDrilla
Flammark Arms
High Street
Abigail
Wood End
Wither Road
Seely Tor
Witherington
Seely Woods

I

A DELIVERY

Scratching.

Like nails on a blackboard. On Emma's front door. Loud enough to hear it from her bedroom.

In the middle of teasing out her wiry hair, getting ready to go out, she paused her hand. Froze. Peered sightlessly at her reflection in the dressing table mirror, every nerve strung tight.

What the hell was going down *now*?

The sound again. Grating. Louder.

Not to be ignored.

The last thing Emma wanted was to investigate, yet she rose and made for the stairs, wincing at the creaking of her door. Because people do, don't they? Like in the movies, where the lone heroine ventures down to the cellar or out into the night to suss out the noise made by her killer. Why the hell did they go? Why the hell was she going? Why not call the police?

Because it's only some scratching. Probably an animal—or a prank. And because the only policeman you'd call would overreact and drop everything, despite being knee-deep in a cluster of graves filled with the bodies of dead teenagers.

She reached the living room, its only light emanating from a small lamp in the corner, dim and suddenly eerie. The noise stopped. Emma froze again, straining her ears.

"Who's there?"

Nothing.

No one.

She edged to the window and slowly pushed aside a slat of the vertical blind. Closing her eyes in a silent offering to whatever god might be listening, she opened them again to peep out at who'd been grinding the hell out of her front door.

Nothing.

The garden lay empty too. She widened the gap and peered out at her little jeep in the driveway, then to the garden path that wound its way to the gate. Rimed with frost, the world glistened in the bright moonlight. All seemed quiet enough. Heart thumping a little easier, Emma stepped slowly to the door.

She stopped to ponder at the bolts, her hand on the cross around her neck, weighing the need to know who it was against the horror of finding out. But she couldn't call Westen, and she was damn-well not going to spend the rest of the night holed up in fear.

That time had passed.

Not quite ready to open up, she crept into the kitchen without turning on the light and peered out of that window too. Nothing out there—at least as far as she could make out. Making a half-turn, she slid out the cutlery drawer and found a small, sharp vegetable knife.

Carried it back with her to the front door.

Taking a deep breath, she slowly drew back the first of the

three bolts then turned the key in the lock. Another breath and she opened the door a crack. Then a little more.

And relief. Nobody there.

But she needed to be sure. She flipped on the outside security lights—one click for both front and back—and grasping her weapon, made a slow and hesitant circuit of the house then down the path to the gate.

Nothing.

Only then did she relax a notch. Not completely, though. She still held the knife in a death grip.

Shivering, annoyed, Emma retraced her steps back to the cottage. Must have been a fox or something. Her teeth started to chatter. It was minus five or thereabouts and with no coat—wearing only slippers too—what had she been thinking?

But on reaching the door, she came to a full stop and grasped the knife even tighter, so hard she felt her fingernails bite in.

Deep gouges scored their way through the lower half of the door, tearing its red paint so deeply they'd splintered the wood beneath. And they had a pattern. Emma crouched and placed her palm against them, their intervals matching almost exactly the finger spans of her own hand.

A shout rent the air, scaring her to her feet.

"Emma!"

The voice came only seconds before the girl that possessed it flung herself at the gate and fumbled at the latch. "Oh, thank God!" cried Abigail. "Are you okay?"

"I think so. But why… ? How are you here?"

"You tell me! I was at Gran's. We were just chatting when I heard—no, felt—this weird noise." She shuddered. "It set my teeth on edge. I knew it came from here."

"Well, you're not wrong. What you felt were these." She pointed at the damage. "Look!"

"Wow," said Abigail, falling to her knees, splaying her fingers over the marks in the same way Emma had done. "Did you see who did it?"

"No. I'd started to hope it was someone playing a stupid game or something. But your arrival's put paid to that." She pulled her arms around her, her shivers more extreme. "You're getting good at this Sight thing, Abby. I'm glad it brought you here. I don't want to call Westen."

"Why not? He might be a superintendent now, but you know he'd come in a heartbeat."

"Let's carry this on inside. I'm freezing."

Emma held the door and ushered her friend in before closing and bolting it again. "Why don't you take your coat off and put the kettle on? I'll throw a log on the fire and get a cardie."

Ten minutes later the two of them were sat on Emma's shabby-chic sofa, the smell of peppermint from the girl's cup beating hands-down the coffee aroma from hers. In fact, for some reason she couldn't bring herself to drink it.

"Spill, then," said Abigail. "Why aren't you ringing Westen?"

"He's a lot on his plate. He's got a massive case on. You know, at Seely Woods."

"Oh, my God, yes!" Abigail's eyes widened. "The village is full of it. How many girls have they found so far... five? All buried alive? It's awful." She frowned and nodded to the door. "But this isn't good either, Ems. I don't like that it caught my attention the way it did. You might not be safe. Westen wouldn't care what case he's on. Call him. Maybe you should stay at his flat."

Emma shook her head. "I'm supposed to be meeting Robbie for a drink at the Flammark Arms. Gabby's coming too. I'll stick to the plan. Whoever did that's gone now." She picked up her cup and, sniffing it, put it down again.

"Besides," she said, wryly, "If Flammark's taught me anything, it's that running away from its weirdness solves absolutely nothing."

"I suppose," Abigail replied. "Still don't like it, though, and it doesn't mean you have to face stuff alone."

Emma glanced at the clock on the shelf and flinched at the time. "Well, whoever did it is obviously gone now, and I refuse to sit and dwell about it. I'll decide whether to call Westen later." She got up. "In the meantime, why don't you come with me to the pub? I don't think you've seen Robbie for ages, have you?"

"No. Or Gabby, for that matter. I've been busy getting through my exams."

"Of course!" said Emma. "I completely forgot! You'll soon be a fully qualified hairdresser! All the more reason for you to celebrate!"

Abigail grinned then drained her cup. "Okay. You get your coat. I'll have a last look round. To be sure."

Emma nodded and headed for her bedroom leaving Abigail to unbolt the door. Hearing it close behind her, she threw the mirror one final glance before grabbing her cherry-red duffel to make her way downstairs. Giving the living room a quick once-over, she shrugged on the coat and opened the door.

There was something on the step.

She cocked her head. Frowned. It couldn't have been there before, she'd have noticed earlier when she examined the scratches. As would Abigail.

Jerking her head up, she scanned the tiny garden, then craned her neck to peer past the jeep over to the green. Useless. Too dark. How could the thing have possibly got there? While Abigail was round the back maybe? She knelt and picked it up. By the look and feel of it she thought it might be a bird's nest, though it seemed flimsier, less solid than that. She'd never seen anything quite like it. What at first it seemed a mess of roughly woven twigs, closer scrutiny revealed they'd been delicately hewn into a flattish circle. Like a wreath. Still crouching—and somehow mesmerised—she ran her finger over its intricate tracery.

And smiled.

Abigail appeared from the side gate. "You ready? I've had a scout around. No sign of anyone."

Her words cut short Emma's fascination. Saying nothing, shielding the wreath from sight, she hastily slipped it into her shoulder bag and clambered up to slam shut her injured front door.

"Coming!"

2

GANG MEETING

After a brisk fifteen-minute walk the two friends reached the Flammark Arms. "So, are we here for any particular reason?" asked Abigail, "Or is it just a work's night out?"

Emma managed a half-hearted laugh. "Just a catch up. Possibly. Robbie and Gabby have been thick as thieves lately so I think something might be brewing."

"The Scooby Gang together once more!" Abigail proclaimed, mixing her allusions by affecting a superhero pose.

"Not quite."

Abigail's face fell. "No. You're right. Still nothing from Will?

"Nope. Nada." She shrugged and grinned to lighten the tone. "And I not sure I like the Buffy reference, by the way. Even Westen's started to call us that!"

"Seriously?" chortled Abigail. "I had no idea he was a fan!"

Ignoring her, Emma stepped into the pub's fairy-lit porch. She frowned at the sprigs of mistletoe dangling over the entrance to the main bar. She hated mistletoe, redolent of those unsolicited advances at the office not too far back in the day when men felt they could appropriate whatever female caught their eye—if only for a moment. Or in her case, longer.

She shuddered and pointed up at it. "Why hasn't the landlord got rid of this? We saw the new year in over a week ago!"

Abigail gave her a quizzical look. "Nothing wrong with a bit of all-healer. It's an ancient remedy, you know, and a ward ... to stop unwelcome spirits from entering. Some of the older villagers keep it up all the time, though it's the first time I've seen Ken do it. Maybe he just forgot to take it down."

The bar was quiet. Very quiet—and it wasn't for lack of people. In fact, there were more than usual present for a mid-week night, but no one seemed to be talking. The murders, of course. The community was in shock about the discoveries in the woods—and frightened, no doubt. Full of questions.

Emma scanned the room and spied Robbie and Gabby in a relatively secluded corner. They didn't notice her; their heads were bowed close to each other, deep in conversation.

"My shout, what're you drinking?" asked Emma.

"Erm ... cranberry juice, please, spritzed with bitter lemon."

Smiling apologetically at the barman, Emma ordered the concoction together with a fizzy water for herself. She didn't fancy anything stronger despite what'd happened earlier.

Thinking about it brought her mind back to the twig-wreath in her bag and, since Abigail mentioned him, to Will and the fact that he wouldn't be there for her, at the vicarage, lending an ear while they pondered over what it might mean.

Since he left them over six months ago, there hadn't been a single day she hadn't thought about him—where he was;

what he was doing. Whether he'd be coming back. Whether he'd forgiven her?

She thought it unlikely, given that he hadn't been I touch.

Drinks in hand they moved over to the corner. Robbie spotted them and stood up, a huge smile bursting all over his bearded face as he drew back two chairs.

Gabby was grinning too. "Emma! And Abigail, too! Lovely to see you! It seems ages since we all got together!" She gave Emma an admonishing glance. "I keep hoping to see you at St Jude's."

"Yes, well. I haven't felt up to a service after Will left. I did go once. They've got a female priest to replace him, haven't they? She seemed competent enough, I suppose. I didn't really have the heart for staying much longer than the sermon. It just wasn't the same without him." She sipped her water. "But you should pop over to Clearview. I'm usually in on a Sunday!"

"I know, I know. But Wyland's been away for a few months. He's gone to America on a woodsman's course. He told you his plans, didn't he, Abigail?"

The girl nodded. "Emma knows all about it. And his ideas for the caravan park when he gets back. He's already got rid of a lot them, hasn't he?"

"He has," Gabby replied. "He'll be building a workshop when he gets back and wants to start a business. *From Tree to Table* is going to be its—oh, what do they call it?—its strapline! He hadn't been able to travel before I came along. You know how..." her eyes flitted uncertainly to Robbie, "...tied to the land he is. It's why I've not been around much. I'm taking over for a while. Keeping the watch, you know."

Oh, they knew right enough.

Pleasantries over, they settled in, chatting and catching up. After a lull, Robbie looked around the room. "Grim business out in the woods. Emma. Everyone's feeling it, you can see by their faces."

"I know," Emma replied. "Believe me, the police are feeling this one too. Westen's sickened by it. Needless to say, they're going to pull out all the stops."

"Do they know who they were, yet?" said Abigail. "Were the girls all local?"

"Westen said they haven't been identified," said Emma. "Anything more, I can't say. I probably shouldn't have said even that!" Her eyes flitted to the other tables. "Can we change the subject? Why don't you tell me why I'm here."

Robbie pressed his lips together and sighed. "It seems a bit petty now in view of what's happened, but—"

Gabby interrupted. "It's Will's replacement. Sandra." She separated the syllables. *San Dra.* It sounded like a mockery.

"Sandra Davis? What's up with her? Her sermon was a bit on the dry side, I suppose, but okay—"

"Okay? *Okay?*" blurted Robbie. "The woman is a bloody catastrophe! An unmitigated disaster!"

Wow.

"Why?" said Emma, taken aback by the outburst. "Because she's a female priest?"

"Don't be ridiculous, woman. I'm a woke man!"

Emma couldn't help but chuckle. "Oh, God, Robbie. There's so much wrong with that statement, I hardly know where to start!"

"Woke?" said Gabby. "What does that mean?"

"To be honest," he replied, "I don't have a bloody clue. All the GPs in the Sandmarsh Health Trust are being made to attend what they choose to call 'sensitivity training.' Woke came up. A damned lot. According to some of the attendees, I am, apparently, a dinosaur. They attempted to educate me." He harrumphed. "I'm not that bad, am I, Emma? The patients like me, do they not?"

"I've not had any complaints, Robbie, if that's what you mean," she said, chortling again. "And yes, most of your patients do like you. Except Mrs Holt, of course."

"That wasn't my fault. I call all the ladies *dear*. The silly woman had absolutely no grounds to take any offence!"

Emma put her glass down, shaking her head and rolling her eyes at him. "*Silly woman? Ladies?!* Tch, you should take the course again, Robbie! Seriously, it matters."

"So what's the deal with this Sandra?" Abigail asked. "Why is she a disgrace?"

"Our new incumbent has plans," said Robbie. "Big plans. I wouldn't mind, but she's only temporary."

"Good," said Abigail. "Obviously, I'm not into the church thing, but we all want Will back. Glad to hear he hasn't been completely replaced yet."

"It's only a matter of time before he will be, though," said Gabby. "*San Dra* is only here on a trial basis—for a year—but if members of the PCC are happy with her at the end of that, and Will hasn't asked if he can return, the bishop will make moves to install her as our parish priest. Permanently."

"Sorry," said Abigail. "PCC?"

"The Parochial Church Council." Emma replied. Then, winking at Robbie, she said, "Will used to call it the mafia!"

"Ohhh. Right."

"Seriously though, vicars can't just do what they want, can they?" Emma continued. "Don't they have to get approval from the PCC for any big changes? That said, Will did get most of his way."

"Because William had the best interests of St Jude's at heart and they knew it," said Gabby. Then added as an afterthought, "And *every*body liked him."

"Well, the bishop must think there's a possibility he might return," Emma said, her heart beating a little faster, "otherwise why wait?"

Robbie glanced at Gabby. "He isn't optimistic. Will handed in his resignation. I'm sorry, lass."

Emma's heart lurched. No. *No.*

Robbie must have read her expression. "It's alright, no need to panic just yet. As I'm the mafia head, the bishop called me in to discuss ways forward for St Jude's. That's when he told me about Will's resignation. He also said he wouldn't be accepting it. At least not yet. He blames himself for Will's situation, you see. Remember, it was he who gave us St Saviour. He's emailed Will to come in and discuss his future, but he hasn't replied yet."

"Yes. Frederick Thomas has to bear some of the weight for what happened last year," said Emma. "Though I don't suppose we can expect him to take all the responsibility. Westen said he'd had made all the necessary background checks, but that Thomas' PA had falsified his employment history." She didn't say any more. Couldn't tell Robbie about Animus and his evil given that everyone thought him a mere terrorist. The repercussions spoke for themselves in the wonderful memorial Wyland had installed for all the victims of that terrible day.

Abigail must have been thinking along the same lines. "How did Wyland get the resources to landscape the Deep-Drilla site? Transporting those bluestones must have cost a fortune."

"He got a government grant," Gabby answered. "Massive, it was, but the least it could do considering it was Deep-Drilla's main sponsor. But it took its toll on Wyland. It's why he decided on the trip to the States. He was exhausted."

"Getting back to Will," Robbie continued, "since he's been gone for over six months, the bishop is going to have to make a decision soon, especially as Sandra Davis has given him a proposal he's finding very hard to refuse."

"Proposal?" asked Abigail.

Exchanging glances with Gabby, Robbie blew out an exasperated sigh. "She wants to sell off the vicarage."

Abigail choked on her drink. Emma's heart missed a full beat.

Dumbstruck, she turned to Robbie, "S-sell off the vicarage? She can't do that, surely? For a start, it's not hers to sell and ... and it's part of Flammark's heritage!" Not to mention a huge chunk of her own ancestry, some great cousins a million times removed, once having the living.

"She doesn't think it's right that a *'modern vicar'*—" Gabby's voice took on a passing resemblance to what Emma remembered as Sandra's tone, "should be living in such a large house. Not when there are more *'pressing ministries to concern ourselves with.'*"

"But ... but ... what about the library?" said Emma.

"And the conference facilities! All the heritage work ..." Abigail's face was livid.

Robbie nodded. "I know. Will's passion. He was dedicated to the history of the village and to the church's ancient origins. Without losing a moment's sleep, he could organise retreats, historical conferences, talk to the TV people, tourists ... Now that's all gone."

"What do you mean, 'all gone?'" asked Emma. "Will was —is—the perfect fit for all that. He made St. Jude's the tourist centre it is, for God's sake, as well as being a fantastic parish priest."

"You don't have to tell me that, lass. He helped me to get over Joanie, after she died." Robbie paused, shaking his head before pulling from his pint. Putting his glass down, he folded his arms and leant in. "The bishop has had to ensure some continuity, so he gave all the heritage stuff to Solomon Barnes. He's a retired archaeologist of some standing. I've known him for years. He lives in Sandmarsh—near the cathedral, actually. Brilliant man. He discovered Tiny Barrow, the burial ground on the other side of Seely Tor. I can't think of a better choice to take over that side of things while Will's away. It suits him, he's been bored out of his skull since he retired from the lecture circuit. He uses the cathedral as a base and organises the tours and so on, from there."

Emma felt afraid to move, as if the slightest tremble would bring more of her world down.

Robbie continued. "Plan was, he'd give it all back to Will once he returned."

"But *now*..." Gabby didn't finish her sentence. Just shook her head in mock despair.

"I still don't understand," said Emma. "What's that got to do with selling the vicarage? And what are these 'other pressing ministries?'"

"Sandra," (*San Dra*), "wants to persuade the bishop to bring forward her installation so she can get stuck into what she calls her youth ministry."

"Okaaaay ... Nothing wrong with that," said Emma, shrugging cautiously.

"Isn't there? Have either of you been down to the church's undercroft?" asked Robbie.

"What's an undercroft?" asked Abigail.

"It's like a cellar," said Gabby. She turned to Robbie and slapped him on the arm. "Why do you have to be so pompous. No one calls these things undercrofts anymore."

"Don't they?" said Robbie. "Well, I don't know why. It's a perfectly respectable word. Perhaps it's not woke enough?"

"Oh, for God sake stop squabbling," said Emma. "People are looking at you. And it's hardly the time, is it?" Everything was going pear-shaped again. The murders, the visitation she'd just had, and now it looked like she might be losing Will for good! Almost in tears, she recalled the door just inside the church porch, from where Will appeared the very first time they'd met. He'd emerged swearing, having tried and failed to fix the boiler. She'd never forgotten that moment; it marked the start of the journey to getting her life back.

But Robbie was on a roll and seemed only partially unbowed by Emma's outburst. "The *undercroft*," he said, lowering his voice and giving Gabby a hard stare, "is hardly a *cellar!* It's a big space. Runs the entire length of the church."

"Aren't there bodies buried there?" Abigail piped up. "You know, old saints and stuff?"

Gabby gave a tipsy chortle. "Flammark never did saints … except for Jude, obviously. Can't think why."

Ignoring her, Robbie said, "No. No bodies. It houses the church's heating system and there's centuries of discarded stuff down there. Old pews and suchlike. Some of its quite valuable."

"Sorry, Robbie," said Emma, her impatience rising by the minute. "I'm not making the link between this and the vicarage having to be sold."

He sighed into his beer. "The Reverend Davis wants to turn it into a youth space. Clear it out. Sort out the damp and put in some lighting, buy the usual sort of equipment; table tennis … that kind of thing. She wants to have … oh, I don't know … what do they call discos nowadays?"

"Club nights," said Abigail. "There's one in Sandmarsh. It's called *Diesel* for dance nights then they tweak the decoration and call it *GrimAce* for the Goths. Lots of places do it."

"Never mind all that," said Gabby. "Sandra had the basement surveyed. Big space like that, it'll cost over a hundred thousand pounds to get it completely renovated and that's before they've done the surveys. My guess the final estimate will come to a whole lot more."

Abigail let out a low whistle. "Really? That much?"

"I'm afraid so," said Robbie. "The floor needs levelling, the ceiling fixed and it's very, very damp. Being a listed building means specialist contractors using specialist materials. And as I said, it's huge. Sandra's already started clearing it." He stared at them gloomily. "The diocese has no money. The woman has been very clever. She's costed everything and has suggested it should sell off most of the vicarage to pay for the work. It'd cover the cost and then some. They'd pocket the change to fund other social justice projects. Even I have to admit, it's an easy sell for a cash-strapped system in need of good PR." Robbie paused then slumped. "I know I'm being cynical. Obviously, the church shouldn't be hanging on to assets it can't and shouldn't support. There's a world of need out there. It's just..."

"Go on," said Abigail.

Gabby cut in. "We think she's doing it for the wrong reasons. Sandra's ambitious."

"Ambitious?" said Abigail. "What do you mean?"

"It's a big project," Robbie replied. "It has ... excited the bishop. She's already suggested to him that if her mission is successful they could expand its reach and get other dioceses involved."

"Oh, I see," said Abigail. "And she'd head it up?"

"Exactly," Gabby said, giving big nods.

Emma went cold. "But ... but whatever the reason behind it may be, getting rid of the vicarage means—" She couldn't complete the sentence. Couldn't *think*.

"You're finally there, lass," said Robbie. "Should the bishop take on board Sandra's plans he'd be minded to accept Will's resignation and there'd be zero chance of him ever returning. It would be irrevocable. Even if Sandra moved on after a few years there'd be nothing here to tempt him back. The library—the conference facilities—they would all have disappeared. She plans to divide the vicarage into three dwellings: one affordable and made available to the sitting priest. The other two are to be renovated to luxury standard and sold off. Sandra's already got an architect friend to produce computerised mock-ups which have really impressed the bishop. I've seen them. The sale would indeed make a pretty penny and would more than cover the cost of the basement conversion."

"Are you sure the diocese would go along with all this?" said Emma. "Surely it can't all be up to the bishop?"

"Well, no. There is a Diocessian ... Diascian ..."

"Gabby, are you drunk?" said Robbie, turning round and glaring at her. "Because if so, you certainly choose your moments!"

"No." Gabby replied, fixing her face straight.

"Oh, for pity's sake," Robbie said, rolling his eyes. Turning to Emma and Abigail, he continued. "What Gabby's *trying* to say is there's a diocesan synod. He's already consulted with them and they're prepared to give the go-ahead. Why wouldn't they? The church is under massive pressure both to sell off its assets and work more with young people. God knows, no one else is opening their pockets for them." As he talked, he took Gabby's nearly empty wine glass and placed it beyond her reach. "I think the bishop's on board. That's why we believe Will may not be coming back. Worse, if he doesn't hear from him in a few weeks, he told me he might have *bring forward* Sandra's installation. Apparently, the synod wants to approve her plans. Will's incumbency is the only thing that's preventing it. And as he doesn't seem inclined to get back to the bishop over his resignation—well, things don't look promising for him. Or for us."

"They might put everything on hold," said Abigail. "You know, with the murders and all that."

"No," said Robbie. "I don't think so. This is a two-year project and it's only in the preliminary stages. Besides, what's happened in the woods is about children. I wouldn't put it past the Reverend Davis to make some sort of political capital out of it. You wait and see!

Emma looked at her friends with absolute horror, eyes suddenly welling. She'd never faced full-on the possibility that Will might never forgive her—forgive them—always believing he'd bounce back somehow. It would be a heartrending and difficult reunion, but they'd work through it. Over time, their deep—no their *profound* friendship—would be restored. At least, that's what she imagined would happen. And if Robbie was to be believed, his replacement sounded horrendous.

It felt like a punishment.

She reached for her bag and rummaged for a tissue. Her fingers brushed the twiggy surface of the thing she'd found on the doorstep. It made her miss Will even more. She yearned to show it to him; to tell of its mysterious appearance. It wasn't as if she could share her discovery with Westen ... And Gabby was in no condition to be told about it now.

Though she wasn't sure why she hadn't told Abigail.

Still worrying at it with her fingers, her thoughts were interrupted by Robbie. "We wanted to ask you something, Emma."

"Okay ... ?"

"Would you pay Sandra a visit? See what you make of her?"

"You mean befriend her? Pump her for information?" She almost laughed out loud. "From what you've told me, there'd be fat chance of that."

"We can't get a proper handle on the woman," said Gabby. "Shomthing's *off* about her." An observation that caused everyone except Robbie to grin. Even Emma, despite herself.

Why not meet Sandra? Couldn't do any harm and she'd

like to get the measure of her. See what they were up against. "Okay. There's an evensong tomorrow. I'll see if I can get her to chat afterwards." Her hand still in her bag, she fingered the twiggy thing yet again before reaching for her purse. "Now, my round. What do people want?"

"Very kind of you, Emma," said Robbie. "I'll have my usual. Gabby will have a lemonade."

"I thought you were a woke man," said Abigail. "Let her have another glass of wine, silly. You'll be taking her home, won't you?"

"No. She can stay with me," said the doctor, shaking his head disapprovingly. "If she behaves herself..."

Emma and Abigail went to the bar leaving Gabby to the castigations of the good doctor. "She's becoming quite the party girl, isn't she?" said Abigail. "Robbie'll have to give her some lessons on holding her drink!"

Emma made no reply.

"You alright, Ems? You look a bit ... pale. We haven't had a chance to talk about earlier. Have you decided what to do? I can stay over if you like."

"No," Emma replied—too quickly. She took a deep breath. "I'll be fine, really. I'm just a bit tired. Worried about Will. Do *you* think he'll come back?"

"Dunno. I'm surprised he's carried it all on for this long, to be honest. You and he were really close and he was brought up in Flammark so I never really thought he'd actually leave us for good. Have we any idea where he might be?"

"Not a clue. He must still be hurting terribly if he's given in his resignation. Oh, I wish he'd at least get in touch! And I wish I'd told him about Animus."

"What happened is not all on you, Emma. Stop blaming yourself. Nothing would have stopped Animus from having Peter killed. Nothing. *He* used him to manipulate Will. *He* was responsible, not you."

Emma only shrugged as she paid the barman.

Abigail returned to what happened earlier. “We should tell Gabby about your door, you know.”

“Yes, of course! Not tonight, though, for obvious reasons. She needs to sleep it off. Besides, I’m still processing all the information about what’s going on at the church.”

“But those scratches were weird. Really weird. We should tell someone and I’m definitely not happy about you being at the cottage alone. If you don’t want me to keep you company, at least call Westen.”

“I will tell someone. Just ... just not tonight” Suddenly feeling a strange, uncalled-for urgency, she reached out and put her hand on Abigail’s arm. “Promise me you won’t say anything. I ... I want to do it in my own time. I need some space to think about Will and that Sandra woman. I don’t want a fuss.”

As Abigail nodded uncertainly, Emma clutched her bag with the thing inside all the harder.

Not wanting to let it go.

3

GRAVEYARD SHIFT

An army of TV trucks, journalists and rubber-neckers had gathered behind two cordons at the entrance to Wither Road, closed since the first body had been uncovered. Westen drove past to the usual onslaught of flashes and calls for comment—as if he'd even think of getting out of his car and give anything to them. They'd have to fucking wait.

They stopped at a gap in the woods, guarded by two uniforms either side of a line of police tape. They got out and after ducking under the tape, started on their second—and unexpected—journey to the burial site.

Though the hoarfrost glistered the trees of Seely Woods, the ground beneath them had not properly withstood the army of polyethylene-covered boots worn by the Sandmarsh Serious Crime Squad and its attendant forensic teams. Westen and Burrows had all but waded from the car to the crime scene, ankles smothered in ice-cold mud. Until, that is, they reached the nexus of the investigation; an area of roughly fifty square yards, paved with a shanty of planks and protective cordons, shielding it from contamination.

"I thought we'd found them all, Pete," said Westen as he stepped on the cobbled-together decking. "Last thing I expected was to be back here. Not after the fucking awful day we had yesterday."

Aiming for a distant stand of maglites, the two detectives took yet another wooden pathway extending out from the main scene by about another fifty yards.

"They found this body in the lee of a fallen tree," said Burrows, "about three or four our feet under. Still deep but not as deep as the others. Probably couldn't deal with the tree roots. The rest were easy to find in comparison. It took the dogs to—"

"I know," Westen rummaged in his pockets and fished out a pair of latex gloves. "I can deal with most things, Pete, but kids ..." He shook his head. "It gets to me when they're kids. Every fucking time."

He groaned as he caught sight of the squatting, baseball-hatted figure of the Head of Forensic Science, his smooth bald head making a brief appearance as he lifted his cap briefly to wipe his brow in the crook of an elbow, before returning it to precisely the same position. God, he detested the man—and the supercilious tone he knew was reserved solely for him.

"Savage?" Westen called abruptly. "What've you got for me?"

Without deigning to lift his head, the pathologist replied, "Just as the others, Superintendent. A young adolescent female. I cannot yet confirm she was buried alive but in this case, I think it reasonably safe to assume so, given the victim's facial expression." He slowly uncoiled his six-foot-four frame into a standing position. "See for yourself."

Westen stiffened and tentatively approached the grave. Definitely shallower than the others. Much shallower. He leaned forward and over to peer at the degraded face of his sixth murdered teenager, starkly illuminated in the overhead maglites: a ravaged face, the flesh starting to rot and already partly eaten, welcome mid-winter food for worms and whatever fucking bugs lurked underground this time of year. The girl's mouth stretched open—wide open—its tendons visibly fixed and strained in one final, desperate, silent scream before her lungs and throat had filled with soil and she'd choked to death.

But, like the others, she was recognisable. Just. To someone.

No eyes.

Westen couldn't help but shudder. Savage had told him they'd have been the first organ to go. Scavenged. Reluctantly, he had to hand it to the pathologist; he and his team had worked overnight on the other five victims to confirm both time and cause of their deaths. The amount of earth excavated from their lungs during the post-mortems led to asphyxiation being declared the COD, confirming what they all knew: the girls—all girls—had been buried alive. Teenagers. No signs of sexual assault.

Westen chewed over how they been subdued during their burial—since Savage's team found no indications from any of the bodies that a struggle had taken place. On the contrary, all had been found in a mockery of restful repose, their hands crossed at their breasts. With no marks discovered that might ascertain how they were rendered unconscious, they were waiting for toxicology to solve the mystery.

But by the expression on the face of *this* poor kid, well … she'd clearly not been subdued enough.

"Fuck, Savage. She must have died in agony."

"Correct, Superintendent. And this body is not posed as the others were." The pathologist reached down and shone his pencil torch on her fingers, their nails varnished an unmistakable red, all broken and filled with crap.

"She came around too early from whatever put her out. Tried to dig her way up," said Westen.

He got up off his knees. "She was the first," he said to Burrows.

"Guv?"

"Whoever did this hadn't got it right," Westen said, grimly. "She woke up. It could explain why she's so far away from the others. The pattern hadn't been established yet."

"I concur," Savage interrupted. "At least in that this body is the earliest of the victims we have so far uncovered. We completed the last post-mortem only a few hours ago, Superintendent. I can now tell you that we believe the deaths occurred between three and four days of each other though we cannot be more precise. Cold slows everything up. Including this new victim, we estimate the murders took place over a period of approximately three weeks. The decomposition in this victim is a little more advanced. But not by much. I will need her on my table before I can confirm."

Westen nodded. He was surprised. Savage had been much less of a trial than usual. Maybe the case had affected him, too.

"Thoughts, Pete?"

"Yes, Guv. That pose we're talking about. Shows empathy. Whoever did this was on a mission. Not a mark on their bodies, and we know they weren't assaulted. Not sexually, anyway."

Westen looked at Savage again. "Same with this victim?"

"Again, I would have—"

"Does this look like the same MO or not?"

Savage sighed. "Yes. Yes it does. But I cannot confirm that until—"

A uniformed copper suddenly rushed in on them, almost

sliding off the wooden planking in his haste. "Sir! Sir! We've found something."

"Alright, Benson," called Burrows. "Stand still. You'll do yourself some damage, not to mention the crime scene! What's up?"

"Something very odd in the woods, sir. We—that's me and Broadhurst—we don't know what to make of it. He said I should come and get you."

"Odd?" said Westen. "What do you mean, odd?"

"You need to come and see for yourself, sir. Don't even know whether it has any bearing on the case, but we think you need to take a look, just in case. You'll need your torch."

Not without some relief, Westen left Savage to it. He was glad to get away from the man. Glad to get away from the eyeless stare of the dead girl.

"Do you think we've got them all, Guv? The bodies, I mean," said Burrows as they followed the copper along a path that led deeper into the trees.

"Fuck knows," replied Westen sharply. He filled his lungs with the freezing woodland air and refocused. "But I think so. Seely Woods is dense in places, though I've seen bigger areas to cover. Hats off to that rambler who discovered the first grave. Not easy when there's a frost, even disturbed earth can look the same as the rest. Why the dogs missed this victim, God only knows. How was she found?"

"Same dog. Handler remembered it had been ferreting about under that tree but when the shout went up about the other bodies, he got distracted, so he came back with it later. He's gutted he missed it the first time. Should have left his mutt to it."

"Have we got anywhere on identification?"

"Nothing so far, Guv. There was nothing found on the bodies and no local misper reports. Tony's on with the national database."

"Well, they must have come from somewhere. Get Donna on it, too."

"Ahead of you on that. Both of them have been working flat out. There is one thing, Guv, but not sure what to make of it.

"Go on."

"Don't know if it's anything but we got a phone call from one of the deputies out at the Phoenix Academy. It used to be the old Raglan Road comprehensive, you know, between Flammark and Ledbridge? They renamed it to rise out of the ashes of the old school, apparently."

Westen rolled his eyes. Another fucking Phoenix! That made, what, three schools he knew with that name? Education was going through more changes than the force—with just as little evidence they improved anything. Except the thickness of a few wallets, of course. "So… this deputy. What did he say?"

"Woman, Guv. A Julie Tarrant. She said one of her students, a Shelley Iveson, hadn't been in school for over a week."

"Why would she report it to us? Schools have their own systems. They'd have contacted the parents, first, surely?"

"They did! Even sent an attendance officer round. The Ivesons said everything was okay and that their daughter had come down with the flu."

Westen sighed. "I suppose there's a point to all this, Pete?"

"The girl's friend had been worried about her. She'd gone to the attendance office and told them they'd planned to go to a concert, and she hadn't turned up. Not being able to raise her on her mobile for the whole time she's been off, her pal turned up at the house but the parents fobbed her off. Said Shelley was feeling better but decided to give the concert a miss which this pal said no way would she do. They wouldn't let her in, either. This Miss Tarrant said her colleague had a really bad feeling about it and with the graves hitting the news..."

"Interesting. Well, it may be nothing but send Donna out. Do it now. See if she can get sight of the girl. May not end up being anything to do with us but worth a look."

They scrambled along the path for another five minutes or so until it smoothed out and suddenly gave way to a clearing and what must have been Broadhurst, directing the beams of his torch at the strangest fucking construction Westen had ever seen in his life.

"What the fuck's that?"

"Beats me, Guv," replied Burrows, as they drew up closer. "They didn't cover things like this in the Inspector's exam."

"Looks like something from the Wicker Man!" said Benson, hardly able to conceal his pride at what they'd discovered.

He wasn't wrong. At first, Westen thought he was looking at nothing more than a tangle of branches and twigs in the gap between two thick-trunked trees. Then he saw they wove together to form a free-standing structure. On closer inspection, he saw the method in it. A large horizontal branch had been braced between two forked verticals at the edges, both struck deep into the ground. It made a stable framework within which whips and sticks and stems were woven. It made a roughly circular frame taller than he was. Even in the torchlight, the hollow centre loomed at them.

Deep. Matt black.

Next to him, Burrows shuddered. "I don't like this, Guv. Don't like it one bit."

"Get a grip, Pete. It's ... it's ... well, I don't know what it fucking is but I doubt it has anything to do with the case."

Benson piped up, "It'll be the pagans, sir. Out of Sand-marsh. They're into stuff like this. Always messing about in the woods. You know," he lowered his voice conspiratorially, "with no clothes on..."

"Thank you, Benson," said Westen, nodding slowly, biting back a grin. "We'll bear that in mind. You can both go back now."

The two coppers moved away. The detectives were about to follow when Westen suddenly stiffened.

"Seen something, Guv?"

"I don't know. I thought I saw a flash of white in the middle of that thing. Hang on."

He walked right up to it; flashed his torch at its dark centre. Nothing. He shivered, not with the cold—something else. Something walking over his grave. For some reason he didn't want to step through the circle, so he walked around it. He still couldn't see anything. No repeat of the white flash.

"Must be my imagination," said Westen, turning his shiver into a shrug. They waved their torches in the general area for a few moments then gave up the ghost. "Come on, Pete, let's get back. Nothing for us here."

4
DOORSTEPPED

Emma left Abigail at the Flammark Arms, though her friend needed some convincing before letting her go home on her own. Difficult to do out of earshot of Gabby, who'd got increasingly tipsy. And Robbie, of course. She wanted to process the events of the evening and a lone walk home would do the trick nicely. Hopefully, by the time she'd got back, she'd have thought of a decent pretext upon which to meet Sandra. She didn't really want to befriend the woman, nor did she relish the idea of having to feign any sort of interest in her damned projects. Anything that would get in the way of Will's return was anathema to her. Even the thought of setting foot in the vicarage with a new vicar in situ made her stomach lurch.

But all this couldn't take her mind off the other thing that bugged her.

Almost without realising it, Emma's slipped her hand inside her shoulder bag, her gloved fingers seeking out the comfort of the little woven wreath. Comfort. What a strange thing to feel! And how had it so mysteriously appeared on her doorstep? It must surely have been delivered by the same hand that caused the damage, but how had they avoided Abigail? Maybe they'd been lying in wait, using the jeep to shield themselves from detection.

Perhaps she should have brought Abigail back with her—it would have been the sensible thing to do, what with a murderer at large and the damage to her door. The two things might be linked, of course, but something told her they weren't, and that she was not in harm's way. Why she thought that she couldn't say, only that she was certain of it even though whoever made the scratches—and presumably, left the wreath—was clearly capable of performing much worse acts, and not just to a door. Abigail certainly hadn't understood why she insisted on returning alone.

She wondered whether Westen would be coming home tonight and what she would say to him about it. Then she marvelled at herself: she seemed more bothered about explaining the gouges to him than by the fact of the damage itself.

To her horror, Emma found she was about to face all that head-on. As she turned into her road, she spied his car parked outside then, nearing the garden gate, saw the man himself adopting the identical position she and Abigail had a few hours earlier. Crouching in front of the door, examining the scratches.

Fixing a smile on her face she took a deep breath and braced herself. "Hello, stranger!"

Westen stood up and, unsmiling, waited for her to come to him. As she neared, she could see his face set in that hard policeman's expression of his; jaw working, eyes glinting steel. Worried.

"Thank God you were out, Emma! With Mason I seem to remember?" She nodded. "I was just about to call you. I think it'd be a good idea if you stayed at the surgery tonight. Or at my flat. Someone's..."

"Scratched the door. I know."

"You *know?*"

"Er… yes. It happened just before I left to meet Robbie. I … I was going to ring but I knew you'd be busy. Didn't want to bother you. It's only a few scratches."

She knew she'd said the wrong thing as soon as the words left her mouth.

"They're hardly just fucking scratches, Emma," he hissed, balling his fists then immediately relaxing them. He took a deep breath and let it out slowly. "Why do you think I'd not be bothered? Serial killer on the loose… you all alone… your door gouged. Words escape me!"

They faced each other in silence, the tension building. She could tell he wanted to shout at her; knew also that he wouldn't. It was one of the many reasons why she loved him. He'd known what she'd been through before she came to Flammark and had vowed he would never subject her to any form of aggression from himself—though she'd heard him giving a dose of the verbals to his detectives often enough. All this didn't mitigate their current confrontation, however. Westen's intensity was full-on.

"Well?" he said, breaking the impasse, jerking his head at the door.

"I've no idea, honestly. It happened when I was upstairs getting ready to go out. Abigail came round but whoever did it had gone by then. And she checked around, front and back, before we left." Her mind flew to the twig wreath in her bag. "No sign of anyone."

"I can't believe Mason let you come home on your own! Jesus, Emma—"

"I didn't tell him what happened."

"Didn't—" he sucked in a breath. "Well, you should have told me."

"I know, but as I said, you're busy. You'd have dropped everything, and I really didn't think there was any need."

"No need? No *need?* You more than anyone should know the world is full of madmen, Emma, and Flammark seems to be blessed with more than its fair share. You've got to be more careful."

Emma moved forward and brushed past him through the already open door. Once their relationship had become a thing, she'd given him his own key. As she passed, she caught his hand in one of hers. "I know. Come inside and we'll talk. It's freezing. I'll make us some coffee and tell you what happened. Are you staying or do you have to go back tonight?"

He softened as she led him inside. Unable to stop a grin forming, he said gruffly, "Don't try to change the subject."

"I'm not. I just want to know how long I have you."

Relenting even more, he replied, "We found another grave so, a few hours—less, maybe. I have to get back. But that was before I found that someone had shredded your front door." He took a breath. "I can't leave now, not until I'm sure you're safe."

"Westen, if anything was going to happen to me, it would have happened hours ago."

He snorted. "Huh. You can't know that."

And yet she did. Unequivocally. Despite the scratch marks, she had no shadow of a doubt that whoever left the twig-wreath meant her no harm.

Life still stirred in the log she'd put on the fire during Abigail's visit. She poked its embers and threw on more. "Come on, sit. How about a drink before you go? Tell me about today—what you can, of course."

He held her gaze a few seconds longer before letting his shoulders relax. "Okay. But not before I call Donna. I'm going to ask her to stay with you."

"No!" The word barked out of Emma's mouth before she knew it. "Sorry, Westen, I … I don't want a fuss—and I don't want Donna to stay. Abigail offered and I refused her, too. So, leave it. Sit. I'll make us something to drink."

It wouldn't be the first time his DC had been called in to babysit, but had she wanted company, she'd have got Abigail to stay. Once Westen had left she would have the house to herself. Could take the twig-wreath out of her bag and hold it. Keep it close.

Connect.

Connect?

She strode through to the kitchen and started the coffee maker. Westen joined her.

"I always knew you were going to be trouble. From the first fucking moment we met." He broke into a reluctant smile. "Okay, I won't call Donna, but I will make sure a squad car makes regular passes your way. *That,* I insist upon." He sat at the table and slumped on his elbows, rubbing his eyes with his knuckles.

"Was it bad?" she said, bringing the cups over.

"Very."

"I'd have thought they'd have expanded your team by now. You've been full-on since your promotion."

"I should be so lucky. Government cuts, Emma. To be honest, it suits me, I'm not another Piper. I could never sit behind a desk all day like he did. I took over from him on that one condition. I like getting stuck in. Gutted that Pete Burrows didn't pass his Inspector's exam, though. Plan was he'd stay and take some of my load and I'd be given another DC."

"Not as gutted as he is, I expect. He's not been the same since his girlfriend died, has he?"

"No. That DeepDrilla stuff was a fucking catastrophe—I don't have to tell *you* that, though, do I? Pete doesn't talk much about Jasmine. She'd dumped him you know … a few weeks before they dug her out with all the others. So, a double-whammy for the poor bloke."

"Yes, Donna told me. She also said he thought Jasmine might take him back."

"Yeah, he did." He gave a sympathetic shake of his head, "Some of the heart's definitely gone out of him. Maybe that's why he failed the exam. But … it's the same with all of us, at the moment, truth be told. All cases are bad but this one …. well, this one's enough to make you think true evil actually does exist. Kids. There's no excuse for killing kids."

"Have you managed to identify any of them yet?"

"That's what bugging me. We haven't a clue who they are or where they came from. Six teenage girls, all buried alive in the space of about three weeks. No misper reports, nothing."

"That does sound odd. Whoever killed them won't have had the time to scour the country for kids that no one would miss—if that was their intention, of course."

"Exactly. The only sniff we've had came from the Phoenix Academy. Told us they were worried one of their students hadn't attended for a while. Parents say she's come down with the flu but is otherwise okay."

"Seems unusual to ring the police. Don't they have their own attendance procedures?"

"That's what I said. But one of her friends pressed the panic button. Didn't believe the parents when she called round. With the graves being all over the news, the school rang us. Donna's onto it. She's gone round to get sight of the girl." He glanced at his watch. "Probably as we speak."

Somewhere in the back of Emma's brain, a light flickered. Hairs on the back of her neck started to rise. Suddenly urgent, she said, "Go back to the school, Westen. Ask them for a list of their other absences, even …"

Westen put his cup down. Raising an eyebrow, he said quietly, "Go on."

"Even if their absence is authorised by their parents. *Especially* if their attendance is authorised by their parents. And yes, make sure you get sight of those kids."

"What's this about, Emma? What do you know?"

What did she know? Nothing. It was more what she *felt*. Mouth suddenly dry, she left her untouched coffee and stepped to the sink to pour a glass of water. After taking a few gulps she turned to face him, an apologetic smile fixed on her face. "I don't know anything. Not really. It was just an idea."

"It's happening again, isn't it?"

"What?"

Westen sighed. "I wish I knew. There's a whole side to you that's a complete fucking mystery to me."

Emma tried to grin. "It's only common sense. You know what kids are like, how secretive they can be. They hunt in packs. If one girl's missing..."

Westen gave her one of his stop-bullshitting-me looks and, still regarding her, flipped out his mobile.

He tapped the screen then put the phone to his ear. "Burrows, are you still at the station... ? Good. Get that teacher out of bed—Tarrant was it? I want the names of any Flammark girls who've gone absent over the past three weeks, authorised by their parents or not... Yes. Same age as the victims to keep the list short, for now. Has Donna called in yet about her visit... ? Well, as soon as she does, get her back in and give her a uniform team. I want every home on that list visited and for us to get sight of the kids. Anyone doesn't let you in—get a warrant."

After a further back and forth, Westen ended the call and put his phone away. Scraping back his chair, he said, "This conversation isn't over, Emma. Whatever this relationship of ours is, it can't survive on secrets and half-truths. Twelve years on the force are screaming that you're hiding something."

What could she say? Anything that came out of her mouth at that moment would have dug a different kind of grave.

His frustrated sigh came out as a growl as she gave no reply. He left the kitchen to head out and she followed him to the door. After opening it he paused; glanced at the gouges. "Promise me you'll lock up as soon as I leave."

"Seriously?" she said, lightly. "You're asking *me* to lock up?"

"Okay." He hovered uncertainly for a moment before turning to her. Taking her in his arms, he whispered, "I'd never forgive myself if anything happened to you."

"Nothing's going to happen, Westen, I promise. I also promise to lock up and if I hear any sign of an intruder, I'll ring you or the station. Go. Those kids need you more than I do."

Together they walked down the garden path, Westen holding Emma close, shielding her from the freezing cold. At the gate he drew her towards him again. Despite herself, she relaxed as he held her and took in the smell of his natural musk, more sensual than any cologne. After a parting kiss, she smiled and waited as he got in the car then waved as he drew away.

Two seconds later, she was legging it back down her path as quickly as the ice would allow. Once inside, she grabbed her phone. Despite the dodgy signal at the caravan, she managed to get through.

"Gabby! Thank God." Her heart sank, suddenly remembering her friend's condition when she left her at the pub. "Oh sorry, are you at Robbie's?"

"No. After you left he bought me some coffee. Two

coffees, actually. I don't like staying away from the caravan while Wyland's away if I can help it. I'm a bit fuzzy—and somewhat embarrassed—but feel much better. What's up?

"I don't want to explain over the phone. I need to come over."

"Now?"

"Yes, now. It's urgent. Really urgent!"

5
CURSES!

Emma left her bedside lamp on before leaving the house for the second time that night. Less likely to suggest to any passing patrol car that she might not be in. She left the security light on too, then climbed into the jeep and set off for Wood End. Twenty minutes later she reached the twin columns that marked the entrance to Wyland's park and saw Gabby's waving figure. Thankfully, she looked sober enough.

Leaning over, she opened the door to let her friend climb in.

"I thought I'd wait here and guide you down to my van since you haven't seen it before," said Gabby. "I've put the kettle on. It's really, really late, Emma. What's up? You've right put the wind up me!"

"I've put the wind up myself," Emma replied, making for the end of the cobbled courtyard.

"Go left. I'm three vans down to the right."

As directed, Emma turned into the hard standing next to the caravan and they both scrambled out. Long, long past midnight, the park shrouded them in winter silence. Not even an owl stirred. Gabby opened the door to her van, immediately assailing them with a blast of heat.

"Wow!" Emma exclaimed. "I can see the appeal of living here now. I imagined you'd be freezing."

"Caravans aren't what they used to be. I've got double glazing as well as central heating. Thank the Lord! I wouldn't last two minutes now, camping on Seely Tor like I did with Michael. There again, I'm not exactly what I used to be so..." She paused, gave her head a little shake. "Come on, let me give you a tour while the kettle boils. Then we can get down to it—whatever *it* is."

The caravan was much bigger than Emma had envisaged. With two bedrooms and bathroom, it also sported a decent-sized kitchen and even a dining area. The tour stopped at a carpeted living room—not enormous, but big enough. Maybe twelvish feet square. The inset radiant gas fire powered away adding to the cosy atmosphere already generated by two generous built-in sofas. It looked very comfortable. Posh, even—everywhere showroom-neat and beautifully decorated albeit in beige bland. Though there was nothing of Gabby's personality stamped there.

Maybe she hadn't found it yet.

"I know," Gabby said. "It's lovely but a bit boring, isn't it? I can't seem to mess it up. Not that I've got much in the way of possessions to mess it up with. I don't do shopping. I have my books and, of course, there's the watching ... and listening, of course. Do sit. I'll make us some coffee."

"Not for me, Gabby, thanks. Just water. I seem to have gone off it."

Watching.

Gabby had been talking about Peter, of course, whose death—whose torture—would stay with them all forever. Impossible for Emma to forget for one minute, how Will offered up the body of the only person he'd ever loved, literally to stand for all eternity, guarding the world against the emergence of another creature like Animus. It had been the most profound act of grace she had ever experienced. And he'd done it even as he blamed them all for Peter's death; for not keeping Will in the loop; not disclosing soon enough the reality of the creature that was St Saviour, the false cleric who tried to unleash all hell upon the village.

Upon humanity.

As her friend returned with the drinks, Emma sighed, "I don't know how you do it, Gabby. Keeping watch."

"It's not what you might think. I don't spend my time gazing through the window at Peter's standing stone. Watching is more about … attuning. Developing a bond with the land. Learning it in a way I never could before." She stared into the middle-distance. "I'm used to being alone with my thoughts. Watching over Peter is a continual reminder that my situation is wholly insignificant compared to what he endured under Animus, and, of course, in the work he's doing for us now. I was … ashamed of getting a bit tipsy at the pub." She smiled. "I've obviously got a lot of learning to do about mortal temptation."

They sat a few moments in silence, letting the quiet seep in. "Okay, Emma," said Gabby. "It's time. Why are you here?"

Emma took a careful breath and put her glass down. "It's about the bodies in Seely Woods."

"Go on."

"There's six now. Another was found this afternoon. Westen came to Clearview for a break before going back to it all. They've had problems identifying the victims all of which have been killed over the past three weeks. Kind of like a spree."

"Pour souls," said Gabby.

"Yes. Thing is no one has come forward to report their children missing. Then a schoolteacher rang the station to say that one of their students hadn't come in. The parents said she had the flu but her friend didn't believe and raised the alarm. I told Westen to check other absences..."

Gabby put her cup down and leaned forward. "Because you think these parents don't know their child is missing."

"Yes. It's like what happened to the village during the Blackstone curse cycle." Her lips trembled. "Do you think it's back? Do you think we're ... I'm ... going to have to go through all that again?"

Gabby's brow furrowed as she considered. "That wasn't how it worked, Emma. The curse put Flammark to sleep so the village would become oblivious to what was going on up at the estate."

"Yes. Like these parents are oblivious to the fact their daughter is gone—or at least might be. I don't know if I'm right—Westen's on with it now—it's just ... I dunno, I have this feeling..."

"Okay. Well, for the moment let's assume you are right. It can't be the curse. I promise you. You captured the evil behind it and Michael and I took it to a place from where it can never return." She frowned. "If this child does turn out to be missing—that her parents don't seem to realise *is* very worrying, I agree. Everyone in Flammark is on high alert after what's been on the news. Why on earth would they keep quiet about it? Parents are hardwired to protect their kids—there's no bond stronger. If something could subdue that protective instinct enough to render them truly oblivious to her disappearance, then whatever has a hold over their consciousness must have a great deal of power."

"I told Westen to make sure they get actual sight of the kids."

"Did you, now. I bet that went down well."

Emma smiled. "We're walking a tightrope. I'm positive he realises I'm sort of tapped into something though he doesn't know what. He asks me how I seem to know things, but I honestly haven't a clue what to tell him. I try not to lie but the best thing I can do is just avoid his questions. He's aware of it. He thinks it'll come between us."

"You know it will, in the end."

"Will it? Does it have to?"

"Time'll tell, I suppose. And you're right, you *are* tapped into something. We just don't know what it is exactly. I've always said, there's something very special about you, Emma, and I still haven't quite worked out what. You have abilities."

"No, I don't! Not like Abigail."

"No. Not like Abigail. In a way, what she has is more straightforward—at least, more explicable. To us, anyway. You, on the other hand my dear, are a horse of a much darker complexion. You not only defeated the Blackstone curse, you helped us identify what St Saviour really was. You saw his essence move in his cane—or rather, it moved when you came near it. You agitated it and that gave us the clue to what would ultimately end him. And it may be happening again with these children. Maybe you're seeing another kind of spirit at work. I have no idea what it might be, but Westen would be right to take you very seriously indeed."

Despite the heat from the gas fire, Emma turned cold. Her eyes flitted to her shoulder bag.

The movement had not gone unnoticed. "What is it, Emma?"

"Hmm? Nothing, I'm just thinking."

"About?"

"If I have tuned in on something, what could it be? It might not be how the Blackstone curse worked before, but it's certainly similar. I agree with you, if their child was missing—and nothing's been confirmed yet, I could still be wrong—the parents absolutely *would* have reported it. So why didn't they?"

"I have no idea, and if you are on the right track, there are five other sets of parents who are in for a terrible, terrible shock, too." She got up, reached for her phone. "We need to get hold of Abigail. Maybe the Orb will tell us more."

Emma's eyes flew to her bag, then just as quickly, she looked away. "No," she exclaimed. "No!" What if the Orb was to pick up on the twig-wreath? She couldn't have that. "Sorry, Gabby. Do you mind if we wait? It's only a half-baked idea and I'm probably being silly. Let's wait for Westen to get back to me." Avoiding Gabby's hooded stare, she drained her glass and got up. "I've got to go. It's really late and I'm at work tomorrow. Then I'm off to see Sandra Davis."

Gabby, having also thrown a puzzled glance at Emma's bag, suddenly relaxed and formed her lips into a half-smile. "Good luck with that one. You're going to need all your wits about you. As I said at the pub, there's something definitely not right there."

"I miss Will," Emma suddenly blurted. "I wish we could bring him in on all this."

"Well, to state the obvious, you wouldn't need to be meeting Sandra if William was here."

"I so regret our not telling him about Animus. Do you think he was right? *Would* he have been able to prevent Peter's death if we'd told him what we knew sooner?"

"Emma, we've gone over this. You of all people should know there's no point. What's done is done. You felt the same way over Ben, if I remember correctly?"

Emma nodded. "Still do."

"It's a kind of survivor's guilt. We think we have agency but usually we don't. Events simply overtake us and we do what we do. Look what happened to me. If I hadn't got so involved with Abigail, I'd still be with Michael."

"Have to say, you're coping very well with it all, Gabby."

She sighed. "My life here does have a pattern to it, and

remember, Michael and I have been posted here for centuries so in that respect little has changed—except now I know my time on earth will eventually come to an end. But I can't deny, I do feel a chasm." She put her palm over her heart. "Here. Separation, you see. It's a terrible thing. You're feeling it with William. If it weren't for the fact that I believe I'm in this human state for a reason—that there was a purpose to what happened to me—I ... I'm not sure what I would do." She hesitated. "And I'm a bit worried at how tipsy I got tonight. I enjoyed how it took my mind off things, so maybe I'm not handling what happened as well as you might think."

"Don't be so hard on yourself. Nothing wrong with getting a bit merry now and then."

"Isn't there? Wyland wouldn't have done it. I ... I don't want to fail at this too."

Gabby suddenly seemed forlorn. Lost. Emma went to her. "I'm so sorry," she said, giving her a hug. "I can't possibly imagine the scale of your loss. I'm still a surface believer and nowhere near as devout as possibly I should be, given what I know."

Gabby pulled away. Smiled. "You mean, that because of me—the fact of my existence—you know that God exists?"

"I suppose. He isn't real to me though, and after what I've been through in my life so far, to be honest I don't think much of your boss. That he could let such ... stuff happen."

"Evil has a mind of its own, Emma, just as we do. We don't exist in a deterministic world. In the end, it's all down to our choices, our judgement and our ultimate path. All we can do is hope we get it right." She sighed and got up. "Now it really is time you were on your way," she smiled and edged to where Emma had been sitting. "Oh, don't forget your bag."

Before Gabby could put even a finger on it, Emma was on her feet too. With a slight lunge she got to it first.

"S-sorry," Emma said. "I didn't mean—"

"No problem," Gabby shrugged, brushing it away pleasantly enough. "We need to get together after you've spoken with Sandra." *San Dra.* "I'll invite Robbie. I've got the keys to Wyland's cottage. It's nice enough here but it'll seem a bit cramped for the four of us."

"Okay. And I'll let you know about those parents, too."

"You do that, Emma," said Gabby as she walked her friend out. "You do that."

6
IDENTIFIED

Six am and the station was not as quiet as it should have been. Though it'd be another hour before the skeleton crew of duty officers left their night watch, they'd already been joined by members of Westen's core team who were slumped at their desks amid empty cups of vending machine coffee and spent crisp packets. Not much in the way of chatter. They were all too exhausted.

Westen came into the bullpen, the knot in his forehead furrowed deep. Jacketless, tie loosened, the sleeves of his rumpled white shirt rolled up, he wore the look of a war-torn general. Having had confirmation from Donna that their first victim had indeed been identified, he'd spent most of the night with his team knocking on doors, persuading parents to let them have sight of their kids. Then came the hysterical aftermath when five sets of those parents discovered they'd been harbouring a totally inexplicable delusion that their daughters were tucked up safe and sound in their beds.

What the absolute fuck?

"Right. Let's do this," he said, jerking his head towards his office. His team slowly scrambled themselves together and, carrying various notepads and screens, followed him through.

His predecessor, Superintendent Peter Piper—otherwise known as Pecker—had preferred a lofty office suite on the floor above. That was before he resigned, a fact due in no small part to Westen himself. But, unlike Piper, he liked to work in close proximity to his people and had turned his old inspector's office into a second conference space useful for briefings like the one he was about to lead.

Westen took his files from his desk and slammed them down at the head of the large table he'd installed in the centre of the room. He took his seat, Burrows next to him. The more senior members of his team sat round it, others leant against filing cabinets or supported the wall. He didn't beat around the bush.

"So, here's where we are. The Phoenix Academy gave us a list of female absences in the same year-group as our victims. All authorised, all with notes from home. Five of those children were not in their beds, their parents now out of their fucking minds. Not that they weren't before, though in a different way. We'll come back to that in a minute."

He paused and pressed his lips together, still barely able to comprehend the meaning behind his own words. "We bagged hair samples, *et cetera*. They're on the way to the lab for DNA testing. Donna, after this I want you down there looking over their shoulders. We need to know yesterday that the missing girls are unequivocally our victims."

"Goddit, Guv." She took in a breath, about to say something else.

"Out with it, Donna."

"The victims are still recognisable. We could get the parents—"

Westen cut her off. "No."

"But—"

Before she could finish Burrows interrupted her. His usually cheery face pale and drawn—eyes like black pools—he suddenly blurted out what they all were thinking. "How, Guv. How could they not have known? I mean, I get it that kids play their parents, sneaking out, that kind of thing. Christ, I did it myself. But this! The first victims have been missing for nearly three weeks!"

"Okay," said Westen. "I can see we obviously need to talk it through now. To answer your question, Pete, I haven't a fucking clue." He looked to the others. "Are we looking at some kind of mass hysteria, or what?"

"Feels like a cult to me," said Stamford. "Maybe the parents were in on it. Maybe their kids were ... sacrificed?"

A mixture of gasps and derisory chortles echoed around the room.

"Did the parents you visited this morning fit that bill, Tony?" said Westen. "Did they look as if they'd willingly let their kids be buried alive only to tell their teachers they had the fucking flu?"

Stamford blushed. "No, Guv. Sorry, Guv, I was just—"

Westen eased off. "I know, Tony. I know." Addressing the rest of the squad, he said, "I'm not sure we can speculate on the psychology of what's happened with these families. It's way out of our skill set." He glanced at Donna. "All I know is I don't want a procession of traumatised and guilt-ridden parents trooping their way through Savage's mortuary. We know we've identified our victims; it won't hurt us to wait for DNA confirmation. I've no doubt some, if not all the parents will want to see their kids. Say goodbye..." Westen paused, himself still coming to terms. "But wherever possible, we'll do it in their time. Not ours. I've spoken to Savage. He understands that releasing the bodies may take much longer than usual."

Sheila Stewart, one of a group of DCs who'd been roped

in to support the investigation, piped up from the back of the room. "Shouldn't we be bringing in a team of counsellors, Guv?"

Westen thought for a moment, then nodded. "Good call. See to it, Pete?" Burrows made a note as his boss continued, "Donna, have you allocated family liaison yet?"

"It's my next job when we've finished here, Guv. Then I'm off to the lab."

"Good. Get the FLOs to find out whether the missing girls were friends. What connections, if any, there might be between them. Same with the sets of parents. Immediate updates to me on anything—and I mean *anything*—that seems out of the ordinary, or left field. There'll be rational explanation for the parents' behaviour. We just have to find it." He sighed and threw a half smile at Stamford. "Tony, do some digging. See if there's any mileage in this cult idea of yours."

The man perked up. "Will do, Guv."

"I'd like to bring Martha Jacobs on board," said Burrows.

"The prison psychologist out at Oakmarsh? She's done some profiling work, too, hasn't she?"

"She has. Gaining quite a reputation. Might be useful on several fronts."

"Get her," Westen said. "No question. We need as much light thrown on this case as we can get." He ploughed on. "Okay, next. Pete, go to the school. From now on I want any absences, authorised or otherwise, male or female to be reported straight to us. As soon as one comes in, get someone out to check on the kids, no exceptions. Make sure they have sight of them."

"Will do, Guv."

"I want friends and classmates interviewed. No time to do it one by one, get them all in one place. We need a solid liaison with the school so make sure that deputy head's there. Miss Tarrant's proved more than sensible, so far."

"Guv."

"And get someone with FLO training there too. Those kids'll need support."

"No can do on that," said Donna. "Everyone we've got will soon be with the families."

"Right. I'll get on to Witherington. Get them to send you some extra support."

"I don't know if it'll help," she said. "but we're being pestered by Flammark's new vicar. Sandra Davis. I say new, she's been there for the last six months. She was at the school early doors as soon as the news broke. She's offered her counselling services. The school isn't too keen. It has no religious foundation and would prefer to use their own professionals—and ours, of course. But she's being insistent. What do you think?"

"What's the harm?" said Stamford. "Some of the kids will know her. Anyone who can offer that kind of support is useful."

"I think it's the school's, call," said Westen. "But if they do let her in, I don't want any of that confessional confidentiality crap. If she's there, she reports back any information she might get from the kids."

Donna nodded and made a note. "Thanks, Guv."

Westen ticked down the sheet he was staring at. "Next, the press. The world and his fucking wife wants to know what happened. With this being sp high-profile a case, the ACC is involved and we've agreed to try to keep this as close to our chests as possible for now, but there will need to be a press conference. That'll be in a few days when we have more to offer. And that's going to be a tricky one. We don't want to reveal anything about our deluded parents—they've all asked us to keep schtum about their seeming lack of vigilance. Are we clear on that, everybody? I don't want anything about that aspect of the case passing your lips." Westen took the time to give everyone the eyeball. "They can't explain it and nor can we. Yet. And I hope I don't need to tell anyone: a reporter approaches, it's no comment. That understood too?"

Nods from around the table.

"That said, the village needs to be made aware their kids are at risk, so until we've enough to go to the press with, emails are going out and there's to be a parents' meeting at the school tonight which I'm attending. No journalists allowed." he turned to Burrows. "All this will frighten the horses. Pete, so make uniform aware. Some gentle presence in Flammark might be called for, and not just to be ready for trouble. People will find it reassuring. And I want every copper in Seely Woods on the lookout for loiterers and repeat rubber-neckers. It's the kill site and means something to someone."

He reached back over to his desk and grabbed a half-empty bottle of water. After taking a swig he continued, "Tony, do some research into the place. See if it brings up any red flags. Past crimes, traumas ... anything. I'm looking for connections; associations. Speed cams have been checked already. Check them again."

Tony interjected. "Guv, I've been analysing the school database. All the victims had just turned sixteen—within a few months of each other."

Westen took a moment before he answered. There was something almost mystical about the number. Sixteen. Kids on the threshold of adulthood, an entire future denied. He let out a long sigh. "Okay. So, a pattern's emerging. All girls, all the same age, all live in Flammark. It's a well-defined target group." He worked his jaw for a few seconds, thinking. He turned to Burrows. "From now on, I don't want any of the girls in this year group to make their own way to and from school. We bus them in."

"Okay, Guv, but ... can't their parents take them?"

"If they genuinely had no fucking clue their kids were missing in the first place, they're the last people we should trust to take them to school. No. Insist they're bussed. Speak to local transport providers. I want them picked up and dropped off at their doorsteps. If they're in walking distance of the school, then everyone goes in twos. Get the kids to call on each other and to report anything untoward. Take registers. Visit any kid who doesn't turn up. And we need to impose a curfew. It'll all be in the email and I'll reinforce everything at the parents meeting."

Sheila put her hand up again. "Guv, with respect, you don't have kids. You can tell them to stay in but getting them to do it is another thing altogether. Wouldn't it be better just to close the school?"

"No. I've spoken to Redmayne, the head of the Phoenix Academy. He's the only person apart from all those around this table who's been told about the parents' role in all this. So, for now, we've agreed the school's the best place for them. And if the kids don't want to co-operate with a curfew, Sheila," Westen's voice had sudden snarl to it. "Then scare the fucking daylights out of them. A few photos from the graves might do the trick. Just make them stay home. End of."

The meeting started to break up, Sheila not even bothering to hide her scepticism at Westen's response. It hadn't gone unnoticed. As his team rose to leave, Westen said, "Look. I know this is hard. But we do hard. And we do what we can—*have* to do what we can. We're on the clock. Everyone's pulled all-nighters but this killer isn't going to stop. Forensics can't be completely accurate about this, but it looks like the murders took place between three to four days apart. Parents can't help us get anywhere near an accurate time of death since they didn't even fucking know their kids were missing. So, if this pattern continues, there'll be another soon. Maybe today, maybe tomorrow, maybe the day after. If you've not been tasked with anything, get some sleep but do it in shifts." He nodded at Burrows. "Organise that for us, Pete? To those who have to stay on duty, the dead girls give you their thanks."

He didn't have to say any more. He knew his team wouldn't stop and probably wouldn't get the sleep they needed, either. Okay by him, nor would he.

With the scraping of chairs, the team left the room without the usual banter. Westen stayed put and mulled in the following silence.

Two things bothered him. First and most obvious was the parents. He was a stumped and bewildered as his team. And it had been Emma that pointed him in the right direction, suggesting he go back to the school to check those absences. No, not suggested; she'd more or less *insisted,* as if she'd intuited something totally beyond his field of vision. Not for the first time.

He fished out his phone and called her.

"Hey, you," she answered. Everything about her voice suggested she was between the warm sheets of her bed. *Their* bed, now. Why shouldn't she be? It wasn't yet seven. Not even daylight. "Everything okay?"

"I'm fine. Full-on with the case. Just checking to see if you're alright. Any more visitations?"

"No. I slept through."

"Good. The patrol I set up did four passes. Everything seemed quiet enough, apparently." He paused, gathering his thoughts. "You were right. About the kids—the parents. We knocked on doors and got them to take us up to their kids' rooms. Six missing and no one had a fucking clue they were gone. You knew, didn't you?"

"Well, I didn't *know* exactly..."

She didn't say any more. Westen refused to fill the

silence, hoping it would force some kind of disclosure. Fucking pointless to ask her. She'd just clam up.

But she didn't give him an inch. He sighed. "Okay, Emma, have it your own way. As per usual." But he wasn't finished. He brought up the second thing that bothered him. "Abigail Chater," he said. "She's a member of the Sandmarsh pagans, isn't she?"

She chuckled, sleepily. "Yes. Why? Thinking of joining?"

"Not immediately," he said, glad of a moment's levity. "Something's come up in the investigation. I could do with her input."

"That's a first."

"Could you get her to meet me at lunchtime? I want to take her to Seely Woods. You too, if you're up for it."

"You want *us* to visit a crime scene?" He sensed her sit up. "I ... I'm not sure I—"

"No. No, we won't be going near it. There's something else I want you both to see at the other end of the woods. Can't make head or tail of it. It may not be relevant to the investigation, but I need to rule it out."

"Okay, I'll get her to come to the surgery round about noon?"

"Yes, do that. And Emma?"

"Hmmm?"

"We're okay aren't we? We're good?"

"Of course, we are. Why wouldn't we be?"

"It's just ... Never mind. I'll see you later on. Love you..."

"Love you too. See you soon."

7
INPUT

Twelve sharp and Emma and Abigail were in Westen's car being sped on their way to Seely Woods. Abigail had been not unpleasantly surprised to hear she'd been summoned. "*My* input?" she'd said when Emma called her, unable to keep the thrill out of her voice, despite the terrible reason behind the request. "Gosh, I'm flattered. Something pagan, eh? I wonder what it could be?"

What, indeed? Emma clutched her shoulder bag, aware of the twig-wreath inside. She'd put it in a small plastic bag and carried it with her all the time—even put it under her pillow at night. She had no idea why, nor could she fathom the reason she hadn't told Abigail about it.

Westen turned off the high street and into Wither Road. It was more of a wide lane, really, skirting most of the section of Seely Woods where the bodies had been found. After another half-minute he drew up next to a gap in the trees. It had been police-taped off, and uniformed coppers were stationed there and every fifty yards or so along the road to ensure no one got in.

A big operation.

The three of them got out and stood for a while, facing the gap.

"Come on, then Westen," Abigail said, eyes glistening with an enthusiasm she clearly couldn't curb. "Spill. Why are we here?"

"We've found an odd structure a couple of hundred yards away from the crime scene and one of my men said it was probably some of your pagan lot getting up to their tricks. I want you to see it. It's probably nothing but I need an opinion on it. Can't think of anyone more qualified than you to tell me what it is."

"Okay. I'm suitably intrigued. Lead on!" She gave a little giggle.

"Abby!" said Emma, almost hissing as she held her friend's arm, holding her back for a second as Westen strode on. "Can you try to look a *bit* more circumspect? You're enjoying this too much. He's been up all night, you know. Can't you see how exhausted he is? This is important! And you should know better."

"Sos," Abigail replied, more than a little crestfallen as they set off again. "I think I'm just pleased he's asked for my opinion. I always think he doesn't take me seriously— you know, that I'm just a kid. Wyland said that to me once. It still rankles."

"I can hear you, you know," Westen called over his shoulder. "And you are just a kid."

Abigail rolled her eyes. "See," she said.

As they continued along the path, Emma started to drag her feet. Abigail forged ahead and joined Westen, matching his stride and chatting away despite everything Emma said, clearly relishing her consultant status. As the gap between them increased, she found herself scanning left and right. Is this where she lived? Would she see her?

Frowning, Emma slowed her pace some more. She? Who on earth was *she?*

A familiar thrumming began in her ears, a sensation she hadn't felt for a very long time. Not since Ben. The hairs on her forearms and the back of her neck were moving. Was she being watched?

Was *she* watching her?

Squeezing her shoulder bag closer—the twig-wreath safely inside—her eyes darted about the thickening skeletal treescape, fully expecting to catch sight of its maker.

Nothing.

She picked up her pace, her shoes kicking up the ankle-deep wealth of dead leaves that rustled and crackled away as she disturbed the surface frost. Her breath coming in short pants, suddenly her mouth filled with saliva. Shit, shit shit, was she going to be *sick?* She gathered her arms around herself and blew out long, deliberate exhalations. It was just imagination. She needed to calm down, and calm down quick, before the other two saw what state she was in.

To her relief, the path opened up. It led to a small clearing.

Abigail was already halfway across the space running up to an assortment of branches and sticks carefully woven to frame what looked like a perfect circle.

"Omigod!" said Abigail, eyes wide, mouth open in wonder. She started to run her fingers over the weave, pushing it sightly to test its stability which was obviously solid as a rock. She scraped the bark of one of the branches with her fingernails. Peered at the scratch.

"Well, what is it?" asked Westen impatiently. "And how long do you think it's been here?"

"Not long, I think. See the places where these branches have been stripped or broken? They're not weathered at all. It's cleverly done. I've seen things like this where there's lots of willow. But these twigs are from a harder wood. Willow's bendy, see, and in the wild tends to grow where its wet. I could be wrong, but I don't think there's any in these woods—too dry. And look," she pointed to where she'd scraped back the bark, "See how dark it is where I scratched it? The sap's not risen yet, so the branches have no give to them." She glanced at Emma. "It would have taken Wyland weeks to build something like this properly."

"Ah," said Westen, nodding in recognition. "I remember Wyland from last year. Owns Wood End, doesn't he? Is he part of your little gang now?"

"Don't know what you're on about, Westen!" Abigail tutted. "He can't have done this, though, it's too recent. He's been out of the country for months."

"So... I repeat. What is it?"

She didn't answer for a while, choosing instead to walk around it. Obviously reluctant to walk through its centre, she took three strides back to take it all in.

"Well, I'm not sure it's necessarily a pagan thing. There are loads of found artists who do this sort of stuff."

"I know," Westen said, drily. "I have been on the internet. So... it doesn't mean anything, then?"

"I wouldn't go that far," she chewed her bottom lip, surveying. Weighing up. "It might be a witch's circle."

Westen guffawed. "A *what*?"

"Don't be like that," Abigail grew dead serious. "You wouldn't have brought me here if you thought I'd just spout rubbish. You might not follow my path, or read the same things as I do, but I suspect you have some inkling of the old ways. You could hardly work—and live—in Flammark and not pick *something* up." Suddenly looking much older than her nineteen years, she fronted up to him. "You're by no means dim. You know what I'm talking about." She jerked her head sideways, towards Emma.

… who throughout the interchange had not moved. She stood, alone and forlorn in her cherry-red duffle, hugging herself as she fixated on the circle, one hand clutching her bag as if her life depended on it. Slowly, she raised her other arm and pointed.

"She did this."

And then her knees buckled.

"W-what happened?" Emma was coming-to, staring up at the horrified faces of Westen and Abigail. She felt cold. Freezing cold.

"She's shivering, Westen," Abby cried. "Give her your coat!"

Kneeling, all colour fled from his face, after a brief fight with his sleeves Westen managed to flap out of his overcoat and fling it over her. "Thank Christ, Emma. For a minute, there, I thought I'd lost you."

"What happened?" Emma repeated, hoiking herself up on her elbows.

"You were pointing at the circle," said Abigail. "You said something like 'she did it' then you bloomin' fainted. What did you mean? *Who*?"

Emma peered at her and frowned. "I don't know what I meant. I… I can't remember saying anything."

"That's it," said Westen. He put his arms under her knees and around her shoulders and in one easy movement gathered her up. "You're going to the hospital."

"I am not. I'm perfectly okay. Put me down," said Emma.

Ignoring her, he started walking. She thumped on his chest.

"Westen, I mean it. Put me down. I'm fine. Just cold. Take

me back to work." She shifted violently in his arms. "Seriously, do as I ask. I want to walk."

Reluctantly, Westen bent his knees to set her down, supporting her for a few moments till she found her feet. "Emma love, I wish you'd let me carry you. You fainted and you're white as a sheet and unsteady."

"I've told you. I'm okay. Just a bit wobbly, that's all."

He'd put her down facing the witch's circle and the recognition hit her again like a blow, knowing she carried a miniature replica of it in her bag.

She shook her head to shake away the thrumming that threatened to assail her once more. "Take me back to the surgery, Westen." He was about to open his mouth again when she reached out and put a finger over it. "You can insist all you like, but I'm going back to work. I'm okay. I'm sorry I worried you and said something stupid. I honestly can't remember." She took an unsteady step forward. "But you can give me your arm, if you like."

He gave an I-told-you-so grunt and held out the crook of his elbow. Slowly, they turned their backs on the circle and retraced their steps along the path and to the car. Abigail climbed in the rear while Westen settled Emma in the passenger seat and fussed over her seatbelt. She slapped his hands away. "Stop it. I'm not an invalid. I can do it myself!"

Defeated, he walked round to the driver's side, scowling. Abigail leant forward and said, "You sure you don't remember anything, Ems?"

"Oh, don't you start. I've already said so haven't I? I just felt a bit queasy, that's all. Next thing I knew, you two were standing over me."

Abigail leaned back in her seat as Westen climbed in, his eyes boring into Emma as he sat a moment without turning on the engine.

Eventually, he spoke. "At least you work for a doctor. I'll tell Mason to look you over."

"You will do no such thing." said Emma. She relented. "Look, I understand you're looking out for me, but I won't be bullied. I'm perfectly capable of asking him myself."

"But you won't, will you?" he replied.

She said nothing.

Firing up the car, muttering something that sounded very much like, "I fucking give up..." Westen took out his frustrations on the gear-changes back to the surgery. After arriving, he parked up and without a glance at Emma, twisted in his seat to face Abigail. "Thank you for your time. You've been really helpful."

"Have I?" she said. "Something tells me you won't give what I said a second thought."

"A witch's circle?" He nodded, thoughtfully. "I can take that on board. Quite easily, actually. It's a matter of record how women got othered back in the day. How they still are, of course. I can quite believe they bought into the mythology and began creating their own myths and artefacts."

Abigail balled her fists. "Westen, that's complete, revisionist bollocks. You're—"

"I know, I know," he interrupted, attempting a smile. "Revisionist bollocks, eh? You *have* been doing some reading!"

"Take that patronising grin off your face. I like you, Westen, I really do but sometimes you can be a total arsehole."

Relieved that the mood had lightened, Emma joined in and chortled, "She's right, you know. You can."

He swivelled in his seat and put his hands up in surrender. "Okay, okay. In my defense, though, just remember I asked you both meet me because I genuinely thought you could help. And believe it or not, you have. I am aware that there's something … off about Flammark and I also know, Emma, you don't tell me everything. It's fucking annoying." His eyes twinkled at Abigail through the rear-view mirror. "Still friends?"

"I suppose," she said. "If you take me back to the salon."

He chuckled. "Okay." Turning to Emma, he said, "Take it easy, you. Don't overdo it. Please ask Mason to give you the once-over. For me?"

"I'll think about it," she replied, knowing she wouldn't, "but I've told you, I'm okay." She shrugged his coat off and handed it to him. "Are you coming back tonight?"

"Not sure. We're waiting for a break in the case. I might stay at the station. We're all there, catching a bit of sleep when we can."

"Right, well just be aware, I'm going to attend evensong tonight. There's someone I need to talk to. If you do decide to come home, it might be late before I get back."

As she opened the car door and swung out her legs she threw a meaningful glance towards the back seat where Abby was grinning at her, mouthing, "Good luck!"

Emma rolled her eyes and clambered out, giving them both a quick wave before she scurried into the surgery.

8
SANDRA

Despite her protestations, Emma still hadn't properly recovered from her fainting fit in Seely Woods and she still felt a bit off when she pulled up outside Clearview after work. She hadn't a clue what caused it, remembering only experiencing some kind of dizzying feedback loop from the noise in her ears. Ben had started all that, of course; a defense mechanism to block out the terror. Its return must have triggered sensory memories. Classic PTSD. Then there was the witch's circle, of course, a macro twig-wreath. She knew something was coming, of course she did. Maybe the dread of it was what finally did for her in the woods.

Getting ready for church didn't feel right, either. When Will had still been around, she'd got into the habit of attending services. Every Thursday and most Sundays. She especially enjoyed evensong since its atmosphere was completely different from the weekly eucharist: the chairs arranged informally in a semi-circle, Will sitting slightly apart from the dozen or so stalwarts who attended. She liked the contemplative quiet he'd created, letting her mind wander in and out of a psalm, or a reading. Or a prayer.

When Sandra arrived in Flammark, Emma thought it only polite to attend her first eucharist. It didn't incline her to repeat the experience. Her relationship with the church—insofar as it could be called a relationship—had not been enough to continue the habit she'd developed when Will presided. Oh, the new incumbent could deliver a sermon well enough, but it hadn't been the same. Emma understood the church wasn't about the priest; *shouldn't* be about the priest. And yet, for her, it was. Pure and simple. She didn't need St Jude's to fan the flames of belief or persuade her of the existence of God. As she'd discussed at the caravan, the fact of Gabby's existence offered all the proof required. It was God's *nature* that was the problem. The sort of nature that could create the monster Ben turned into, or that could permit the defilement of such a man as Peter. He had been beautiful in every way she could think of: kind, intelligent—devoted. Not to mention the love of Will's life. She shuddered at the memory of his hanging, tortured figure, and then what followed: Will's anger and rejection because of what she'd kept from him about the man behind his murder.

Animus.

It was too much to hold together and Jude had been no help whatsoever.

Soon, she was ready. It surprised her that despite everything, she was quite looking forward to the service—if not to meeting Sandra. A bit of quiet contemplation might well do her good. Though far too early for the service, Emma felt too antsy and wired to hang about. Better to spend some time walking the church grounds, familiarising herself with them again.

She put on her duffel, grabbed her bag and unbolted the door but before slamming it shut behind her, she glanced down at the step. Nothing there. There'd been no more scratchy visitations, no more gifts. She envisioned the little twig-wreath resting snugly as she carried it, finding it impossible to be parted from it. She could feel its much larger counterpart in Seely Woods calling to her, though she pushed it to the corner of her mind, unwilling to confront the idea that yet again she seemed to be the centre of someone's—or something's—attention.

Maybe she'd try to visit it again tomorrow, *if* she could slip past the police cordon.

She set off for the church.

Emma had made the journey across the green a thousand times. It had become second nature to her, even by torchlight, and to walk it in the dark held no fear for her. Progress, compared to when she'd first arrived in Flammark. Goodness, had it only been eighteen months ago? Then, she'd been unable to leave Clearview without looking over her shoulder, day or night, in constant fear that Ben had rooted her out.

She thought of him as she faced the church's lewdly carved entrance with its Romanesque carvings of bare-breasted women, leered at by goblins, fauns and antlered men, caught *in flagrante* by the porch's overhead lantern. The first thing people saw on entering their place of worship.

"I want to replace it, but the diocese won't let me."

Emma spun round.

Sandra Davis.

"Awful, isn't it?" she continued. "It might have listed status, but I don't think it belongs around the door of a church, do you? People don't see it for what it really is."

"You're probably right," Emma replied, "But Will told me it served a purpose. Helped to ease the transition from the old Celtic forms of worship to the new Christianity."

Sandra gave a knowing little smile and nodded her head.

"Ah, William Turner, my predecessor. Well, yes, he's right, of course. But that was over a millennium ago and a totally different world. The only purpose it serves today is to confirm our internalised misogyny. I'd rather see it prised out and replaced with something more appropriate. You're a friend? Of Turner's, I mean?"

Clever of Sandra to switch the subject mid-stream. It prevented Emma from launching a defence—both of the carving and Will's attachment to it. Which of course was completely the point of the tactic. And something about the word *predecessor* upset Emma, almost as if Sandra regarded herself as the true incumbent because Will would not be back.

"Yes. Will and I were—are—friends. I live in his cottage across the green. Clearview."

"Then you must be Emma Blake. The bishop told me about you."

"Did he, indeed. In what context?"

Sandra shrugged. "Will must have talked about you. Frederick said you'd been a great support to him and suggested I might look you up when I arrived. You know, in case being a woman priest scared the pigeons, and all that."

Did she just call the bishop, Frederick? *Frederick!*

"But you decided to give me a miss."

"Yes, I did." Sandra stepped back to let one of her congregation pass, her face creasing into an instant smile that never quite reached her eyes. "Good evening. Lovely to see you." She switched off the smile and continued, "I think the days of animosity towards female ministry are pretty much in the past. I haven't found the need for the kind of support Frederick suggested and I've never been much of a fan of … shall we say *sisterhood,* in the modern sense of the word. So far, I've found everyone very welcoming and amenable—at least most of them."

Emma had imagined this conversation taking place around the table in the vicarage kitchen. Had hoped she might be invited, envisioning herself and Sandra hugging cups of coffee, dunking biscuits; laying the foundation for some kind of friendship perhaps. She hadn't expected it to happen outside the church, freezing their socks off, interrupted by the arrivals to the service.

"Most of them?"

"I'm no gossip, Emma. Though I expect you've heard of my plans. If you had a cosy friendship with William Turner, you'll also be close with Robert Mason our, oh-so-conservative leader of the PCC. No doubt he's told you about my intentions for the future of St Jude's?"

No point in hiding it. "Yes. Yes, he has."

"So... are you here for the service or to suss me out?" That smile again, cold as the weather.

Emma felt completely wrong-footed, Sandra making no attempt to get her on-side nor forging the barest effort to be friendly. And she sensed an empathy gap. Interesting, given this priest was throwing herself behind huge plans to develop youth ministry in the parish. Kids pick up on that sort of thing. There was hostility, too. Maybe Sandra suspected Emma of spying for the enemy.

Which, of course, she was.

"People just do not seem to understand the importance of what I'm proposing. We need to work with children more than ever. They are disaffected and feel they have no future. They need to know the church is behind them, supporting them in every stage of their lives. *This* is what the church is for, not to act as an ecclesiastical handmaiden to its fossilised heritage."

If Emma had been prone to violence, right then and there she'd have slapped Sandra right in the middle of her self-righteous smirk. Unfortunately, she wasn't, which meant she had to listen to more of her patronising crap.

"The church needs this kind of progressive mindset, Emma. People respond to it. It's why I've been asked to join the police in their efforts to counsel the friends and classmates of those poor, poor, murdered children."

Emma's eyebrows reached for the stars. Westen sanctioned *that*? Asked for *her*?

Against such self-aggrandisement, Emma knew she'd be on a hiding to absolutely nowhere if she argued. Now certainly wasn't the time or the place. She merely set her face in a stiff smile and said, "That sounds very worthy, Sandra."

The woman narrowed her eyes. "Why did you come? Was it to sound me out? To see if Robert Mason and his cronies were right about me? I can hear from your tone we follow different agendas."

"Do I need an agenda to come to one of your services?"

Sandra made no reply.

"I had wanted to meet you," Emma continued. "And believe it or not, I was looking forward to the service but now I'm pretty sure I wouldn't be welcome. You seem to want to pre-judge me and I get the distinct impression you don't want me here. Which is odd, given your vocation.

Sandra merely moved the corners of lips upwards. It wasn't a smile. "I think most people who are going to arrive have done so." She looked at her watch. "I have to get ready. So nice to meet you, finally. I hope you enjoy the service—if you do decide to join us, that is. Good evening."

Taken aback at the brush-off—at the whole encounter, if truth be told—Emma stared aghast as the priest turned her back on her and strolled into the church. She supposed she couldn't blame the woman for being defensive, after all she was right in calling out her motivation for being there. It had nothing whatsoever to do with cultivating sincere friendship and it probably showed. Still, the tenor of the entire encounter stung. There seemed a kind of ruthlessness in Sandra. Not what she expected and definitely not priestly.

She hovered on the threshold, unsure whether she wanted to go in. Stepping aside as a few stragglers passed her —no one she knew—she took out her phone to check the time. Nearly seven. She shivered. It had become a very bleak outing indeed.

Eventually deciding to step inside. Emma peeked into the nave as the assembly of exactly eight people took their seats, scattered on the front row like crows on a fence. No semicircle. The chairs remained in the position they were locked into for the Sunday eucharist. Sandra sat facing them, next to the only source of heating in the church, a single calor-gas heater. Will would have fired up the boiler. Under his stewardship and with tourists aplenty, there'd always been a weighty collection box to empty at the end of the day. The accumulated funds were more than enough for the parish to afford to heat the church one night a week, even in winter.

But maybe all that had passed. Based in Sandmarsh, this Solomon Barnes fellow wouldn't be able to tie the church into the heritage work in quite the same way Will had, and Sandra clearly had no interest in it.

Not good. Not good at all.

Clear beyond any doubt that she would not feel a welcome addition to this particular party—and certainly couldn't be any kind of friend to Sandra Davis—Emma turned on her heels and headed home.

9
CONFAB

The next evening, the friends were gathered around Wyland's log fire, in Wyland's sitting room drinking from Wyland's cups. Except for Robbie. His turn to do a stint at the local hospital.

"So, you're in charge of the place, Gabby?" said Emma.

"Yes. And I have some big news."

"Oh," said Abigail, curled up on the big floor cushion. "Do tell!"

"Wyland's not coming back. For a while, anyway."

"Not coming back?" Abigail repeated. "I thought even a holiday was a bit of a stretch. He's a Guardian. Isn't he bonded to Wood End?"

"Of course, he is! He wouldn't be able to stay away forever. This place will pull him back soon enough." Gabby took a swig from her coffee mug. "He's got caught up with a group of Native Americans in Minnesota. They're fighting against an oil pipeline some big corporation is building on their tribal lands."

"Don't they have their own Guardians, for that?" asked Emma.

"They do. But Wyland heard of their plight and couldn't resist paying them a visit—"

"—and got himself sucked in." Abigail grinned. "Well, I suppose they need him more than we do especially as you're here to take the watch."

"Exactly," said Gabby. "To be honest, I'm glad. It's given me some purpose. Wyland said he doesn't know when he'll be back but that I can have the run of the cottage if I want."

"You've moved in?" said Emma.

"No. Believe it or not, I quite like my caravan. It's all I need and its cosy and warm. And it gives me a clear view of Peter's henge."

She stopped speaking and the three of them fell silent.

"I still can't get over what happened to him," said Emma. "What agony he must have gone through."

"He was a true martyr, for sure," Gabby replied. "We've all been changed by it. I have to say though, Emma, he's not the only one to have fallen foul of what Flammark has to offer. You've come through everything it's thrown at you much better than anyone had any reason to expect. And I'm not just talking about what happened to last year. Most people would have upped sticks by now."

"I've thought about it, believe me. But … how can I explain it? It's like Wyland's situation. I was drawn to the place by my forbears—albeit the evil that resided in them—and now, come what may, I'm not sure I can leave even if I wanted to."

"Then there's Westen," said Abigail, giving Emma a sly glance. "That all seems to be going very well."

Emma smiled. "It is. He's … wonderful. He makes me feel safe and I trust him. I'm very lucky. But…"

"You have to keep things from him," said Gabby. "I can see how that could be awkward."

"Yes, it is. He senses something, I'm sure he does. But I

can't tell him everything. It is a worry. I was pushing it when I suggested he investigate those school absences a bit further."

"What absences?" Abigail asked.

Emma took a moment to put her in the picture.

"Oh no. Sounds like what happened to Grandad, and all the others. You know, when the Blackstone curse was raging about."

"That's what I thought," said Emma. "Gabby's less convinced."

"Hmm. I've been thinking about that. Absolutely I don't think the curse has returned. I told you, Michael and I got rid of that box you put it in once and for all. But I didn't say these awful murders—or more specifically the reactions of the poor parents—had nothing to do with the Blackstones. There's every likelihood there *is* a connection, I simply don't know what it is yet." She put down her cup. "So, in the meantime, tell us how you got on with Sandra." *San Dra.*

"You managed to talk to her, then?" asked Abigail. "How did it go?"

"Awful," Emma replied. "It couldn't have gone worse. She was unfriendly—hostile, even. I got to the church early, hoping to catch her before evensong started, maybe get her to invite me to the vicarage for a chat afterwards."

"She didn't?" Abigail leant forward, elbows on Wyland's low coffee table, cupping her chin in her palm.

"Closed down as soon as she realised I was a friend of Will's. From what transpired, I think she's feels assailed by detractors and thought I might be one of them. Any hopes you had of me gaining her trust or pumping her for information are well and truly dashed. If I'm honest, I couldn't stand the woman and it very soon became clear she couldn't stand me."

Abigail sighed. "That's a shame. Maybe her shields are up."

"Oh, they were. It felt like she didn't want friendship at all—and not just mine. She's on a crusade, for sure, but ..."

"Go on," Gabby urged.

"Westen sent a team of police officers with family liaison training to the school. You know, to help the kids come to terms with what's happened to their classmates? Sandra said she'd been invited. That's not true. I spoke to Westen earlier. He said she invited herself. He was more than prepared to go along with it, no problem there; it's just not what she said had happened."

"A liar, then. And an insecure one, to boot. She has to big herself up." said Gabby. "Didn't I tell you there was something off about her?"

"Oh, I don't need converting on that score. You should have heard what she said about Will's heritage work."

"I can imagine. Par for the course," Gabby sneered. "It's what primitive thinkers do. They have to kill off the last idea."

"Still, you'd think she'd be about making friends, not pushing them away," said Abigail. "If she's got big plans, she'll need people on her side."

"Will she, though?" Emma replied. "What she's proposed is, essentially, about money. Oh, there's the youth ministry aspect and all that but it wouldn't surprise me if the diocese will consider any worthy proposal if it also happens to fill their bank accounts."

"Cynical much?" said Abigail.

Emma shook her head. "Perhaps. But practical, too. I used to work in HR for a big city firm, remember? I can't tell you how many tears were shed over lost causes because they weren't cost-effective. We all know the established Church is, in effect, a corporation. It owns thousands of acres of land, yet its influence and reach is dwindling. Money talks, even there." She frowned. "But you were right, Gabby, I don't see Sandra working well with kids. Not at all. I didn't sense any kind of empathy there. It wasn't just in our conversation, there was hardly anyone at evensong and even the few that were there sat well away from each other. And the church was freezing." She shuddered. "The whole set-up seemed to reflect her personality. Kids are sensitive. She may be providing them with facilities, but if she runs her youth ministry in the same manner I saw last night, they won't go anywhere near. Her youth mission will fail and the renovations to the church—and the vicarage—will be a tragic waste of time and money."

"Just what Flammark needs," said Abigail. "Murders, witches and now a neurotic vicar."

"Witches?" said Gabby.

"Westen wanted our opinion of something near his crime scene out at Seely Woods. We went there with him yesterday," Abigail explained. "It was a witch's circle. Emma passed out."

Gabby sat up. "A what?"

Abigail chuckled. "Interesting you honed-in on that and not Emma's reaction to it. But yes. I think so." She picked up a book from one of the piles on Wyland's huge, low coffee table and started riffling through the pages. "It was a huge circle framed by masses of twigs and branches woven together. See … like this." She held up the book at a page containing half a dozen pictures of similar constructions.

"They're not really witches' circles," said Emma, quickly, glancing at the pages she held up. "They're purely decorative. Found art. They don't mean anything."

As one—astonished—Gabby and Abigail turned to her.

"What makes you the expert?" said Abigail, sounding almost offended.

Emma bit her lip. Tried not to side-glance at her shoulder bag.

Gabby kept the silence for a few moments before saying to her, "And you passed out when you saw the one in Seely Woods?"

"Yes. It was nothing. I just felt a bit queasy."

"Queasy?! That's a complete understatement!" Abigail exclaimed. "Gabby, the blood completely drained from her face then she just crumpled to the floor. You should have seen Westen! He was out of his mind!"

Gabby made no reply, regarding her friend through hooded lids.

Emma shifted in her seat. "What are you looking at me like that for? Honestly, it wasn't worth the fuss. I felt better almost straight away."

"True witches' circles are very rare," said Gabby. "And Emma had a reaction to it, you say?"

Abigail nodded.

"Then it probably was."

"Eh ... What ... ?" came the scattered replies.

Gabby smiled. "*Witch* is a bit of a catch-all term, a name that's given to an old woman; a crone—usually pejorative and hardly ever used nowadays in that way. It's also used to describe followers of a certain path—like yourself, Abigail. You have certain ... shall we say, mystical energies that set you apart. And I think also, you quite like the term?"

Abigail grinned. "Yeah. I do a bit."

"But occasionally places can be visited upon by a particular kind of malevolence—usually female—and definitely not of this world. Often they return because of some past torment."

"Why do they build circles?" Abigail asked, eyes sparkling.

Gabby shrugged. "I don't really know. I haven't had

personal experience of their ways. But all creatures like to make their mark. Like to announce their presence. I doubt this one is any different."

She turned to Emma. "Interesting that she's honed-in on you. We talked about it the other day, didn't we? The way the Blackstone curse found you and brought you here and that business with Animus' essence. I can't say for sure what's in Seeley Woods, but if Emma reacted to it like that, then we can assume the worst. And judging by her opinion of the pictures in that book, she certainly seems to think it's a genuine witch's circle. Am I right, dear?"

Emma did not like the sudden attention. She could have kicked herself over that comment. Her mind flew to the twig-wreath, unable to get over the feeling that the remark had cost her in some way; that it meant trouble.

"You seem very attached to that bag," Gabby observed. "You haven't let it out of your sight all night."

"Haven't I?" Emma replied. She should have been more careful.

"Is there something you want to share with us?"

Emma tried a laugh. "Like what?"

"Emma. Dear..." Gabby replied. "William leaves, a new incumbent threatens us with a radical change of direction, and there've been a spate of truly awful murders. A witch's circle appears in Seely Woods, and it is blindingly obvious that you are hiding something."

"I-I don't know what you mean," said Emma careful to keep her eyes on nothing but Gabby.

"Oh, yes you do. What is in your bag?"

"I... I can't."

"Can't or won't?"

Tension crackled in the air. Abigail looked from Gabby then to Emma and back again, clearly both fascinated and alarmed at the turn the conversation had taken.

Emma broke first. Shrinking back on the sofa, she said, "I can't explain it. I mean, I physically can't. It's like it's in my head all the time. Whenever I try to say something about it, I get this… this thrumming. Here… " She rubbed her temple. "I used to get it with Ben. Caused by stress, I suppose." She grabbed her bag; held it close in.

"Have you told Gabby about what happened at Clearview, yet? The night we all met at the Flammark Arms?" Abigail asked. "You said you would."

"What's this?" asked Gabby.

Damn Abigail. Damn all of them. Why couldn't they all just leave her alone?

"I'd come to the pub with Ems because I'd turned up at Clearview about an hour before. I had some kind of premonition; a sense Emma was in danger. Turned out her front door had been damaged—deep scratches gouged into the paintwork, as if something had taken a screwdriver to it. Odd thing was, they were finger-widths apart, as if the scratches had been made by the fingers of a hand —though it would have to have been a bloomin' strong hand."

"Why on earth didn't you tell me?" Gabby sat open-mouthed, frowning at both her friends.

"I wanted to!" said Abigail. "I expected Emma to have a word that night but, well, you were a bit the worse for wear. Said she'd tell you later." She turned to her friend, "But you didn't, did you?"

Slowly, Emma shook her head. "It felt wrong. It felt like … a betrayal."

"A betrayal of what? Who?" said Gabby. She narrowed her eyes. "Do you know who made the scratches?"

Again, Emma shook her head. "No … At least …" She slumped, defeated. Gabby wasn't going to let up. "On one level, perhaps," she admitted. "There's familiarity there, certainly, but beyond that I can't say. I certainly can't put a name to her."

"*Her?*" Gabby leant forward as if sniffing something out. "Abigail ...Take Emma's bag away. I think she wants you to, but she can't ... allow you to. Isn't that right, my dear?"

Head suddenly pounding, Emma blinked. Gave the tiniest of nods. All she could manage.

Slowly, carefully, Abigail rose from her cushion and stepped towards the sofa. One by one, she unclenched Emma's fingers that clung onto the bag's shoulder strap and slipped the whole thing out of her grasp. She carried it over to Gabby.

Emma let out a cry as fear mingled with relief. A weight off. But there was an awful kind of emptiness, too ...

...as if she'd lost Will all over again.

Gabby opened the bag and reached inside; gasped as she drew out the twig-wreath encased in its plastic bag.

Abigail drew in a breath too. "Ems! Where did you get that?"

Emma swallowed hard as she tried to use her words. "It was on my doorstep. I found it on the way out to the pub that night."

"But I was there then. We left together. I didn't see anything!"

"Yes. I know. I didn't see anyone, either."

"I rather think this settles it," said Gabby, grimly. "We may have a witch on our hands. If so, I doubt very much she's of the Wiccan kind."

The room fell quiet, the silence interrupted only by the rhythmic ticking of Wyland's home-made clock.

"Are you sure of this, Gabby?" Abigail murmured. "You're leaping to a lot of conclusions. And if a witch is responsible for the murders, then that's a completely different ball game.

"It is, but you can't deny that an obvious pattern is developing here. We're nowhere close to joining the dots but this little wreath and Emma's attachment to it, together with the circle, the scratches you described—the deaths of those poor children—we have to seriously consider the possibility. If I'm right, then she's malign, deadly and definitely not human."

Emma couldn't bear it. A tsunami of emotions assailed her and as if from nowhere she suddenly burst out crying! Abigail immediately jumped up and sat next to her, putting a comforting arm around her. "Sh... shush, Ems! It's okay. Whatever this is, we'll sort it. You know we will. We've done it before."

Emma, a mess of tears and snot turned to her bag for a tissue and growled in frustration because it wasn't there. The girl gestured to Gabby to throw it back. Rummaging inside, Emma sniffed, "I'm sorry. I don't know what's wrong with me. Now you've taken it away it's like a connection's gone. Like I've lost someone."

"That'll be her doing. The witch." said Gabby. "She's singled you out, Emma. Gave you a gift. Something she made herself. For some reason, you're important to her."

"Important?"

"Yes. But this is a good thing. Now her gift is not in your possession, she'll seek you out again and try to reconnect. Maybe it'll allow us to find out what she wants before she murders anyone else."

"You think she *wants* something?" asked Abigail.

"Oh yes, witches of this ilk always do."

Then to her own enormous surprise, Emma made a sudden lunge at Gabby. Tried to snatch the twig-wreath away. "Give it back. Give it back! I need it."

Gabby jerked it away out of her reach. Though smiling, she shook her head.

Then threw it in the fire.

10

JENNIFER

Come with me, sister.

Jennifer Grey opened her eyes and not realising where she was for a moment, frowned. Despite a weird kind of buzzing—from behind her eyes of all places—she looked around for a moment then grinned. They were in the second seat from the back of the coach—snoggers corner—returning from their day trip to Lanchester. She snuggled deeper into Mark's arms as he dozed next to her, but couldn't settle now she'd woken. Extricating herself, she sat up and tapped the heel of her hand against her temple. That stupid buzzing was pissing her off.

"Okay, everyone, wakey wakey!" Sweaty Colin was striding down the aisle of the coach using the backs of the seats to brace himself as he held out a large black bin liner. "Rubbish in here, please. Don't leave anything behind. We've had a great trip. Try not to let yourselves down now."

Mark, having shaken himself awake too, checked near his feet. "What the hell?" Annoyed and tutting, he scrabbled about on the floor snatching up an armful of coke cans and empty sweet packets. "You nobheads!" He turned round to face the row of grinning loons on the back seat and threw the rubbish back at them. "Get rid of your own shit."

"Ha, ha!" chuckled Macturd, hurling the cans back. "We wondered when you'd notice, Yatesie! First you were busy chewing Jen's face off, then you fell asleep. Get a rooooooom."

"Sorry, sir." Macturd said, sing-song, grinning contemptuously as the teacher scowled at him. "Just giving Mark and his new girlfriend a bit of relationship advice."

Jennifer jumped onto her knees and threw herself over the seat at him, grabbing at a crisp packet and slapping him over the head with it. "Shut yer face, dickhead!" She would have laughed with him, though, had the bee inside her head hadn't got so freakin' painful.

The coach stopped on the zigzags outside the school left clear by the bank of waiting cars. As they got off, Jennifer said, "Mark, sos, but I'm not going back to yours. I'm going home. I feel weird."

"Aww," Mark replied, his voice heavy with disappointment. "Alright. I'll walk you."

"Better not. If dad spots you, he'll go mad. I told him I'd be staying over with Theresa. I'll ring and get him to pick me up."

"Okay. I'll wait with you, then."

She fished out her phone and waited until the coach door hissed shut and it pulled away. She was just about to press the call button when a shout echoed across from one of the cars.

"Oi, Yatesie!" It was Macturd. "Wanna lift? We're going your way."

Mark hesitated. Jennifer, on tip-toes, plonked a kiss on his lips. "You go," she said. "Dad'll come as soon as I call him."

"Well, if you're sure? Don't want to leave you here on

your own. Not with ... you know, not with what's been going on."

"Yeah, I do. Shelley was in my art class, remember? But I'm sure. Dad won't be more than five minutes. Better that than a fifteen-minute walk home. I'll stay right here till he comes, promise."

He kissed her again, long and slow.

"Oh, for Christ's sake," Macturd shouted. "Do me a bleedin' favour! Give the girl a rest!"

Mark abruptly broke off the kiss and swivelled round, giving Macturd the finger. "Shut up, wanker."

Sweaty simpered towards them, flapping his hand and shushing, asking them to keep it down.

"Now look what you've done," said Jennifer. "Just go. I'll be okay."

She wondered how long she would remain in his head after Mark's long legs had skipped over the road to the car that waited for him. With a painful grin—that fucking bee!—she watched the lads get in what looked like some kind of sports model. Macturd senior fired the engine, pulled out and gunned away.

Apples don't fall very far from the tree.

Sweaty closed in. Freakin' perv. Jennifer shivered at the thought of him in class, leaning over her enough that she could, feel his breath on her shoulder as he took the pencil from her hand to sort out a bit in her picture. Go away ... go away ... go away.

"You alright Jen? Do you want a lift?"

"It's Jennifer, Mr. Sweeting. No, it's alright. Dad'll be here in a minute!" She lifted up the phone. Lying, she said, "I've just called him."

Sweaty put a hand on her arm. She recoiled as he stooped over her, a simpering grin on his soft face. "I can't leave you on your own. Not after everything that's happened."

"Honestly sir, I'll be fine." Jennifer shrugged his hand away. She'd seen the cops at the school, had even spoken to that vile vicar woman. She knew the score. The last thing Jennifer wanted was to be waiting in the dark on her own with this idiot. A thought crossed her mind. Shit, what if it's him? What if he's the sicko that took her mates and buried them in the freakin' woods? Half worried, now, debating quickly with herself whether Sweaty Colin had it in him to commit serial murder, she said, "Please, sir, will you just … go. Leave me alone."

Sweaty frowned and took a step back, looking around at the empty street. "Shhh. Not so loud, Jen."

"I've told you, it's Jennifer. And you're making me really, really nervous." A spiteful smile formed on her face, as with increased volume she cried. "If you don't go, sir, I'll scream. I'll scream really, really loud. Then you'll get the sack. Which is what you deserve." Going in for the kill, she shouted, "Paedo."

With a smirk, she could see she'd hit home noting the flash of fear in his eyes as he backed away.

"Why are you being like this?" he cried. "Why does everyone think I'm … after something? I'm not, you know."

"Because you're rubbish. You're a rubbish teacher. You can't handle us. And just look at you." Her lips twisted in disgust. "You're ugly and your breath smells like shit. And you look at us weird."

Sweaty's face crumpled and he backed away, tripping slightly on the kerb. "You little bitch," he said. Defeated, he shuffled to his car.

And drove away.

Jennifer grinned to herself and gave a spiteful little chuckle. Well, that sent him packing. Now, what was she supposed to be doing?

She looked down at the square of black plastic and glass

in her hand. It had something to do with that. She cocked her head, trying to fathom it, vaguely aware she had to use it—that it was *important* she use it—but she hadn't a clue what it was for.

She tried to lift it—wanted to fathom it—but... Shit. *She couldn't move*! Not a leg. Not a hand. Not a finger.

Then, one by one, the streetlights dimmed. Heart pounding, her brain desperately tried to remember what she should be doing with the device; the thing she grasped like her life depended on it.

A noise.

A scratching, shuffling kind of noise. Behind her. Jennifer tried to turn but nothing would work!

The scraping sound neared. Rhythmic, crackly—like someone walking on a dry forest floor. And in her head... words came.

Do not fear, sister, for I have come to save you.

Heart beating so fast, Jennifer's breaths came in tiny, shallow gasps as she felt someone—something—rustle-in next to her.

There, there. I am with you. He won't find you now.

A touch.

On her hand.

Head locked, Jennifer could only move her eyes. She glanced down at the shiny thing she held. She felt a muscle relax—with no permission from her—and it dropped out of her grip and onto the pavement.

A hand took its place. A long-fingered hand with filthy broken nails. She glimpsed white, parchment-dry skin glowing sickly in the dimmed streetlights as it snaked in and around Jennifer's manicured fingers.

She felt another touch on, then around her shoulders. Still inexplicably frozen, only her guts could recoil as she strained her eyes to track the movement of another hand. Felt it flex on her other arm to hold it like a vice.

You have nothing to fear from me. I am here to protect you. I have found a place where you can be safe.

Jennifer suddenly found her legs were moving. But only her legs. Desperate to see in whose embrace she'd been caught, she strained her eyes sideways, managed with all her strength to unlock a neck muscle and gain a millimetre of traction.

Which is how she saw.

In profile, the makings of a face.

Skin pitted. Dirty-white like chalk. A cavernous black eye socket stared relentlessly ahead, a pinprick of white light the only sign that life stirred within.

But what kind of life?

They seemed to walk for miles, Jennifer spending twice the energy the journey needed in resisting the force that drove each step. It was exhausting. Where was everybody? It was late, but not that late. Why didn't anyone stop them? Why couldn't they see what was happening to her? Why couldn't they see … it?

No one is interested, sister. No matter how loud you might cry no one will hear. No matter whose door you knock upon, they will not answer. No matter how much you beg for help, no one will care. This much I know.

What the freakin' hell? A new fear flooded in with a certainty that made her heart quail. This was what happened to the other girls! Jesus, oh, sweet, sweet Jesus. Hadn't they been buried? Hadn't they been buried…

… alive?

Summoning every last ounce of strength, Jennifer screamed inside for her legs to stop. And they heard her! She paused mid-step and was about to tear away from the creature's bony grasp when the bee in her head buzzed stronger, filling her head with white noise, cutting her off from herself.

Inwardly she sobbed, for no sound passed her lips as they resumed the march along Flammark's deserted High Street, past the pub and onwards. Where the fuck was it taking her? Jennifer's muscles shrieked they were tired, oh so freakin' tired—yet still the creature wouldn't let her go; wouldn't let her speak. She stumbled and its grip changed, keeping her upright, keeping her going on and on and on.

... And on to the church. To St Jude's. Where the white noise changed. Changed into words...

Soon, my sister. Soon we will be there.

The graveyard. Jennifer recognised it from her grandmother's funeral. They passed her burial site with its white marble memorial, long-dead daisies in the vase on top. Then older tombs, with huge black headstones twice her size, looming this way and that in the moonlight.

To a corner. A corner the furthest away from the church. To another tilted tombstone, black as the dead it watched over.

Its grave was open.

An ebony maw.

The creature took her bony arm away—no need to guide what couldn't walk—and the white noise spoke again.

I wanted you to rest with our other sisters, but they are discovered. His henchmen have them. I know others in this place. They will welcome you, too. You need fear no more.

Every muscle, every sinew, every nerve in Jennifer's body made futile war against what they were forced to do next. Slowly, inexorably, her legs took her to the graveside where they knelt, then seated her, then swung over the edge of the pit. Terror and dread and horror and revulsion fought head on with the creature's compulsive grip on her psyche.

She knew what was coming.

Like an automaton, she dropped down into the grave, her feet crashing through the corroded metal of the ancient casket below. Explosions of agony coursed through her system as her ankles shattered. Still—somehow—they supported her, as her broken feet cracked through more of the coffin on her way to the end of the grave where her legs were forced to bend and she was made to lie; lie on top of the old bones inside.

In excruciating pain Jennifer felt her arms bend at the elbows and rise. Then they crossed and her hands sank to rest upon her bosom. Overwhelmed by agony and exhaustion —barely conscious—Jennifer fixed desperately on the rectangle of moonlit sky above and at the silhouette of a figure that was kneeling over the graveside, two pinpricks of dead light peering at her. And on its head, some kind of ... nest?

Jennifer tried to scream. Tried to implore. Strained every sinew and vocal cord she had to hurl one last plea for her life.

But all she could manage was silence.

It was then she knew.

She was going to die.

The creature disappeared and soon freezing soil rained down, spattering her broken ankles; her exhausted limbs, her face, her clamped-shut mouth. Unable to resist the soil's inevitable ingress before long, she was covered.

Buried.

Smothered.

In the time it took for her heart to burst, all Jennifer perceived was her inside self, alone with the receding white noise and the words in her brain.

There, there, my sister. There, there.

11
TICK, TOCK

Ten o'clock, Monday morning and Westen's squad was back in his office. The man himself entered, jaw set, face grim, folders in one hand and a bottle of water in the other. "Settle in, everyone," he said, taking his usual place at the head of the conference table with Burrows. "You'll have heard by now, we've another victim, so let's get on with it. First, I need to introduce Dr Martha Jacobs, a clinical psychologist based at Oakmarsh. She has some profiling experience. She hasn't been fully briefed yet, but I've asked her to sit in, anyway." He turned to her. "Welcome, Martha. Any questions, feel free to ask."

Jacobs, a small, neat, suited figure gave the assembly a terse smile and nod. She didn't look much older than the victims.

"Okay, Donna, you have the floor," said Westen.

"Guv." Donna cleared her throat and began. "This morning, Julie Tarrant rang in to report three absences. Schoolmates saw two of them that morning, though both were unwell when they were called for. The third is a different story. Jennifer Grey."

The detective pointed at her photograph, newly added to the victim board.

The assembly murmured and shifted in their seats to look.

"An hour ago, I called on the Greys. Jennifer wasn't there. As with the other victims, the parents were completely unaware their daughter was missing. I've got a FLO with them now."

"How the hell … sir?" Stamford sat, head shaking. "I still don't get it. How could they not notice?"

"Nor do I," said Westen, grimly. "Martha, that's going to be one for you."

Brow furrowed, the profiler nodded as she scribbled in a file.

Donna continued. "Thing is, Jennifer could have gone missing as early as Friday. She'd been on a school trip to Lanchester with a member of the art department—a Colin Sweeting, and two support staff. Got back late. Given the problem we have with the parents, we can't be sure that she didn't return home after the coach dropped them off. However Jennifer's boyfriend, a Mark Yates, said he'd left her with Sweeting and that she was supposed to call home and get her father to pick her up. He hadn't seen her for the rest of the weekend, though they had no plans meet up." She paused and looked around, significantly. "Her phone was found outside the school by a student. The screen was smashed. It wasn't passworded so it was easy to get in. She never made that call."

Westen waited a few moments for the information to sink in, then took over. "Pete, I know you're on with looking into Sweeting," said Westen. "Anything yet?"

Burrows shook his head. "Nada. He's not on our system. No record, not even a parking fine, Guv."

"Well, since he's the last person we know of to have seen

Jennifer alive, I'd like to say he's gone right to the top of our list of suspects. But that'd be a bit fucking rich because so far, he's our *only* suspect. I've spoken to the ACC and he's agreed we can't put off a press conference any longer. It's after this meeting. Then Pete and I are off to the Phoenix. I want to get a picture of what this Sweeting is like before we haul him in."

"And a picture of how that bloody trip was allowed to go ahead," Sheila muttered loudly.

Westen nodded. "Abso-fucking-lutely." That was the second time the DC had made her presence felt in one of his briefings. Westen liked it. She had grit and would be an asset to his squad—assuming he'd get the funding to take her on permanently.

Donna's phone vibrated. Peering at the screen she suddenly stiffened and cried, "He's here, Guv! Sweeting! He's just walked in!"

Westen raised his eyebrows. "Has he now? Well, good. Get downstairs to put him in an interview room and give him a cup of tea or three. Find someone who can keep him chatting. We've a busy morning and we need him to stay." As Donna started tapping on her phone, he turned to Burrows. "Pete, change of plan. Once this is over, go down and take his details. Ask him why he's here. Keep him busy. I'll go to the school on my own. I want to make sure he's here when I get back."

"Right you are, Guv."

"So … back to our latest victim," said Westen, briskly. "Sweeting is only a suspect at the moment but as we go over what happened with the Grey girl, let's see what we think of him for the other murders too. If we can tie him in, this all may be over sooner than we'd hoped."

He opened one of the files. "Okay. Jennifer disappeared three days ago. Given the frequencies of the murders, we think it safe to assume we won't find her alive. We've called the dogs out but I'm not optimistic we'll find anything else in Seely Woods. Uniform hasn't reported any suspicious activity and, of course, the killer must know we've discovered their burial site. Likelihood is, they've found a new one."

Martha interjected. "I agree. From what I've read so far, there are elements of ritual and pattern here. The killer is highly organised. Adaptable too. When the first murder didn't go as planned, they tightened up their MO."

"Blimey, Guv," said Stamford, "Most of Flammark's rural. She could have been buried anywhere."

"Yes." Westen replied. "If we knew what the woods meant to him, we could refine the search for Jennifer. Martha? Any ideas?"

"A few things first, if you'll bear with me. About these timings. Has Savage been able to work out the exact intervals between the burials?"

"More or less. He can only pinpoint the times of death on the most recent murders, but he does estimate all the girls died within no more than four days of each other." Westen handed her a sheet of paper. "Except for Jennifer. If she is dead—and I'm stone-cold certain she is—it's been a full seven days since the previous victim was buried."

Martha raised her eyebrows as she perused the document. "The murderer needed time to find a new site. That's what I mean about being adaptable. I also see that Savage found no toxins in any of the victims That would discount the use of Rohypnol as a subduer, of course. Potassium chloride or calcium gluconate then? They don't leave traces."

"Possibly," said Westen. "They're both prescription drugs. We've had a team onto that from day one, but they've come up with nothing from surgeries or chemists—or the hospital. Either the killer is very well connected or—"

"Not local," Jacobs finished for him. She shook her head.

"But that would be anomalous, Superintendent. The victimology and where they were found all suggest the perpetrator *is* local."

"Agreed," said Westen.

"And the victims," Martha continued, "All of them sixteen, all girls. Unmolested I understand?"

"Yes. Everything intact. Clothes intact. Hands crossed at the chest. No sign of sexual or physical assault."

"Yes. I saw that from the pictures you emailed." She put her pen down and faced the squad. "I think we're looking at a complex psychopathy. By the way the victims were posed, it is clear the killer is not motivated by rage and I believe is without sexual motivation as well. The fact that the girls were unmolested, together with their positioning, speaks to compassion, despite the brutal nature of their ending. The killer does seem to be putting these girls to rest in some way. A working-out of a past trauma, perhaps? That in ritualising their victims' murders, they are somehow putting themselves at rest too. At least temporarily. Until the urge to kill again becomes too strong to resist." She looked across at Westen. "There's very great empathy for the victims, here. We should look for that in Sweeting. But, in all honesty, weighing the facts, I think it's possible our killer is female."

Shocked murmurs hummed through the room. Sheila—again—piped up, "That's a bit of a stereotype, isn't it?"

Jacobs gave her a long look. "That's what you do every day on the job, is it not? You put together a picture of a perpetrator based on well recognised patterns of behaviour so as to predict their next move? My work is no different, if a little more … refined. Though it might be possible for a man to exercise the degree of care this particular perp gave their victims, the absence of any sexual aggravation clinches it for me. I could be wrong, of course. I'd certainly be interested to see what your suspect has to say for himself."

"Aside from Sweeting, Martha," said Burrows, "if we are looking at a female, that gives us another problem. The site's a good two hundred yards into the woods and no car could access it. There were no track marks to indicate a trolley or a barrow of some sort had been used. The victims must have been carried. It'd need some strength to haul a live victim—incapacitated or not."

"Why do you think they were carried, Pete? Couldn't they simply have walked?"

"Lured?" Westen replied, raising his eyebrows.

"Can't see it, Guv," said Tony. "Well, maybe one might be persuaded to go into the woods. But, all of them?"

"Dunno," said Donna. "Kids'll do a lot for a pretty face with a plausible story. Hell, not only kids! What I can't get my head around is what happened when they got there. Did they just willingly lay down and wait to be buried ... *alive*?"

"No, not willingly," said Martha, "But at someone else's will ... certainly."

"What do you mean?" said Westen, drumming his fingers on the table. He suddenly stopped. "Christ, you can't mean the girls were fucking hypnotised! Surely not! No one can hypnotise anyone to do something that would kill them."

Jacobs, unruffled, replied, "Why would they think they were being lured to their deaths, Superintendent? A skilled practitioner can get their victims to do almost anything, once under. Think about it. All he or she would have to do is direct them to walk, climb into a hole and lie down. They'd have no awareness about what was *about* to happen to them."

"Surely they'd struggle!" said Sheila. "Their reflexes would kick in."

Jacobs shrugged. "I don't have all the answers. All I can say is, I think it's a possibility. It might also explain the parents' ignorance. The killer might have got to them as well."

Sighs and scoffs murmured throughout the assembly. "That's seriously fucked up," said Stamford. "No serial killer I've ever heard of has ever done that before, they're too focused on their victims."

"It's worth considering," Jacobs answered. "Perhaps, in their delusion, they were trying to alleviate the parents' suffering in some way too—or to give them some time before the bodies were discovered. I don't know for sure. All I can offer is a different perspective." She turned to Westen. "I presume this is why I've been invited, Superintendent, because the clock is ticking and, apart from this walk-in, so far you've come up with nothing."

"I'm still not buying hypnotism," said Westen. "It's too … bizarre. Too rare."

"The technique itself isn't. Many health professionals use it. Psychiatric practitioners, therapists—some counselling services. Entertainers too, don't forget. And enthusiasts, of course."

"Okay," Westen said blowing out his cheeks. "I understand you can stay with us for a while? Dig into the cases. See if you can find anything that might verify this hypnosis theory of yours."

"Have you changed your mind about closing the school, Guv?" asked Donna. "We can't carry on like this."

"No," Westen replied. "Still can't the trust the parents. I think the school's the safest place for them. I want you and Sheila to base yourselves there. Arrange an assembly each morning where this one year group can register. Just the girls. I think it's now safe to say boys are not within the killer's target group." He glanced at Martha and she nodded. "As before, straight away knock on the doors of any absentees. But I want an extra layer of security. We need sight of all these girls after 10pm either by video link or, if necessary, a physical visit. Tony, big job, I know, but can you make sure all the parents have the right technology and know how to use it? We're talking about seventy-five households. Girls make up just over half the year group."

"Will do, Guv."

"And we're still bussing them. No exceptions unless they're walking to and from the school in pairs, at least. And the curfew is to stay."

Westen sat back and addressed his team more informally. "I've only got one more thing before we all go. Upstairs has sanctioned overtime on this and all leave's been cancelled. Seven girls, people! Seven girls in four weeks and a very frightened community." From out of his office window he spotted Thelma Reid, the press officer, approaching through the empty bullpen. He got up and strode to his desk to remove his jacket from his chair. Swinging it round his shoulder, his last words marked the end of the meeting. "And after this press conference ... they'll be a hell of a lot more frightened."

~

More frightened than he'd bargained for, as it happened. Half an hour later, he emerged blinking from the room full of journalists and press photographers to find Tony waiting for him.

"Guv," he panted. "You really opened the floodgates. The conference barely began before the phones started ringing. About Sweeting. Words got round about the trip. Parents have concerns."

"That's to be expected ..." Westen started.

"Yes, but they're not complaining about the trip itself, Guv. More about how he gives their daughters the creeps. Gets a bit too close, bit touchy-feely. Calls are still coming through but thought I'd give you what we had so far, seeing as you're going to the school."

Westen took the file and scanned through its contents. "Fucking hell, Tony."

"I know, Guv."

"Try to keep all this on the down-low. Could be a pile-on. Sweeting's obviously in the frame but we don't want to fan the flames any more than we have to, though that was always the risk with press conferences, as these phone calls demonstrate. I want to get the measure of this chap first. The last thing we need is a fucking witch hunt..."

12
SWEETING

Half an hour later, introductions over, Westen found himself in front of the Phoenix's Academy's executive head teacher, Marcus Redmayne. Sitting behind a huge rosewood desk, with what must have been the entire school's timetable pinned to the wall behind him, he seemed youngish, despite his greying hair. Where do they get them all from? This chap didn't look as if he could run a piss-up in the proverbial, let alone a fucking school. Pen-pusher, probably. Couldn't wait to get out of the classroom.

"Glad you're here, Superintendent. We've another, I understand. Please, sit." As Westen complied, Redmayne moved over to a set of cupboards on top of which rested a kettle and a tray of mugs. He lifted one aloft to Westen, but on seeing the detective shake his head, walked empty-handed back to his desk. "I'm fully aware I have to bear some of the responsibility. Colin—that's the member of staff who organised the trip—reminded me of it the day before. Since it would take the children out of the area, I thought it would be safe." He bowed his head. "A good idea, even."

"Well, you were wrong," Westen replied. "Maybe if you'd

made sure a senior member of staff had been on board to ensure the kids got home safely—and at the very least informed us of it too—things might have turned out differently. Jesus, man, we were bussing the kids to and from your school for a *reason*!"

Redmayne hung his head. "I know, I know. It's a decision I'll regret for the rest of my life. If it's any consolation, I'll probably lose my position."

"The parents have grounds to sue, you know."

The man slumped. "I was afraid you might say that. I suppose it's no more than I deserve."

Westen let him stew for a moment. "Except, like the others, they seemed not to notice their daughter was missing. We haven't made it public knowledge, though, to protect the parents from vilification. They're ashamed enough as it is. I just held a press conference and skirted the issue. Made a big thing about vigilance."

The head nodded and pushed out a breath of relief. "Thanks for that. This—what is it?—this *oblivion* certainly is very strange. A good thing the press hasn't got hold of it yet. Can you imagine the headlines! *Village sleeps while its children are murdered*. It beggars belief!"

Strange? Fucking bizarre, that's what it was. And it reminded Westen again about what happened during Ben Cregan's spree. Flammark shut down then, too.

"The situation has changed though, with Jennifer's murder," Redmayne continued, "When we discussed keeping the school open I was sceptical but, given all the circumstances, it turned out to be a good call. And we had some measure of success in helping the students through this. But Colin's in the frame, now, isn't he? Since he was possibly the last person to see Jennifer alive? The students know all about it and are understandably angry. It's an anger we may not be able to contain."

"Parents have been in touch with us too. Press conferences have a habit of opening things up. Hopefully, it'll be much harder for the killer to attack again now everyone's fully alerted. Sweeting's at the station now, as it happens. Came in of his own volition. Whether he is involved at a deeper level than leaving that poor kid on her own at silly o'clock at night with a killer on the loose, remains to be seen. But the lid's been lifted which all-in-all is a good thing. We still need you to keep the school open, though. Believe me, the kids are best served here. Work is always the best distraction."

"Okay, Superintendent," Redmayne sighed. "We'll do our best, but if things fall apart I may have to close—at least for a few days. The staff are at breaking point too, you know."

Westen nodded. Shifting his position, he changed the subject. "Tell me about Colin Sweeting."

Redmayne heaved another sigh and shook his head. Steepling his fingers he leant forward, elbows on his desk. "Colin returned to teaching relatively recently. He's been here just under two years. He experienced a great loss. It all came out in his interview—there'd been a gap in his employment history which we had to ask about. Turns out his wife was killed in a terrible accident. A nurse, apparently. Her hospital was short-staffed and she'd been working a double shift. They think she fell asleep at the wheel. He told us he'd had a nervous breakdown—tried to take his own life, in fact. Spent some time in an institution. It took a lot of courage for him to tell us and even more to rebuild his life and face the classroom again."

"I see," said Westen. "Well, as I said earlier, parents have been contacting us." He tapped on the thick file he'd placed in front of him. "There've been complaints. A lot."

Redmayne made his lips into a pencil line. "I can guess what they'll be about. It's mischief, Superintendent.

Mischief. He isn't … popular. He still hasn't completely mastered the science of behaviour management. Believe it or not, students like the structure a well-ordered classroom gives them. Its absence breeds disrespect, I'm afraid."

"So, why's he still here?"

Redmayne shrugged. "Education cuts, Superintendent. Constant change and churn. Most schools experience staff shortages nowadays—haven't you watched the news?" He smiled grimly. "Sweeting started off as a cover supervisor, what used to be called a supply teacher. Most have difficulty with classes—comes with the territory. But at least he was reliable. When a permanent position as an art teacher came up, we thought we'd give him a chance. The field wasn't strong and he's actually a very good artist in his own right. The portfolio he showed us was brilliant. He's exhibited, you know. But … you're right, things are clearly not working out. We put him on an improvement programme and he's been set targets. The way things have been going, and especially after what happened on Friday, he won't make it to the end of term."

"Have *you* had to field complaints?" Westen asked. "Inappropriate behaviour, that kind of thing?"

Redmayne hesitated. "He has, shall we say, an unfortunate … demeanor. Amongst other things, he's not good at eye-contact—"

"But he's better at physical contact. At least, that's what the parents who've rung in are implying. Last time I heard, that was certainly inappropriate!"

"Other than the odd muttering, we had one formal complaint, Superintendent. One. Colin put his hand on a student's arm."

"A female student?"

"Yes, but that was a while ago, not long after he'd joined us. We immediately sent him on a safeguarding course to get him up to speed on current dos and don'ts. There's been no repetition."

"So how do you account for these?" Westen handed Redmayne the file containing the wad of telephone notes. The head took a minute to flip through each sheet. Giving them back, he said, "It's kids, Superintendent. It's what they're like. I assure you, there's no foundation for any of this. Just embellishment. Probably as a result of your press conference. Parents are frightened and they are angry. Their kids too. And now they've found a scapegoat."

"Because he was with Jennifer Grey the night she died."

Redmayne, dipped his head. "There is that, of course."

"Did Sweeting come in this morning?"

"Yes, he did. Because of your investigation and involvement with the academy, we hold a staff meeting every morning before school starts to keep everyone appraised of the changes you asked for; details of counselling sessions, classroom changes and so on. I found him before he got to it and asked him to stay in my office while I broke the news that Jennifer had gone missing. It was news to him too, of course. The man was devastated when I told him. Burst into tears, actually." Redmayne shook his head, sadly. "I sent him home. There's no way he'll be able to stay here after all this. Hell, he'll probably never return to teaching. He blames himself." He lowered his voice. "As do I."

Westen said nothing. Seconds later, he started at what sounded like a loud, ambient doorbell.

"It's the bing-bongs," Redmayne explained. "Lesson change. Can I be of any further help? I'm teaching. I'd rather not find a substitute."

"No, no. You go ahead. You've been helpful, thank you."

Redmayne grabbed a large spiral-bound book and a box full of pens and markers. Westen looked at them quizzically as they made their way out, somehow glad he'd been wrong about the man and that he wasn't as tied to his office as he first thought. Redmayne spotted his expression and shrugged as he followed Westen's gaze. "I know, right? They never bloody bring their own!"

~

Twenty minutes later, Westen was back at the station. He found Burrows at his desk in the bullpen. "Sweeting still downstairs?"

"Yes, Guv. Left him twenty minutes ago after taking his details and having a bit of chat. Kept it light, nothing about the case. When I'd finished with him, he said he was happy to wait. He didn't look as if he had anywhere else to go, to be honest."

"First impressions?"

"A bit wet. Seems harmless enough but we know that doesn't mean anything. Said he knew we'd want to speak to him seeing as he'd been on that trip. He certainly seems upset. Thinks he might have been the last one to see the Grey girl alive."

"No shit!" said Westen. "You didn't take a statement, did you?"

"No, Guv. He wanted to get into it but I cut him short. Told him to save everything until you came back."

"Right, with me then. Let's get this over with."

The two men took the stairs down to the suite of interview rooms. Burrows jerked his head at a door and Westen gripped its handle and noisily pushed his way in. Inside, a grey-faced man waited behind a metal table. He jumped at their entrance. Shadow beard, receding hairline—forty-ish. Shakily he rose out of his seat as Westen drew near and moved for a handshake then stood uncertainly as the detective refused to take it. Letting his eyes slip, he sat down again, retracting his birdlike neck back into his shoulders.

"Good afternoon, Mr. Sweeting. I'm Detective Superintendent Westen. I think you've already spoken to my sergeant?"

The man swallowed and attempted a smile as he nodded, his gaze sliding off to a spot somewhere to his right. How this man could ever have been considered capable enough to manage a class of teenagers was beyond him. The school should have known fucking better.

The two detectives sat down. Burrows set the tape, informing a startled Sweeting that all police interviews have to be recorded as a matter of procedure. Then Westen began.

"So, tell me why you're here, Mr. Sweeting—may we call you Colin?"

The man nodded. "I … I came in because I'm responsible. Sorry, I *feel* responsible for Jennifer's disappearance. I organised the school trip she was on—" He stopped and managed to rest his eyes on Westen for a full second. "Have you found her yet? Is there *any* chance she could be alive?"

"Did you know any of the other missing girls, Colin? Did you teach any of them?"

"Erm … Yes. Some of them. Sh-Shelley. I taught Shelley. She was in the same art class as Jennifer." Placing an elbow on the table, he raised a shaking hand to his temple. "I knew you'd think it was me. I'm sorry. So sorry."

"Sorry about what?"

"Sorry they're missing. Sorry I organised the trip. I'm sorry—"

But Westen didn't want him there just yet. He needed to mix it up so the man wouldn't get into a rhythm—not that there was much chance of that. He was a fucking bag of nerves.

"How long have you been teaching at the school, Colin?"

"Erm. Nearly two years. I started as a c-cover supervisor." Sweeting's knee started pumping. "I'm a suspect, aren't I?"

"What was Jennifer like, Colin?" Westen continued. "Good student was she? Did as she was told?"

"I wouldn't go that far. She could draw quite well. Had some talent. But I think she saw art as an easy option. So many of them do, you know."

"Did that upset you?"

"Not really. One gets used to it."

"Only your headteacher told us there'd been a complaint," said Westen, opening his file and taking out a sheet of paper. He made a pretence of reading. "Apparently, you grabbed a girl's arm. Made her very distressed. Was that Shelley's?"

"No. It was a year nine student. She ... went too far. Started throwing pencils around the room. I was only trying to stop her." He lifted his chin. "She wasn't distressed, Superintendent. She was deliberately winding me up!"

"Like they all do?"

"Yes, like they all do."

"Made you angry, did she? Colin..." Burrows intervened. "Made you want to hurt her?"

Silence. Then Sweeting nodded. "For a second, perhaps. I'd grabbed her to get my equipment off her. Maybe I gripped her a bit too tight." He shook his head. "I know it was wrong and I apologised to the girl and her parents. It hasn't happened again."

"But you still get angry, don't you, Colin?" said Westen. "I'm not sure I'd blame you. Things haven't been easy, have they? Mr. Redmayne told me about your wife. I'm very sorry about your loss."

"Are you, Superintendent?" Sweeting glanced his way, eyes suddenly glittering. After a few seconds he gave up the effort and switched his gaze back to the wall.

Westen returned to his file and fanned out the wad of

complaints. "We've received quite a lot of phone calls about you, Colin. Parents seem very concerned." He picked up sheet after sheet, randomly reading out loud: *"Joanne feels uncomfortable with him … Mr Sweeting behaves inappropriately … Annabelle doesn't like him to come near her … My daughter doesn't like the way he looks at her … Janine sits at the back near the wall so he can't lean over her shoulder …"* And this one from a student, *"Mr Sweeting sometimes puts his hand over mine when I'm drawing. I've told him not to, but he keeps on doing it."*

"I do that to help them develop a muscle memory of the drawing process. Nothing more," Sweeting cried. "I know I'm unpopular. It's not my fault. I try to get them to like me."

"Did you try to get Jennifer to like you. On Friday night?"

Sweeting managed to raise his voice. "No! … I—"

"Go on."

"I'd promised the school I'd make sure everyone had a means of getting home. And they did. Jennifer said she'd called her father. I wanted to stay with her until he came, to make sure she was safe. I tried to be pleasant. I just wanted to keep her company."

"What time did he arrive?"

Sweeting slumped into himself again. "He … he didn't. The children left. I saw Jennifer was on her own. I went up to her, asked her if she needed a lift. She was rude. Really rude. She tried to upset me. Called me all sorts of terrible things. Told me to go."

Both detectives stared at him incredulously.

"Are you saying you *left* her?" Burrows exclaimed. "Kids going missing, kids buried alive, kids from your school—your class!—and you left Jennifer alone?!!"

Sweeting recoiled as Westen banged on the table and leant forward. "Bullshit. *Bulllshit* he left her alone. You grabbed her, didn't you, Colin. Forced her into your car…"

"Then what, Superintendent?" Sweeting managed,

momentarily locating his backbone. "I took her away kicking and screaming, dug a hole and put her in it alive? Do you seriously believe I'd be able to do that? Apart from the sheer *lunacy* of thinking me capable of doing such a thing to another human being, it's been a freezing cold winter. I wouldn't have the strength to dig even a shallow grave. Not without power tools."

Westen froze. The man had a point.

"Where did you go after you left her?" Burrows asked.

The man shrank into himself again. "I ... I went to my mother-in-law's. We keep each other company. Takes our mind off our loss. I had intended to go home but I was so upset at what Jennifer called me, I didn't want to be on my own."

"What did she call you, Colin?" asked Westen.

The man hesitated; looked down at the table.

"Well?"

"Paedo," he replied in a voice barely above a whisper. "She called me a paedo."

Westen sat back with grim satisfaction, letting the words of his own incrimination hang in the air.

In the silence that followed, Burrows handed Sweeting a sheet upon which was highlighted the only dates Savage had felt confident enough to offer as time of death for the most recent victims. "What about these dates? Can you tell us your whereabouts during any of them?"

Sweeting glanced over it. "I was either at the school or at home. I paint, you see. I don't go out much." He stabbed the sheet with his forefinger. "But I was at my mother-in-law's then."

Burrows asked for her name and address and noted it down.

There came a knock on the door. Tony entered, whispered in Westen's ear.

After he left, Sweeting said, "I came here voluntarily. To be of help. But I want to go now."

"And you can," said Westen, gathering up his file. "We appreciate you coming in voluntarily, Colin. We'll make some checks after which we may want to talk to you again." He turned to Burrows. "Take him through to the back door. Put him in a squad car." He answered the question on his sergeant's face by turning to Sweeting. "According to my colleague there's quite a crowd gathered in front of the station. Parents and press, mostly. It might be an idea to contact your mother-in-law. I don't think going home is your best option at the moment."

Sweeting looked at him in horror. "They know I'm here? You *told* them?"

"No," Westen replied. "But word has a habit of getting around. Do you have your phone on you? I'd ring her now, if I were you. Get her to pick you up."

Sweeting, a very worried man, nodded and they left him to his call. Outside, Westen said, "What do you think, Pete? He our man?"

"Dunno, Guv. I can see why the kids think him a bit on the creepy side. But ... he rang true to me. Kids—especially girls—can be cruel. I've friends who are teachers and some of them haven't lasted. Kids can smell fear a mile off and make a teacher's life hell. I wouldn't be one for anything."

"Agreed. And he may have an alibi, so we need to talk to the mother-in-law. Put Sheila on it. Then ask Donna to go back to the school. Get her to have a friendly chat with the students whose parents called. We need to gauge if there's any proper foundation to all these accusations. Redmayne told me he's only ever had one formal complaint. We may be looking at nothing but fucking smoke."

13
SHITSTORM

Sandra Davis stared dully out of her bedroom window. The winter sun gleamed just above the horizon, promising a bright, if frosty day. It didn't matter. In her mind, each day felt no different from the rest. Bright, cloudy—raining—her life would still be the same no matter what the weather.

Barely sufferable.

When she'd arrived at Flammark, she'd hoped the change of scenery coupled with a new challenge would change everything for her; show people what she could really do. No one ever saw her potential; her *ambition.* Her old city parish hadn't appreciated her; hadn't allowed her to prove herself to them. They were as glad to get rid of her as she was of them. And now? She sighed, pressing her brow to the cold glass, misting it with every exhalation. Now petty-minded parish politics threatened to undermine her yet again. She was sick of it. *Sick* of it.

Take Robbie Mason and that friend of his, Gabby whatever-her-name-was. They'd been against her from the start. No doubt they'd sent Emma bloody Blake over to *have a quiet word*. If that stuck-up bitch hoped to befriend her in order to get her to drop her plans or continue Turner's heritage garbage, she'd another thing coming. Maybe he'd got sick of them all too. Maybe they were the reason why he'd done a runner in the first place.

This place. This bloody enormous vicarage. She supposed it had been useful when it'd been used as a training centre, but no one could convince her it was worth all the resources the diocese had shoved into it. And what use were all those damned history books downstairs? Once the bishop confirmed her as permanent priest-in-charge they'd be first thing to go. Let them languish in the cathedral library. Those who had the time to read could find them there. The way forward for the church was ... well ... forward. Mission was not about the past.

Why couldn't people see that?

And why was she always so exhausted?

She lifted her head from the glass. She should have known her plans would be treated with hostility. At least by some. Especially the old guard, the stick-in-the-muds. Parishes don't like change. It meant getting people on side, flattering them, opening their dull minds to her vision. The church needed kids, or it would have no future; and they needed the church, now more than ever. The past few days she'd spent at the school had done nothing but strengthen her conviction. Those students were lost, lost in a sea of cruelty and ignorance and *social media*. They needed a lifebelt. Needed *her*. Especially now. Someone had to help them through the awful trauma of what had happened to their classmates.

Pressing her lips together in certainty, she nodded at her reflection. Finally! Finally, God had revealed himself to her. Shown her the way by giving her these murders. She was on the right path. Had been accepted by the school and by the children there, supporting and guiding them through this terrible time. Soon she would get them to church, fill St Jude's with new blood. Everyone would see what she was capable of!

And if she could do it in this god-awful village she could do it anywhere in the diocese. Anywhere in the country!

Then the dark came again and she slumped; returned her forehead to the freezing window. This time, she couldn't seem to lift it.

Why did everything have to be such a struggle?

And why couldn't she talk to God about it?

As she eventually turned away, something caught her eye. Catching the hem of her sleeve, she cleared the glass; glimpsed the merest flash of white in the darkest reaches of the graveyard. What was it? Some kind of reflection? Not from her. Whatever it was didn't move when she moved and, glancing behind her, she couldn't see anything in the room that remotely corresponded to the object outside. She turned back to the view, narrowed her eyes, squinting for focus.

She jerked back.

It was a face. She was sure of it. A white face with impossibly huge, black eyes.

Staring back at her.

Shit. Another bloody down-and-out. Another reason she'd left the city. Knocking on her door for handouts, expecting the church to cough up to reward them for their laziness. Sandra's lips curled as she watched the figure, standing still in its reciprocal regard before it moved away, towards the drive. She sneered in contempt. A deplorable. Someone who'd found a kind of strength in their weakness, preferring to exploit her goodwill rather than face the consequences of their own bad choices. Well, good riddance.

Drawing away from the window, Sandra shivered as if someone had taken a stroll over her grave. She looked around the room. Why the hell had she chosen this one to sleep in with *that* view of the churchyard? It wasn't as if this awful place hadn't plenty of other rooms!

After making her way downstairs she fired up the coffee maker, wishing her mood would lift. She had been looking forward to the day. After her stint at the school, she would be off to the bishop's palace to meet with Frederick. He had some queries about the renovation budget.

She reached for a mug and almost slammed it down on the worktop. For God's sake, why couldn't he just let her get on with it? Did he think she didn't know what she was doing?

Still, he had been very optimistic about the chances of her staying on. It was a vindication, a sign that he wanted her to see things through. She'd managed to win over enough people on the PCC to her way of thinking. Robert Mason and his cronies were isolated. With a bit of luck, he'd resign. Find another place to worship in.

The latest project plans were laid out on the kitchen table. Sandra liked seeing them there. They reminded her of what she was about; what she was *for*. The conversion had run into some expensive issues—the listed status of both church and vicarage meant limited alterations could be made to the interior but the facades had to remain intact. For the church, the architect had come up with an imaginative solution which involved the adaptation of an old entrance she'd found. All good. But it did mean further delay and a longer wait before she could launch her youth club.

Coffee in hand, she stepped over to the table and ran her finger over the architect's renderings. About to sit down, she heard a loud *POP*.

Startled, she spilled her drink, some of it going over the plans. Tutting at her clumsiness, thinking nothing of what she'd heard, she scurried to the sink to put her cup down and grab a cloth.

Another pop, louder now. From the window. Then another; something bouncing off the pane. A stone? The glass was intact. Possibly a stick or something. Was it kids? She pressed her lips into a line. Typical. After all she'd done at the school. Well, she'd give them a piece of her bloody mind!

Determined to see the buggers off, Sandra took a few steps towards the door. Then, for some reason, she paused. Looked back at the window.

She would remember that moment for the rest of her life. As a hiatus. A second of quiet before her world turned upside down.

Like a hailstorm, objects hit the glass, a deafening battery of sound that made her fling her palms to her ears. Bewildered—terrified—she slid down the front of the sink unit, heart racing as she gaped at the onslaught of missiles which pocked and cracked and splintered the glass seeming for all the world as if they wanted to get in.

What the hell? Make it stop. Make it *stop!*

But it didn't. On and on it went, cracks spidering their way across the pane thick and fast before the whole thing detonated, sending smithereens of glass to join the avalanche of sticks and twigs that continued to spew through the mullions, covering the floor, showering the crouching, quaking woman with shards and forest litter...

... burying the table and the plans that rested on it.

It felt as if she was screaming, but she couldn't hear above the weird white noise that suddenly filled her ears. Fuelled with adrenalin, breaths panicked and shallow, face cut, hands bleeding—still stuck to her ears—Sandra pedalled her legs towards the door and into the panelled hall. Battered and bruised she half-walked, half-dragged herself to the front entrance ... then through the porch ... scrabbled at the lock ... dropped the key ... put it back in the hole ... turned it and ...

Got out.

Deafened—shell-shocked—eyes wide with pain and terror, she scanned the landscape. Where to go? What...?

Who the hell...?

Dashing round the church appeared a girl, long black hair flying behind as she ran towards her, mouth open, clearly screaming at her. But the din in her brain was too loud to hear and all she could do was hold her bleeding, aching head and stand in stupified paralysis as the girl grabbed her and pulled her away from the vicarage, into the graveyard, over to the largest headstone, then down against it.

Where she was held in the stranger's arms till the white noise went away.

"Sh... sh... Sandra, is it?" said Abigail, who after ten full minutes still held the shaking, keening woman. "Calm down, I have you." She relaxed her grip. "It's okay. I know you can hear me, the noise has gone."

"H-how? Who...?"

"My name is Abigail. Abigail Chater. I heard the noise in your head. Used it to find you."

"I think I was attacked! The kitchen..."

"I know. At least, I know something happened, but not exactly what. Your hands and face are grazed and you're covered in bits of leaves and stuff. I think there's some glass, too? Doesn't look anything too serious, though. I don't think we need to call an ambulance, but we should get you to a doctor."

"R-Robert Mason?"

Abigail nodded.

"No. No, I don't want ... I don't..."

"Well, we can't stay here, can we? You're in shock and it's freezing plus you need to get cleaned up. I'm not sure what happened at the vicarage, but it might not be safe to go back." She thought for a moment. "Hang on." She dug her phone out of her coat pocket and pressed a button.

"Emma, are you up?" Sandra's face screwed up in horror and she frantically shook her head. Abigail put the phone to her chest. "It's alright. I know you two don't get on. But trust me on this, we're going to need her." Phone back to her ear, she continued, "We've a problem at the vicarage ... Yes, with Sandra ... No. You stay where you are. We'll come to you."

Whether because of the cold, or the shock—or maybe the thought of having to deal with Emma—an uncontrollable shaking had taken over the woman. Abigail fiddled with the toggles on her duffel and shucked out of it. "Sandra, you need to get away from here. We need to do something about the state you're in and you may not be safe. Here, put this round you." She threw the coat over the woman's shoulders—it was way too small for her to ever get into it properly. "Come on. It's not far."

Reluctantly, eyes scanning the landscape, Sandra complied and still shaking, huddled against Abigail as she led her away.

"You and Emma B-Blake are f-friends?"

"Yes. And, just so you know, Robbie Mason and Gabby too."

"And William Turner?"

"Yes."

Sandra groaned. "Was this a p-practical joke? S-staging something to teach me some kind of lesson? You all want me out of the parish, d-don't you?"

Abigail felt Sandra tense; knew she would have broken

away from her if she could. She held her more firmly, reassuringly. "Of course not, Sandra. We'd never do anything like that. But what you have to understand is … Flammark is an odd place. Bad things happen here, very bad things. We can help, if you'd let us."

"I don't s-suppose I have much choice, do I?" The woman threw a terrified look back at the vicarage. "I don't know what happened but … but we can't call the police, can we?"

"No, Sandra. I don't think we can."

They turned the corner onto the green to find Emma running over to them, full pelt.

"Oh, my God, Sandra!" she cried. "Look at your poor face! What happened?"

Putting her arm around the woman's free side, Emma took some of her weight. "You're freezing too! Let's get you inside." She looked over Sandra's shoulder to Abigail. "What happened?"

"It's bad, Emma. I was getting ready for work when suddenly the world felt, I dunno, out of phase. Then I got this screaming in my head and knew there was trouble so I just legged it. I thought it was you at first, but when I got to the cottage realised it was coming from over the green. I found Sandra in front of the vicarage, covered in crap and screaming something about sticks and windows."

Emma raised her eyebrows. Mouthed, "The witch?"

Abby nodded and mouthed back. "Think so."

Another two minutes and they'd reached Clearview. Once through the door and in Emma's warm living room, the two friends deposited their charge on the sofa.

"Abby, can you pop upstairs and grab the duvet off the spare bed?" said Emma. "You'll be safe here, Sandra. We'll get you warm and I'll sort out those cuts. They don't look too deep. I don't think they'll need stitches. I'll call Robbie."

"You'll do no such thing!" Sandra said with a determination that belied her quivering lips. "Pains me to say it, but you'll do."

Emma stilled a second, taken aback. She raised her eyebrows at Abigail who'd returned with the duvet. "Leave it, Ems. She refused to let me call him when we were in the churchyard, too. She didn't want to come here either but, well, she didn't have a lot of choice."

Abigail placed the duvet carefully around Sandra, swallowing her annoyance as the woman, equally carefully—and deliberately—adjusted it more to her liking.

Emma brought in a bowl of warm water and began to bathe the Sandra's wounds—at least those she would allow. "You know, there may still be glass in one or two of these cuts. You really should go to the hospital."

"No. No. I'm alright. You can see for yourself, nothing's gone deep."

So, she carried on cleaning. It was an awkward process since Sandra resisted every one of Emma's ministrations. Neither did she seem to want to talk and Abigail had run out of things to say. The silence got so awkward she decided her efforts would best be spent making the ungrateful so-and-so something hot to drink.

A few minutes later, Emma's ministrations over, she came in with a tray. "It's tea," Abigail said, offering Sandra a mug. "Hot and sweet." Sandra took it and drank, her face softening momentarily as the tea did its trick. "Do you feel able to tell us what happened? Take your time."

Still cradling the mug, Sandra shrugged. "I honestly don't know. I'd just got up. I went downstairs and into the kitchen and was about to sit down when someone threw a stick at the window. Then lots of sticks. I thought at first it was one of the kids from the school—I'd been there recently to help. You know, counselling the young people who'd been affected by the recent murders..."

"The superintendent in charge of the investigation—Westen," said Abigail. "He's Emma's—"

"—friend," Emma finished for her, narrowing her eyes at the girl with a barely perceptible shake of her head.

"My, this *is* a very tight-knit community, isn't it?" Sandra said, handing Abigail an empty mug.

This was the snarkiness Gabby had told them about. "All villages are," Abigail said. "You just need to know how they work."

"And you do?" Sandra replied.

Abigail nodded. "Pretty much. Though Flammark still has its surprises. So, after someone threw sticks at your window, what happened next?"

"I don't know. Literally, I don't. What started as a few objects turned into a barrage. It went on forever. I don't understand where it all came from. A kid couldn't have done all that - not even ten of them! It was like a whole forest floor was being sucked into my kitchen. It buried the table and nearly buried me."

"Was that when the noise came? In your head?"

"Yes. It started like a bee in my ear then it got worse. Like tinnitus on steroids." She glared at Abigail. "What was it? And how did you know about that? In fact, how did you know to come in the first place?"

"Abigail has a gift," said Emma with a wry smile. "You get used to it."

"To answer your first question, I'm not sure what it was," said Abigail. "Like I said, I heard it too. It's how I honed-in on you. And it ties-in with other stuff that's been happening." She glanced up at Emma. "We need to go and have a look."

"No need," Sandra scoffed. "I feel much better. I'll go back on my own, thank you very much." Visibly pulling herself together, she peeled away Emma's duvet. The woman had nerve, she'd give her that. But despite badly wanting to she knew she couldn't leave the woman to make the journey alone.

"Trust me, Sandra, you need us to come with you."

Sandra scoffed. "Trust you? I'm not used to trusting anybody." She directed her next comment to Emma. "Everyone has an agenda, don't they?" The corner of her lips twisted upwards. "He's not coming back, you know."

This? Now? Abigail couldn't get over it. What a piece of work! And after everything Emma had just done for her!"

"Perhaps you should try to get some rest," her friend said, abruptly. She made for the kitchen with the used bowl of water. "I'm going to get ready for work. If you change your mind about going back, you are welcome to stay and use the sofa. If you can bear it, that is."

"Sandra," said Abigail, as Emma departed, "Will left in very difficult circumstances. I don't know if you have the whole story, but Emma's been really badly hurt by it so try to ... oh, I dunno ... can't you at least be polite?"

Sandra just curled her upper lip. "I have to go back to the vicarage. There's things to do and I've a meeting with the bishop this afternoon."

"Seriously, I *can't* let you go back on your own. We don't know what happened, yet. You may be in danger."

"Well, you'll be the one to tell me, won't you? After all, it's you that has—what did *she* call it?" Sandra jerked her head towards the kitchen door, "—the 'gift?' Now I've had the time to think, I wonder if I was right after all. This has all been part of some elaborate plot to get me to change my plans, hasn't it?"

Abigail almost laughed and was about to retort when Emma returned. "Save your breath, Abby. She won't listen."

But Abigail wouldn't be thwarted. "I'm sorry you feel that way about us, Sandra, I really am but it doesn't change the fact that you can't go back alone. Honestly, you could be in a lot of danger. There's a killer loose, don't forget."

"You think what happened to me had something to do with that? Don't be ridiculous!"

Not bothering with a reply, Abigail glanced at the clock on its shelf. "It's nearly half-eight. Emma, you'll be late for work. I'll stay with Sandra. I'll get Mandy in to cover me, she's been looking for some extra hours."

Emma made no objection and headed for the stairs. Once she was out of earshot, Abigail rounded on Sandra. "You're wrong, completely wrong about us. But whether you believe it or not, something terrible *is* happening in your parish. So, suck it up, I'm coming with you."

14
A GRAVE DISCOVERY

The two women made their way across the green. Though they walked together they could have been miles apart. Sandra looking uncharacteristically chic in one of Emma's coats, had grown very quiet after her outburst at Clearview. Though she knew the woman was silently fuming, Abigail was glad of the silence.

It didn't last long.

"Are you sure you're up to this," said Abigail, as they neared the church. "Whoever you think might be responsible, you've had a real shock. Emma would have let you stay at the cottage, even though you were really rude to her."

"Huh," Sandra scoffed. "Absolutely sure. Couldn't stay there another minute. She can't abide me, you know. I can tell. Besides, I need to see that mess again with my own eyes. Make sure I wasn't imagining it. Then I'm off to the school, then to the cathedral. The Bishop will want to know the extent some people will go to oppose our plans."

"Oh, so you're going to tell him what happened in your kitchen, then?"

Sandra hesitated. "I-I'm not sure what happened there

yet. We'll have to see. He'll definitely want to know what happened to my face."

Abigail only nodded. Words failed her.

As they rounded the corner of the church, the vicarage in sight, Sandra suddenly started to hold back, her strides becoming less determined. And Abigail raised her chin, as if sniffing the air.

"What's the matter?" said Sandra, eyes flitting across the landscape, suddenly whispering despite all her earlier bravado.

"Not sure. Something. Can't place it." Abigail stepped up the pace. "But nothing from the vicarage. Whatever was there is gone now."

Almost as if to convince herself, Sandra replied, "You can drop the act now. You can go. I'm sure I'll be fine on my own."

"No, I told you, I'm seeing you home. End of." Something didn't feel right. Abigail didn't know what yet, but she wasn't going to leave till she found out what it was.

As they drew up to the vicarage—all doors still wide open—Sandra couldn't hide her nervousness. "You okay?" Abigail asked. "Do you want me to go in first?"

Sandra replied with a tight nod.

They entered through the front porch and Abigail led them through to the kitchen. Stopping at its threshold, she gaped in astonishment.

"Oh. My. God."

Every surface lay covered in twigs and sticks and bits of moss: the floor, the cooker—worktops. But it was to the middle of the room where her eyes were drawn. An impossibly perfect pyramid loomed there, floor to ceiling, comprised of the same material, the occasional fragment coptering down, loosened by the gentle draft that wafted through the shattered window.

Abigail swung around to Sandra, eyes blazing. "Look. Look properly. Do you still think this is a stunt? That … what? That someone drove a wood-chipper here and aimed its crap through your kitchen window? That's the only thing that might explain all … *this*! But it doesn't really, does it?" She pointed at the pyramid. "Because it doesn't account for that!"

Sandra didn't reply, her gaze also fixed on the pyramid. Open-mouthed, her eyes followed the perfectly formed pile of debris right up to its apex at the ceiling.

"That's where the kitchen table is, isn't it?" Abigail said. "Under that?"

"Yes. The plans were on it. Plans for the vicarage conversion and the church undercroft."

Only the sound of a twig dropping disturbed the silence that followed.

"Well, something didn't approve of them, that's for sure," said Abigail. "I think it's fairly obvious you can't stay here. Wouldn't you agree?"

Sandra tore her eyes away from the debris and stared at her. "What is it? I don't understand. I don't understand what's happening."

"Nor do I," said Abigail. "Yet. I think whatever's behind it is sending you a message. You need to get out of here—and stay out till we find out what it is."

She lifted her chin again, as she'd done near the church.

"What?" said Sandra. "What now?"

"Don't know." Abigail went into the hall. "I'm being drawn this way. Something else, outside."

Sandra let out a low, keening moan.

Abigail didn't like this woman. She was both offensive and defensive and completely wrong for Flammark—probably for the priesthood too. Shame on Frederick Thomas' appalling judge of character. But she couldn't help feeling sorry for her. "It's alright, Sandra. I don't think there's anything ... imminent. But ... there is *something*. Stay close to me, just in case."

They moved outside, and Abigail raised her arm slightly as if being pulled by some unknown force. She picked her way through the graveyard, past the smaller headstones, towards the larger, mossier monoliths that leaned into each other. One of the graves—at the back, in the corner—had been disturbed, its turf loose and uneven as if it had been dug up and put back again.

"I don't like this, Abigail. Not at all. I—"

"Actually, nor do I. Sorry, Sandra," she said, fishing out her phone. "There's someone I have to call."

~

For the thousandth time, Westen asked himself what the fuck it was with Flammark? That it seemed such a focus for psychopathy and murder. Even terrorism! As a copper who loved his job, he didn't know whether to feel blessed or cursed. Nor did he quite know what to make of the Chater girl's phone call. There was a depth to her— a kind of wisdom he'd sensed which was partly the reason he'd asked her to come with him to look at that thing in Seely Woods. If she had discovered something suspicious about a grave, it was worth taking the hit for a possible false alarm.

Because it fitted. It *fitted!* It was *exactly* what they'd been looking for. Another burial site, in reasonable proximity to the first. Somewhere significant; somewhere that spoke to the kind of twisted logic he knew they were dealing with. But could it have been Sweeting's logic? Having met the man, he doubted that very much.

Sirens wailing, Westen and Burrows sped up the church drive followed by Donna and a squad car full of uniformed officers. Skidding and crunching to a stop in the gravel car park in front of the vicarage, he could see Abigail with a woman he didn't recognise in tow. They were at the far corner of the graveyard, the girl waving as if he was landing a fucking airliner.

Signalling to the rest of the team to stay put, he and Burrows made their way round the headstones. He briefly took in the stranger—noted the cuts and grazes to her face—before following the direction of Abigail's gaze to the upturned clods of the old grave.

"Westen," Abigail began, "this is Sandra. Sandra Davis. She's replaced Will as the vicar of St Jude's. She, that is we—"

"Let me stop you there. You told me over the phone that it was Ms Davis here, that discovered the grave had been disturbed?" Abigail nodded. "Then let's hear it from her."

The girl hesitated then stepped back, throwing the woman a look he'd seen many times before … on witnesses summoning whatever psychical forces they could to make sure everyone got the story straight.

"Right, Ms Davies, out with it."

Hesitantly, eyes never leaving the Chater girl, the vicar told him how Abigail had come round for a chat. How someone—a kid probably—had thrown something through a window and broken it. They'd decided to give chase so they ran out of the vicarage and…

Then it was if a dam burst. The woman started crying and shaking. All she could manage was a semi-hysterical jumble of… *someone in the churchyard … couldn't see properly … definitely came from here … a face … white …*

He put his hand up for her to stop. "Burrows, get a crew out here and have this dug out. Establish a perimeter around this whole area. I want the grounds searched as well as the church and the vicarage. And call Savage." He lowered his voice and muttered in his sergeant's ear, "I think we've found the Grey girl."

"Guv? You sure?" Burrows muttered back, looking from the grave then back to Westen, clearly perplexed. "She hasn't given us much grounds to believe there's a body here. Anything could have done this—an animal maybe?"

Westen threw Abigail a knowing look. "Yes, I'm sure."

"Okay, then," said Burrows, partly under his breath. Still nursing his baffled expression, he strode back to the car park, and waved the team out of their vehicles.

"Ms Davis—can I call you Sandra?" Westen started.

A tremulous nod.

"Okay, Sandra. Tell me more about this white face you saw."

Abigail opened her mouth but he fixed her with a hard gaze. "Abigail, can you wait for me near the cars? I'll be there momentarily."

Dismissed, Abigail stomped away, but not without eyeing the vicar woman again. Westen moved to block her sight of the girl and said, "Go on ... Sandra. Tell me what you saw. Take your time."

"I ... I don't really know. It was just a glimpse. But definitely a face. A really white face. I got the feeling it had been watching me."

"Feeling?"

Sandra shrugged. The tears were coming back. "I can't say any more. I don't know. I don't understand anything that's been going on!"

"What do you mean? What else has been going on?"

She recoiled under his scrutiny and started to cry again. Fucking Abigail! He wanted to push it but he knew it'd be useless. The woman was mess. He got Donna's attention and waved her over. Drawing her aside, he said quietly, "Drive the reverend here, to the station. Make her some tea and see if you can get some fucking sense out of her. Find out what happened to her face. Then take a statement. Something went on here she's not telling us."

As the two women left, he turned on his heel and made for Abigail who was waiting for him next to the church entrance.

"So come on, young lady, what happened? And I'll warn you now, you'd better tell me everything!"

Innocence personified, she said, "Of course I'll tell you everything. Why wouldn't I?" After an indignant toss of her head, she began her story. "Like Sandra told you, I'd come over for a chat when someone threw something at her window. It broke and we rushed out to see who was behind it. That's when she found the grave. She wasn't sure whether to phone you so I did. You gave a press conference where you said we should all be on the lookout for something suspicious and ... well, I thought this was suspicious."

"What time did you arrive?"

"About eight o'clock."

"Why aren't you at work?"

"I've some holiday owed," she lied. "I took the day off."

He stood in silence, his jaw working as glared at her.

"Is Emma involved?"

"Why would she be?" Abigail frowned, looking askance.

"Abby, stop bullshitting me. Is Emma involved? Was she here too?"

"No, she wasn't. Honestly! She'll be at the surgery. Ring her! Ring her now if you don't believe me."

He gave a frustrated sigh. "I know you aren't telling me everything and it's got to stop. This is a murder investigation. If I find that you're obstructing it in any way, I'll take it further. Are you clear about that?"

She nodded at him far too fucking enthusiastically for his liking.

"Okay," Westen sighed. "That'll do for now. Ms Davis is being taken to the station to give a statement. I want one from you too, but something tells me it would be a waste of an interview room. Find Pete Burrows, he'll get someone to talk to you and take a print off your shoes."

She gave him a quizzical look.

"To eliminate your footprints."

"Oh. Okay."

"Then you can enjoy the rest of your day off."

In the end it was Burrows himself that took her statement. After she got her the soles of her boots printed he made the mistake of leaving Abigail to her own devices. Creeping around the back of the church, she made her way over to the vicarage. Unnoticed by anyone, skirting its walls, she arrived at the broken kitchen window. She had just enough time to scan the room, now cleared and roughly swept, before jerking back as two policemen entered. She heard them rustling about before coming to the window. Holding her breath, she pressed herself flat against the adjacent wall. After a few moments, one shouted, "Clear!" then they both left. Letting out a slow sigh of relief, she peered around again to give the kitchen one final glance and nod of approval.

Shaking back her long, black braids, the expression of pure innocence back on her face, bold as brass she left the vicarage. Satisfied their mission had been accomplished, she chose the obvious route and picked her way through swarms of police and technicians and dog handlers that had suddenly arrived before finally making it to the church drive. A few reporters had turned up there, too.

Yellow police tape was being unfurled by two uniformed coppers. Way behind them stood a woman, small and plump in wellington boots, her dirty-blond hair plastered on a face puce with exertion. But she wore a smile of triumph as she spotted Abigail and jerked her head to an upturned wheelbarrow, seemingly abandoned on the edge of the green.

The kitchen duly liberated from its ordeal, all that remained for the two conspirators to do was to go their separate ways, crossing their fingers in the hope that Sandra wouldn't stray too far from their fragile and very hastily concocted story

15

COGITATIONS

Gunning it back to base, Westen and Burrows left the rest of the squad in the graveyard with hours of sifting and searching still to do. It hadn't taken long to confirm they had indeed unearthed the body of Jennifer Grey.

Donna had rung through. She'd managed to get some kind of a description out of Sandra Davis and had been working on it with Martha. She wanted Westen to see what they'd come up with.

Breaking the tense silence between them, Burrows said, "So, if you don't mind me asking, Guv, how *did* you know the Chater girl had called it right, getting us in? I'm not sure I'd have—"

"Taken her seriously? Brought in the troops?"

Burrows nodded.

"Remember when Benson brought us to that circle thing in the woods? I didn't tell you at the time—thought I was fucking seeing things. When the Davis woman started spouting something about seeing a flash of white, that's when I knew..."

"Because you'd seen one too?"

Westen nodded; a quick, embarrassed thing. "I should have called out a search team. It might have saved the Grey girl her life."

Burrows shrugged but gave no reply.

"Then there's Abigail Chater," Westen mulled. "I've no doubt she's a bit of a flake—haven't a clue what goes on inside that head of hers—but she's been part of every Flammark murder investigation I've been involved in. As, of course, has Emma. Much as I hesitate to say it, I'm getting used to trusting their instincts. Then, suddenly, he blurted. "There's always more than meets the eye with those two; always something they aren't telling me. They've another friend I haven't met yet. Someone called Gabby; don't know her last name. She's close to Robert Mason too. Acts like some kind of fucking guru."

"A guru? In *Flammark*?"

Westen rolled his eyes. "Shut up, Pete."

Burrows buried a grin but said no more. Westen was glad of it. He let out a long, exhausted sigh. Maybe tiredness was behind his outburst. Maybe he needed a fucking friend. This morning had been tough, very tough: seeing the girl smashed up like that, laid on crushed metal and old bones—covered in soil and crap, eyes wide open and mostly present enough not to have lost their sheen of full-on terror. Christ, what a way to go! And it looked like Martha Jacobs had been right about the victims going to their death under their own steam. Other than the presence of three sets of footprints by the graveside—which they'd already established belonged to Abigail, the vicar and the victim herself—the crime scene had been completely devoid of any recent tracks or footprints.

Worryingly, Savage had found another print next to the grave, with two handprints either side of it. Made him tentatively suggest that Jennifer might have sat on the edge of it for some moments before jumping into it. The answer as to whether she was pushed would come after the post-mortem. But he wasn't holding his breath; after a preliminary exam, the pathologist had found no evidence of bruising—actually, no signs anywhere of any form of coercion.

His thoughts drifted to Colin Sweeting again. Though he was their only suspect, Westen just couldn't bring himself to believe the man capable of this kind of murder. Of any kind of murder, truth be told. And he was still mulling over his comment about how he could have broken frozen ground—how anyone could. But that wasn't enough to rule him out.

Burrows was on the same lines. "Do we bring Sweeting in again, Guv?"

"No. No, not yet. We've grilled him enough for now and I think we have the measure of him. We need more. Something that ties him into the other murders, apart from just being the victims' teacher."

They left the car. Taking the station steps, Westen said, "We need to brace ourselves, Pete. The killer is running out of burial sites. There won't be many that possess the kind of significance a sick mind like his—or hers—is looking for."

"Agreed, Guv. They'll devolve. The murders could escalate."

Westen almost laughed. "Devolve? Where did you get that from? Homework?"

"No, Guv. The telly."

Westen rolled his eyes. Fucking actors. Now everyone's a profiler.

They reached the bullpen to find Donna and Martha, both huddled together over a file. Grabbing chairs, the two men joined them.

"What've you got for us?" said Westen.

"We're wondering whether the killer was wearing a mask, Guv," said Donna. "Or some kind of make-up."

"Go on."

"As I said over the phone. We didn't get a whole lot out of Sandra Davis. She was mess. Hope you don't mind, but I brought Martha into the interview. She helped me calm her down enough to get that description."

"What makes you think mask?" Burrows asked.

"I've done lot of work on memory reconstruction techniques," Martha explained. "She wasn't a particularly tough nut to crack. It was merely a matter of putting her back in same place she was when she saw the suspect and getting her to talk about what she's looking at. In real time, as it were."

"Cognitive interviewing," Westen nodded, gratified at the surprised expression he elicited from both women. "Okay, good. So, what did she remember?"

Martha went through it. "She'd been looking out of her bedroom window. Early. Just after dawn. Good visibility. She saw a face, a white face, watching her from the corner where we found the Grey girl."

"Watching her?"

"That's what she said," Donna replied.

Martha continued, "After I got her in the zone, I was able to drill down to a better description. Usually when we say a face is white, we mean that it's *pale*. But she kept repeating white, as if the face had been, in her words, *painted*. She also mentioned the eyes, Westen. To be more precise, eye *sockets*. Black. Not dark, not like after a hangover or if someone is ill, but black. She said they didn't look human. And she described a mouth. Thought it might be malformed in some way."

"Jesus," said Westen. "I see what you mean. Anything else? Clothes?"

"That was as far as we could get. She said everything else seemed to meld into the trees, somehow. Thought whoever it was might have had something on her head but she couldn't really tell."

"So, she saw the figure just after she got up and not after her window was put through?" said Burrows. "I got a different impression."

"No, it was definitely earlier," said Martha. "But she saw it near the grave and when they gave chase *after* the window was stove in, she told the girl about it."

"And Abigail being Abigail, she wanted to ferret about," said Westen, nodding.

"Why didn't the Davis woman call us in when she first saw the figure by the grave?" Burrows asked. "Why wait until Abigail turned up?"

"Because at the time, she didn't think anything of it," Martha replied. "She thought it was just a down-and-out. Her words, by the way."

Donna chimed in. "That got to me, to be honest, Guv." She narrowed her eyes, her face slipping into annoyance. "She's a bloody vicar! I asked her whether she went out to see what they wanted, and she just sneered. Said it didn't matter how much she gave them they'd only come back for more."

Martha agreed. "Yes. She was pretty vehement about it. Surprised me, too, considering her vocation."

"Well, I can't speak to that but I do know masks are bad news," said Westen. "The fucker could be anyone, could be walking freely amongst these kids—Jesus, might even be one."

"It fits the psychopathy, Westen," said Martha. "These murders are emotionally brutal. Burying a victim alive requires a … disconnect. However, the way they were posed suggests the reverse. Empathy. I'd posit the murderer feels some kind of connection to the victims but needs to wear a mask to go through with the actual act of killing."

"Let's take a step back," said Westen. "Why was the Chater girl there in the first place?"

"Davis said she'd called in order to talk to her about some plans that were afoot to convert the vicarage." Donna smiled, grimly. "I got the idea it wasn't going to be a friendly chat, Guv. From what she said, there seems to be a lot of opposition in the village. She's got the people who matter on her side—her words—but there's a lot of resentment. I think Abigail's in the latter camp."

"What happened to her face?" Burrows asked.

"That's when it all started to break down again, Guv," said Donna. "When I asked her, she said it happened when the window broke. Said she'd caught a few splinters. But it didn't make sense. Her face looked more grazed than cut, as if she'd been through a bramble hedge."

"Yes." Westen replied. "Yes, it did."

"She mentioned Emma, actually."

Westen stiffened. "Oh?"

"Yeah. She said Emma cleaned her up after the window incident but when I asked her about that she quickly changed her tune to Abigail." Donna sighed. "Her story began to get very sketchy. And the timings didn't add up."

"That's because after the first part of her statement—the bit where I took her back to remember the face of the intruder—she started to lie. Through her back teeth. Began to get hysterical, though I think that was largely self-induced to avoid us digging deeper."

"It tallies with what Abigail told us, though, Guv," said Burrows.

"Of course, it does." Westen replied, grimly. "I wouldn't expect anything else!"

Donna continued. "We knew something was off when Davis told us the window was put in at about eightish—"

"Eight o'clock?" Westen exclaimed. "Abigail didn't call me

until half-ten! What the fuck had they been doing? Even if there was some compelling reason they had to get their story straight, it wouldn't take over two hours!"

Donna nodded. "That's what I said. And that's when she got hysterical. Started raving about how everyone had it in for her, that they wanted her to bury her plans. When she started babbling about the pyramids, we ended the interview."

"Jesus," said Burrows. "Where is she now?"

"I didn't think staying at the vicarage was an option, Guv." Donna gave an apologetic smile. "I did suggest she could maybe stay with Emma..."

"Oh, did you now! Thanks for that."

"Don't worry, she refused point-blank. She's gone to stay with the church warden." Donna consulted her notes. "An Albert Reed. He's got a spare room, apparently."

"Right. Get a sketch artist out there. See what the Davis woman can come up with. It'll be tricky. We may not want to release it. The press would lap it up and if it's as weird as it sounds, there'd be a panic. For police eyes only, got that? Tell the rest of the squad. No leaks!"

"I'd like to be there with the artist," Martha said. "I managed to gain some rapport with Sandra. I think my presence will help calm her. Remembering trauma needs skilled handling."

"Yes, but no prompts, Martha. The image she comes up with needs to be completely authentic."

"Of course!" she replied with an ironic twist to her lips. "I'll try to get over the implication that you think I might be less than professional."

"No implication intended," said Westen, a faint smile playing on his lips. "You've done well for us so far. Just making sure it continues that way."

Some kind of atmosphere was building between them.

Burrows and Donna looked at each other, their eyebrows slowly rising.

"Donna," Burrows said, breaking the tension. "Pay a call on our Abigail, will you? See if she can shed some light on what happened between when she arrived at the vicarage and when she called in."

"Okay."

"She gave Pete a statement at the scene," said Westen. "If she departs from it by one syllable, I want to know about it."

16
REGROUP

Emma was having a pig of a day at the surgery. She'd called in to tell Robbie she'd be late—something she'd had to do far too often—though he'd been decent enough about having to cope alone. She was puzzled and upset by what happened to Sandra, but that was nothing compared to the fury she felt at the way the woman had treated her.

Having rolled in half-an-hour past her usual start time, she had to wait until Robbie was between patients before she could apologise.

"Don't worry, lass," he said, as he wrote some notes on his ancient laptop. "It's not as if it's the first time, is it?" He peered over his specs at her, his beard not quite masking the irony in his smile. "What's up?"

She decided on a half-truth. "Abigail brought Sandra Davis over. She was in a bit of state, having been weirded-out about something that happened in the graveyard."

"Really?" he said, his expression fighting a battle between concern and glee. "Was it enough to make her want to leave St Jude's?"

"Unlikely. She had a bit of a … fall and was disorientated. Nothing serious, but she needed a bit of first aid. Gabby will have told you how things went down at evensong?"

"She did. She's appalling. *Appalling*!"

"Well, after I'd fixed her up, things got unpleasant again. I think it's fair to say I never want to set eyes on that bloody woman ever again."

"My fault, lass. Gabby and I should never have asked you to get involved. I'm sorry you've had to deal with her." He moved his laptop aside and got up to call in the next patient. "Anyway, you sorted it. Any chance of a coffee?"

After making one for both of them, Emma spent the rest of the morning playing catch-up and wondering how things had gone down on Sandra's return to the vicarage. It wasn't until mid-afternoon that she found out.

Abigail rang.

Emma snatched up her phone as soon as she saw the girl's name on the screen.

"Emma! It's all gone tits-up …" For the benefit of the waiting patients, Emma fixed a terse smile on her face as the girl offered a garbled account of the scene that greeted her at the vicarage and how she sensed something off outside, which led to them finding the disturbed grave.

"A great pile of leaves! And the grave …?"

"As soon as I saw it I knew straight away there was another girl down there so I rang Westen."

"Westen? You got *Westen* there?"

"Well, I called Gabby first and she taxied over. Sandra wasn't holding it together and she wouldn't believe me about there being a body buried. She was really good with Sandra, actually. Firm, but kind—you know how she can be when she wants to. She said the police had to be called because if I'd said there was a new body in that grave then there would be and they needed to know. She also told her not to say anything about what happened in the kitchen and also not to mention you."

"Oh, my God!" Heads turning in the waiting room, Emma lowered her voice. "*Another* girl?"

"Yes. I didn't call the cops straight away. Once we explained what happened, Gabby started clearing the kitchen while Sandra and I rehearsed what story to tell your boyfriend. That was a job in itself!" Abigail took a breath. "She started losing it, so I had to call Westen before Gabby was even half-way through! But we calmed her down and I think it went alright. And Gabby got the job done just in time. They hadn't actually found the body by the time I left, but I know it's there. Westen seemed pretty sure, too. You may get a call from him, by the way. He was really keen to know whether you were involved in some way."

With her phone stuck to her ear, Emma got up and backed into the kitchen area behind reception. Screaming a whisper down the phone she said, "Involved!!? What, with the murder?"

"No, silly. With what happened before we discovered the grave had been disturbed. He asked if you'd been there. I said no, which was true, of course. We left out *a lot* including us going over to Clearview to get Sandra calmed down and cleaned up. I still have my fingers crossed she's able to keep to the story. We said if she gave a statement about what really happened in the kitchen she'd be a laughing stock. Seemed to work."

"Okay. Well, I haven't heard anything from Westen so far. Maybe I'll ring him."

"To be honest, I'd leave it. I got a visit from Donna and had to go over it all again. I think she was satisfied though I had to lie some more to account for how long it took to call in the cops. Sandra is one worried woman, I can tell you that. We think the—"

The landline in reception started ringing. Emma hastily closed down the conversation and returned to her seat, her mind churning. Then a text Abigail pinged through:

Flammark Arms with me and Gabby. After work

Ravenous, Emma ordered food when she arrived at the pub. No sign of her friends yet. Being early evening, the huge public bar was nearly empty. She took a glass of sparkling water over to the log fire and waited.

Abigail came in first. She leaned in at the bar and pointed at this bottle and that, then brought a puce-coloured drink to the table. Without preamble she sat down and said, "Did Westen ring?"

"Yes, just before I left the surgery. You were right, of course. They did find another body. It'll be on the news soon. He wanted my opinion of Sandra—he remembered I'd told him I was going to evensong that day at Seely Woods. I didn't tell him anything except that we didn't get on. He didn't mention anything else about this morning."

Abigail let out a huge sigh of relief. "Then I think it's safe to assume Sandra stuck to the story."

"So … was it bad? You know, at the vicarage?"

"Yeah. Really bad. Looked like Sandra had been hit with a literal shit-storm. From the moment we left Clearview, she'd been convincing herself it'd been all a huge stunt. When we got back, well… you should have seen it, Ems. As I told you, the table had been literally buried in a massive pile of leaves and twigs. But here's the thing," Abigail leant forward, unable to hide her excitement. "That pile … it was shaped like a pyramid. Held under its own weight and everything!

And it was only... leaves and stuff! Bloomin' impossible! She couldn't explain it because—"

"—because it was inexplicable." They both jumped at the sound of Gabby's voice behind them.

"Finally!" said Abigail. "I wonder where you'd got to."

"Had a bit of reading to catch up on," Gabby replied, her face grim.

She put down a glass filled with what looked suspiciously like gin and tonic—or something similar—and sat down to join them but could say nothing more. The barman had arrived with a plateful of burger and chips.

"Seriously, Ems?" said Abigail, ogling the food in disgust. "You're eating that crap? What's up with your usual salad?"

"Shhh," Emma said, conscious the man hadn't taken more than a few steps back to the bar. "I'm starving. Had to work through lunch to catch up. Salad won't cut it." Filling her mouth, she let out a satisfied groan.

"Never mind that," said Gabby. "Are we all up to date with events?"

"I think so," said Abigail. "Glad you managed to get the kitchen cleared before Westen arrived. I could have called him a bit later but Sandra—"

"No. I think we got our timings just right," Gabby replied. She took a sip from her drink and gave it a surprised nod of approval. "And I couldn't bear to leave that child in the ground for a moment longer than was necessary. Sandra kept her end of things together, I trust?"

"Must have done," said Abigail. "No come-back so far."

Emma swallowed hard and reached for a napkin. "Westen told me Sandra was staying with the church warden for now. Albert Reed?"

"Ah... Albert." Gabby said resignedly. "He's a fool. One of Sandra's true believers. Goes hand in hand, I suppose." She shrugged her shoulders and tried a smile. "Abigail told me it didn't go well between you and her this morning."

"Nope. Couldn't have gone much worse. I mean, she arrived in a hell of a state, and I did my best to help, but she hates me, Gabby. Hates me. I don't really know why. I've only met her twice."

They fell silent, musing to the crackle of the massive log fire.

"It was the witch, wasn't it?" said Emma eventually.

Gabby nodded.

"She's pissed-off," said Abigail. "Because of what you did the other night, Gabby. When you threw that little wreath in the fire."

"Perhaps. But she had Emma in her thrall. It had to be broken." She cocked her head. "And I don't think we're the only ones she's … pissed-off at. She's upset at Sandra too. Do you know what was on the kitchen table before it was buried?"

"Yeah," said Abigail. "The renovation plans."

"Wow," said Emma. "You think the witch knew about them?"

"I do," said Gabby. "I think this creature is very wedded indeed to the church and doesn't want to see it altered. Emma, you said before this might have something to do with the Blackstones. I think you were right. They used to own St Jude's. Many an ancestor is buried there."

Emma put her fork down. "And now it has a new body. Everything that's happened … I suppose it proves everything's connected, doesn't it? Like you said the other night, Gabby. My visitation, the wreath, the circle in the woods and, of course, the murders. She's definitely responsible, isn't she?"

"Yes. I think she is."

Gabby sipped her drink; almost placed her glass down

before she changed her mind and took another. "My guess is, the witch brought this latest child to the graveyard because the police have cut off access to Seely Woods. Makes me wonder." She took another sip.

"Well, go on!" said Emma. "And if you're not careful you're going to get tipsy. Like the last time you were here!"

Gabby, a little shamefaced, pushed her glass away. "Witches are deeply bonded to the place where they originated. This one clearly belongs to Flammark and is apparently attuned to Seely Woods. I think something very bad happened there. Something that made her the creature she's become."

"Omigod," cried Abigail, struck by a thought. "I'm guessing but, suppose ... suppose *she* was murdered. Maybe buried alive? It would make sense, wouldn't it? Killing all these girls the same way?"

"It *is* a guess," said Gabby, weighing the possibility. "But a good one. Plausible."

The three women fell silent again as they let Abigail's idea sink in.

Emma broke the silence. "Since the murders began nearly a month ago, are we assuming this ... *bad thing*... happened recently?"

Abigail shook her head. "No. I think she's old. Very old. Don't ask me how I know, I just do."

"I agree," said Gabby. "Then there's Sandra's description, of course."

Emma's eyes widened. "She *saw* her? You never told me *that!*"

"It's why she ended up at the police station," said Abigail. "After we found the grave, she told me she's seen someone earlier that morning. We incorporated it into the story we told Westen. Better to tell the truth where we could. Plus telling him she'd seen something—granted, a bit later than she really had— helped us explain how we ended up at that particular grave in the first place. It was so far at the back of the graveyard, we'd never have come across it if I hadn't been drawn there. 'Course I couldn't tell him that."

She paused as a thought struck. "Bit of a weird moment, actually. Sandra was burbling on about a white face when Westen stopped her in her tracks and got Pete Burrows to order more teams in to dig out the grave and search the grounds. Right then and there. *Then* he asked for a proper description and got Donna to take her to the station."

Emma frowned. Definitely odd. She'd have to ask him about that when—if—she ever saw him again!

"That's when she told him about the eyes," Abigail continued. "Something about them being buried deep in their sockets. Great big black ones, she said."

"If this witch is so old, why is she suddenly here?" Emma shuddered. "More to the point, how do we get rid of her? Westen can hardly arrest her!"

"I have no idea on both counts," Gabby replied. "She can't be killed—"

"Because she's already dead," Abigail nodded. "Can she be burned? Decapitated?"

"I doubt it," said Gabby. "She can't be corporeal. She obviously has the semblance of a body—Sandra proved that—but she may be able to manipulate it to appear and disappear at will."

"Bit of a relief then." Abigail smiled, wryly. "Can't say I'd be up to any of that. I'm too squeamish."

"Said she who ploughed into the crowd at DeepDrilla with a massive truck!" said Emma. She'd have laughed had the subject not been so awful.

"We need more information," said Gabby, moving on. "We have to find out where the witch came from and why.

Who she is—or was. Abigail, can you connect with the Orb tonight?"

Abigail hesitated. "I'll try. Mum's away with the folk band, so that's no problem..."

Gabby frowned "So ... what is?"

"The Orb can be pretty random. Sometimes it wants to connect, sometimes it doesn't. Everything's on its terms, like a dodgy Bluetooth signal. I can't guarantee I'll come up with anything."

"It's not interested in making your life easy," Gabby replied. "If you can find answers or solutions by your own undertakings, it won't speak to you. But I think you'll find it'll co-operate this time. This problem is right up its street. Give it a go." She grinned. "Classic example of using a witch to catch a witch, eh? Has a kind of symmetry to it."

Abigail rolled her eyes and tutted. "Okay. It's my half-day tomorrow. I'll try then. We can meet again afterwards. Here or Wood End?"

"There's a sign up at the bar," said Emma. "Tomorrow's quiz night."

"Wood End it is, then."

17
THE ORB

Abigail arrived home about one-ish. She decided against lunch—even though she was starving, knowing better than to have anything before a session with the Orb. She rang Josie to find out how the tour was going, making small talk, genuinely glad her mum was enjoying life again. But that wasn't the purpose of the call, of course. Abigail wanted to check she was still miles away and wouldn't be making a sudden appearance and interrupt her connection.

Assuming the Orb was in the right mood to chat.

She was well-versed in the vagaries of the crystal. From the very first moment it connected properly with her, all those months ago when it showed her the arrival of Animus' forward troops and later as it paired with her to enable Will's terrifying rescue ... she knew its power. But, as she said to Gabby and Emma, such displays were made at a time and place of *its* choosing. It made an unpredictable and annoying ally.

She made herself a light brew. Green tea as usual, for calm and focus, then she climbed the stairs and into her bedroom. Opening the door to her alcove closet, she rummaged underneath the hanging clothes for a bright green bucket, necessary for the trial by vomit that would happen once the Orb had finished with her. Happened every time. Why on earth she'd chosen that colour though, escaped her. It made her queasy just looking at it.

Hugging it closely, she took a step sideways and gave the crystal an adversarial stare. Abby had to admit to a reluctance—no, more like borderline fear—of what it might reveal, knowing that behind its implacable presence, true horror could lie in wait.

"Alrighty, then," she said, cracking her neck from side to side. She set the bucket down and took a deep breath. "Let's do this!"

She took her place in front of the sphere and steadied her breathing; concentrated on its rhythm. As the minutes passed, she aimed to become as waves on a beach, her present thoughts washing away. Clearing her mind. Making her a blank page. A blank canvas.

A blank.

Attuned.

As one.

In the zone.

She opened her mind; let in the carousel of images she wanted to share with the Orb to let it know what she needed from it. The twig-wreath, the pyramid of leaves, the grave and lastly a vaguely conceived picture of a white face with black eye sockets.

Perfectly relaxed, still continuing the rhythm of her breathing, each exhale longer than each inhale, Abigail gently scrolled the images. Calling them forth one by one, she lingered for two, maybe three breaths before sharing another, trying to avoid needless reflection or speculation or—

Everything cut to black.

The familiar pin-prick beam of concentrated light arrived front-and- centre to Abigail's consciousness. Careful to control the incipient burst of excitement she always felt when the Orb accepted her, she waited for the light to expand, ready to take in whatever it wanted to show her.

So she wasn't ready for the panic.

DEVIL'S WHORE … BLIGHT … AWAY, GET THEE AWAY, ABOMINATION … No … No! Fader, tell them. Help me! For the love of CHRIST, MAKE THEM LET ME GO!

The tiny beam burst wide into a visual cacophony. A door … trees …

Men.

Lots of men.

She was walking. Walking barefoot, dragging herself forward. Tired, so tired. Exhausted. Cold. On and on she trudged, pushed on her way, made to trip. Laughing, they kicked her …

GET UP, YOU BLASTED WHORE …

The trees thickened, the path crackling as she trod over sharp twigs and dried leaves, her feet aching, bloodied by thorns, toes stubbed on root and branch. *Stop … please stop …*

SHUT UP, YOU WHINING BITCH …

Then they did stop. And it was *worse.* They circled around her, jeering and laughing, passing her between them, shoving her forwards then backwards, prey to the hands that grabbed her and tore at her blouse, her skirt, her undergarments.

Naked.

Still thrown from one to another, she shrieked. Tried to cover herself. She yelled—pleaded—at the sneering faces … *Let me go … let me go, you BASTARDS … Fader, Fader … WHY ARE YOU LETTING THEM DO THIS TO ME?!!!*

Her words enraged them more, and they threw her down, and to her screaming horror covered her with their bodies … one after another, after another, after another. Entering, laughing, rutting, grunting as she shrieked and spat and bit and keened and kicked until she had no fight left.

Time passed. Minutes or hours, she couldn't tell the difference; she was too filled with agony and shame and horror and exhaustion to keep track, her torture ending only when the fader yanked the last one off her ...

Enough! That's ENOUGH!

Racked with pain and trauma she dragged up her shaking body. Had to flee... had to... She made for the path, tried a limping, agonising run for it—but all she found was a fist. A fist with a heavy ring that exploded her face and sent her reeling.

And she was back on the forest floor, writhing, excruciated as they kicked her some more: her ribs, her sex, her breasts.

She wanted to die. She was going to die, and in that moment, barely conscious, barely *thinking*...

...she saw the hole in the ground.

No. NO! I am innocent, I am not what you say!!! But the words came as little more than croaks, for her tongue had swollen where she'd bitten it. But the Fader heard them.

You are a liar, girl. A curse. A scourge. You bring us nothing but evil!

Then hands again, grabbing her ankles and snatching her wrists. They swung her; long, sickening lurches over the black maw now beneath her. Loosening their grip, they let her go and her ravaged body plummeted deep and long—a millisecond of weightless relief—until it crash-landed so hard on the pit's dank bottom, her back broke.

She felt nothing. She could move ... nothing. But her eyes were still open, and with them she saw the rectangle of light and treetops above her. She could hear, too; hear the bastards sneering and cheering ... then suddenly fall quiet. She sensed rather than felt a growing heaviness on her feet, her legs, her belly. But she felt it when the soil hit her face. She gagged. Tried to spit as the earth filled her mouth. And her nose. Eyes.

They buried her body, so deep it would never be found.

And it made her rage.

18
LATE

"We did say same time as yesterday, didn't we?" said Emma as she sat on Wyland's cracked leather sofa, glancing at her watch for the umpteenth time. "Where could she have got to?"

"Yes. It's not like Abigail," Gabby replied. "Could she have been kept late at work?"

"She'd have let us know, surely? Hang on, I've got the salon's number." Emma took out her mobile and scrolled through the contacts then pressed a button. Phone to her ear, she listened for half a minute then shook her head. "Voice-mail. Salon's closed. I've a really bad feeling about this, Gabby," she said as she ended the call. "Really bad. She was supposed to have linked with the Orb. Could something have gone wrong?"

"I doubt it. She got through it all remarkably well when they connected over Animus. And there've been other, more recent successes. There is—"

"What?"

"Well, there's always the possibility the crystal showed

her something she couldn't handle. There's not a great deal we can do about that, of course. Comes down to experience."

"Yes, but Abigail's still a teenager. A mature one, for sure, but still very young. You know, I always thought giving her something that powerful to play with was a bad idea. Like giving matches to a toddler."

"Oh, don't say that," Gabby cried. "I feel bad enough about what happened with Will. I'd never forgive myself if I made something happen to Abigail too!"

Emma rang Josie's.

Nothing.

"I think we should go to the house," said Emma, getting up. "Double-check she's alright."

Twenty minutes later they drew up outside. No lights to the front and the curtains were left undrawn. Emma rang the bell.

No answer.

She knocked on the door. Then again, more loudly.

Still no answer.

"I'll go round the back," said Gabby.

She returned almost immediately. "The curtains are drawn in her bedroom, but I think her light's on. The back door's locked."

"They always leave the key in the lock. I could pop the window."

"Okay," said Gabby, suddenly whispering, suddenly a burglar.

They stole around the house, palms to the wall—hardly any light now the streetlights couldn't guide them. At the door, Emma took off her shoe and smacked it against the tiny pane above the lock. She reached in and down, found the key and turned it.

"Tch. That was far too easy," Gabby muttered, as Emma swung the door open.

"It was," she replied. "Westen's always going on about Flammark's village mentality." She slapped the heel of her shoe to check for glass, then put it on and stepped over the threshold.

Emma hadn't a clue what to expect. Heavens, the girl might only be asleep. But something didn't feel right; didn't feel right at all.

"Shhh," Gabby hissed. "Hear that?"

Whimpering. Upstairs.

Careless to any lurking danger, they rushed into the hall and up the stairs and burst into Abigail's room.

They stood aghast the state it was in: dressing table overturned, chairs shattered, all Abigail's precious things strewn and broken. It was as if a bomb had landed.

But she wasn't there.

More whimpering. Emma cocked her head. "She's in Josie's bedroom!"

As Emma flung the second door open she froze at the sight of the shaking, trembling figure on the bed, huddled in foetal position, cocooned in a duvet, head buried in a pillow. A jolt ripped through Abigail's body as Gabby called her name and she began to keen, a terrifyingly guttural sound, full of shock—full of fear.

Emma recognised it, for Emma had once cried like that herself.

Slowly, she stepped towards the bed, signalling Gabby to stay put. "Sh… sh… It's me, sweetie. Emma. Gabby's here too. It's alright, you're safe now."

The keening stopped. Slowly, Abigail lifted her head from the pillow and turned towards her, eyes wild. Frantic. Stray locks of wet, matted hair stuck to her face. Emma hardly dared to ask what happened, yet knew she had to. The girl wore a look she was all too familiar with.

"Abigail, we can go into details later. But we need to

know… Has there been an intruder? Do we have to call the police?"

The girl swallowed and sobbed. Shook her head.

"You sure?"

She nodded.

"Has *anyone* been here?"

"Nnnno."

Then Gabby murmured, more by way of observation than question. "The Orb…"

Emma spun round at Gabby, raising I-told-you-so eyebrows. The woman backed away; headed for Abigail's room.

Carefully and very deliberately Emma lowered herself onto the bed. She reached out her hand to brush the hair away from Abigail's face. "We're here now. You look very poorly, sweetie. Shall we call Robbie?"

Abigail shook her head again, managing only to say, "N-no. You c-can't. I w-wouldn't know what to t-tell him."

"Are you sure? You look terrible. Have you been like this all afternoon?"

"D-dunno."

"Okay," Emma said, gently, "we won't call Robbie. For now, at least." She raised her head and called, "Gabby, can you get Abigail some water?" Hearing footsteps thunder down the stairs, she turned back to her friend. "Come on, sweetie, let's see if you can sit up. Can I put the lamp on?"

Allowing Emma to switch on the light, Abigail clung on as her friend lifted her shoulders to arrange the pillows before letting her lean back. The girl still quivered from head to foot, and it worried her. Pulling the duvet right up, she considered calling Robbie whether Abigail liked it or not. This was starting to look a lot like shock. Real shock. But … the doctor would want to know what happened, and since

Abigail's condition had clearly been caused by her connection to the Orb, their ability to come up with a plausible explanation would be well-nigh impossible.

Desperately, Emma racked her brains to come up with something that would calm the girl. Something prosaic. "Is there a tea we could make for you?" she asked. "What sort of flavour would help?"

It seemed to work, for despite her shivering, the corners of Abigail's mouth made the tiniest journey upwards. "C-Chamomile and V-Valerian."

Emma smiled too and at that moment Gabby came in with a glass of water. Squeezing her hand she said, "Sip this first. Take it slowly. I'll go down and make you that tea."

Leaving Gabby to sit with the patient, Emma rummaged around in the kitchen looking for the requested infusion, then popped it in a mug and boiled the kettle. What the hell happened? Although she did have reservations about the girl's abilities to handle the crystal, she knew full well nothing would have stopped her trying to connect with it. And she did have some experience. So, what could it possibly have shown her that would reduce Abigail—optimistic, beautiful, confident, Abigail— to the jibbering mess they'd found upstairs?

Kettle boiled, she filled the cup and made her way back to find Abby entwined within her mentor's arms, sobbing as if the world had ended. Good. Much better out than in.

It took another hour of soothing noises and ministrations before Abigail showed any real signs of calming down. She said she needed the loo, but getting up seemed unaccountably painful and she winced, her hands flying to her ribs and private parts. Collapsing back onto the bed she whimpered, "I ... I can't. You'll have to help me. Everything hurts."

"This is unusual," Gabby murmured. "The Orb showed

her something so traumatic, she's developed a physical memory of it."

"It didn't show me," Abigail exclaimed, anger edging her voice. "It *put* me there. I felt *everything*. I don't ever want to go near it again. Never. Take it back, Gabby. Smash it up!"

After a long and agonising journey to the bathroom, it became clear that sleep wasn't yet an option. Abby didn't even want to close her eyes, as if, maybe, she'd have to relive whatever she saw behind them earlier. So, Gabby heated some canned vegetable soup and took it upstairs where the three of them partook of the quietest of picnics. While Abigail mostly listened, Emma and Gabby chatted about something and nothing, well into the early hours until at last Abigail's eyes began to droop and finally, thankfully, she fell asleep, wrapped in Gabby's arms.

Emma whispered, "She's going to need a lot time."

"Yes," Gabby nodded. "Though I'm not sure how much we can give her. God knows what she saw, but if Abigail can be reduced so, we must be looking at some terrible precipitous event. If everything that's happening to Flammark now came from the vision she experienced—we *have* to know what it is."

"I agree with you. But we can't force questions on her. Not while she's in this state. And she can't be left alone."

"No. And though it pains me to say it, we need to keep her away from that crystal," said Gabby.

"Is the Orb still intact? I don't remember seeing it."

"She covered it. And yes, it's still whole. It can't be destroyed—Abigail knows that no matter how much she'd like it me to smash it."

She put her hand through the girl's long black hair, a world of affection in every stroke. "Why don't you go home, Emma?" she murmured. "I'll manage from here. You've work tomorrow."

Reluctantly, Emma rose from the bed. "Okay. I'll ring you first thing. I can't take any more time off, I always seem to be leaving Robbie in the lurch, but I'll be back after work. Hopefully she'll be recovered enough to tell us what we're up against."

"Once she's feeling better, I might take her back with me to the caravan. It'll put even more space between her and the crystal until we decide what we should do with it."

"Abigail clearly wants rid."

"Yes, well Abigail isn't herself, is she? Let's wait. She may change her mind."

Emma wanted to throw something at her. Though it was difficult to keep her tone both hushed and angry, she managed it. "But if you take it away now, as she's told you to, she'd never be exposed to it again and this," she waved her hand at the sleeping girl, "could never be repeated."

Gabby didn't reply at first, just shook her head and smiled as she looked down at Abigail. "I love this child with all my heart and with all my soul. I can't explain why. For centuries, I've looked after this village and no one, *no one,* has ever had this effect on me." She looked up at Emma. "She's special. Very special. As you are special. The Orb is vital to us and will eventually reveal everything. Whatever she saw has to be borne. *Has* to be."

Emma had no answer. All she could do was glare at Gabby with all the force her frustration and impotence could muster. It occurred to her that maybe *she* should take the Orb. Throw it in the river and let the Flam swallow it. But she knew she could never do it. Fundamentally, she also believed the crystal was too important.

With a defeated sigh, she nodded. Before leaving the room, she placed the back of her hand against Abby's forehead, smiling as she realised her feverishness had dissipated.

Then, on a sudden impulse, she moved around the bed

and kissed Gabby on the cheek. These were two of her best and closest friends. It looked increasingly likely that she'd lost Will. She couldn't—*wouldn't*—risk losing the friendship of anyone else.

19
THE WITCH

To her shame, of all the things Emma could have thought about as she drove home, the overwhelming front-runner happened to be a yearning for *The Flammark Fish* to be open. Strange. She *never* bought fish and chips. Stranger still, she'd have bought them to eat now instead of waiting to get them home and put them on a plate. What was wrong with her? She could almost smell them!

It was an effort, but she managed to drag her thoughts away from food and turned them instead to what should have been foremost in her mind. Abigail. She wondered again at what nightmare the Orb had shown her. She knew how the thing worked; remembered Abigail describing how it put her in the centre of the action, placing her in a kind of bubble, as it had done when it showed her the arrival of Animus' first horde of demons. Well, that bubble had been well and truly broken for her now.

Had Abigail encountered the witch? Had she done something to her in her vision? And why had it seemed to crave connection with *her?* Emma shivered at the thought of the scratches on her front door and the twiggy present on the step, baulking at the memory that somewhere deep in her psyche, she once craved connection with *it*.

She must get the door replaced. Too deep to be sanded out, those gouges demonstrated the power of this creature. If they ever met, she'd have no chance against it.

Emma's heart sank as she rounded the corner into the tiny lane that Clearview fronted onto. All the lights were off in the cottage, so … no Westen. He must be busy. She badly needed company. For the thousandth time, she glanced over the green towards St Jude's.

Where Will used to be.

Suddenly, she realised how bloody alone she was. She loved Westen; knew the time was fast approaching when they'd have to decide whether to properly move in with each other. Even then she found herself equivocating. The problem lay in not being able to talk about the other side of her life, the side she had to keep concealed. He'd think she'd gone mad!

Emma liked it that he'd asked Abigail to consult on the circle in Seely Woods. It did suggest he might be open to other ways of thinking. But she'd be kidding herself if she thought he'd actually accept that a real witch had created that thing; that Flammark was a place of dark and arcane secrets. It would … undermine him. Take away the one thing that made him so strong: his *certainty*.

She idled the jeep for a while under the streetlamp outside the cottage, strangely dim for some reason. Not wanting to go in just yet, she turned off the engine and got out to peer over the green. Why she did this, she couldn't say. Perhaps to seek communion—or guidance from her absent friend.

She shivered. Really cold now.

She made to turn round, to get back in the car and put it in her drive. But …

… she couldn't move.

Thrumming. The sensation she associated with her time with Ben. It made her stomach lurch and her heart race. She tried to lift her arm; wanted to reach back and fumble at the gate latch but … she couldn't. Couldn't lift even a finger. Still facing towards the green, a kind of impotent panic set in. She wanted to run but was rooted to the spot, her lungs heavy, managing to expel their air only in quick, shallow gasps.

Out of the night a pale shape loomed. Disembodied. Oval. Faint but clearly visible.

Emma's breath caught in the back of her throat—a preamble to a scream—but no sound came as the shape drew closer. It clarifed into a … face? Above the thrumming, she made out a rustling. No … more a crackling, like the sound of feet on a forest path; the sound she herself had made on the way to the clearing in Seely Woods. Where the circle had been.

The witch's circle.

And suddenly she knew. She was about to meet its progenitor.

Unable even to blink, her eyes fixed on the creature. Slowly—inexorably—it came towards her. Increasingly discernible in the moonlight, its limbs and torso seemed somehow in flux; a churning cascade of what looked like … twigs and thorns and dead leaves. Each facet shifted in endless sussurating movement, forming and reforming into a suggestion of lower limbs, making steps, propelling it forward …

… until it came to a dead stop less than yard in front of her.

Gasps coming quicker—shallower—Emma still couldn't move: not a limb, not an eye, not a muscle could prevent her from taking in the full horror that was the witch. Its head—the only solid thing about it—seemed overlaid with only a semblance of skin, chalk-white and pocked. Lights for eyes, faint beams thin as pins. They regarded her for what seemed a millennium, shining dimly from dark abysmal sockets black as the void, dead as the pit.

It leaned in.

Too paralysed to recoil, Emma could only scream inwardly at its face and the tangled crown that moved with it, a huge medusa of twig and branch. It cocked its head in seemingly curious regard and its mouth began to open, expanding into a black, yawning chasm framed more by teeth than lips. Wide. Wider. No words, just a deep, sickening compost stink that turned Emma's stomach.

The thrumming in her head shifted. No ... *morphed,* became a warping, backwards-tape sibilance that uttered ...

Sister. At last.

Still as death, Emma tried to press every muscle she had into the service of escape, but the thrall—and the terror—was too great. All she could do was gaze mutely at the horror as it lifted an arm towards her, the bone and forest matter it comprised stilling and solidifying. Angling its skeletal wrist, it placed a shrivelled hand on her belly.

The creature seemed to be thinking. Considering. Shook its head in some semblance of sorrow. The stinking maw stretched open again and in her head she heard:

Sister, I am sorry. It is a girl, and she cannot be.

The hand twisted and a sharp pain pierced Emma's gut, and another. Then, as suddenly as it had landed upon her, the hand resumed its oscillation and lifted away.

And she was suddenly freed from the witch's thrall.

But she didn't run, didn't even step back. Instead, Emma remained rooted, grasping at herself where the witch's hand had rested. Another spasm of agony ripped through her and a torrent of soupy bile streamed into her mouth. Bent double, she disgorged it onto the road, the onrush of vomit burning her throat. She managed to cry out—grab the gate—but she missed and crashed to her knees.

Something warm and sticky oozed between her legs.

The witch nodded slowly before turning. Emma, in the throes of collapse, reached out, desperate for any support—even the creature's—but it had started its return over the green. The last thing she saw before unconsciousness took her was the branches of the witch's woody dreadlocks … gleaming like sin in the moonlight.

20
CARRIED AND MISCARRIED

"Jesus fucking Christ! Emma!"

Once he'd drawn up to see the only person in the world he had ever cared about lying prostrate in front of the garden gate, Westen flew out of his car and flung himself on the ground next to her. Heart in mouth, he checked Emma's neck pulse and heaved a sigh of relief before carefully feeling about her body. No visible injuries and, as far as he could make out, nothing broken. She must have fainted again. He fought his way out of his coat and laid it over her before gently lifting and holding her to him as he carried her down the path. Shifting her weight, he managed to fumble for his door key and got them inside.

He laid her like precious cargo on the sofa and lit the kindling under the fire. It was only after he'd gone into the kitchen to find the brandy bottle and saw blood on his hands that he rushed back in. Lifting the coat, he saw a creeping red stain making its way across the white cushions.

Realised where it was coming from.

Jesus. Was she… ? Had she… ?

He whipped out his phone and used his squad ID to call

an ambo. It would make them get a fucking shift on. Then he threw himself to his knees by her side. This was no faint. She lay still, cold. White. Totally unresponsive. Christ, he should have been here earlier. What if he hadn't come at all?

He leaned his face against her cheek. Despairing, he whispered, "Emma! Emma love! I'm here. Everything's going to be okay. Please, *please* be okay…"

Then: "Why didn't you tell me?"

Ten minutes later the ambulance arrived, and suddenly the room filled with bustle.

Jaw working, Westen watched helplessly from the corner. "I think she's had a miscarriage."

"What's her name, love?" the female paramedic said.

"Emma. It's Emma." He swallowed hard. He'd witnessed some shit in his life, but nothing—*nothing*—had ever made him feel like this. Useless, functionless. Terrified.

The woman knelt next to her patient as the other paramedic made a quick examination. "Emma? Emma, can you hear me?" She shook her head at her partner. "She's out of it. Pulse is racing, though. This feels off. We need to get moving."

Soon they were in the ambo masking Emma up and wiring her to a monitor, Westen gripping her hand for dear life as they gunned it down the Sandmarsh Road.

The paramedic sat on the drop-down seat next to her charge and asked Westen questions about Emma's general health, age, and so on, typing each answer into her field laptop. "How far on was she?"

Westen stared back, completely lost for words. He gave his head a little shake then dropped his eyes. Despite everything, a curl of anger crept inside as he avoided the medic's gaze. Had Emma been keeping this from him, too?

Twenty minutes later they'd reached the hospital and her stretcher was rushed through the doors to what must have been a suite of operating theatres. A nurse stopped him in his tracks. Westen, left alone and traumatised, none the wiser about anything, wanted to punch a fucking hole in the wall. Was she going to be alright? When did she know? Why didn't she—" No point. No point in jumping to conclusions until he could talk to her. If she pulled through … He shook his head. It was a miscarriage. Miscarriages happen all the time. The medics know what they're doing.

She. Will. Be. Fine.

Yet his mind returned to the state he'd found her in. He didn't know how long she'd been there, or what had caused it or why she was still unconscious. That wasn't normal, was it? The paramedics had thought so too…

He flipped out his phone.

"Mason? Mason … sorry to call this late. It's … It's Jamie Westen."

The doctor, clearly struggling out of sleep replied, "Westen! What's the problem?"

"It's Emma. I'm at the hospital. Could I possibly ask you to get over here? Can't—" He swallowed. "She's had a miscarriage. I can't get any fucking sense out of anyone and I … I …"

"Oh, laddie, I am so sorry. Say no more. I'm on my way."

Pocketing the phone, Westen finally accepted there was nothing else he could do but wait. He loosened his tie and slumped down on a flimsy blue plastic chair. He put his head in his hands and began the long, dark wait, every second of it expecting the worst.

He was still in that position when Mason found him. The man sat in the next chair, his giant frame making the seat squeak and wobble.

"How're you doing, laddie?"

Westen looked up. His bloodshot eyes answered for him.

Mason put a steadying hand on his shoulder. "Thankfully,

she's my patient, so they let me see her notes. It was a bad one, for sure, but she'll come through it, lad. She will. She's a survivor."

"You didn't see her, Doc. She was completely out of it. So fucking white..."

"She's lost a lot of blood. That's to be expected."

Westen tried a smile, wanted to believe Mason was right. She'd been through hell and back before—and after—they'd met. He had to believe she'd pull through this.

"You didn't know?" asked Mason.

Westen shook his head. Unable to keep the edge out of his voice—even now—he muttered, "She never said a word." Then suddenly he stiffened. "You? Did she tell you? Did you examine her?"

"No, lad. I didn't know either. Try not to read too much into it. If the pregnancy was still early, she may not have known herself."

"You're right.," Westen replied, relaxing a little. "I know I shouldn't be thinking about that, but I can't help it! Jesus, she looked bad, Doc, really bad. Even the paramedics were worried."

"Yes. Yes, they were. But she's in the right place now. And it's perfectly natural for you to have questions. Just ... leave them until we know more and until Emma's in a state where she can answer them. She will, you know."

Westen nodded.

"She has no family, am I right?"

"Yes. Her mother and father are both dead."

"Then she'll need you all the more. Have you contacted anyone else? Abigail? I know Will Turner's still out of the picture."

"Yes ... No, I've only called you so far. Turner's cut Emma off completely. She doesn't know where he is."

"Okay. I'll let Abigail know. And Gabby, of course."

"Thanks, Doc. You know, I've never met this Gabby woman. Emma doesn't talk much about her, but I know they're close."

"They are, we all are. Gabby pulled me through something similar." Haltingly, he told Westen about Joanie and her two-year fight with cancer, how it had left him devastated and depressed and how this Gabby had found a way of letting him talk it through. "Bus trips," he said, with a little chuckle. "We took buses and trains and travelled the country. Taking our time. She has a knack of knowing how people tick."

As did Mason. Westen knew he was trying to make the time pass, pulling his mind away from the edge. And to a degree, it worked. When all this was over, he'd take the doc out for a pint.

But for all Mason's efforts, after another hour had passed, Westen found it almost impossible to hold things together. "What's taking so fucking long?"

A woman in scrubs appeared at the door. Both men leapt up.

"She's fine. The procedure took longer than we expected, but she's come through it well. We put her in Recovery and she'll no doubt come round shortly. We'll be taking her up to the ward soon."

"Oh, thank Christ!" Westen exclaimed.

This time, a huge smile of relief on his lips, Mason put his whole arm around Westen's shoulder, almost giving him a bear hug. "See? I told you!"

Feeling lighter, Westen asked, "Has she come round? Does she know … about the miscarriage?"

"I'm not sure," said the medic. "She hadn't regained consciousness before we operated. Unusually for a pregnancy this early, there was quite a lot of internal haemorrhaging. It would have been very painful. She might have realised what was happening then." She gave a little shrug. "In situations like this, we think it's kinder to leave it to the family to break news like this."

"She has no family. I'm her partner. Can I tell her?"

The doctor smiled. "Of course." She turned to go. "It's this way."

"I'll leave you to it, lad," said Mason, almost pushing Westen through the door. "Give you some privacy. I'll come back later. It'll mean a lot to Emma that you're there when she opens her eyes. But … go easy. Leave the questions. The last thing she wants is an—"

"… interrogation. I know, I know." For the first time, Westen cracked a half-smile. He took a few steps then stopped dead and spun round. "Mason, could I ask … that is, can I give you my sergeant's number? I'm in the middle of an investigation but … I'm not leaving here till I know Emma's okay."

"Not a problem. Pete Burrows, isn't it, if memory serves? I'll let him know and I'll also gather the rest of the troops. Emma will want her friends around her. But for now, laddie, I think you'll do on your own."

Westen gave the doc Pete's number, then throwing him a grateful nod, left him to walk along the corridor with the surgeon. Half-embarrassed at having to ask, he said, "How far on was she?"

"Very early, probably no more than seven, possibly eight weeks. It's a very good job you found her when you did. Her vitals caused us a lot of concern. She's through it all, now, though."

"Was it … a boy? Girl?"

The doctor paused at the threshold of the recovery room. Smiling kindly, she said, "Sorry. I'm afraid it was far too early to say." She pointed to the corner of a large unit, empty except for a bay in the corner, where a nurse fussed around a bed. "I'll leave you to it. Good luck to you both!"

At first, Westen didn't move. Didn't know what he was going to say; what he could say. But he didn't have a great deal of time to think about it because the nurse was nodding him over.

"She's coming out of it," she said. "She'll obviously be a bit woozy. Give her some water to sip—but not too much. It might make her sick."

The nurse bustled out. He found a chair and dragged it to Emma's bedside. Picking up her hand, he leant towards her, bidding the cosmos a silent thank you for not taking her away from him.

But it nearly had; he nearly lost her. As he sat next to her, gazing at a face white as the sheet she was lying on, he remembered how he'd found her. Thank Christ he'd decided to take a few hours off the case. Any later, it might have been a different story.

Her eyes fluttered and he smiled, determined to greet her re-entry into the world with his best face. The questions will come later. They didn't matter one jot.

Coming fully into consciousness, Emma returned his smile, uncertainly. His grin widened and he leant in further to give her the kiss he had so fervently promised himself he would. But before he could get within reach, her brow furrowed, and she glanced down at the bed, then at the walls. Suddenly, she froze as if struck by a blow, and sat stock still, eyes fixed on the middle distance as her memories loaded up. Her eyes flew to the door, chest heaving. She tried to sit up; began thrashing about, recoiling from Westen's hand as he tried to steady her. "Take that thing away from me. Getaway ... Get off ... Get *off*... !" Putting her own hand on her belly, she began swatting at him with the other, crying, keening, still glaring at his hand as if it was some kind of fucking atrocity.

He tried to calm her, but it made her even more agitated.

Glaring at him—her yes like pinpoints—she curled her lips and formulated a snarl that came right from the back of her throat.

"Get away from me, you *fucking* creature*!*"

Westen froze a second, then stricken and utterly mortified, he leapt up and to the door. "Nurse! *Nurse*!" he thundered. Not one, but two ran in, pushing past him as he stated the obvious. "Something's happened. Something's … *wrong*—"

By this time, Emma was on her elbows, angling herself backwards. She dug her ankles into the mattress, glaring daggers at him as she strained away. One of the nurses spun around at him, as if he was the fucking cause of it all, shouting for him to wait outside. But he couldn't move. Nonplussed, helpless, he heard nothing; saw nothing except Emma's eyes blazing at him as the two nurses held her down.

A doctor arrived; was suddenly herding him out, hand on his elbow. *No. Fuck, no.* But he had no authority here. No expertise.

No fucking idea why Emma was screaming at him.

21

JIM

Abigail woke to find herself lying in her father's arms. She breathed in his scent; a preciously familiar combination of tobacco and fabric conditioner. She leant into him closer; buried her face in his wide chest as he held her to him like a baby. "Shhh… shhh… I'm here, sweetheart. I'm here. It's all going to be okay."

"Is it?" she said.

"Of course, it is. I won't let anything happen to you, my sweet girl."

"Promise?"

Jim gave her a little squeeze. "I promise."

"It was … terrible."

"I know. I know it was and I'm so sorry you had to witness it."

"It wasn't just that, dad. I was there. I felt it all. What they did to her … it was as if they did to me. I felt every touch, every kick; could feel the soil in the back of my throat … my lungs bursting." She stirred in his arms, started to gag.

"Shhh… shhh… Be still, little one. It's over now. Steady yourself. I'm here. Breathe. You are still very young—the Orb didn't realise ... didn't understand. It presumed too much. It'll try to be much gentler next time."

"Next time?" she shuddered. "There won't be a next time. I won't go through that again. I won't let it."

"I think you will. If I know anything about it, nothing will stop you from doing the right thing, the courageous thing. You're so brave and I'm so proud of you. So proud!"

"You are? You never told me."

"Didn't I? But you always knew it, didn't you? My girl. My precious girl. I'd do anything to protect you."

"I know. Of course, I know." She frowned, stirred in his arms. "You died to protect me. Tried to get away, to leave the village. Because the curse wanted you to hurt me."

"Yes. That's right."

She thought about this for a while. Took the time to listen to her heartbeats. Then she *knew* and relaxed back into his embrace. "You aren't him, are you? Aren't my dad."

"No, sweetheart. I'm not."

"So ... who are you?"

"You know who I am. You know what I am."

She nodded. "I think so. You're my Orb."

"Yes."

"What are you doing?"

"I'm calling on your memories of your father—borrowing him. It is the only thing I could think of to try to heal the damage I did to you." She felt his arms tighten around her. "Tell me, sweetheart, did I do right? Do you mind me being your father for a while?"

She felt as if there might be tears in her eyes. "No. No, I don't mind."

"You see, I want to us to carry on. I am bonded to you and I think you are bonded to me. I fear that if you ignore me, I will call to you more loudly. And that may do you great harm. Also..."

"Yes?"

"I cannot be destroyed."

"I ... I don't want to destroy you. But I don't want you to destroy me, either. What happened last night, I—"

"I know. I am sorry. It was too much. You weren't ready."

"No. No, I wasn't."

To her surprise, Abigail felt no anger towards the crystal. Instead, she decided to bask in the simulation of her father's presence, luxuriate in it. She called up her favourite memory of him; when he used to lift her half-awake from his van after she'd gone out with him on a job. Always she would beg him to take her with him and he used to let her hand him things; be his proper little helper, his shadow, his little girl.

His sweetheart.

Now she was with him again, she didn't want him to go. Couldn't bear the heartache of being parted again.

The Orb read her mind. "He never left you, Abigail. He will always be in your heart and in your memories."

"Will you bring him back to me again, like this?"

"You won't need him, at least not in this way. You will become stronger. I will make you stronger—if you can learn to trust me again. Can you learn to trust me, Abigail?"

"Yes."

It seemed an affirmation much weightier than the word itself, for the instant she uttered it in the zero space of this dream, or vision, or whatever it was, the hurt—or rather, the *abstract* of the hurt went away. Just ... left. And all that she heard was her father's delicious, gravelly, beautiful voice as he said,

"That's the spirit, sweetheart. Now, it's time you woke up."

Slowly, Abigail opened her eyes They felt sticky and puffed-up. She found herself wrapped in a pair of arms. Not her father's.

Gabby's.

Eyes tight shut, the woman's mouth lay wide open, a little trickle of saliva oozing from its corner as her head lolled on the pillow. Careful not to wake her, Abigail gently extricated herself and came to a wobbly standing position. No pain. Her ribs felt fine, the raw soreness in her vagina gone.

And so had the shame.

Feeling able to tackle the stairs on her own, she chose not to take them at her usual thundering speed, but painstakingly, alert for the sudden onrush of pain. Reaching the kitchen without anything untoward happening, she grabbed a glass and filled it with water. Glugged it down. Then she put the kettle on and fished out a little packet of ginger tea. As it brewed, she leant against the worktop.

And took mental stock.

At first, she thrilled at the memory of her dad's arms around her. His voice. His smell. His words. Abigail knew they weren't his, of course, but she didn't want dwell on that; instead, she wondered at what the Orb had done for her. Not only had it understood that she needed to be healed, it had known how to do it; known what *mattered* to her. It seemed their bond was true. Real. She faintly remembered coming round to a room full of mayhem, where she must have thrashed around as the vision took hold, then dragging herself to the bed to find something to fling over it. She'd have thrown the bloody thing out of the window right there and then had she'd either the strength or the nerve to touch it. Amazingly, after all it had put her through, now all she could feel was ... gratitude.

She made her tea and took it upstairs—still a bit wobbly, but a whole lot better—and stood at the threshold of her room. It looked more like a war zone, her things thrown everywhere as she must have fought like blazes with that *fader* character and his henchmen. Whoever they were. Tentatively, she stepped further in and kicking aside the debris, righted a chair and sat in front of the crystal. Putting her cup down on a goddess coaster—miraculously still resting in its place—she pulled away the first thing that must have come to hand to cover it up. A pillow case.

Abigail didn't imagine the faint glow that faded in and then out. She knew it to be a salutation. She picked up her cup, signalling to it that she didn't want to fully connect. Too soon. She didn't want to risk another Sighting.

But remembering the last one at least felt possible now.

So, she closed her eyes and sipped her tea while she only partially opened her mind to the crystal, mentally slipping her hand into Jim's.

And that's how Gabby found her, seated serenely in front of the sphere, cup in hand, eyes closed.

"Abigail Chater, you never cease to amaze me," Gabby said. "I cannot begin to comprehend the horror of what you were shown. All I know is, judging by the state you were in, it must have been truly terrible. That you can sit here calmly drinking tea in front of the glass… I'm speechless!"

The girl opened her eyes and gave a crooked smile. "Yeah. Yeah, it was terrible. Horrific. But the Orb did something wonderful, too." With a thready sigh she rose from the chair. "I've realised I'm missing a day's work. Can you ring the salon? Tell them you found me with a temperature, or something? It's not as if you'd be lying! Then … let's go downstairs. I think I can tell you what I saw."

22

BAD NEWS

Abigail and Gabby had only just ensconced themselves on the living room sofa—gas fire on full—when someone started pounding on the front door.

"Who on earth could that be?" cried Abigail, startled. She looked at the mantle clock. "It's still early."

She was about to get up when Gabby put her hand on her shoulder. "No. You stay there. I'll see who it is."

There were mutterings in the hall, followed by th soon of Gabby crying out. She brought Robbie in, his face a raincloud.

"Something's happened to Emma," said Gabby. "Something terrible."

Abigail, looked from one to another. "To Emma? W-what?"

"Westen found her lying outside Clearview," said Robbie. "She's had a miscarriage. He called an ambulance and went with her to the hospital. He rang me and I waited with him. He's still there."

"A miscarriage?" exclaimed Abigail. She gaped at Gabby. "Emma was *pregnant?*"

Gabby flopped down by her side. "There's something else, isn't there? I can see it in your face."

Robbie nodded. "They performed a small procedure. There were complications, and she's lost a lot of blood, but the surgeon was satisfied with the outcome. Westen went into the recovery room to be there with her when she came out of the anaesthetic. We weren't sure whether she knew she was pregnant or not. The lad was girding himself to tell her the news that she'd lost the bairn. I was on my way out of the hospital when he rang me again, beside himself. Emma had woken in considerable confusion. Screamed at him, apparently."

"Oh my God," said Abigail. "That's awful. Emma, screaming? That's not like her. Do you think something happened? Something that caused the miscarriage?"

"My thoughts, exactly," Gabby said, grimly. "Sounds to me like trauma."

"Agreed," Robbie said. "They've sedated her. Heavily. She'll come out of it this afternoon, but she'll be very, very groggy."

Gabby's eyes flitted to the door. "I want to go—need to go and see her—but…" she bit her lip as she turned to Abigail. "I can't leave you and you're definitely not well enough to come with me."

Robbie peered over his glasses at Abigail. "Are you poorly, lass? You do look a bit flushed."

"No, yes … that is, I came down with something overnight but I am feeling a lot better now."

"Sit you down," Robbie said. "My bag's in the car."

As he left to retrieve it, Abigail said, "We should go. I'm fine, really." She got up but dizziness overtook her, and she stumbled back into her seat, just in time for Robbie to return and witness the performance.

He took her temperature and blood pressure. "Well, I don't think it's terminal, young Abigail, but you are a bit on the warm side. Stay put. You'll be no use to anyone if you caught a chill and Emma wouldn't thank you if you passed something on to her. She's enough to cope with. Besides, there's nothing either of you can do. No point in being there until she wakes up and even then the hospital will probably restrict visitors until they've made their assessments."

"How's Westen?" Abigail asked.

"They told him to go home and get some sleep. He refused, of course. We've both of us been at her bedside more or less since she was admitted. Wild horses wouldn't keep him away. The man's in pieces."

"When did all this happen?" asked Gabby. "She was with us until well past midnight."

"Westen found her about two o'clock this morning. I've phoned his sergeant because he's still in the middle of this damned case! They've put her in a quiet side-room. I've been trying to ring both of you, but your mobiles were off for some reason. I thought I'd see if at least one of you was here, since it's on my way to the surgery."

"Oh, poor Westen. And poor, Emma!" said Gabby, wringing her hands.

"I think she'll be in for a few days. They'll want to keep an eye on her. She needs zero stress, ladies. I'll let you know when you can visit." He heaved a sleepless sigh and glanced at his watch. "I have to go. I'm late."

"Yes, go. *Go*!" said Gabby." Thanks for letting us know. And you get some rest, too!"

He grimaced. "I'm fine. It's not the first time I've pulled an all-nighter and it won't be the last." Snapping shut his medical bag, he turned to leave. "I'm away, then. You both stay put. I can see myself out."

After the door banged shut, Abigail cried, "It was the witch! That's why Emma woke up screaming."

"Yes, I think you're right." Gabby replied, somberly. "It must have shown itself to her. The shock must have caused the miscarriage."

"The pregnancy explains why she fainted at the circle."

"Yes," Gabby replied, "and why she's been so hungry lately. I should have guessed. She usually picks at a salad." Distracted, she stepped towards the window and stared out. "This is my fault."

"What do you mean?" said Abigail.

"I burned the twig-wreath. I said it would seek her out, didn't I? I should have known something like this might happen," Burying her face in her hands she wailed, "Oh, Abigail, what if William was right all this time? That I'm more part of the problem than the solution? Look what happened to you! I gave you the crystal. And now this. Now Emma."

"Stop it, Gabby. Stop it! Things have been going down in Flammark for centuries. It's why you were put here. Every solution to the kind of crap we're dealing with carries risk—real human risk. And we learn."

"Yes, but I should have been more careful with Emma. I left her unprotected."

"What could you have done? You don't have that kind of power any more."

"I could have not burned the wreath."

Abigail had no answer to that. Gabby was probably right.

They fell silent. Gabby stared out of the window again, no doubt mentally castigating herself. Abigail was busy trying to join the dots.

"What I don't understand," said Abigail, "is why Emma?

Why is the witch so obsessed with her?"

"Haven't I said all along there's something special about her?" Gabby replied. "She's like a magnet. The curse found her; Animus feared her. Now, a witch is on her case."

Abigail went over to the window and catching Gabby's hand in hers, led her to the sofa. "Come on, Gabs. Let's sit down. We've got to get to the bottom of this before this creature does even more damage. We owe it to Emma. Let me tell you what the Orb showed me. Then you'll see giving it to me was the right thing to do. But I need your help to make sense of it."

"Are you sure you're up to it?" said Gabby.

"Yes." Sitting next to her, Abigail told her why. Told her how the crystal called upon the memories she had of her father's physical presence; how it had used them—used him—to heal the pain it had put her through. "I trust it, now. Completely. In a weird kind of way, I think it cares for me, empathises. What it revealed was ... horrendous. Awful. Of course, none of it really happened to me, but it happened to *someone.* I *was* her. I heard everything, felt ... everything."

After taking a few deep breaths, stuttering at first, Abigail recounted how a band of men had taken her and for what seemed hours, had marched her to some woods—Seely Woods, maybe? Then she described what happened there.

She dry-swallowed. Could hardly frame the words. "But it wasn't me, of course. It was a felt vision. I think it was the witch. How she used to be ... before." She swallowed again. "They ... stripped her. Then raped her, Gabby. Then they threw her into an open grave. Afterwards they filled it. I could feel the weight of the dirt raining down on her; in her mouth, her lungs...

Abigail had to stop, catching the back of her throat as she tried to breath down the edge of rising agitation. She closed her eyes and behind the lids saw her father, smiling at her tenderly. Heard him murmur, *'It was not real'* so that the pain and trauma became once-removed, the proxy-experience it truly was.

The relief must have shown in her face, for Gabby said, "Jim?"

Abigail nodded.

"What the Orb did for you is extraordinary. I have never seen anything like it before. That it conjured your father to take you through these moments is wonderful. Powerful. It will free the crystal to show you what it needs to show you."

"Gee, thanks," said Abigail, giving a wan smile. "And there's me thinking it gave me my dad back because it cared about me."

"Oh, that too," Gabby grinned. Her expression turned serious again. "Did you get a read on who those men were?"

Abigail concentrated. "They weren't modern, that's for sure. They wore wristbands and strappings. I got the impression of leather. Erm ... studs too. Soldiers, maybe?"

"Possibly. Is your phone handy? Can you do a search?"

Abigail nodded. Then frowned. "It's in my bedroom so there's no guarantee it won't be broken. Mum's laptop's in the kitchen. I'll use that."

"Stay put." said Gabby. "I'll get it."

She returned with it, using it to balance a tray of more drinks and a packet of biscuits.

Abigail tutted as she held the tray aloft for Gabby to put the laptop on her knee. "Mum would kill you if she saw you doing that!" Refreshments secured, she opened the computer. "Okay, what am I looking for?"

"Brigandines," said Gabby.

After a few taps, up came a screen full of images. "Yes!" Abigail exclaimed, "I think that's what I saw!" She tapped again and began reading. "It says they're a kind of armour. Knights wore them—and archers." She looked up, frowning.

"My God, Gabby. Did I go back to the fourteenth bloody century?"

"Give or take. I seem to remember brigandines were in use for at least three hundred years." She flapped her hand. "Anyway, never mind that. We've a rough idea of *when* we're dealing with. But not about *who*. Is there anything else you can remember about them? Even the slightest detail?"

Abigail closed her eyes again, tentatively replaying what happened, desperately hoping not to feel any of it. But the Orb's healing strategy had worked, and with no after-effects, she raised an image. "A ring! One of them had a ring. A big one!"

"A signet ring?"

"Yeah, but bigger than I've ever seen."

Gabby gave a knowing smile. "It'll have been a proper one. One that was used to seal documents. So, we're looking at—" The grin left the woman's face as her expression darkened.

"What?"

"Aristocracy. Only people that could write—who were educated—wore signet rings and only the very rich needed seals. It's all coming together now. Remember, how I said that witches were bonded to the place from which they came and that usually they return because of some past torment? You said she was buried alive ..."

"Oh, wow! God, I'm so stupid! I should have made the connection. The murders!"

"You've been too busy processing everything. I think the Orb took you back to Seely Woods and to the moment the witch was created; the moment when a man buried his daughter. And, given the period, and that ring, I think that man might have been Oswald Blackstone."

"Blackstone?"

"Yes. The Orb must have re-enacted a Blackstone murder.

Oswald was born in 1486—a very, very ugly baby, as I remember." She paused a moment. "The more I think about it, the more this feels right."

Abigail gasped. She typed into the search bar again then as the result came up, grabbed Gabby's wrist. "Fader. She—I —kept screaming at this Fader. I didn't get it at first. It's not spelt the way I thought. It's *f-a-i-d-e-r.* She was talking about her *father*!"

Gabby nodded."Yes. Faider's a medieval form. It confirms what we've just been saying."

"So ... this *is* about the Blackstones and the curse is definitely back?"

"No," said Gabby, working it through. "It's truly impossible. Michael and I buried it in the outer regions. Obviously, there's a connection but I promise you the curse cannot return. But I do think you saw it in action. In Oswald."

"Okaaay," said Abigail. Something had popped into her mind, a half-formed idea she was trying to grasp. "Let's keep with the curse for a minute. Go over exactly how it all started."

Gabby nodded. "We—Michael and I—saw it as a distillation of misogyny. The Blackstones nursed such a hatred for the female sex hardly any daughter survived. Wives were tolerated only insofar as they bore the line its sons. Over the centuries, this hatred took on a life of its own—became essence—a scourge, a true curse. You experienced it in Oswald; how, in his cycle, it consumed him with such hatred for his daughter he ... did what he did to her. And, of course, the curse came with the sleeping sickness. It literally eradicated even the slightest awareness in the village about what was going on."

"And this hatred. Remind me where *that* come from..."

Gabby frowned. "You know the answer to that. Misogyny was baked into the entire social system of the period—and it's still here in some form or another. Oswald's time was getting perilously close to the Inquisition—at least in its English incarnation. Fear of women was stoked up; witchcraft used as an excuse to vilify, torture and scapegoat. Particularly powerful women. They could be brought down in a heartbeat by the slightest malicious accusation. And innocence couldn't be proved, of course, unless it was through the agency of death."

"But that was everywhere. What made it so intense with the Blackstones?"

"I'm not getting where this is going, Abigail. Why are you asking?"

"Are you sure it was just misogyny that fuelled the curse? What if it was something … more? What if … What if it was something *else*?

Gabby sat back, her mouth flapping open. "What on earth do you mean?"

"Do you remember the name of Oswald's daughter? Whose shoes did I walk in?"

"Margaret. Her name was Margaret."

"What if Margaret really was a witch even before she was buried?"

"Eh? I don't follow."

"After the soil came down, she—I—felt … angry."

"Understandable…"

"No Gabby, you're not getting me. I said *after* the soil came down. After Margaret *died*."

You could have heard a pin drop, Gabby silent as she processed Abigail's bombshell. Abigail, too, fell quiet, mentally circling the very edges of her memory trying to recall—but not re-experience—the moment that had been bugging her all through Gabby's narration; the rage, the incandescent hatred once the soil had covered her and she'd stopped breathing. The more she thought about it, the more certain she became. Margaret Blackstone had been like her. Had the Sight.

Had been a witch long before she was buried

"My God, Abigail. All these years—all these centuries. Michael and I believed the curse had no foundation; that these daughters were ... ordinary."

"I felt her. In the cold and silence and," she shivered, "the deadness. At the very end—*after* the very end. I felt her ache for revenge."

Suddenly, she frowned and clutched at Gabby. "What about the other Blackstone daughters? Did they have the Sight too? Were they witches? And me ..." She swallowed. "I have the Sight—and, as you're so fond of saying maybe Emma has something like that too. We're both fruit of the same tree. Are we witches like Margaret? Will we become like her? Will we not be able to die?"

Suddenly her whole life took on a different quality. Her obsession with paganism and its artefacts that she so loved: her candles and wands and orbs and goddess posters seemed nothing more than vain frippery now. Margaret was the big league and certainly no role model. It was as if Abigail was suddenly realising the *potential* of her chosen path; how precarious and dangerous it might become.

Gabby locked eyes with her. "Absolutely not. You are nothing like Margaret. She was brutalised where you are nurtured; reviled where you are loved. But no doubt she was very powerful—as I believe you and Emma to be. The *manner* of her death was what kept her from passing. *Oswald* was responsible for what Margaret is now. This will not happen to you, and you *will* die." She smiled. "I promise."

Abigail smiled too, gruesome though the promise was. "I do feel nurtured, you know. I do feel I'm being allowed to ... I dunno, be myself."

"And so you should. Difficult back in the day, though.

Acknowledging the gift would have meant certain death possibly for the entire family. They suppressed their secret so well even Michael and I didn't fathom it. Fear like that makes fertile ground for evil to breed."

"So *how* is Margaret back? If she never … passed, where has she been? And why choose now to appear? And why did she go after Emma?"

"That last question is the easiest to answer. I think she wanted to reach out. That's what the twig-wreath was all about. She's a blood relative, remember."

"She hasn't reached out to me."

"You weren't pregnant."

"Omigod, Gabby! If the baby was a girl …"

"Exactly! That the witch caused the miscarriage is obvious, but I wonder if was brought on by more than just a shock encounter. I can't help but wonder if the witch might have deliberately triggered it, though I'm not there yet as to exactly why." Gabby grimaced. "Whatever the case, we can add Emma's baby to the list of Margaret's victims. We have to get rid of her. *Have* to!."

After a long moment of silence Abigail whispered, "How? If she can't be killed…?"

Gabby sighed. "I have an idea, but you aren't going to like it."

Abigail raised an eyebrow.

"Oswald wouldn't have left it at a mere burial. That only dealt with Margaret's body. If he thought his daughter a true witch, he'd have had her spirit driven out too." She pursed her lips. "The only person qualified to exorcise a witch is the spiritual leader of its territory. In our case … it's the parish priest."

"Oh no," said Abigail.

"Oh, yes. I'm afraid we're going to have to talk to *San Dra*."

23
AWAKE

Westen hadn't budged an inch from Emma's side. That's not to say he'd managed to stay awake. It had been a hard day and a harder night—hard fucking month—and he just hadn't the physical resources left to stay alert.

He sensed rather than saw a change in her. It jolted him awake and he found himself hunched over the side of her bed, his head cradled in the nook of his elbow, his other hand over hers.

As before, Emma's eyelids fluttered.

"Emma! Love! I'm here. How are you feeling!"

Her eyes opened. Clearly battling for focus, she looked at him; even tried a smile but didn't quite manage it. The doctor had warned him she might be like this, confused, disorientated. The sedation had been heavy, and they'd wanted her to come out of it gradually.

Then, suddenly, her respiration started to increase—not quite as it had before, but noticeably. Her expression slipped as with a slight frown, her eyes fell away from his and slowly scanned the room. The haunted look was back.

"Shhh, sweetheart. You're safe. You've had some kind of a trauma. Try not to think about anything, just rest."

Giving her hand a reassuring squeeze, he pressed the call button to let the nurse know she'd wakened. But he was worried. Whatever had got Emma into this state hadn't been banished by the cocktail of drugs they'd given her. This was not a straightforward miscarriage. Something had caused it. Something that had terrified the fucking daylights out of her.

He knocked the smile off the face of the nurse who entered. "She's getting agitated again. The sedation hasn't worked."

The nurse checked Emma's vitals on the screen they'd wired her to. "I don't think you need to be too concerned. Everything looks normal, though her heart rate has picked up a little. That's to be expected, she's just come round. I wouldn't worry. The doctors are already on their rounds. They'll be here shortly." The smile returned. "Sit tight, Superintendent. "She'll be okay."

Emma certainly seemed calmer than she'd been a few minutes ago. Reassured, he resumed his seat and started talking. About nothing, really. Just words. He'd been told often enough that trauma victims respond to the sound of a familiar voice. But after ten minutes had passed, he'd started to worry again. Her position hadn't changed, her eyes fixed on a spot just north of her feet.

"Emma? Emma, sweetheart, look at me."

She didn't move.

The doctor arrived with the nurse in tow and he stood up. "She's not taking any notice of me, " Westen said. "She's just ... staring. Been like that since she woke up."

"The nurse said you'd reported some agitation?"

Westen nodded. "At first, yes, but now—"

"Now she's fixating on that one spot. Hmmm." The doctor raised his hand to his chest pocket and unclipped a pencil light. Shone it in Emma's eyes. "Emma? Emma, can you speak to me?"

Nothing.

"I wouldn't worry too much at this point," the doctor said, putting his light back. "It's the sedation. It was pretty strong. Her pupils are responsive so there doesn't seem to be any physical impairment."

"Why won't she speak?"

"I'm sure she will. Give it a bit longer, eh? Try not to worry."

"Why don't you pop down to the café and get a bite?" the nurse said. "You've been with Emma all night and must be shattered. You'll be no use to her if you don't look after yourself."

He shook his head. "No. I'm not leaving her. I'll be fine."

The doctor understood. "Make him some tea and maybe send someone to get him a sandwich?"

The nurse nodded. "I'll make some toast. We're quiet at the moment." As she bustled out the doctor moved on, leaving Westen once more alone with Emma.

"Sweetheart," he whispered. "Try. Try to talk to me. Give me something. I'm out of my fucking mind."

For a moment, his heart leapt as her eyes welled. At least that was something! But she continued to fix on her point, never once looking at him, and all he could do was watch impotently, as the tears rolled down her cheeks. Though he couldn't be certain she knew he was there, he suspected it. And worse—fucking worse—he began to think she wanted him to leave.

The nurse returned with a tray and set it down, glancing at her patient.

"There, it may not seem like it, but tears are a good sign. She's probably coming to terms with it."

With what? The baby? Did she even know about the

baby? The way she'd swatted at him like that, trying to protect her belly at the same time, told him she did. And her tears suggested she knew well enough that she'd lost it. But this was Emma. The Emma who'd been through the hell Cregan had wrought upon her; the Emma who'd found the tortured remains of Peter Martin! She was strong. A warrior! With him at her side, surely she could face this? The could face it together! And they could try again, if she wanted.

He kept coming back to it. A growing certainty. There was something else.

An hour passed. The weeping stopped and started but still Emma made no sound. And he couldn't get any sense out of the fucking medics. They kept insisting everything was perfectly normal; that she'd come out of it soon, but by mid-afternoon even they were talking about calling in psych services.

He rang Mason again.

"My advice?" the doc said. "Go home. Get a shower and something to eat. I agree with you that something's off. This is not like the lass. You found her outside the cottage, didn't you? Could she have been attacked?"

"Yes, that's my thinking, too. Someone had done some damage to her door a few nights ago. But you know how fucking stubborn she can be. She refused to have anyone stay over. Best I could do was put her on the squad watch-list for regular patrols. Fuck, this is my fault. I could have done more!"

"No, laddie. I know what Emma's like. If she doesn't want to do something, she won't."

"I know. Still, I should have insisted she stay with someone. There's a fucking murderer on the loose!"

"And it's your job to find him," said Mason. "She knows that. You are not to blame."

Westen wanted to believe him but in his heart he knew

this was all down to him. "Thanks for getting in touch with my sergeant, by the way. When you told him what happened, he treated it as an assault case. He sent a someone out to canvas Emma's neighbours. Talk about bolting the stable door. Too little too fucking late!"

"Calm yourself lad. It sounds as if Burrows has everything in hand. Get some rest. You've barely slept. We know how strong Emma is. She probably just needs time to process things by herself. I'm getting a locum in to see me to the weekend. It'll take me an hour or so to set it up, then I'll be over. I'll talk to her doctors. See what's what."

"Thanks, Doc. Appreciated."

Westen ended the call and peered at Emma's motionless figure. He fixed his face into a smile. "Mason says I should go, love. Give you some space. I don't want to, but I think for some reason, I might be upsetting you more by being here. But if you can hear me, I need you to know that I want us to be together. For ever. No matter what."

He got up. With no little hesitation, he leant over her. Seeing no sign of her earlier recoil, he tenderly kissed her cheek. "I love you, Emma."

He hovered a moment and then left the room, the taste of her tears on his lips.

"Guv?" Burrows exclaimed, looking up from his computer in astonishment. "I … we thought you were still at the hospital. How's Emma?"

Westen shrugged. He didn't fucking know. He'd taken Mason's advice. Gone home. Had a shower. Tried to get some sleep but couldn't. The doc messaged him to say he'd got his locum and was at the hospital and that there'd been no change.

He couldn't think of anything else to do but turn up at the station.

"She's awake, Pete, so that's something. Did you get any joy out of her neighbours?"

"No. Nada. Nothing from any of the patrols either."

"Well, get them out again. I've said before, I'm not a great believer in co-incidence. What happened to Emma may somehow linked to the murders. That gives us all kinds of headaches if the MO's changed that much!"

Burrows frowned and shifted uncomfortably in his seat. "Sorry, Guv, but … well, Emma's had a miscarriage. Why link her to the investigation?"

"The doctors believe her reaction is … extreme. They're beginning to think some kind of trauma might have brought it on. If I'm right and what happened to her *is* connected to the case, then perhaps the killer is, as you say, devolving. They've already changed burial sites, maybe the victims are changing too."

Burrows returned a thin smile. "Okay, Guv. I'll get uniform out again. See if we can turn over some new stones."

"This is down to me," said Westen. "I told you about the damage to her door. I should have moved her into my flat. Should have insisted. Fuck it!"

"She wouldn't have gone, Guv. That lady of yours has a mind of her own."

"That's what Mason said." Blowing out his cheeks, Westen slumped. "She won't talk to me, Pete. Won't talk to me."

"I'm sorry, Guv. But … anything you need, just say."

"Thanks, Pete." He heaved another sigh. "Well, I'm obviously no fucking use at the hospital at the moment, but I can be here, so … where are we?"

Burrows pulled a face. "Wasn't sure when to tell you, Guv. The assistant chief con's been on the blower. He wants to bring in the review team to see where we are. He said with you being distracted, like, he thinks it might be best if they—"

"Take over." Westen nodded grimly. "Over my dead fucking body they will. Update me, then I'll get back to him.

"To be honest, we're in a slump. We're keeping an eye on Sweeting. He hasn't left his mother-in-law's since we interviewed him. She told Sheila there was no sign of dirt or exertion when he arrived home after that coach trip; nothing that might indicate he'd been digging. We got the lab results back from the clothes he was wearing that night—which he gave to us voluntarily, remember. Nothing to suggest he made any physical contact with the Grey girl. The dirt under his shoes didn't match up with the samples we took from the churchyard, or Seely Woods. Doesn't look good, Guv. We've nothing that ties him in. The only development is he's given the Phoenix his resignation."

"Good. He should never have been near a fucking classroom though that doesn't make him a murderer. None of this cuts it, and now we've got the review team breathing down our necks. As if I didn't have enough on my—" He shook his head angrily. "Never mind. Whose heading it up?"

Burrows winced. "Frank Marshall."

"You're fucking kidding me!"

"Yeah. Thought that'd go down well. I know you two don't get on."

"No, we do not! Jesus, Pete, it's all I fucking need."

24
PERSUASION

Exorcism.

Abigail didn't know whether to be excited or terrified as she played with the word in her head. There were other images there too, of priests and crosses and incantations and girls with rotating necks. She could hazard a fairly accurate guess at what Sandra's reaction to performing one would be. Thank the stars she'd managed to get a decent night's sleep, they were going to need all their wits about them for the encounter to come. Gabby more so since she and the vicar pretty much detested the sight of each other.

"I'm dreading this," Gabby fretted, as they walked to Silver Blossom Drive. It was at the far end of the village, near the Tor. "You saw her face when I turned up at the vicarage. She didn't once look at me—not the entire time I was there."

"She doesn't need to like you. She did what we asked of her," said Abigail. "Even lied to the police. Although she couldn't do much else given the state of her kitchen—and that great pile of leaves."

Gabby almost chuckled. "Yes. If she'd spouted about that,

it would've shot a hole in her credibility for sure—which she couldn't risk, not with all those plans she's hatching."

"Talking of which, are they still there? On the table?"

"I suppose so. I didn't move them. Just swept all the detritus away." She took a moment. "It's an interesting question, though. If she hasn't gone back to retrieve them..."

"Then she may not go back at all." Abigail finished for her. She grinned. "Result, then!"

They stopped in front of a small sixties semi and pausing to give Abigail a wry glance, Gabby creaked open the tiny picket-fence gate that led up the narrow, flagged path towards Albert's front door. A white—and dirty—uPVC affair it was, with stained-glass lights. Lifting a finger to the doorbell, Gabby muttered, "Here goes nothing!"

Albert answered almost immediately, his expression clouding over as soon as he set eyes on Gabby.

"Oh. Oh, it's you. I wish you'd called before you took the trouble to come all the way out here. Have you come to see Sandra?" He shifted his head as if he thought to look behind, his eyes flitting sideways. With no subtlety whatsoever, he raised his voice, "She hasn't been feeling very well. She's not up yet."

Abigail almost laughed at his crude warning. Seconds later, she heard light footsteps inside, presumably taking the stairs.

"Albert," Gabby pressed. "We need to speak to her. It is very urgent."

"I'm sorry," he said in his flat, reedy voice. "She is a guest in my house, and I won't have her disturbed."

Abigail tried not to enjoy the interchange, but she couldn't help it. She loved it when Gabby did formidable.

"Now listen to me, Albert Reed. You may be church warden, but there's things going on you know nothing about.

Sandra's in the middle of it all and she's needed. She did tell you what's happened, didn't she?"

"Of course, she did! She's devastated by it all. Having kids put her window through, finding that body, then calling the police. Thank God she had her wits about her! She told me Superintendent Westen thinks her discovery broke the case."

Abigail gasped. She knew about spinning yarns but she hadn't expected *her* yarn to be spun in that way!

"Did he now? He must indeed be thankful for Sandra's considerable wits. But we really, *really* need to see her. Pastoral business."

"Pastoral business? Oh. Is someone in trouble? Well, why didn't you say so earlier? Come in. I'll put the kettle on and get Sandra. I'm sure she'll be awake."

"I'm sure too," said Gabby. Before he could change his mind, she hopped over the plastic doorframe tripping only slightly into a tiny, cluttered hallway.

He led them into the front room. Clearer than the hall, it was dominated by a mustard-coloured fringed three-piece suite. A slight whiff of lavender polish lurked in the air. The place had a visitors-only vibe. It made Abigail shudder and not only because the radiator she was standing near delivered next to no heat.

"Who's this, then?" Albert said, smiling at Abigail as he indicated for them to sit down.

"Oh, sorry, I should have introduced her earlier. This is Abigail Chater, I think you knew her father, Jim? He died in that terrible road accident a few years ago."

His face softened as the light dawned. "Ah, yes. Yes, I do remember that. Pleased to meet you, Abigail and … I'm sorry you lost your dad. He was a good man."

"Yes. Yes, he was. Thank you."

"Make yourself comfortable, then. I'll see if Sandra's well enough to see you."

As one they sat on the edge of the sofa. There'd be no comfort here.

Without speaking, they rolled their eyes at each other as muffled voices came from above. It was as clear as anything the woman didn't want to come down. Yet Albert must have prevailed, because after a few minutes they heard slow, reluctant footsteps on the stairs before pausing behind the door. Then Sandra edged into the room.

Abigail broke the ice. "Hi, Sandra. How are you feeling?"

"What do you want from me now? More lies? The police sent round one of their artists, you know, and the woman who interviewed me at the station. Couldn't face them. Albert said I was too unwell. There's another lie right there!"

Gabby snorted. "Everybody lies, Sandra, as you well know. And telling the police the truth would have got you nowhere. Have you completely rationalised yourself into denial about what happened at the vicarage?"

Their stand-off was interrupted by the sudden entrance of their host who'd taken that moment to back through the door with a tray in his hands. Setting it down on the low teak coffee table, he said, "There you are, ladies." He shivered as he stood up. "I'm sorry it's so cold in here. I don't get many visitors which is why the radiator's turned down. I'll put the gas fire on."

He fished out a lighter from his back pocket and lit a spill that trailed from a bright red plastic cone-thingy on the hearth before turning on the gas and placing it at the bottom of one of the radiants. "There, you'll be warm in no time. Give me a shout if you need anything else."

"Thank you, Albert," said Sandra. "We won't be long."

After he left, she hardened her expression. "I'm not denying anything. I can't explain what happened, but that doesn't mean there *isn't* an explanation. But I do know you made a liar out of me, on sacred ground and before a grave that contained the remains of a young girl! God rest her poor soul and shame on you! Shame on me too, for going along with your nonsense."

"She's why we're here," said Abigail, trying to find a gap in the woman's defenses. "Well, she and other potential victims. We want to talk to you about how you can help make sure no one else suffers like she did."

"I can't. I won't." Sandra stuck out her chin and stared sightlessly out of the window. "We don't have to talk about anything. I don't *want* to talk about anything."

"Sandra," said Gabby. "It all must have been a terrible, terrible shock. I understand how you must be feeling."

The woman scoffed. "No you don't. You don't know a thing about me. You've been against me all the time. Against my ministry, against my mission, against my plans."

Gabby bowed her head, "Yes. Yes, I admit, I've been less than ... enthusiastic about your vision for St Jude's—"

"Less than enthusiastic?! You've been obstructive and rude. Opposed my every move. But I got the plans through despite you and Robert Mason. Thank God Bishop Frederick knows the way the wind's blowing for the church. Targeting the youth is the only way forward, to reinvigorate the church, bring new blood into it. New life—"

She broke off. Even she must have realised how rote and crass she sounded. Her face crumpled.

Abigail jumped up and stepping towards Sandra, slipped her hand in hers. Jerking her head to signal Gabby to shove up, she led the poor woman towards the sofa. "Come on, sit down. It's been awful for you and you're not over it yet."

Sandra did as she was told and slumped back, automatically taking the cup and saucer Gabby pushed into her hand. She swallowed a sip and in the smallest of voices—almost like a child—she cried, "What was it? What caused that thing in my kitchen to happen? Was it the same thing that killed that poor girl?"

Gabby nodded. "We think so. Sandra. We think it also hurt Emma."

"Emma Blake? What happened to her?"

"She's had a miscarriage," said Gabby. "A terrible one. Her partner found her collapsed outside Clearview cottage. She's still at the hospital. She ... she's not talking."

"I'm very sorry to hear that. I didn't get on with her, but no one should have to go through that. But I still don't see how I can help. It's all a mess. I don't understand any of it and I *don't* want to talk about it."

"We wanted to tell you at the vicarage what we thought was going on," said Abigail, "but you were upset, and we had to get our story straight before the police came. We didn't think you'd believe us. We understand even more now and know what we have to do, but we need your help to do it."

"*My* help? You seem to do very well without it. In fact, when Gabby came to clear up that ... that mess in the kitchen, you didn't seem to need my help at all. She just took over!"

"You were in shock," Gabby said. "Not only did you have to cope with that avalanche of stuff coming into your kitchen, you ended up discovering another murder victim! That you could stick to our story showed a lot of courage, Sandra. My hat goes off to you."

Sandra straightened her back slightly and raised her chin at the praise. "So, what caused it then? What possible explanation could there be for my garden to hurl itself through my window and build itself into a pyramid over the kitchen table. All by itself?"

The two friends glanced at each other. Abigail nodded. As if about to dive off a cliff, she took a deep breath. "We think it was a witch."

A pause. Probably the longest pause in all of recorded time.

Sandra threw her head back and laughed. More a cackle, really, causing her to spill her tea. Gabby hastily jumped up and took her cup away.

"You've got to be kidding me," Sandra cried, taken by great heaves of mirthless guffaws. She held her sides, tried to catch her breath.

Couldn't.

Abigail took her by the shoulders and shook her hard—she probably ought to have slapped her face but couldn't bring herself to do it. But shaking did the trick and Sandra came more to her senses again.

And judging by her body language, her shields were back up.

This time, Gabby ran the gauntlet. "We think we know who the witch actually is—or ... was. Do you know anything about the Blackstone family? Centuries ago, they used to own the village. That includes both the church and the vicarage."

"Nothing," Sandra replied. "Absolutely nothing. And I don't want know. In fact, what I want is for you to get out. Truly, I mean it. Both of you, *get out*. All of this is part of your plan to get rid of me. It's what you've wanted all along. And guess what, it's working. I hate this place. Hate the vicarage, hate the village, hate the people."

Wow.

"Sandra," Abigail said. "Look at me. *Look* at me. What about the girl in the grave? Did we make that up? And how could we have done that thing in your kitchen? Listen to Gabby, she's lived here forever. She knows about these things. She knows about Flammark."

"Oh, I'm sure she does. I'm sure she knows everything. What have you dreamt up for me next? An exorcism?"

Less of a pause, more a … blanket of silence.

Sandra looked from one to the other; at their faces set in grim acknowledgement.

"No. *No!*"

"Flammark is a … challenging parish," said Gabby. "It has a history of this kind of thing."

"Has it?" Sandra replied, her voiced laced with sarcasm. "Has it *really*?!"

"Alright," said Abigail. "You explain it then. You explain what happened to you. Explain how your plans got buried, explain the tower of leaves, explain how the body got in that grave."

"It got there because someone dug it out and put the girl there then put the soil back. As to the rest, I have no idea. And I don't want to have an idea. But, for what it's worth, you've won. You've had your way. I'm leaving. Leaving the parish, hell, I might even leave the church. Just like William Turner, I've bloody-well had enough."

"You can't!" said Gabby. "You *can't*. At least not now. We need you."

"To perform an exorcism?" Sandra gaped at them. "No chance. Anyway, we'd have to get permission from Bishop Frederick. And it wouldn't be an exorcism, the Church of England doesn't recognise it as a legitimate service. They'd only allow a deliverance ceremony."

Gabby had none of it. With an impatient shake of her head she said, "I know all that, and usually that would suffice. Deliverance ministry nods more to the issues of mental health than any supernatural incursion. The Church of England doesn't feel anything more is necessary because evil on the scale we're dealing with is rare."

"Huh," said Abigail. "Not in Flammark."

"Yes. well, perhaps not in Flammark." Gabby flapped away the interruption. "The village is special and we're nowhere near at the bottom of finding out why." She gave Sandra a hard stare. "Your first duty is to your people. Your *flock*. Not to the Bishop. Already some of them have died. It is your sworn duty as priest of this parish to protect them."

Sandra didn't answer, only shook her head slowly and gazed at the wall, her face set and stubborn.

The two friends sat for what seemed an age, saying nothing, letting Gabby's words sink in, hoping they'd made some impact, some mark on the woman's intransigence.

But it didn't look as if she was budging an inch and she certainly wasn't speaking. Shrugging a silent '*we tried*', Gabby rose to her feet. Abigail stayed put for a moment but eventually followed suit, realising they were on a complete hiding to nowhere. They hovered a moment in front of Sandra—still staring at the wall, still completely closed-off—then, defeated, made for the door.

All that remained was to find Albert and thank him for the tea. Gabby chatted for a few minutes about church business while Abigail wondered if she might nip back into the front room and have another go at Sandra. She didn't, of course. Deep down she knew there'd be no point.

Pleasantries over, Albert led them through the cluttered hall. As he reached out to open the door for them, like a ghost Sandra suddenly appeared from the sitting room.

Hovering at the threshold, her face pale and resigned, she raised her shoulders in a sigh of surrender.

"Okay, you win. There are some things I can't explain. If you're right about them—and God knows I don't think you are—I suppose I do have a duty. What do you want me to do?"

25
NO CHANGE

Westen half-dreaded visiting Emma again. Or rather, he dreaded having to face that fucking … blankness. He rang Mason first.

"Sorry, lad. No change. She's still staring into space."

"You think she needs a shrink?"

"Possibly. This is reaction is certainly … unusual. It can't do any harm. They'll make a decision on whether to call in Psych Services later this afternoon."

When Westen did arrive at the hospital, he found Mason hovering at the nurses' station. The Doc greeted him with a nod and jerked his head to indicate he should go straight through.

They'd got Emma out of bed and into an armchair, one of those large, high-backed jobbies with wooden arms. She seemed smaller, somehow. Shrunken. Her face appeared so pale her skin seemed almost transparent. It struck him how prominent her cheekbones had suddenly become. Her beautiful hazel eyes, bereft of spark, lay dim within their bluish sockets, fixed in the middle distance, gazing at fucking nothing.

He made a play of being cheerful. "Hello, love," he said as he bent over to kiss her cheek. "Brought these for you. Thought they might cheer the place up a bit."

No response.

Fool. He looked at the sorry bunch flowers, hastily bought from the petrol station on the way in. She deserved better. She deserved *him* to be better. What were they, anyway? Lilies? He wrinkled his nose, suddenly aware of their pungency. Ugh. They smelled like a fucking funeral.

They were the wrong thing to bring her. He should have bought ... he stood there like a prat. What flowers *did* she like? He should know that. *Why* didn't he know?

He looked around for something to put them in and, failing, almost threw them down on the side-cupboard. He drew up another chair and sat in front of her.

What to say? He could almost touch the wall she'd built between herself and the world. He couldn't breach it.

She didn't want him to.

No, don't go there. This wasn't about him. What do people say? Being there is sometimes all that's needed? They were probably right, because he hadn't been there when she needed his protection the most and look where that had got her.

"Come on, Emma. You'll get through this. *We'll* get through this. But you've got to *try*."

Nothing.

Falling silent, he found her hand. It felt limp and hot. Tenderly rubbing her palm with his thumb, he decided that if just being there was enough, then that would be fine with him.

Which was okay in theory.

After only a few minutes of sitting, trying his best to match her rhythms and be the man she needed him to be, he discovered Colin Sweeting had crept into his mind, stirring his rage at what the man might have done to those girls—what he might have done to Emma—and how fucking impotent it made him all feel and how he fucking hated Frank fucking Marshall and how he wanted to tell his fucking review team where to fucking stick it…

WHAT THE HELL HAPPENED TO HER?

If he didn't get answers soon, he was going to climb the fucking walls!

Luckily, Mason chose that moment to join him. Westen's face must have said it all. "You need to calm down, laddie. You're no use to Emma like this. No use to anyone."

"That's what people keep saying! But it's no good! I need to know what happened to her, and I need to *do* something!"

"We don't know if anything did happen to her. This could simply have been nature taking its course."

"No. You didn't see the state she was in when I found her—and you didn't see how she was when she woke from the anaesthetic. There was nothing fucking natural about that. You've said yourself there was something's off about—" He gestured towards her. "About *this*." He laughed scornfully. "There's got to be more to it, Mason. Much more."

"What do you mean?" Then suddenly Mason's eyes widened. "Dear God, man, are you thinking Emma might have seen your murderer? That she might have been a potential—"

"Victim? Possibly." He gave Emma a rough smile; squeezed her hand again. "You're going to think I've gone do-fucking-lally saying this but … every time the shit hits the fan in Flammark, she's been right in the centre of it. First Cregan, then St Saviour and now this. I don't know how she's involved, Doc, I just feel it. Feel it here." He thumped his chest.

"Okay, lad. Try to calm down. At least there's progress. At least she's out of that damned bed."

"And not much the better for it as far as I can make out." Westen closed his eyes. "We should get the shrinks in. Push for it. Look at her, this isn't normal, Mason."

"No. No, you're right, laddie, I don't think it is. I'll talk to the consultant and get it written into her care plan. I'll do it now." He turned to leave.

"Doc, wait," Westen said. "I have to do something for her. I can't just sit here. I have to make a difference. Tell me what to do!"

"I'm sorry, lad. I don't know that there is anything … except—" The doc paused. A lightbulb had come on somewhere.

"What? What are you thinking?"

"Maybe there *is* something you could do. I'm not sure you'll take kindly to the suggestion, though."

"What? Come on, out with it, man. I'll do anything. *Anything*."

"Find Will for her. Find Will Turner."

26
THE EXORCIST

It had just gone dark when the three women entered St Jude's. Sandra hung back, fiddling with the mortice lock long after she'd opened the door, while Gabby turned on the lights.

Abigail didn't often come to the church, and only then it had been to see Will, never for a service. It wasn't that she didn't believe; more that she walked a different path, one that *embraced* the supernatural potential of the universe rather than shying away from it. Which meant, of course, shying away from her ilk. She used to tease him about the nature of miracles and how they cropped up everywhere in the New Testament, yet his church would die a death rather than admit their *actual* existence.

There was irony there, somewhere. Or hypocrisy.

Still, she got it; wasn't unaffected by the atmosphere of a place well- prayed-in. She felt it to her bones. After all, St Jude's had been founded many centuries ago, here in some form well before the Normans arrived; she couldn't simply ignore a millennium of tradition.

She lit the candles they'd brought—in case the lights

failed for some reason, Gabby had said—and as she put them flickering on the stone sills of the mullions, breathed in the church's scent. Not as laced with incense as it used to be—that had been Will's thing—but there, nevertheless. Like it was embedded in the walls.

Gabby was feeling it too. Abigail could tell by her expression; how the stress she was under seemed to fall away as she took a sideways step into one of the rows of chairs. Taking off a tapestried cushion to kneel, Gabby carefully put down the items she'd brought in a plastic carrier and rested her hands palm down on the seat in front to place her forehead on them. For her, it must be like coming home every time she stepped into the place. Before her fall, it would have acted as a direct line to the boss. Now she was like everyone else, consigned to the great Uncertainty, not really knowing if her prayers were even heard, let alone be answered.

After her lengthy prevarication at the entrance, Sandra walked down the nave. Unlike Gabby, she didn't stop to kneel. As she reached the transept she stood as a woman lost, literally not knowing which way to turn. Had this been Will, without a moment's hesitation he'd have made straight for the altar.

But Sandra was no Will.

Gabby used the seat in front to help get herself to her feet. "If this is what growing old feels like, you can keep it," she said with a faint smile. It wasn't there for long: one glance at Sandra's surly face and she wiped it away. "I think for this we need to go into the sanctuary, don't you? We need the power of the cross for what we're about to do."

Sandra shrugged. "Very well. Do I … do I need to wear my garb?"

Gabby gave her a long look and shook her head, letting out a resigned sigh. "No, Sandra. We can do without it. It's you we really need."

They went through into the smaller and most intimate section of the St Jude's. Accessed through a stone arch, it comprised the entire third section of the church—and Abigail's favourite part. A domed space, it housed the altar table on a small dais. No chairs. It was the beating heart of the church, the place where communion was given and received. She didn't have to be a Christian in order to appreciate its sanctity.

Gabby had brought two cushions. She set them down near the far wall of the sanctuary and well behind the altar. "When we're ready, here is where we will kneel, child. We are only witnesses and must not get in the way. We support the priest but allow the priest to confront the witch head-on."

Priest. Weird. Though Sandra was now Flammark's vicar, Abigail never thought of her in terms of her priesthood. She didn't know why that was, exactly, but now she thought about it—now they needed her hotline to God—it occurred to her just how ungodly she actually was. Like Sandra was somehow ... a dud. The realisation made her heart sink.

This exorcism was not going to work.

Gabby nodded reassuringly to Sandra, who shuffled towards the altar dais and hesitantly stepped up to take her place behind the polished silver cross. With neither preamble nor prayer nor obeisance, she roughly pushed it aside and took out a small book. It had obvious age to it, so mottled and pocked were its covers. Must be one of Gabby's.

Sandra lifted the black ribbon that marked a page inside and the book fell open to it. Her hand shook only slightly as she held the little tome and scanned it, her lips moving silently as her finger moved across the words.

"You don't have to memorise them, you know," murmured Gabby. "God won't mind if you read from the book."

"These words, they're wrong. They aren't ..."

Gabby smiled. "Protestant? No, they aren't. The Anglican church never formulated its own answer for the excision of evil, except for what it borrowed from the Catholics. As we too are about to do."

"I can't do this," said Sandra, putting the book down. "You do it, seeing as you know so much about it!"

"We've been through this. I can't. At one time, perhaps, but not anymore. I'm not qualified. You are."

"I'm the wrong person, you must know that. I'm not even sure we should be doing this. It's ... blasphemy."

"It is *not*," said Gabby. "Be it in words or actions, blasphemy challenges the word and wisdom of God. We are not here to do that. We're here to banish blasphemy itself. We're here to get rid of the witch."

Sandra's mirthless laughter rippled through the sanctuary. "I cannot believe I'm here. I cannot believe I'm even entertaining the possibility there's a witch in this parish—or that one could exist anywhere, for that matter!"

"I think you'd need to dig pretty deep for anywhere near a better explanation for what happened to you at the vicarage," said Abigail

Gabby gave an impatient sigh. "Enough. It's too late for second thoughts. We're here now and we must do what we *have* to do, what we're *called* to do."

Moments of sullen silence followed. Gabby broke it by rustling inside her carrier bag. She took out three phials and placed them on the altar table. "Bless the water, Sandra. Make it holy."

"Will it work for an ... exorcism?" She could hardly form the word. "I only ever use it for baptisms."

Gabby nodded grimly. "Yes. Exorcisms reference the doctrine of baptism. You will be calling the evil that plagues us to renounce itself and choose innocence instead. It presents an attack on the witch's entire being leaving it no choice but to go. So ... go ahead, bless the water."

Haltingly, flatly, Sandra began the prayer:

We praise you, loving Father,

for the gift of your Son, Jesus Christ.

He was baptized in the River Jordan,

where your Spirit came upon him...

It struck Abigail how rote her utterance seemed. Were all priests the same, so used to their ceremonies that their words came more from a place of habit, rather than truly meant? That would never happen in her pagan group. Never.

And it wouldn't have happened with Will.

...Now, Father, we ask you to bless this water,

That those who are baptized in it

May be cleansed in the water of life,

May know that they are loved as your children,

Safe in Christ forever.

"That do?" said Sandra.

Gabby let out a long, slow breath, heavy with irritation. "I don't know, Sandra. You tell me. An *amen* would have been nice!"

"How can this possibly work?" said Abigail, really worried now. "If words are all we have..."

"They're not, thanks to you." Gabby rustled once more in her bag and took out three twigs. She placed them next to the phials.

"What're those?" Sandra asked.

"We have to summon the witch. I was hoping words will be enough but now ..."

"Now you're not sure, are you? You're not sure I have it in me."

Gabby made no reply.

Nose wrinkling, Sandra hesitantly peered at the twigs. "So, what are they? What's their significance?"

"We think the witch made something out in Seely Woods. I asked Abigail to go there and bring us a sample from it. We only need a token. Something she's touched. She gave something similar to Emma. Used it to bind her to her. Luckily, we were able to realise what was going on and took it away. I think we might be able to use these to summon her; bind *her* to *our* will."

"You think?" said Sandra. "You think?"

Gabby's lips wavered in pure frustration. "At times like these, Sandra," *San Dra,* "one has to find one's way. Each encounter with the Other has its own logic. There are no hard and fast rules. But of this, I am stone cold certain, the accoutrements matter less than the sentiment behind their use. Belief is everything. *As you well know.*"

Sandra held her gaze for a moment before looking away. "Yes," she muttered. "Yes, I do know that."

Then Abigail suddenly realized. She didn't need the Sight to get the implication of Gabby's words. She'd sussed Sandra and they were deeply screwed. For now it all made sense. How she rode roughshod over everything Will had worked for, the obsession with her plans, cosying up to the bishop, bigging herself up.

She alienated people, too, Abigail's mind flying back to the morning at Clearview when she'd been so vindictive with Emma after she'd washed her wounds. Sandra had completely lost sight of her priesthood—if she ever had it in the first place. She just didn't seem to have an inkling about developing real, authentic relationships, which is surely the main thing about being a parish priest? And she hadn't knelt on entering the church, as Gabby had. As Will would have. All this together with the way she blessed the water—rote, emotionless, lacking in conviction—pointed to only one thing.

Sandra had lost her faith.

This was useless. They should call it a night and go home.

Abigail shivered. Sandra's teeth were chattering, and Gabby was shivering too which she never did. It was really cold in the church, but they'd dressed for it.

This was something different.

"Sandra," Gabby said, her voice quietly urgent. "Give me the phials. Start the prayer. I think Margaret knows what we're about." What little colour remained in Sandra's face drained away. She didn't move.

"Now!" Gabby's bark reverberated around the sanctuary making not only Sandra jump. She grabbed Abigail's hand and led her to the cushions where they both fell to their knees.

Sandra reached out to grab the phials, her fingers trembling so much Abigail doubted she could ever pick them up let alone open them.

"Oh, for pity's sake," Gabby exclaimed. Hastily, she clambered up and almost ran to the altar and grabbed each of the phials, pulling out their stoppers before resting them back on the table. "This water is precious. Do not spill any of it." She braced herself and took three deep breaths. "I'm sorry, Sandra. I don't mean to make this any worse for you." Reaching at reassurance, she gave a quick and wholly unconvincing smile. "You will be fine. We'll all be fine. Have faith."

She returned to her cushion. The temperature in the Sanctuary kept dropping and Abigail found it hard even to speak. "Gabby," she whispered. "G-Gabby, go easy. You're not h-helping."

"I kn-know. I tried but …" Suddenly Sandra glanced back at them and her knees buckled, her hand grabbing the altar table and making it shake. Gabby groaned and got to her feet yet again and found a place of safety for the phials. She spun round and grabbed the trembling priest by the elbow. "Get up. Get up! This is no time for supplication. We need a show of strength." She grabbed the little book and shoved it back into Sandra's hand; yanked it up to her face. "Read! Read now!"

The terrified woman climbed to her feet, her hand quivering violently now. To her credit, Sandra tried, *really* tried, despite Gabby's bullying.

In th-thy name, O Lord…

G-God the F-Father com…mands you, God the son c-commands you, G-God the Holy Spirit—

Abigail felt her ears go weird, like when a train enters a tunnel.

And a rustling sound. It reminded her of when her mum swept the flagstones outside the house. A steady *sh … sh … sh…*

And then she saw.

Through the sanctuary arch, at the back of the church two faint pinpricks of light. Moving. Coming into focus. And a stench. A stench like rotting leaves; like the pyramid of forest litter piled on the table in the vicarage kitchen.

Breast heaving, trying to dampen her panic, Abigail got off her knees and cried out to Gabby and Sandra. They looked up from the book they shared to where she was pointing.

Sandra stopped praying and collapsed to her knees in a movement too strong for Gabby to withstand. Herself wide-eyed and pale, Gabby tried to lift her up. "Face it. Face it, Sandra." But Sandra had nothing. The terrified priest collapsed sideways onto the altar step, landing on her backside. Mewling, knees to chest, she buried her head and started to rock.

Gabby gaped at her and then at Abigail, palms to the sky in despair. Abigail stood ready to fly to her aid but found she couldn't move. Sandra's wails were suddenly cut off, as the vacuum in Abigail's ears deepened, hurling her into a world of silence.

The witch reached the transept, and the stink strengthened. Stomach lurching, Abigail's heart a bass drum in her chest, she stood transfixed as the creature made for them.

Against her will she had no choice but to stand and wait on its approach; no choice but to take in the oval, patchy-white face, its parchment skin stretched almost to transparency by cheekbones so protuberant it seemed hardly clothed in flesh at all.

The witch's hair was a nest: black, motionless snakes of interwoven branchlets jutted before and behind, tangled, heavy. And below, a shimmering, morphing, ever-moving cascade of leaves propelled it forwards—the same stuff it'd hurled through Sandra's window. With a kind of horrific splendour, the creature sailed onto the altar dais on the other side from where the astonished Gabby held onto Sandra, its shifting mass only hinting at the possibility of arms and legs. It stopped not two feet in front of Abigail, from where its pinlight eyes bored into her from deep black sockets made out of midnight.

This is what had become of Margaret Blackstone.

Abigail held her breath. The Orb had taught her about connection; taught her how to possess herself; how to listen. How to keep her wits about her even when the world turned to chaos. And as the witch crept into her mind—as the Orb had done so many times; *as it had done the other day*—something deep inside told her she was still under its protection. A feeling that her father was near; that he was holding her hand.

That they would meet this thing together.

The tunnel-silence altered, changed into a kind of white noise that shifted as words came.

You cannot have me, sister. The force in this priest-woman is weak. And my work is not yet over.

- Sister?

Yes. We are blood, are we not?

- Your father was Oswald?

My father is a fool. He thinks that by killing me, he will kill the spirit that resides within me. And that can never be banished.

- And yet you were. For many centuries.

The creature did a thing with its head. Angled it sideways as if Abigail had said something that didn't make sense.

Centuries?

The witch seemed to pause.

You do not fear me?

- I do. I do fear you. You hurt our other … sister.

It was for the best. She carried a wench. It faced the same fate as I. As all our sisters do. Better to die quick in the womb than in the cold embrace of a grave dug by our faider.

- *Our* faider? But Oswald is long gone.

Its head tilted again. Then some of the leaves solidified; became a true arm complete with a ravaged skeletal hand, its long bones visible under its cellophane skin

The witch stretched it towards Abigail who tried to step back. Away. But still she couldn't move. It placed its hand on her belly. Seconds passed—she didn't know how many before she took it away.

You have nothing to fear from me, sister.

- I-I haven't? Why?

You cannot bear a child.

Then the figure once more began its leafy churn. Effortlessly—as if it floated—travelling backwards the way it came without even a glance at Gabby and Sandra, it withdrew out from the sanctuary, into the transept then to the nave. Not once did its pinlight eyes ever waver from Abigail's horrified gaze.

Until it reached the exit and disappeared.

Then suddenly, Abigail was released and blasts of shrieking assailed her. She gave herself a second to shake away the residual numbness in her head and shifted her gaze to Gabby who was trying her very best to calm Sandra down —or, more accurately, trying to *hold* her down.

"I'm so sorry, Abigail!" Gabby shouted above Sandra's din. "There was nothing I could do to help you. She won't *shut up*!"

Abigail took a breath, wobbling a bit as she came out of Margaret's thrall. Not even trying to assimilate the awful thing she said to her, she moved to the altar step and sat at Sandra's other side. Prising Gabby's arm away from the distraught woman she said, "I've got her, Gabby. Leave her to me."

Holding her, gently stroking Sandra's hair, she said, "Sh… sh… It's okay, it's gone. The witch has gone. At least, for now. We're safe, you're safe."

"I-I-I'm sorry," Sandra blubbed. "I couldn't do it. I …"

"Sh-sh. I know. You've don't have to explain. I see it now. This was never going to work. This is our fault and I'm sorry."

Her words seemed to comfort the woman—at least she stopped that terrible wailing. But not her tears. She couldn't stop those from streaming down her face.

Just as Abigail couldn't stop hers.

27

RECOVERY

The exorcism had been an unmitigated disaster. Thoroughly exhausted, the two women returned to Abigail's. But not before they'd managed to get Sandra into a taxi, returning to the much-alarmed Albert a pale, subdued and utterly played-out shell. It had taken them ages to calm her down—freezing as they did it in the church drive, since Sandra refused to stay a minute longer in the church.

Abigail could sympathise. She'd felt drained and exhausted too. Worse than that, she felt ... violated. Again! Margaret Blackwood had looked inside her—had in some way *been* inside her—and had found her ... lacking. Beyond that she didn't want to think about it. Pushed it to the far recesses of her mind. She didn't want to process it. Too much. It was all, too much.

Thankfully, Gabby didn't try to press her about it. Instead, they spent both Saturday and Sunday morning at the hospital, taking turns at Emma's side when either Robbie or Westen couldn't be there. But just as she'd been with the men, their friend remained unresponsive. Seeing her so sunken and reduced mortified them even further after their failure at the church.

Between visits, they divided their time between sorting Abigail's wrecked bedroom and sleeping. But, come Monday, Abigail knew she couldn't put off the inevitable discussion about her exchange with the witch any longer. She'd been surprised Gabby had managed to avoid the subject for that long. Maybe she was ashamed of how brutally she'd harried poor Sandra.

The salon being closed on Mondays, Abigail had legitimate time off. She couldn't delay the conversation any longer. Not that she wanted to; she was ready.

With no sign of Gabby stirring, she got up, chose one of her favourite long skirts to wear and added some braids to her hair. Warpaint also applied, she felt more herself than she had for a long time. Giving the Orb a quick, affectionately remonstrative glance, she left the room to wake Gabby and prepare some breakfast.

Once they were settled at the kitchen table, Abigail finally broached the subject. "Albert looked totally out of his depth when we dropped Sandra off, didn't he?"

"Didn't he just!" said Gabby, "I wonder what she told him?"

"Poor woman. I felt sorry for her in the end."

"I didn't. She brought it all on herself. Coming to Flammark for the wrong reasons, using the church to further her own interests without listening to those who know what's what! Tch. I've no sympathy, Abigail. None whatsoever. If she has a problem with her faith, she had no right to come here. It's put everyone at risk."

"Yeah. The witch—Margaret—said she was weak. She didn't fear her at all."

Gabby stopped munching. Leant forward an inch. "Are you up to telling me what else she said to you? I could see you were distressed but we had Sandra to deal with and—"

"Distressed doesn't go near it, Gabby, but Sandra was in a much worse state. Besides I couldn't bring myself to talk about it. Too much to process." She took a breath. "The witch. Margaret. She knows we're related. Called me *sister*. She sort of ... got inside me. I don't know whether you saw but she put her hand ... here." Lips trembling, Abigail placed her own hand over her belly. "It was ... awful, *awful*. Gabby, she must have done the same to Emma. She caused the miscarriage because she ... she wanted to kill her baby."

"She *told* you that?"

"Sort of. We talked, inside my head. It was weird. Said she wanted to save it from having to go through what she went through. You know, with Oswald? She told me something else, too..." Abigail was afraid this was going to happen; her eyes filled with tears. "She ... She told me I'd never bear children, and because of that, I had nothing to fear from her. I think it's why she left me alone."

Gabby instantly scraped back her chair and went to her, embracing the seated girl as best she could. "Oh! *Oh!* I am so sorry, Abigail. So sorry. I don't know what to say." Sobs coming hard and fast, the girl rested her head against Gabby's ample stomach. "There now. There. Cry it out. What a thing to be told! And by that creature, too!"

"I don't really know why I'm so upset," said Abigail after a while. "It's not as if I ever really thought about having kids. I'm not even sure I want any. But it's like something's been taken away from me. Choice, I suppose. I'm a done deal." After a moment, she stilled herself, the sobs reduced to tiny hiccups. "M-maybe Emma is too."

"Possibly. Robbie said her womb was very damaged. They couldn't really explain why. Now we know."

Abigail blew out an enormous shuddering sigh then gave

her shoulders a little shake. “Okay. I’m over the worst.” She tried a smile. “Sit down. Finish your breakfast, I’ll be alright. I’ll make us more tea. I’m not finished yet.” She got up and flipped the switch on the kettle.

Cups replenished, she resumed her place at the table. After a few sips of chamomile she collected herself and continued her story. “I think, no, I’m *sure*—Margaret believes Oswald is still here.”

“Does she indeed!”

“Yeah. She used the present tense all the time. Talked as if he was still a threat. I told her he was long gone and she just kind of tilted her head, you know, as if it didn’t compute. I’ve been thinking all weekend about it. She’s misguided, obviously, and what she did to Emma was wicked, but if she thought she was saving Emma’s baby from what she had to endure, ultimately she was trying to be…”

“Kind?” said Gabby.

“Yes.”

“It’s what Oswald and his cronies did to *her* that was wicked, Abigail,” Gabby said, patting the girl’s hand. “I must say, this has all been very enlightening. At least now we know for sure why she’s killing all these teenagers. She obviously thought she was saving them too. They were, after all, the same age as she was when Oswald murdered her.”

“But why did she wait this long to come back?” said Abigail. “She’s been gone for nigh on seven centuries! She would surely have appeared before now?”

“I don’t know.”

The two women pondered in silence while they drank from their cups. Gabby even managed another piece of toast.

“How do you do it?” Abigail said, after a while. “How have you been able to come to terms with what’s happened to you?”

“Losing my wings?” Gabby smiled, grimly. “To be honest,

I'm not sure I have—or ever will. I'm trying not to think about Michael abandoning me. Sometimes I miss him so much it aches. It's overwhelming. But … I like to believe he still watches over this place in some way. Watches over me."

Abigail cast her mind back to the debacle Animus had wrought at DeepDrilla; how at the end of it all, once the earth had returned from the sky, he'd come upon them to heal the fissure—and Will, of course. But she also remembered the understanding he'd bestowed on her; that his presence there was to stay secret. Abigail had thought him cruel, but later on she thought differently about it; realised Gabby would never learn to move on with her mortality if she knew he'd been there for them.

"I've decided something," Abigail announced. "I've decided I'm not going to dwell on what Margaret said to me about … about not having kids. It's like Wyland used to tell us in the pagan group. What will be, will be. I'm learning there's some things we can't change."

"Well, I'm not sure about that," said Gabby. "If the universe was that deterministic there'd be no point in having Guardians, and Messengers. Or teachers, or priests." She grinned. "And that Westen would be out of a job too!"

Abigail tried to laugh, but deep down she knew. Margaret had spoken true and fate would brook no argument.

"So, what are we going to do now?" she said. "How *are* we going to get rid of Margaret? Sandra's no use. She's a spent force—if she ever was one in the first place. Her prayers had zero effect."

"To be fair, she didn't get very far with them before she started screaming. But, yes, she was useless."

"So, we're screwed!"

"Are we?"

"Well, aren't we? You said yourself, a witch can only be exorcised by the priest of the parish."

Gabby made no reply, only raised her eyebrows and smiled.

Then it dawned. "Ohhhh," said Abigail. "She isn't the only priest of this parish, is she?"

"No," Gabby replied. "She is not. She hasn't been permanently installed yet. William is still the formal incumbent. We can try again."

"Another exorcism? Okay. But we don't know where he is. And even if we did ..."

"Yes. There's no guarantee he'll want to return. Slight problem, I admit," said Gabby, chewing her lip.

"I can't believe he'd still be angry at us. It's been months."

"Robbie said the bishop didn't hold out much hope of him wanting to come back. And didn't you say Sandra had said he was thinking of leaving the priesthood altogether?"

"The bishop!" Abigail cried. "He's bound to know where Will is. We could ask him!"

Gabby shook her head. "Even if he knew, which I admit is a distinct possibility, he wouldn't tell us. William was—is—in a state of retreat. I know Frederick Thomas. He wouldn't betray his trust."

Abigail slumped. "Yeah. Not like we did."

"That was all down to me," said Gabby. "All of it. From the very start. If I hadn't got so close ..."

"To me? Don't you dare say that. If it hadn't been for you, I'd be dead by now. Will wasn't himself when he said that. You know that. I know that."

"And so do I."

The two women froze. Stared at each other for a nanosecond before spinning around.

"Did no one ever tell you how dangerous it is to leave your front door open?" said Will. "You never know who might walk in..."

28
PRODIGAL

"*W*ill… !"

Squealing, Abigail jumped up and threw herself at him, flinging round her arms and pressing herself to his chest.

"Gosh, Abs, if I'd known I was going to get crushed like this, I would have definitely knocked. My bad." He smirked. "When I saw the door ajar, I couldn't resist the surprise."

"That was me," Gabby cried, myriad expressions crossing her face. She stood up, then sat down again, totally at a loss. "I must have forgotten to close it properly when I brought in the milk."

Trying hard to extricate himself from Abigail's embrace, Will said, "There, there. Abs, It's okay. Please, please don't cry. You'll set *me* off."

But she couldn't help but cling on and embraced him even tighter. "Don't ever go. Don't ever leave us again. I couldn't bear it. We're in a mess, Will. A terrible mess."

Totally immobilised, he looked over her head to Gabby. "What does a man need to do to get a cup of tea these days?"

"I-I'm sorry, William," she said. "Of course.I'll … I'll find another chair then sort out a drink. I'll be two minutes. Don't move."

"Fat chance," he grinned, waltzing Abigail towards one of the vacated chairs. She let him go and they plonked themselves down.

"Your mascara's all over the place, Abs. Not a good look." He grinned and she smiled too, gulping as she angled the tips of her fingers to wipe beneath her lashes. "Nope, not gonna do it. Full facial reconstruction, required, I'm afraid!"

Abigail laughed and then started hiccupping. But Will cocked his head and held up his palm and she somehow managed to suppress the next outburst. "Shhh," he said. "Listen. That's not a sound you hear very often."

"It's Gabby!" she whispered, eyes wide in surprise. "She's crying. She hates crying."

"I know she does. I only ever saw her do it once." They grinned at the sound of her feet thumping up the stairs. "We'll let her have a minute, shall we?"

Abigail chuckled, still drinking in the sight of him. Thinner than before. Gaunt, even. And she suddenly realised his faint, musky incense smell wasn't there. His dark, brown eyes returned her gaze with not a sign of their usual twinkle, despite his smile. His thick black hair hung much longer than she remembered, nearly to his shoulders. No flash of white at his throat, just a dark shirt open at the neck under a heavy black jacket. A decorative pin adorned its left lapel. Drawn to it, she peered more closely.

It was a flower. A white daisy.

She lifted up her hand and reached over to touch it.

"Peter."

He let out a thready sigh. "It still hurts, Abs. Cuts me to the core every time I think about him, which is all the time. What really hurts—really, *really* hurts—isn't just that he was taken away from me, that ... bastard ... did away with all the good memories too. Now, the only thing I see when I think of Peter, is his body, with that bloody flower stuck to his..." He swallowed, his turn to swipe at his eye. "Arrgh. I promised myself I wouldn't do this, and here I am, blubbing as well. We'll be swimming out of here, soon!"

"Why do you wear it then, if it upsets you so much?"

"To be honest, I'm not really sure. I think maybe I owe it to him, to remember him at his very, very worst moment. It's the nearest I can get to sharing it with him."

Abigail sat back, holding and squeezing his hand. There wasn't anything she could say that would ease his grief and it was obviously still very raw. So she kept silent, and they mused quietly together, listening to the sounds of some very muscular nose-blowing that came from the bathroom.

A few minutes later, Gabby appeared, red-eyed and smiling. She found a cup and started filling the kettle. Put more bread in the toaster.

It was only when she brought everything over that they realised they were still a chair short. "Sos, Gabby. What was I thinking?" Abigail grinned. "You sit here. I'll sort it!"

Soon all three settled in. Will and Abigail didn't eat. But Gabby did. Mouth half-full with crumbs, she said, "So how did you get here, William? How did you know we needed you?"

"Westen found me."

"*Westen?*" the two women exclaimed, Abigail adding, "How did he know where to look?"

"To quote his exact words to my very similar question ... 'because I'm a fucking detective, Turner!" They all chuckled again. "He never changes, does he?"

Abigail smiled. "No, he does not. I expect Robbie asked him to find you, didn't he? Something tells me he probably wouldn't have thought of it himself."

"Yes. And it was an awkward conversation, to be sure. At least at first. He told me what happened to Em. That's when he asked if I'd come back. As if he needed to!" His expression darkened. "I did a lot of damage there, I think. Emma didn't deserve to be treated like that."

"You did," said Abigail. "You really did. But I don't think now's the time to talk about it. Later?"

Will nodded.

"What else did Westen say? Did he mention anything about the case?"

"Yes, he did as a matter of fact. I had no idea. The place where I ended up doesn't do television so I never got to see the news and I was never one for smart phones. Those poor kids! Westen looked terrible. Stressed. Not surprising, having to deal with Em on top of having such a high-profile case."

"Where are you staying, William? I could open one of Wyland's caravans, if you like?"

"No, that's okay. Robbie's kindly invited me. Westen arranged it. Seems like he and our Scottish friend have become quite thick. I'm going to the hospital later." He put his cup down. "What happened to Emma? I mean, what *really* happened? Westen told me the doctors think the miscarriage was caused by some kind of trauma."

"They're not wrong," said Gabby. Her eyes strayed to the tiny flower on Will's lapel. "William, I want you to be honest with us. What kind of shape are you in?"

"What do you mean ... shape?" He looked at her puzzled, his face hardening as he caught her drift. "Okay. Tell me. Tell me everything. It doesn't matter where I'm at, the only thing that matters is Emma. Don't worry about me and don't you dare spare me the details."

So, between them they told him all about Sandra, the spate of murders, how one of the victims had been found in the churchyard—and what had transpired in the vicarage kitchen.

And they told him about the witch.

"It was Margaret Blackstone, Will," said Abigail. "The Orb showed me what happened to her. As if I was there—as if I *was* her. She was kidnapped and beaten up by her father and his henchmen. They ... did things to her then buried her alive." She lowered her voice. "It was ... it was horrible. It nearly broke me." Then she came back from the memory and gave a wan smile. "But the Orb found a way to heal me. It knows what to do to protect me in future. And I'm stronger now."

He squeezed her hand. "I often wondered if that thing would turn out to be a menace, but Wyland told me it helped you all to obliterate—" The corners of his mouth twitched. "I can't bring myself to speak his name, even now."

"Animus?" Gabby murmured. "Yes. Wyland was right. It showed us—or more accurately it showed Abigail—how to defeat him."

Will shuddered but quickly moved the conversation on. "Margaret Blackstone..." He frowned, tilting his head as he considered. "Fifteen hundreds? Oswald's daughter?"

Gabby nodded. "Yes. Abigail described what Margaret's attackers had worn. That's how we were able to pin down the date and from that, who she was."

"She's back, Will," said Abigail. "Margaret's back."

"But ... how? Why now? Oswald was centuries ago? Why choose now to return?"

"That's what we've just been asking ourselves and we haven't the foggiest idea," said Gabby. "But we do know she's the one killing the teenagers. We think it's some kind of re-enactment of what she went through. Of what her father did to her. "

"She's trying to save the kids, Will," Abigail cried. "It's

twisted and cruel and it's all mixed up with how he murdered her, but she's killing them before Oswald can get his hands on them. And I'm pretty sure she thinks he's still alive. She may even believe she's still in the same century she was born in."

"And she went after Emma! Caused the miscarriage?"

"She came at me in the church, too," said Abigail. "We were trying an exorcism—"

"Whoa! Slow down. You were *what?*"

"Calm down, William, we were only—"

"Don't tell me to calm down, Gabby. Don't," Will said sharply—so unlike him. Deliberately, he calmed himself. "Look, I am still angry. I'm trying to deal with it and, for the most part, I'm keeping it under control. It's taken a lot of time and a great deal of counselling to work through it all. I … I've been considering leaving the priesthood. I'm not sure I'm the right fit any more, not in my current frame of mind."

"William—"

"No. Let me finish." A tone had crept into his voice Abigail hadn't heard before. He seemed more … hardened. Tougher. Weirdly, she quite liked it. "If Westen hadn't found me, if that terrible thing hadn't happened to Emma, I doubt very much I'd have come back. I didn't want to see you again and by that, I mean specifically you, Gabby. Truth be told, I'm still holding onto a lot of blame and I'm afraid a lot of it's centred around you."

"I know…"

"Do you? You're still going off half-cocked. I come back and the first thing I find is that you've held a bloody exorcism, for God's sake. You don't know what you're doing. You could cause all sorts of unintended consequences because, let's face it, you've done it before. You, above everyone knew what Animus was capable of, and you didn't tell me. Now Peter is dead. In my head—as a friend, as a priest—I forgive you, of course I do. But in my heart? I'm sorry. I'm trying, but I'm not there yet."

Gabby didn't know where to look. Her eyes roamed anywhere rather meet his excoriating gaze. Reduced to utter silence, she could only sit, nodding her head to herself, trying not to cry.

Abigail reached out and put her hand over his arm. "But you *have* come back to us, Will. Probably way too soon, but you are back. You're going to have to find a way to deal because we need you. *Really* ... need you. Gabby does get things wrong—after all, she's human. Hasn't that been enough punishment for all her past mistakes? She misses Michael, terribly. Misses everything about her old life. But despite that she still puts all she's got into this place and most of the time gets it right. I know you're still angry with her—with all of us—but you have to find your way through it. Emma needs you to."

Will's face softened. "Wow, that's quite a speech. When did you suddenly become the grown-up?" The girl felt him relax—relent—and she took her hand away. "I'm sorry, Gabby," he continued. "I can't say I didn't mean what I said, but I promise I will try to work through it. I know everything you did was because you cared, and of course I know that you've dedicated your life to Flammark for a very, very long time. Leave it with me. I will get there. If it's any consolation I blame God too—a lot more, as it happens. After I left St Jude's, Bish sent me to a retreat house belonging to a monastic order in the north. They brought me back from the brink. It's a process. Or so they tell me."

For the first time since his outburst, Gabby looked back at him. "I understand, William. There's nothing I can do to put the clock back. I'll just have to wait until you can bring yourself forgive me—but I want you to do it with *all* of your heart please, no half-measures."

After holding his gaze a millisecond longer than strictly necessary, she gave a little shrug and reached over to picked up a slice of cold toast. "Now," she said, tearing off a bite, "this exorcism…"

Will narrowed his eyes and wagged his head. "You. Are. Bloody. Incorrigible."

Regardless, she carried on. "I honestly couldn't think of anything else that might've worked. Flammark *has* to rid itself of Margaret, William. She's killing its children! So … at the church, we were going to try one of the Catholic prayers—"

"We?" asked Will.

"Myself, Abigail and Sandra."

"*Sandra?* You roped *Sandra Davis* in? She knows about the witch?"

Mouth full, Gabby managed, "Uh-huh."

"It went badly, didn't it?" said Will.

She swallowed. "As it happens, it did."

Will sighed. "Go on."

"She's the priest of the parish so we had no choice but to get her to officiate—I certainly couldn't do it. She's not an easy woman. She needed *a lot* of persuading. But despite her denials, she had first-hand experience of what Margaret Blackstone was capable of and though she tried to pass it off as a prank at first, deep down she knew something was very wrong. Eventually she came round to the notion of exorcism. That was Friday night."

"Bloody hell! It didn't work, then?"

"It was a disaster. Oh, the witch put in an appearance, alright…"

Will's eyes widened. Clearly drawn in, he couldn't resist asking, "What … was she like?"

"Terrible," Abigail butted in. Tremulously, she described Margaret Blackstone; what she was made of, how she got around. "She kind of paralysed me so I couldn't move, and she has this way of blocking out sound."

"Yes," said Gabby. "I felt that too. Like my ears were filled with sand. Still heard Sandra screaming, though. I doubt the devil himself could have shut her up!"

"She—Margaret—laid her hand on me," Abigail continued, swallowing hard. "I felt it inside me even though I knew it wasn't, really. Then... then she said I had nothing to fear from her because—" She stuck out her chin. "Because ... apparently, I'll never have children."

Will's face fell. "What? What a devastating thing to be told! My God, Abs, you've really been through the wringer, haven't you?" He squeezed her hand again then turned to Gabby. "Could Margaret be right? Do we believe her?"

Glancing at Abigail she said carefully, "It's possible, yes."

"Abs, I'm so, so sorry. And here I am, bringing nothing to the table except anger." After a moment's silence, he said, "After what she did I understand now why you might think she triggered Emma's miscarriage."

"I know she did," said Abigail, with sudden certainty. "I think Margaret laid hands on her too, found there was a baby and killed it. For the same reason she's killing the teenagers. They're all girls and Margaret specifically said Emma's baby was a wench."

"You think she's confusing them with her own sisters? I'm sure she didn't have any. Even by Oswald's time, the line was pretty-much all male. Daughters were a rarity. I'll look it up."

"Well, all Westen's victims are the same age she was at her passing," said Gabby, "Sixteen. Maybe she thinks any Flammark girl is prey to her father. She probably wouldn't be far wrong if she was actually in her own time. Or perhaps she's just doomed to re-enact her own passing. We don't really know."

"Poor, poor Emma. I should have been there for her."

"Yes, William. I rather think you should've," Gabby said. "Emma missed you terribly—we all did—but you of all people know what Flammark is capable of. Emma still has most of her friends around her—and Westen, of course—but to her, you're irreplaceable. She'd had an encounter with Margaret before the miscarriage, you know. She'd left something on her doorstep. Emma didn't tell us about it. But she would have told you. Then maybe we'd have got to where we are earlier."

Gazing steadily at Gabby, Will replied, "It doesn't stop, does it? Blame, recrimination—not a good place from which to fight the evils of the world." He gave a mirthless chuckle. "At least how they appear here in Flammark. What is it about this village, Gabby?"

"Something, for sure. Michael and I were literally put on this earth to guard it. We clearly hadn't even scratched the surface of its troubles."

"I do regret leaving like I did. But I was grateful for the time the bishop gave me. The retreat house was marvellous. Allowed me to think about the future."

"And did you come to any conclusion?" said Abigail. "Have you really decided to leave the priesthood?"

"That I can't say. I'm not sure. I'm might go back to university. The way I'm still feeling, I've no right to stand in a pulpit."

"Blame and recrimination," muttered Gabby. "You said it; it doesn't get us anywhere, does it?" Suddenly she slapped her hand on the table. Raising her voice she said, "You *can't* give it up, you *have* to come back. Whatever you bring to the pulpit—to Flammark—Sandra brings it worse. *Much* worse. You do realise she's got Frederick Thomas thinking about developing the vicarage and selling it off!"

"I had heard, but not being sure if I ever wanted to come

back—let alone be a priest again—it wasn't my place to say anything."

"I wish you had," Gabby continued. "The woman's a nightmare. Robbie said she's all but cleared out the undercroft at St Jude's. Granted a lot of stuff was just useless tat, but some of the old furniture was quite valuable. Robbie and I were incandescent when we saw it in the skip."

Will smiled. "I bet ..." Then his face changed completely. Thunderstruck, he exclaimed, "Hang on… Did you say she's been clearing the undercroft?"

"According to Robbie, yes."

"What is it, Will? What do you know?" Abigail asked.

"Has she cleared all of it?"

"I'm not sure," Gabby replied. "She's had the church surveyors in—"

Will put his head in his hands. "Oh. My. Living. God."

"Will!" Abby cried. "What is it? You're frightening me."

"I know where the witch came from."

"What do you mean?" said Gabby.

"I could be wrong. I'll have to look. But I think Sandra might have opened the Devil's Door."

29
THE DEVIL'S DOOR

An elephant could have parachuted into the room and no one would have noticed.

Mouth like a fish, Gabby stared at Will. "Oh, my goodness, the Devil's Door! You could be right! I'd forgotten all about that." Tapping her forehead with her palm, she said, "I'm so stupid nowadays."

Abigail frowned. "Okay, spill. What's the Devil's Door?"

"You know how ancient St Jude's is? Just after the war, Solomon opened up a trench opposite the graveyard and found evidence for what historians had long known; that the site had been in use as a place of worship long before the church was built."

"I think I met Solomon Barnes once," said Abigail said. "He came to a moot and gave us a lecture. It was brilliant."

"He's a brilliant man," Will smiled. "Anyway, a lot of churches like ours had small doors or gates built into their north walls. Worshippers from the old religions still visited the site, even though the Christians had muscled in, and were encouraged to enter the church. They'd do so via this north gate. The priests or elders would allow them to continue to worship their pagan gods in that part of the church."

Abigail tutted. "How very kind of them!"

"I think it mostly worked. There'd be market stalls and other things going on, too. It was different world, remember. As the years went by, the worship did become more integrated." He picked up his cup and put it down again. "Ugh, cold tea! Anyway... at its inception St Jude's wouldn't have looked anything like it does today. It wasn't much more than a massive hall. It was left to the Normans to improve and extend the building. They added another storey to create what the nave is now, leaving the space under it to become the undercroft—where the Devil's Door is. Then they slapped on the sanctuary and gave us the three sections we know today."

"So ... why were they called Devil's Doors?" Abigail asked.

Will smiled, getting into his stride. "The Church—especially as it developed with the Catholics, of course—was exceedingly superstitious, always on the alert for any kind of wickedness."

"Any work of the devil," said Gabby, "and then later, of course, their specialism. Witches."

"Right. Formal Church doctrine—what was actually *written down*—eschewed the notion of witches; they weren't officially recognised as entities that existed in the real world."

"Then the Inquisition came along," said Gabby. "The sitting pope had got his knickers in a twist about the Cathars in France—they were ascetics, had a stripped-down attitude to Christianity which didn't suit Rome at all. So, they set up a tribunal to weed them out. Twelfth century?" She tilted her head at Will.

"Around then, yes. After that the Inquisition escalated big time and got political. Basically, it turned into a Jewish pogrom. Then it adjusted its sights to target anyone they considered heretics and spread right across Europe. Inquisitors were very well paid and took great pleasure in their endeavours. Very great pleasure."

"Fascinating though this is," Abigail interrupted, "What's this got to do with anything?"

"Sorry, yes. Well, while the Church wouldn't *formally* acknowledge the existence of witches, it still clung on to its superstitions. The Inquisition had sort of gone rogue and had set its sights on a whole host of heresies, witchcraft being one of them. By the fourteenth century it was pretty much unstoppable. Rome hedged its bets on whether witches were actually real, recognising that evil existed and yet didn't go as far as to admit it could in any way be … personified."

"But evil's mentioned in loads of prayers, isn't it?"

"Oh yes. Nowadays it's mostly symbolic, though. Not much more than a nod to the past. Different story back in the day. Self-righteous, superstitious priests in thrall to an Inquisition now completely out of the control of Rome, would incorporate all kinds of iffy practices into their ceremonies, including a subverted use of these gates. Take baptism. The priest would begin the baptismal ceremony at the church entrance. Any evil the child might possess would be exorcised and given its marching orders by way of the north gate —or the Devil's Door as it came to be called—they'd have opened it before the service began. Then the congregation would move inside to the font. At the point of sprinkling the water—or ducking in it, as some churches still did—the door would be banged shut and the evil banished. Job done."

"Why couldn't it just leave through the front door?"

"Because most churches—not all—but a significant number in those days had their porches facing the wrong way. The spirit had to leave on the *north* side, north being the location where spiritual darkness resides. The superstition was rife in the Dark Ages and went on for centuries. It wasn't long ago that paupers and criminals used to be buried in the north side of graveyards. The belief fed into racist xenophobia: fear of Northmen, or Norsemen. The Scots, too."

"Yorkshire folk," Gabby, muttered, nodding sagely.

Abigail looked puzzled. "But … but I've never seen a door like this at St Jude's. I always thought the porch was its only entrance—oh, unless you count the small one near the vestry at the back."

"That was made later. A lot later. Our Devil's Door is tiny, less than four feet high. All you can see from the outside is the top of its archway. Back in the day, richer patrons used to be buried inside churches—under slabs. Larger churches and cathedrals buried families in vaults, too. After the Reformation all that stopped and there was a massive increase in earth burials *outside* the church. That's when graveyards were developed or extended. The old pre-Reformation footprint of St Jude's is in my library—at least it was. Fascinating stuff. The grounds were raised significantly as the village grew and earth burials became more frequent. That's how our Devil's Door got buried and forgotten. But—and here's the thing—it's still intact and visible from inside the undercroft."

"Wow," said Abigail. "God, I've missed you, Will. All this stuff just trips off your tongue and you know our history so well! You can't seriously want to leave Flammark for good?"

He squeezed her hand. "Let's not get into all that again, eh?"

"Yes, let's not," Gabby had the bit between her teeth now. "It's all starting to come together. From what Abigail told us, we can assume Margaret had the Sight. Oswald would have certainly considered her a witch. I know the door was bricked up around his period. I didn't make the connection."

Abigail suddenly got agitated. "Hold on, I'm remembering

now ... There *was* a door. At the start of my vision I—that is, Margaret—was definitely dragged through one before they took her to the woods."

"I think that rather settles it," said Will. "Oswald will have got his priest to perform a basic exorcism. He'll have used the Devil's Door to banish the spirit and maybe Margaret was physically pushed through it too for good measure. Then he had it sealed."

Gabby joined more dots. "And then they took her to the woods. Margaret's end was extreme. After the trauma of her burial and the exorcism she'd been put through, her spirit probably got stuck in some kind of limbo. Once the door had been sealed tight, it couldn't return to this plane to find the peace it needed to move on." She shook her head in annoyance. "You know, it's all very well dismissing artefacts like these doors as superstitious nonsense. Sometimes they're rooted in lived experience. As we are seeing now."

"So, Margaret's back because of Sandra's renovations," said Abigail. "Are we sure?"

"I'd have to look first," Will replied. "But when you said she'd cleared the undercroft, I thought of it straight away. It all adds up."

"I'll come with you," said Gabby.

It was only the smallest moment later that Abigail asked to go too.

"Are you sure, Abs?" said Will. "Haven't you had enough of St Jude's?"

"More than enough, believe me. But I need to follow this through. I want to see if it's the same door I—Margaret—was pushed through."

"Okay. But it'll have to wait until tonight. There's someone else I have to visit first."

30
NICKED

Westen's weekend had been foul. He'd spent most of it tracking down William fucking Turner. It'd pissed him off when Mason asked him, largely because, deep-down, he knew it was a good idea. But finding him hadn't helped him sleep. Despite the stresses of his job, he'd always slept well, never letting a case get to him. But with Emma the way she was, he just couldn't find a rhythm. By six am he'd given up the ghost and was at his desk an hour later. Burrows was in early too. Carrying a sheaf of papers, he all but ran into Westen's office. "Got a problem, Guv."

"What?"

"There's a bit of a posse gathered downstairs. Parents. They're baying for Sweeting's blood." He held out the papers. "After we interviewed him, he took your advice and has been staying with his mother-in-law. Some of his pupils took it upon themselves to pay his house a little visit last night. Trashed the place. No one would have been any the wiser, but they found pictures. One of the kids showed some to his dad, then the grapevine did its work. They're drawings, Guv. Look."

Burrows handed them over. About forty of them. Life drawings. *Nude* life drawings. "Hang on," Westen said, peering more closely. "This one looks like—"

"Shelley Iveson, I know. And this one—" Burrows leant over and pushed at the papers, "—this one is Jennifer Grey. Three more of our victims are here and others students from the school. The parents are in uproar."

"I bet they fucking are," said Weston. He felt his gorge rise in disgust as he scanned each picture, but he breathed it down. He felt permanently on the edge and too easily liable to go over it. "It's a pity they were stolen. We can't use any of these in court."

"I know, Guv. Uniform's chasing up the kids who broke in. I've asked them to downplay it. Even though they interfered with an investigation, I'm going to suggest cautions?"

Westen nodded. "Sounds about right. And, let's face it, they've pointed us in a direction. Whether we can use these or not, they're a game-changer. They give us the first tenable link between Sweeting and the other victims—apart from the school, of course."

Burrows shrugged. "We can't even ask him about them, though. Especially if he lawyers up."

Westen raised an eyebrow and smiled grimly. "The fuck we can't."

"Guv?"

Westen found his phone and called Martha, and asked if she was free to come in. The answer in the affirmative, he flipped his phone shut and said, "She'll be here in half-an-hour. Good call of yours that, Pete. Getting her in. With her help we might be able to use these drawings yet."

"Not sure what you're up to, Guv, but okay. What do you want me to do about these parents?"

"Get rid of them. Tell them we're on it."

"I'll do my best, but it won't be easy. Flammark's had enough."

But he managed it and was soon back in Westen's office in time for Martha's arrival. She was handed the drawings.

"So, what's your take?" Westen asked. "They were found in Sweeting's house."

"Tastefully done. Skilful too. Very skilful." In a repeat of his reaction earlier, she took one and peered at it more closely. Then another. "Are these—"

"Yes. Some of the victims. I need to know what they tell us about Sweeting. They're not the usual kind of artwork we see in cases like this."

"No, indeed," Martha replied, angling each picture, deep in thought. "Did the girls pose for these?"

"We're not sure. They've just been handed in," said Burrows. "The parents say not but, well …"

"Quite so," she said. "You can't necessarily trust what a teenager might say. But …" She riffled through the sheets, counting them under her breath. "This is a lot. Surely word would have got out that his students were modelling for him? Someone would have blabbed once the investigation got underway."

"I agree," said Westen. "Something doesn't sit right. For one thing, he isn't popular with the kids and for another, we've met him. I can't see any teenage girl wanting to take their clothes off for him."

"Unless he paid them, of course," said Martha.

"Possibly," Westen nodded. "Pete, get Sweeting in. We're going to have another go at him."

"Using these?" said Burrows. "You sure 'bout this, Guv? They're tainted evidence."

"Why?" said Jacobs.

"Because they were acquired illegally." Westen took a minute to update her about the break-in.

"Ah, got it," said Martha, "But be careful. I don't want to rain on your parade, but I'm not sure these drawings point to Sweeting as our killer."

"You've got to be kidding me!" said Westen.

"The victims' bodies were found carefully posed," Martha explained. "Arms crossed. Speaks to empathy—or familiarity with the girls. So, yes, the drawings support that. They're ... tender more than sexual. Nonetheless, the MO was brutal, the deaths agonising. I'd expect any artwork coming from someone who would bury a child alive to reflect that brutality in some way. These don't."

"Sweeting's an artist, don't forget," said Burrows.

"Artist or not, he wouldn't be able to mask his ... proclivities. If he meant harm to the girls he drew, I'm confident we'd see it in his work. He wouldn't be able to help himself. This is a complex presentation, Westen. These drawings are cleverly done but they are also anodyne. Straightforward."

"You still think it's a woman, don't you?" Westen said.

"I've been wrong before, but it's still my best guess. Yes."

~

A few hours later they were facing Sweeting in an interview room. The man looked terrible. He obviously hadn't slept. Face sunken, eyes red ... he was a flaming mess. When Westen entered with Martha, he blanched.

Westen slammed his file down on the table as he took his seat. Sweeting jumped. Running his fingers through his thinning hair, he said, "Please, Superintendent. Why have you brought me in again? I've done nothing wrong."

"You sure about that?" said Westen. "Absolutely sure?"

"Of course. Do I need a solicitor?"

"I don't know, Colin. Do you?"

"No! At least, I don't think so. As I said before, I know I shouldn't have left Jennifer, but she became abusive."

"You're the last known person to see her alive, Colin. Either at the coach stop or next to her grave. Which was it?"

"I told you, I went home."

"Yes, you did tell me that. Now tell me about the drawings."

The room fell silent, Westen sending a silent prayer that Sweeting would take the bait. "What ... what drawings?"

"How did you get them to sit for you? The girls. Did you pay them?"

Suddenly Sweeting slumped. "I know which drawings you mean now. How ... how did you know about them?" Then his face cleared. "Ah, my briefcase. I left it in my classroom. I didn't think it appropriate to go back into school to get it. I suppose one of the kids found it and went through it? I knew it was tempting providence to bring them in."

Westen said nothing, just silently noted there was a briefcase in play.

"No. I didn't pay them. I didn't need to. It's not what you think. They never *modelled* for me. I'm good at likenesses and I'm good at what I do. I-I..."

"... *imagined* them with no clothes on." Westen finished for him.

"No! *NO!*" Sweeting glared at Westen for all of two seconds before his eyes slid away. "Since my wife died there's been no one. What I did was completely harmless." Tenderly, he picked up one of the drawings. "This is her. Mostly. She used to pose for me." Barely audible now, he muttered, "I gave her their faces."

"You ... gave ... her ... their ... faces. Do you realise how fucked-up that sounds, Colin?"

"Yes."

"You liked them, didn't you? You *wanted* them."

"No. *No* I *didn't!* I don't know why I did it. At first I was just messing about but, somehow it made me feel less..."

"Less what?" Martha asked.

His eyes welled. Swiped at a tear. "Bereft. Lonely."

Westen let her carry on.

"Do you get on with your students, Colin?"

"No. I wish I did. They don't like me."

"It does seem a very unusual thing to do." Martha was in full shrink mode now. "Drawing the faces of your students on your wife's body."

"I suppose it is. But..."

"Go on."

"Doing that somehow made her ... live again. Every time I saw one of the girls—at school—they sort of ... brought her back to me."

Martha raised her eyebrows and sat back, nodding thoughtfully.

"That's even more fucked-up, Colin," said Westen. "So much so, I'm finding it very hard to believe."

Sweeting swallowed. "I know. I know." He wiped his eyes and nose with the back of his sleeve. "But I had nothing to do with any of the murders!"

"See, this is the problem," Westen sniffed. "Here's a man with a tragic past, I geddit. Very sorry. You get back on the horse, get a teaching job. You're still grieving. It's a loss you'll never get over. So, you start drawing pictures of your dead wife, giving her the face of the kids you teach. You're on a school trip and you end up alone with one of these kids, who later turns up dead. Tell me what's wrong with that picture, Colin. Tell me why I'm wrong in thinking we don't need to look any further for her murderer."

No answer.

"Are there more pictures, Colin?" Martha asked.

Sweeting nodded.

"At home?" said Westen, holding his breath.

"I brought them into work occasionally. For when I had a free lesson."

"Anything else we should know about?" Westen asked. "Magazines? Drugs?"

"No! *No.*Nothing like that. Search my house if you like."

Westen relaxed. "Thank you, Colin. We will."

Having got what he wanted, he nodded at Martha and they both rose to their feet.

Sweeting said, "I can't go home, can I?"

Westen shook his head. "Sorry, Colin, no. We'll be detaining you for a bit longer. *Now* you need a solicitor."

31

AWAKENINGS

Something in Emma's brain stirred.

No. No it couldn't be. Will?

It wasn't that his voice came into focus straight away. Rather, she heard him, at first, at a distance. Miles and miles away, so far off, his words came to her like a dream. A dream of Will as he used to be when she could tell him everything and everything would be okay.

Imperceptibly at first, his words started to cut through, gradually penetrating the fog of her consciousness. Even then she didn't have the wherewithal even to acknowledge he was there. She wanted him to be—wanted it more than anything—but the numbness was paralysing, and she didn't have the strength to push through.

She was too wrapped in the comfort of distance and denial. She'd been there before, with Ben; when the only thing she could do to endure his terrible violations was to take her *self* away from them; to journey somewhere in her head. Yet even that, even what he had put her through, was nothing compared to—

Will's words faded and the blackness came back. Great, soothing waves of it. She wasn't waking up.

Not ready.

Except the voice kept bringing her back. She felt herself warm to its cadence, its tone. It could only belong to one person and he was *there,* waiting for her. All she had to do was open her eyes.

And see him.

Her two minds battled each other. One drawing her back to the dark place, the other bringing her to Will's light. She'd wait and see which prevailed. She didn't have the energy to do anything else.

Except listen.

I'm so, so sorry I left like that. Left you. I know now it was an awful thing to do. But, in my defence, Em, I was in a terrible state. I had to get away.

But … I should have come back sooner. I know that now.

You may not see it, but despite everything that's been thrown at you, you are strong. Stronger than I am. You can come out of this. You bloody-well have to!

I was angry. Angry and desperately, desperately sad. I couldn't bear my own company never mind anyone else's. Had to get away. And now I can't bear to see you like this. I was a fool, taking my bat home like that. I'm still trying to work out where my place is, where I belong. Maybe it's here after all, I don't know…

I so miss talking to you! You always make things clearer, help me decide.

I know I'm terribly late, but I'm talking now. And, so help me, I'm going to jabber away till you bloody wake up. If it takes all night—all week—then so be it, that's what I'll do.

Want to know where I've been?

Bish got it absolutely spot on. He knew I needed some peace and quiet, somewhere people wouldn't get in the way or tell me what to do or how to think. So much to process, so much to grieve! But he also didn't want me to be on my own. I suppose he was frightened I might … you, know, join Peter.

So, he sent me to a retreat house in Yorkshire. Gorgeous place. Peaceful. It belonged to a monastic order that knew all about the power of silence. So, although I was never really on my own, it felt like that.

After a month or so, the abbot—Abbot John—took me aside. He's a trained counsellor, you know. He suggested we take some walks. We even fished in one of the streams! I've never touched a rod and line in my life, but I'm a true convert now. Such a fantastic man. Grounded. Empathetic. He made sure we met every day and he just let me talk. Talk it out, you know? I couldn't tell him everything, of course. That was part of the problem. I couldn't tell them who—what—that bastard really was. I'll never say his name. Never.

So, I followed the police line—you know, that he'd had been a terrorist. Poor Bish. He still blames himself for giving that… for giving him so much power… Blames himself for Peter, and of course for all the others who lost their lives too. Most of them were so young, their future wiped out, just like that.

… The future! God, it doesn't bear thinking about, Em. Up till now, I've been considering jacking it all in… you know, the priesthood? But then … then this happened to you and it was a no-brainer. I had to come back, at least for now.

Anyway, for what it's worth, I am feeling … better. No, that's wrong. I'm feeling more centred. I'm still not right; still sinning in my anger against God. I'm up against a brick wall with that. I haven't spoken to Him. I've tried, don't get me wrong. Abbot John and I, we knelt together in his chapel most days. But the words … they seemed to turn to dust in my mouth. How can I talk to Him when he made Peter's death happen and happen in the most horrendous way possible? Oh, I know. I know. As the monks kept trying to drum into me, it wasn't God that killed Peter. But he bloody well let … him do it!

Didn't he?

The bloody doctrine of omnipotence! How many times have I coun-

selled people on it? People who've had loved ones taken away. Now it's my turn to ask the same question … If God exists, how could he let evil happen? How could he, Em? How could he?"

At first the only conclusion I could come to was that God Himself must be evil. Given the existence of Gabby and Michael, I can't damned-well deny He exists, can I? But as Abbot John said, I've been focusing on His omnipotence when what I should really be thinking about is His omniscience. Not only does he have the capacity to control everything—free will aside—he also knows more than I do. Knows there's a reason behind things that we humans cannot possibly fathom. The question is, do I buy it? Do I want to? Look what's happened to you? Now and in the past. Did He want this for you? Is our heartbreak serving some higher bloody purpose? If so then that means we're nothing but pawns in some kind of bizarre game of chess.

I'm sure you don't want to hear all this. It doesn't exactly make for cheery banter, does it?

But … Whoa… Emma? Am I mistaken or are you looking a bit more pukka? There's colour in your cheeks! Em? Emma. EMMA?

"W-Will?"

"Em! Jesus, you're looking at me …" Will squeezed her hand. "Are you coming back? Come back to me, Em. It's Will. It's me!"

She could barely move. The muscles in her face didn't seem to want to work. And her mouth felt soooooo dry. She managed to move her head enough to signal for him to come closer. Raising her chin she began mouthing something.

Will leant over and put his ear near her mouth. "What? I can't hear, you Em. What are you saying to me?"

In the faintest whisper of a voice, she replied, "That was all bullshit."

His face broke into a huge grin and he chuckled out loud. "What? Omnipotence or omniscience?"

She twitched her lips upwards. "Both."

He jumped up from his chair. "Hang, on. Hang on, Em.

I'll get someone. Do you … do you want something to drink? Something to eat? I'm not sure what to do, do you—"

"Drink." The word came in a rasping whisper.

Will scurried to the bedside table and sloshed water from a plastic jug into a red sippy cup. He held it to her mouth, and she started to take it. Somehow it came down her nose and she snorted, and it sprayed out, so he had to scurry over to the table again to get a tissue.

Gently, he wiped her mouth and she smiled at his touch. It made her feel … restored. Minutes later she found more of her voice and soon—remarkably soon—was laughing and crying in his arms, clinging onto him as if he were a piece of wreckage. In fact, they were making so much noise, a nurse came running in, the concern in her own face giving way to a huge smile when she saw what was going on. No sooner had she arrived than she about-turned and ran back out again, muttering something about telling the doctor.

"I thought you'd never come back," croaked Emma. "I have missed you, so, so much."

"Me too. I'm so sorry, Em. I'm so sorry I left you." He held her more tightly. "And I'm sorry about the—"

She finished the sentence for him, though she could barely form the words. "The baby?"

He drew away slightly. Still holding her, he caught her gaze. "Yes. The baby. We, we weren't sure how much you knew. This is the first time you've come round properly since—"

"I remember everything. I remember what that … thing did. I have no idea why I'm not crying the house down right now. Maybe it's because you're here. Or maybe it's because I've only just woken up."

"Or maybe the shut-down helped you to face it. Like mine did with me. But you will cry, and very soon, I should think.

Though I have to admit, I'm glad it's not now. You'd get me blubbing too!"

"Has Gabby told you about her. About the—"

"Witch? She has. We've pieced together most of what we think happened to you. There's no need to talk about it just yet—unless you want to, of course."

She felt his arms tighten. For now, it was enough that he was back and that he *knew*. Of course, he knew. He always did.

"How long have you been here?" she said.

"I came back late last night. I spent the morning with Abigail and Gabby. They told me everything. But I'm not actually sure what you know. We've a lot of catching up to do, but let's do that later. And not here, either. You still need to rest. It can all wait till you get home."

"What day is it? How long have I been out of things?"

"It's Monday. You had your … encounter last Wednesday."

"Did I? I remember I was coming home from Abigail's. She'd had some kind of bad experience with the Orb." She grabbed his wrist. "Is she alright? Is she better?"

"She's fine. Right as rain. The Orb put her through the wringer, but then found a way to make it right. She'll no doubt tell you all about it when you see her."

"Have she and Gabby been to visit me?"

Will nodded. "This weekend. They restricted visitors at first. You lost a hell of a lot of blood. Then, after they patched you up, you went a bit doo-lally so they sedated you. You came out of it alright, but then dropped into a bit of a fugue." He grinned. "Not even Gabby could get anything out of you, and that's saying something! And as for Westen—"

"Oh, Westen!" she gasped. "Where is he? How is he?"

"At work. Still on the case. Burning the candle at both

ends, worried to death about you. It was because of him I'm here. He came to find me."

"Did he?" She smiled in a kind of wonder. "Oh my, I'd liked to have been a fly on the wall for that meeting!"

Will chuckled. "It went okay. Sort of. He's always been a bit jealous of me, hasn't he?"

"Yes," she said, grinned. "He has. That is, not so much *you*. I think he resents our relationship—our friendship. There're things I don't tell him and he knows it. It upsets him."

"You could have knocked me over with a feather when he appeared at the retreat house, gruff and sweary as ever. 'Get your fucking act together, man,' he said. 'Emma needs you,' he said. Who was I to disobey?"

Will laughed and Emma did too, hand in hand, forehead almost to forehead...

... and that's the scene Westen witnessed, the smile on his face freezing as he stared on at the two of them, unnoticed at the door. The love of his life and her friend. A friend she preferred to wake up to instead of him.

He tightened his grip on the flowers he'd brought, roses and tiny white frothy flowers—bought from a fucking florist this time while he had some time to spare before facing Marshall and his review team. Feeling like a fucking idiot, he backed out of the room before either of the pals realised he was ever there.

32

CLUSTERFUCK

Westen floored it back to the station, churning over and over the scene he'd just left, trying to persuade himself he'd done the right thing in finding Turner. He wanted to believe he'd seen evidence of nothing other than a close and platonic friendship. It *couldn't* be anything more, could it? The fucking man was gay, wasn't he? Or was he—what do they call it nowadays—sexually fluid?

Either way he couldn't bear seeing them together another minute. Days he'd spent out of his fucking mind with worry; talking to Emma, barely leaving her side even though he had a child-killer on the loose. One minute with William fucking Turner and she was wide awake, as if nothing had fucking happened. Bright as a fucking button.

Well, fuck her. Fuck everything. Fuck, fuck, fuck.

He glanced at himself in the rearview mirror to see two glittering eyes staring back at him in a face blistering with rage. And there was a hard lump in his throat that just wouldn't swallow down. How could she fucking do this to him?

He drove into the station car park and turned off the engine. Breathed. Breathed again. This is what he had brought Turner back for. To make Emma better. And it had worked. The Doc knew it would do the trick, so ... what was the fucking problem?

He knew well enough; he wasn't stupid. Exhaustion. Fear he'd lost Emma. And he'd lost being a father too, something he never knew he wanted but now wanted more than ever. *This* was behind his sleeplessness, the loss—both of the baby and what might have happened had he not found Emma in time. Now he had that fucking reconciliation to contend with —he just couldn't get the image of the friends reunited. It should have been *him* that brought her round. What future could they possibly have together if she couldn't open up to him like she was obviously able to do with Turner?

Then there was the case! Something was off. Very off. He knew they were on dodgy ground; couldn't shake the feeling that despite growing evidence to the contrary the man they'd detained this morning was innocent. Westen couldn't see him carting—or mesmerising—a series of sixteen-year-old girls to the woods, or a graveyard for that matter, in order to bury them alive. Just couldn't. But all the evidence suggested that's exactly what he did do, and Marshall would push for an arrest.

Still chewing things over, Westen left the car to stand glowering outside the station entrance, nowhere near ready to go inside. The review team was due in half an hour. He needed his wits about him. Needed his composure. Needed his fucking life back.

Needed Emma.

He heard a rapping above him, from one of the stairwell's windows. He looked up to find Pete taking the stairs using the bannisters to rappel himself from flight to flight before shooting out of the entrance.

"Guv. Thank God you're back! The—" he stopped himself in mid-flow. "Sorry, Guv, how's Emma?"

"Fanfuckingtastic, Pete. Couldn't be better." He drew in a breath. "What's up?"

"The review team's early. I've put them in the big conference room."

"And the day just keeps on giving. Are we ready?"

"Yep. More than ready. Sweeting's looking good for the murders. We're still searching his house, but we've already turned up more drawings, plus we found his briefcase. Something else, you'll like, too, Guv. Masks. Plain white paper masks. Some of them were painted. They could be used for art lessons, of course, but … well, Martha got a bit excited when they phoned that in. We've got him, Guv."

Westen's heart sank a notch further. "Right, well, at the very least, I suppose that'll get Marshall off our backs."

"You don't seem pleased, Guv. We can put these new drawings in evidence now. And the masks. Ties in with what Martha thought after the Davis woman's statement. Sweeting was the last person seen with the Grey girl and has a questionable alibi from a family member. Plus the murders have stopped since we had him in our sights. It all adds up."

Westen could barely give him a nod. "What's the mood in there?"

"They look a bit grim, but that's par for the course. We won't be in there long, Guv. Not now we've got Sweeting."

"You don't know Marshall. We've history. We could have the Son of fucking Sam in custody, he'd still make it heavy weather."

They took the station steps and made their way to the main conference room. Marshall sat at one end of the table, two empty chairs at the other. Burrows had already stacked the case files in front of them, ready for Westen's arrival.

"Ah, Superintendent," Chief Superintendent Frank

Marshall said, a derisive smile playing around the corners of his mouth. "Good of you to join us."

"You're early, Frank."

Marshall curled his thick lips further upward. "Let's get on, shall we?"

Westen grunted. Taking off his jacket, he took his seat, ready for the long haul. Burrows sat too and opened his laptop.

"I don't have to tell you, Westen," Marshall began, "with a murderer at large for this long, we owe it to the parents and to the community to check that everything that should be done has been done. I understand you have a suspect in custody?"

"We do."

"The case against him is solid?"

"Circumstantial, but we're almost there. We're searching Sweeting's house right now and it's looking good."

"Enough for an arrest?"

Here we go...

Marshall looked over his glasses, waiting for a reply.

Westen swallowed. "I think so."

"So..." said Marshall, addressing the room. "We'll be going through the case file page by page. Any questions, folks, speak out. Remember, we're not here to criticise, only to verify and offer suggestions for any future actions. Okay. Over to you, Superintendent."

Westen was about to open his mouth when Tony Stamford burst in.

"Guv. You're needed."

"Can't it wait, Stamford?"

His DC gave a tiny, tense shake of his head, eyes transmitting loud and clear that something else was about to hit the fan.

Westen pushed back his chair. "Give us a moment, Marshall."

"What?" he barked, closing in on Stamford who'd waited way along the corridor.

"It's Sweeting, Guv. He's tried to top himself. In his cell. The duty sergeant found him ten minutes ago."

"The fuck?" Wasting no time, Westen started for the swing doors and hissed, "Get Burrows. Say *nothing*."

He legged it through the doors and thundered down the four flights of stairs that led to the small block of holding cells. There he found a group of worried uniforms gathered around the charging desk, the sergeant screaming down the phone. "I don't care if he's throwing up his bleedin' heart and lungs, I want him 'ere now!"

Westen shouted at one of the lads. "Take me to him."

Jumping to it, the copper led him—and Burrows who'd just arrived—through the steel door that led into the cell corridor now buzzing with the cries of other inmates who'd smelled something was up. One door at the end hung open. They bolted down to it, only to stop dead at the threshold. Beyond any shadow of a doubt, Colin Sweeting was dead. Lying on the floor, arms outstretched to forty-five degrees, his palms lay upwards revealing vertical slashes to both wrists. He had a smile on his face. A fucking smile!

Donna was inside too, sitting on the bunk covered in blood. Jacobs, also drenched in it, sat on the floor with her back to the wall, shell-shocked, all colour drained from her face.

"Martha wanted to clarify something he said in his interview," Donna said, looking up at the two men. "That's when we found him. He was still alive. I gave him CPR while Martha blew the whistle then tried to rip the blanket to bind his wrists."

"Made out of some kind of plastic fabric. Couldn't tear

it." Martha muttered, devastated. "No use anyway. He was too far gone."

Westen could barely take in the scene. His eyes were drawn to one of the walls where he saw something—painted? —on it. A woman. A nude. Exquisitely rendered with lines of blood. In the same red-brown medium were the words:

I WILL SOON BE WITH YOU MY LOVE

"How?" said Westen. "How the hell did he do it?" Turning to the poor copper that brought them down, he shouted, "Wasn't he fucking searched?"

"I-I dunno, Sir. I've just come on duty. I think so." He splayed out his hands, uselessly.

"Of course, he was bloody searched!" the sergeant yelled as he too, came striding down the corridor. "But he'd brought in a scalpel blade. No way would we have found it."

Donna pointed to a small, shiny flat object just visible within the lake of blood. "He's an art teacher, Guv. My brother's an illustrator. Uses scalpels all the time to cut paper or scrape paint. They've plastic handles and a simple groove to hold the blade. He always has one in his pocket. They come with a tiny cover. Dead easy to take the blade out, push it into the hem of a shirtsleeve. Sweeting could have slipped it in there before we took him in."

Martha chimed in. "He must have been at the end of his tether, Westen. Thought he knew the way the wind was blowing. You only have to look at that—" she nodded at the painting on the wall, "to see what was in his mind." She threw Burrows an angry look. "I said he should be put on suicide watch!"

"He was!" Burrows exclaimed. "Saw to it myself."

"Yes, well, I've just got off the phone," the sergeant said, more subdued now. "Chewed the ears of one of mine. I'd sent him home early. He … he must have missed a round."

Westen couldn't believe his ears. "No. This was down to you, Price. I'll have your fucking badge for this. I'll—"

"What kind of a shop are you running here, Westen?"

He spun around. Marshall! The Chief Super was also making for them, and with murder on his face. He peered into the cell. "What a fucking mess. This is bad. Very bad. A death in custody is on us—on you—whether the man was guilty or not."

With no choice in the matter, Westen, could only stand there and take it, balling and unballing his fists. Not much he could say. Marshall wasn't wrong.

"Okay," the man continued. "You've got half an hour to wrap things up here, Westen. Then I'll see you back upstairs."

33
UNDERCROFT

Abigail was not looking forward to returning to St Jude's. Truth be told, she'd be happy never to set foot in the bloomin' place again.

They arrived in Will's beaten-up VW. They clambered out of it and stood gaping at the silent church as if in some kind of communion. Then Will turned on the torch he'd brought and passed its beam over the building. He rested it on its Romanesque entrance.

"Did you miss it?" Abigail asked, hooking her arm through his.

"Of course, I did," he replied, a catch in his voice. "How could I not? St Jude's has been in my life for as long as I can remember." He moved the beam towards the vicarage but it wasn't strong enough to illuminate anything more than a few adjacent headstones. "And I miss that place, too. I didn't think I would, actually. Part of me never really thought of it as home. You said Sandra had plans to split it up and sell it?"

"Yes," said Gabby.

"I'm not sure I'd oppose it, to be honest."

"You're still not quite right in the head, are you?" Abigail tutted. "Maybe you came back too soon?"

"Not soon enough for Em! Broke my heart earlier, to see what state she was in. I've been stupid. Selfish. I should have known something like this would happen. Since she arrived, Flammark's gone a bit, well ... bonkers."

"It certainly has," Gabby replied. "I think you put your finger right on the spot. Since Emma arrived. There's much, much more to what's going on than meets the eye. Still, you're back and that's what matters. And it's great that you saw Emma and managed to bring her round."

"Yeah. It's the first thing I've felt good about since ... since, you know..."

Abigail shivered. "I'm cold. Can we get on with it?"

"Of course," said Will, patting his jacket pocket as he started walking. "I've still got a set keys. Couldn't bring myself to hand all of them in."

He opened up and flipped one of the heavy switches next to the door. Nothing happened.

"The electricity's been turned off," said Gabby. "At Sandra's behest. She told Albert she didn't want to encourage squatters."

"Squatters?" mumbled Abigail. "What's up with the woman? We don't get squatters in Flammark!"

"That's what Robbie said when Albert told him," Gabby replied. "But the man's really worried about her, apparently, and decided to humour her. He said she hasn't been well since we dropped her off, you know, on the night of her exorcism. He thinks she's not up to running a parish at the moment and that it might be a nervous breakdown. He wanted her to let Robbie see her but since she hates him almost as much as she detests me, she refused point blank. He and Albert have both decided to have a quiet word with the bishop."

"Have they?" said Will. "Well, sounds like it's for the best. Flammark's hard. Going by what you've told me, I doubt Sandra will come back. She's too brittle and she obviously needs help. Some kind of counselling, perhaps. Not that she'll take it, I don't suppose. Not if how you've described her is in any way accurate."

He opened the door to the undercroft. "Right. Give me a tick and I'll have the electricity back on."

He disappeared down the stairs. Suddenly, Abigail's gorge rose. The sound of his footsteps had been replaced with a familiar rustling, crackling. Shit. Had he come across the witch already?

"Will, are you okay?" she called.

"Fine! Hang on, just—" She heard the sound of something being rammed home and the entrance flooded with light, making the two women blink wildly at each other.

"Bloody hell!"

At Will's shout, Gabby disappeared through the door and galloped down the concrete steps. Since it was completely unknown territory for her, Abigail followed more carefully. She stopped on the bottom step and gaped with the others.

She hadn't really known what to expect. Even though Robbie had told them Sandra had begun a clearance operation she'd still envisaged the space to be a bit cluttered. Remnants of old pews, maybe. Shelves. Somewhere that might house old candlesticks or somesuch—she didn't really know. But she hadn't expected the sight that lay before them now.

They beheld … nothing. Just a vast, low-ceilinged space—the entire footprint of the church interior—completely cleared and emptied. She was quite impressed actually, and could see Sandra's point. It really would make an excellent youth space, easily adaptable either for games and table tennis or for a full-on club night.

Had it not been for the sea of twigs and leaves that covered the entire floor, easily to the depth of a few feet. Will and Gabby were knee deep.

"Margaret," said Gabby, as she stared down and around. "It's her signature and the same material Sandra had to deal with in the vicarage kitchen, though that was a more ... formidable experience. She's definitely been here, William."

"Look!" he cried, pointing to an archway at the far side of the room. They waded through the leaves and stood in front of a low door, its ancient oak hardened and blackened with age. He cast about, kicking the litter away to reveal two neat piles of old stones on either side of the door, their white-washed faces matching exactly the shade and patina of the walls.

"Sandra must have noticed the arch and realised it contained a door," said Will. "Then had the brickwork taken down."

"I think I know why," said Abigail. "If she wanted this place as a youth club, there'd have to be an emergency exit."

"Yes," said Gabby. "I bet she was over the moon when she saw this. She'd have had difficulty putting one in, St Jude's being listed and all that."

"It's open!" Will cried, running his finger along the edge. "See? It doesn't fit flush to the stone frame." He pulled it towards him, and it came away from some kind of metal barrier. "She must have tried it and got it part-way open then couldn't get it back."

"Or maybe she didn't even bother, since it's blocked from the outside too."

Will was running his fingers over it, his eyes filled with awe. "It's beautiful. Oak gets harder as it ages. They must have bolted that barrier to the walls—iron probably—so it could never be opened from the outside. It stopped the door from rotting, too, as the level of the churchyard was raised."

"Sandra probably planned to cut into the ground outside and install steps down." Abigail mused. "It'd make a pretty cool entrance, actually."

"She's a nightmare," said Gabby. "A complete nightmare."

"Perhaps," said Will, then shrugged. "But she wasn't to know."

"Hmm," Gabby muttered. "It was her *job* to know! All she had to do was ask me!"

Abigail grinned. Like that was ever going to happen.

Frowning, she looked hard at the door and the walls next to it. "I think I do remember this! I—Margaret, that is—was pushed out of here before the long march to the woods."

"So, pretty much confirming what the Orb showed you, Abs," said Will. "Oswald used the gate not only as a spiritual portal but a physical one too."

"William," Gabby started. "You know where all this is leading, don't you? Abigail and I, we've talked about this. We going to need to perform another exorcism. Get it done *right* this time. We *have* to get rid of her once and for all before she does any more damage. But ... but *you're* going to have to lead it."

At first Will made no reply, just started to hoick the small oak door back into its arch. Then he gave up. "Yeah. I sort of realised where this was all going. It went wrong, but the first exorcism was an understandable call." He placed his hand on the pin on his lapel; started twirling it around. "Thing is, I don't know if I'll fare much better than Sandra. It was only a few days ago I was thinking of jacking everything in. Now you want me back in the saddle..."

"Once a priest, always a priest, William. Ordination's a lifetime commitment, whether you're practising or not."

Will dipped his head in acknowledgement. "You're right. I know that. I'm pretty sure I can call her here, the prayers are powerful. She even came for Sandra..."

"They are, and Margaret will have to obey again, she'll have no choice. But actually, we never really got to start the summoning. Sandra was too closed off to it. We started the baptismal prayer *after* we sensed she was here. It was almost as if she wanted to be."

"But I'm not sure I'll have any better luck at holding her here. I don't know if *my* faith is up to snuff." He baulked at Gabby's sceptical expression. "I explained this to Emma, I believe God's up there, right enough. But I'm not sure I believe *in* Him, and I certainly don't trust in Him. Not like I used to. And an exorcism is not the same as a simple deliverance ceremony."

"Yeah, we know," said Abigail. "We got the low-down about that from Sandra." She took his hand. "I'll be there. I think that'll help. She's already had me in her sights. She believes I'm her sister. She said as much."

"I've been thinking about that. You know, it might have been the thing that stopped her killing," said Will.

"What do you mean?" asked Gabby.

"Something Westen told me. There've been no murders since the last body was found in the graveyard, and that was ten days ago. Before that, the intervals between the deaths were fairly consistent. Three or four days. If you're right, and Margaret's twisted imagination really does believe she's protecting Oswald's daughters, finding two *real* blood relatives might have been the thing that stopped her in her tracks."

"So … we're *next*?" said Abigail. "Cheers, Will."

"That's not what I mean. She's met you both. If she'd wanted to kill you, she had ample opportunity. That doesn't mean she isn't a threat. Look what she did to Emma."

"You could be right about Margaret finding family." said Gabby. "Except she tried to make contact with Emma much earlier than her last encounter outside Clearview."

"I remember you said something about it but I don't know the details."

Gabby explained about the twig-wreath.

"So, let me get this straight," Will said, suddenly glaring at her. "Emma was gifted this wreath thing which somehow bonded her to the witch. And you threw it on the fire. Tell me... How in the world did you not expect her to try to bond with Emma again? *As in pay her a visit?*"

His face suffused with a sudden anger and the air crackled with tension. Gabby said nothing. Unable to hold his gaze, she turned away.

Abigail was caught in the middle. She wanted to comfort Gabby but also knew that Will was right. Besides, there was no use taking sides. Their conflict derived from a deeper source than their current problems.

She decided to move things on. "So, what do you think, Will? Are you up for doing a second exorcism?"

He blew out his cheeks, visibly managing his emotions. Taking his eyes off Gabby, he said, "I'm thinking about it. I wish we had more time. For one thing, it's going to be a job and a half keeping Emma away."

"Why?" Abigail said. "She's in hospital!"

"She's champing at the bit to get discharged. She may even manage the escape for tomorrow, now she's got her voice back. The doctors are very pleased with her, surprised even, at the rate of her progress."

"Yay! That's great news!"

"It is," Will replied. "But now we're starting to understand what's what, we could have done with her staying there a few days longer. While we—while *I* get my act together." He glanced at Gabby. "I just pray to God we can protect her properly this time."

34
HOME

Emma had more success with the doctors than she could have hoped. After Will had left, they'd told her if she managed a good night's sleep and if her blood work came back okay, they couldn't see any reason why she shouldn't be allowed to go home. It would be the best place for her.

As it happened, she hadn't been able to follow all their instructions. Sleep had always been problematic ever since Ben, but they weren't to know that. As soon as the first nurse appeared the following morning, she resumed her campaign but had to wait until the afternoon to be told the bloods were fine and that she was good to go. She called Westen to come and get her.

He didn't pick up, so she texted him. After drumming her fingers waiting for a reply, she called Will.

As she cleared her bedside cupboard, she mulled about Westen. For some reason he hadn't visited yesterday, either. Perhaps he'd wanted to let her have time with Will.

Emma said as much in an earlier voicemail. He hadn't returned her call then, either. She understood it might be difficult to take time off to bring her home—knew he hadn't broken the case—yet couldn't help but feel let down that he hadn't been in touch.

It was then her phone rang. Westen, finally!

"Hey you," she said.

"Emma, love! I got your messages. Fantastic they're letting you out. Turner did the trick then?"

"He must have," she chuckled. "I… I've rung him. He's picking me up. I hope you don't mind but with you not answering I assumed you were busy, so I asked him."

Two beats of silence. "I know. Sorry … and to be honest, you're not wrong. Busy doesn't go near to it. I'm in the middle of a clusterfuck, Emma. Something happened yesterday. I've been trying to sort it out ever since. I'll tell you about it later. I want to be there for you but…"

"No problem," she replied, quickly. "As I said, Will's coming for me."

More silence.

"Thank you for finding him, by the way," she said. "I think he made all the difference."

"So it seems."

"Are you okay? You sound … tense."

"Yes. No … I'm fine. Relieved you're feeling more like yourself. I've been … I've been very worried." Emma frowned. He sounded as near to uncertainty as she'd ever heard him. "I don't suppose I'll be able to convince you to find somewhere else to stay other than the cottage?"

"No. And there's really no need. Will said he could stay over, and I suspect Abigail and Gabby will muscle in too. I don't want to be anywhere else. I need to be in my home."

"Right. Well. I'll be over as soon as I can, then. I'm sorry, love. I know I'm letting you down."

"No, no. Not at all. I always knew your job would get in

the way sometimes. Don't think twice about it, Westen. I'll be okay. Gotta go, the doctor's here."

"I'll ring you later—"

She rang off. Didn't want to hear any more. Because, let's face it, if he'd really wanted to be there, he'd let nothing —*nothing*—get in his way.

Well, at least he was fine. She was fine too. Totally fine.

Twenty minutes later, Will was whisking her away in his VW. "Are you sure you want to go back to Clearview? Gabby told me that's where—"

"Westen found me? Yes. It'll be hard, no doubt, but what am I supposed to do? I'm not living anywhere else, and I have to face it sometime. Besides, you're coming with me. That makes all the difference."

Will fell silent.

"What?" said Emma. "What else?"

"Nothing. Just ... just I think this might not be the safest option. She might, I mean the witch might..."

"Try again? There isn't much more she could do to hurt me, is there? No. I need to be here. I *want* to be here, no matter what."

But words are easy. As they made the turn into the road and Will slowly drove the car up to the curb, her stomach gave a sickening lurch. He got out and opened the door for her. Gave her his arm.

She made it. Made it out of the car, even stopped herself looking over her shoulder at the green, where *she* came from. Got to the door.

His key to the ready, Will let them in. She couldn't wait to get inside and sit on the sofa. But it didn't look the same, somehow; the cushions seemed wonky and the colour wasn't right.

Will must have seen her hesitation. "New covers. Bit tight, I'm afraid. Abigail and Gabby scoured the shops and these were the best they could come up with before you got back."

"Yes. I see. Of course, they'd be stained." She fixed a smile on her face. "Absolutely. I'm just going to pop upstairs. Need the loo."

She all but ran to the bathroom, took great heaving breaths as she grabbed the sides of the sink and stared in the mirror. Maybe she had come back too soon. Why did she think it would all be so easy?

She turned on the cold tap and cupped some water to her face. It helped. After drying herself, she took a few more breaths. She could hear Will messing about with the fire then heard the coffee-maker gurgling in the kitchen. The sounds calmed her and soon she felt able to take tentative steps back down the stairs. Trying not to overthink it, she sat herself deliberately and firmly on the sofa and put her feet up. She was going to make this bloody work.

Will came in and handed her a mug. "Here, drink this. You're doing really well, Em. Really well. I'm proud of you."

"Are you?" she chortled, grimly. "Can't deny, it's a struggle. And I don't think Westen's coming."

"Whaat? Why?"

"I'm not sure, exactly. Some problem or other at the station. I'm okay with it."

"No, you're not. I can tell. Nor should you be. That's not like him. You know he loves you to bits, right? You should have seen him when he found me. Tearing his hair out doesn't get near to what he was like. You're his world."

"No. I'm not his world. I'm *in* his world and that's different." She sighed. "We'll no doubt talk it through."

But what *was* she to talk through, exactly? She could hardly tell him what had really happened to her—she couldn't even tell the doctors, and certainly not the shrink. It took all her effort not to think about the witch and what she did; to not let *that* image in. Yet still it came: those long, skeletal fingers reaching out to her, flattening out on her belly. Twisting.

She gasped—nearly spilled her coffee. It was all she could do not to mirror the memory by lifting her own hand and cradling herself … there. It had been better at the hospital. Maybe she'd been wrong in coming out so soon.

"Em? *Em?* You alright? You zoned out for a minute."

"Yep," she replied, attempting a smile. "Just tired."

"So long as that's all it is. Thought you might be having a relapse."

"I was just thinking… I'm not sure I want Westen to come."

"What? Ever?" smiled Will.

"Perhaps. There are things I can't tell him and keeping the truth from him just takes too much energy. I don't have that to give. And it's not fair to him. What kind of relationship is it that can only ever be based on lies and omissions?"

He opened his mouth to reply when the doorbell rang and sounds of low chatter came from outside. Will screwed up his face in mock dread. "We both know who this is. Are you up to them? Would you prefer I sent them away?"

"No! The more the merrier. It'll take my mind off things."

Gabby looked a little subdued as she entered, but Abigail was all smiles, hugging Emma bright as a button. Either mood was okay with her, she felt hers lift.

After the wave of greetings was over, they settled down. Emma said, "I thought you'd be at work, Abigail."

"Yes, well I had to take Friday and Saturday off. No biggie —tell you later. Thought I'd make the week of it. The salon's given me the time—they can't complain. It seems I've attracted more than the usual shampoo-and-set crowd they had before I joined them. Business is booming."

Before Emma knew it, the old times were back. The

banter, the jokes, the do-you-remembers—though for some reason Gabby didn't seem to be joining in as much as Abigail and Will. She'd craved this for months, the four of them together, and she basked in the company. It was almost enough to make her forget.

Almost.

She fell quiet, and so did the others.

"I want to talk," Emma said, trying to lighten the altered vibe. "I do, but I'm not sure I can."

The three friends spoke at once. "No, no … It's alright … no one's expecting you…" They glanced at each other, and gave little, uncomfortable laughs. One by one, their eyes fell expectantly upon Will.

He squirmed uncomfortably. "Emma. There's no easy way to say this, but … we need you to dig deep into those monumental resources you have. God knows you've been through a lot. If Westen hadn't found you—"

"You'd have died, Ems," whispered Abigail. "You'd have become another of her victims."

Emma's heart sank. She knew something terrible was coming—that it wasn't over—but hoped she'd have more time. More time to come to terms with the encounter she'd had with that … thing. And her loss. Especially her loss. Her head wasn't anywhere near straight enough; she still jumped in panic at the slightest thing. My God, Ben had been bad enough, but this? This was on a different scale of horror. Every time she closed her eyes that bony hand returned. White, gleaming sickly in the moonlight, floating front-and-centre in her mind. She shuddered.

"We're on the horns of a dilemma," Will continued. "A lot's happened while you've been in hospital. We … erm … we know who the witch is, and we know why she's here." Emma felt her head move up and down, nodding on automatic. "We think you might still be in danger. We're not sure how much to tell you because you've only just come back, and you need to heal. But … thing is, I honestly don't think it can wait."

She pushed out a breath. "Hold my hand, Will. If you say I have to hear things, then go ahead. I trust you."

"Okay," he said, reaching out to her. "Abigail, can you start?"

Nodding, Abigail got straight to it. "She's related to us. To you and me, Ems. Her name is—"

"Margaret," Emma said. "I know. That is, I didn't know until you just spoke. It's as if part of her is in here." She tapped her temple lightly. "She spoke to me. Called me … *sister.*"

"That's because she's a Blackstone. Her father—Oswald—buried her. Alive."

Emma nodded. "Like the teenagers." More an observation than a question. She could do this. She could sit here without running for the hills. Of course she could …

"Yes, like the teenagers," said Gabby. "We managed to persuade Sandra to perform an exorcism and Margaret did appear—"

"She got in my head," Abigail interrupted. "Called me *sister* as well. She … did something to me, but I don't want to talk about that. What's important is, the exorcism didn't work."

"Sandra went along with it?"

"She didn't want to at first," Abigail said. "But we managed to persuade her. Try as she might, she couldn't very well deny what happened in her kitchen, could she?"

Gabby shrugged. "It didn't work because the woman's lost her faith. It's probably why she threw herself so enthusiastically into the plans for the church." She sniffed. "Overcompensating, if you ask me."

"Cut it out, Gabby," said Will, sharply. His tone surprised

everyone and made the woman jump. He turned to Emma. "There's an old door in the church's undercroft. We believe Sandra opened it when she cleared the place for the renovations to start. She obviously didn't know its significance."

"Right. Right. Sorry, I'm trying to keep track of it all. I think Robbie mentioned something about an undercroft."

Will squeezed her hand tighter. "Yes, well, the door's down there and its how we think Margaret came back. Seems she murdered the girls in the same way she'd been done away with somehow thinking them to be her sisters. We think she believes her father was after them and she wanted to save them from him. Thing is, she's stopped now, and we think it might be because of you, and possibly Abigail. Because unlike those girls, both of you are true family."

Her mind was slowly working it out. "So let me get this straight. You think Margaret was saving those kids from being buried alive, by … burying them alive?"

"Well, a lot worse happened to her, believe it or not," said Abigail. "That was why I was so poorly after the Orb incident. But, yeah, it is all a bit twisted isn't it? Being locked into behaviours she can't help but repeat," said Abigail. "I expect Westen would call her a typical psychopath, if she wasn't actually dead."

"You've been watching too much telly, Abs," said Will, rolling his eyes. "Westen would probably tell you there's no such thing as a typical psychopath."

Emma shook her head at them, impatiently. "So, if she's stopped her killing spree, then … what does she want from me. Or Abigail?"

"There's the rub," said Will. "We honestly don't know. But given her state of mind and how powerful she is, we think she's still a real danger to both of you. Belonging is a powerful attractor. It brought me back here, and it's what's keeping you in Flammark, too, Em—despite all the crap that's happened to both of us. She's clearly been attracted to you both. It's that family angle we've been talking about. It's inevitable she'll want to make contact again. We need to put her to rest before she does any more damage."

"You're going to do another exorcism, aren't you?" Emma surprised herself at how calmly she was taking all this. "When?"

His smile wavered. "We've been trying to decide. And, truth be told, I'm struggling with it. I'm not sure I'm ready."

"Of course you're ready!" Emma exclaimed. "No question."

"In your mind perhaps," Will replied. "It's been a while. I told you, God and I aren't on the best of terms."

Emma squeezed his hand, her turn to give him support. "I understand that, Will, but you said yourself, time is of the essence. If it needs to be done ... there's no one else. Sandra's obviously not up to it. Tomorrow. Do it tomorrow. I'll be there."

"No, you bloody-well won't," Will replied. "This is what we were afraid of. You're not well enough. I definitely won't go ahead with it if you decide to come. I'm flat-out serious about that."

Silence.

"He's right, Ems," said Abigail. "You know he is. Margaret's too terrifying to be confronted with again. Not after what she put you through."

"She put you through it too, didn't she? I don't know the details, but I was there to pick up the pieces after you'd connected with the Orb." She sighed and looked at Will. "But ... you're right. I'm exhausted. Perhaps it would be better if I gave an exorcism a miss."

"Good," he said. Surveying the friends, he took a huge breath and announced, "I'm doing it. I'm doing it tomorrow. It'll have to be late as I need to do some reading and prepare.

Abigail, I know you said you wanted to be there, but will you stay with Emma while it's going on?"

"Totally. It's a bit of a relief, to be honest."

Will looked at his watch. "You were right, Em. That man of yours doesn't look as if he is coming! I was sure he'd be here. It's getting really late. I'll text him and find out what's happening then maybe order a takeaway? After that it's an early night, for everyone."

He dropped Emma's hand and made for his mobile. She felt its absence in a little frisson. Nothing sexual, of course, more ... as if some kind of electrical charge had been broken.

Then her phone rang.

Westen.

Looking knowingly at the others, she took a breath before swiping the screen.

"Hi ... Yes, thanks ... A little tired ... Oh, did I cut you off? Didn't meant to, sorry ... Yes, much better. It's great to be back home ... *What ...?* Oh, no! Westen, I'm so sorry, you should have said. I feel really guilty now. Poor man ... Are you in trouble ... ? Absolutely no problem. You *have* to go. Have to. Don't worry about me, I'm being well looked after ... Yes, they're all here ... No, no there's no need, honestly, I know you must be up to the eyes in it ... No. I don't want Donna to come. I told you Abigail said she would sleep over if necessary and Will and Gabby are staying too ... That's very kind of him, but it really isn't necessary, he's better going with you, isn't he... ? Okay, well, if Pete wants to spend the night in his car for me, who am I to put him off ..." She googled her eyes at her friends. "Will it put your mind at rest ...? Okay then ... Yes. We're having a takeaway then I'll be off to bed. Yes ... yes, I promise. See you when you get back ... Love you too."

Blowing out her cheeks, she swiped her phone off to

address the sea of expectant faces. "Westen's suspect killed himself in his cell."

Everyone gasped.

"That's terrible!" Gabby exclaimed. "He was completely innocent!"

"I know," said Emma.

Will pursed his lips. "Poor, poor man. God rest his soul. Another of Margaret's victims."

"Still don't know why Westen can't at least pop in," Abigail grumbled. She looked singularly unimpressed despite the news. "Not after all you've been through!"

"As you heard, I told him not to. A death in custody is really serious and he's already under scrutiny because it's taken so long to break the case. It's his first major one since he got his promotion, remember. He's been summoned by the assistant chief constable himself, who only happens to be at a conference in London. Westen has to catch the overnight express."

"He'll be absolutely gutted not to be here for you," said Will. "You've surely got to know he'd have blown the meeting off for you, if you'd let him."

"Yes, I do know," Emma said quietly. "But that wouldn't help anyone. And he's best out of the way, considering what we ... what you have to do." She pushed out her fingers in little starbursts, trying to offset a sudden tingling sensation. "You know, I really do feel a great deal better. If I get a decent night's sleep, I may be up for tomorrow after all!"

"Absolutely not. You'd only be in the way," Will teased.

"Like his sergeant," said Gabby. "I gather he's keeping watch?"

Emma nodded. "Westen thinks my miscarriage wasn't ... spontaneous. He believes it was down to the same person who put the scratches in the door." She gave a dry laugh. "He's not exactly wrong, is he? Apparently, he'd never been a hundred percent convinced his suspect was guilty—which is another reason why he's so cut up about what he did to himself. Said he wasn't going to take any chances with me while he was away. Pete Burrows has volunteered to stand guard. Wouldn't hear of not doing it, apparently."

"Good man," said Will. "From what Westen told me, he's been a bit of a rock for him all through what happened to you, Em. Above and beyond, and all that."

"Probably won't do any harm, having someone outside," mused Abigail. "You know, in case Margaret does decide to pay us a visit!"

It was a quip but no one responded and her smile froze on her face. "I'm sorry, that was a bit stupid. She might, might she!"

Gabby's eyes flitted to Emma. "I wish you'd stayed in the hospital, dear. So much safer."

"No way," Emma returned. "No. Way. This is where I belong, and no witch is going to budge me." She smiled wanly. "Good job Pete's going to be here. He's bound to put her off!"

Just then, they heard a car draw up. Will strode to the window and found a gap in the blind. "Talk of the devil." He waved and put up a thumb. "Doesn't look as if he wants to come in. He's just held up a flask and a packet of sandwiches." He came away from the window.

"He's obviously set up for the night."

35

DISAPPEARED

"I've started to have a really bad feeling about this," whispered Abigail, her slight frame taking up only a quarter of the double bed in Emma's spare room. On the rest Gabby lay beached on top of the covers, fully clothed as they'd all agreed to be. At the ready. Just in case. "I wish we had more time. What if Margaret does come? We're not ready. Will's not ready."

"I know he isn't," Gabby murmured. "That worries me too. But … we have to trust in his resilience. He's been through a lot but he's back. That counts for something. William's strong. He always has been.Actually, he's not the one I'm worried about. I wish Westen's sergeant hadn't insisted on posting himself outside."

"Margaret wouldn't do anything to him, would she? So far everyone she's touched has at least some tenuous connection with the Blackstones."

"Honestly? I have no idea. All I know is, we've two people to look out for now. I'm going to be awake all night with worry. And not just about that. I can't get what I did with that twig-wreath out of my mind. William was right yesterday. Throwing it in the fire was a mistake. It may have released Emma from Margaret's thrall, but it put her in even more danger. I also wonder if that poor girl would've been buried in the graveyard had that connection with Emma been kept. No wonder William's angry with me."

"Will is angry full stop. He said as much. Okay, you may be the focus of it at the moment, but he can't really blame you for what happened to Emma just as he should never have blamed you—us—for what happened to Peter. No, Gabby. Whatever you did or didn't do, Margaret's the one who's responsible for all the harm, not you."

"Thank you, Abigail. Maybe I am being too hard on myself, but I still think William has good reason to be upset with me."

They fell into a brooding silence, Abigail's nervousness increasing by the second. She pushed the covers back.

"Where are you going?" whispered Gabby.

'To check on Emma. I can't settle."

She crept out of the room and into Emma's where she was relieved to hear regular, heavy breathing. Poor thing must be completely exhausted.

She edged to the window and drew aside the curtain. She saw Burrows' car, but with no light on inside it was hard to see anything of the man himself. And for some reason the streetlamp outside had gone dim. But she could just make out a shadow bathed in a faint blue light. He must be on the phone. Probably to Westen.

For the second time she wished he'd at least called in before he left. Emma needed him—adored him. But she knew things had started to get difficult. Her gaze wandered to the sleeping figure. How on earth did Emma cope with such a relationship, with the constant juggling of truth and circumstance it entailed? She certainly wouldn't be able to. If ever she was to find anyone, he would have to be someone who shared her path; understood its possibilities. Someone like Wyland. Only not as old, obviously.

Sighing, she returned to the spare room and to the faint sounds of snoring. Tch! So much for not going to go to sleep! Abigail shivered and got in next to her friend, shuffling her bum into Gabby's to win a bit of space. Honestly, the woman was a bloomin' nightmare!

She lay there for ages mulling things over. Unbelievable, how greatly Margaret had suffered at her ending. As a witch, she was utterly, utterly terrifying, but as a young girl—only a few years younger than she was now—Abigail could feel nothing but pity for her.

It relieved her to find that she could reflect on what the Orb had shown her by putting her in Margaret's shoes. In fact, her heart swelled with pride and even gratitude for what the crystal had done to mitigate the aftermath, for it had brought her father back to her. And he was still there, in the hinterland of her mind. Whenever she wanted him, calming her, soothing—

Her eyelids flew open. Had she dropped off? What time was it?

A noise!

In one seamless movement she nudged Gabby and jumped out of bed, quietly making her way into Emma's room again. Still asleep and peaceful, thank goodness. Once more, she stepped to the window. Burrows' car was still there, but this time she couldn't make out anything within. The streetlight had gone out completely and there was no faint blue light inside. No telling whether Pete was there or not.

And there was that noise again!

Gabby's shadowy figure appeared at the door. "What is it?" she whispered.

"Sh-shhh—" Drawing a finger to her lips, Abigail crept

past Gabby and stood at the head of the stairs, straining her ears.

To where Will slept on the living room sofa.

Nothing.

"I could have sworn I heard something. Twice." Abigail murmured.

Then they heard scratching.

Like nails on a blackboard.

"Ow … OW!" Suddenly, she slapped her hands tight against her ears. "She's here. Margaret's here," she hissed, trying to swallow down the pressure. "I can feel her." She looked up in panic. "She's at the front door!"

Gabby, dumbstruck, also wincing, mouthed, "William!"

Abigail barrelled down the stairs, not waking Emma the very last thing on her mind. Gabby followed. "Will, Will!" the girl shouted, slamming on the light switch. "Are you awake? Where are you?"

They faced an empty room.

"Shit," she said, squinting with pain. She put her hands over her ears. "Ow! This is really hurting!"

"Me too," yelled Gabby, "And I can hardly hear you."

Casting about the room, Abigail yelled, "*WILL!!!*"

"Here!"

She felt more than heard his voice as he ran in from the kitchen, his face screwed up in pain. He ran to the window and screamed something she couldn't make out, then made a run for the door. He grabbed one of the bolts, but Gabby held him back, furiously shaking her head and pointing to the stairs in which direction Will then ran only to collapse before he got there.

Then the noise in Abigail's head morphed.

You cannot keep me from her, sister. She belongs to me. You belong to me. I will come for you later.

Frantic now, palms pressed tight against her ears, adrenalin pumping, Abigail stared wildly at the others as Margaret piled on more pressure. Will, on his knees, seemed to be howling—torment written all over his face. Likewise Gabby. She'd tried to make it to the sofa, but only managed to squat in front of it, elbows digging into her knees, two pudgy fingers plugging both ears.

"Stop it, Margaret. Stop it!" pleaded Abigail. "We can't bear it. Stop! Please, stop! *You're hurting me. You're hurting my friends!"*

Then she too toppled, dizzy and nauseous. Crashing to the floor she threw up, the pain so intense she had neither the skill nor control to summon the Orb—or her father—to lessen the agony.

Eyes barely open, her anguish multiplied as suddenly she glimpsed Emma at the foot of the stairs. She tried calling out but had nothing. *Nothing.* Utterly immobilised, all she could do was watch her friend move like a robot towards the front door, calm as anything, hands to her sides, seemingly free of any pain or noise or inward distress.

As if her life depended upon it, Abigail screamed, "Emma! *Emma! STOP!!!"*

No response.

Like a sleepwalker, Emma drew back each of the three bolts and turned the mortice. Without a backward glance at her tortured friends, as if going for nothing more eventful than an evening stroll, she stepped over the threshold and into the freezing night.

36
COLLATERAL DAMAGE

Abigail had no idea she'd lost consciousness until she found herself on the floor barely able to open her eyes. She tried to get up, but her head thumped like a jackhammer. Breathing through the pain, she squinted round. She was at Clearview. With ...

She sat bolt upright, then immediately wished she hadn't, assailed by a dizziness almost too extreme to control.

Why was she so cold?

Hardly able to lift her eyelids against the pain in her head, she turned to where the stonking great draft was coming from. When her eyes fell on wide-open front door, everything came flooding back.

Emma had gone.

Will! Gabby? Scanning around, she caught sight of them, both prone on the carpet elbows akimbo as, slipping into unconsciousness, their hands had fallen away from their ears.

No. *No!* Fighting the nausea, she scrambled over. Will was the nearest. She grabbed his shoulder. Shook him. "Will! *Will!* Are you okay? Can you get up?"

He stirred. Groaned. Oh, thank God! She turned to Gabby

and did the same. After more pummelling they eventually came round and began the long haul to sitting up, nursing their heads as they tried to open their eyes.

"Where... What happened?" Will asked. "Ow. My head's bloody killing me."

"Mine too," grunted Gabby.

"We're at the cottage. Emma ..." She couldn't say the words. Her eyes filled with great globules of tears which splashed on Gabby as she helped her up.

Will blinked at her, tried shielding them against the harsh light of the ceiling lamp. "Where is she?"

"G-Gone."

"Gone?" At last it dawned, and despite his pain Will rocketed to the stairs. Abigail could hear him blundering first into Emma's bedroom then the spare.

His pace was much slower as he came down. Wearing an expression of utter defeat he said, "What happened?"

"I'm not sure," said Abigail. "It was Margaret, of course. We were all overcome with the noise she put in our heads. I saw both of you faint. I must have too, but not before I saw Emma leave. Honestly, she was like a zombie. Took no notice of me even though I was screaming the house down. She didn't seem to be in pain or anything. Not like we were." Ruefully, she rubbed the back of her neck. "Are."

"She immobilised us while she took Emma," said Gabby. "Sounds like she put her in some kind of thrall." Her voice edged with panic, she turned to Will. "I've no idea where she might have taken her."

"How long have we been out?" asked Abigail.

Will frowned at the clock. ""I remember hearing a noise and you both coming down the stairs. About two-ish." He slumped. "That was over four hours ago. Emma's long gone." Swallowing hard and wincing, he started for the kitchen. "I can't think straight with this bloody head. Does anyone know where Emma kept her aspirin? If I don't take something, I'm going to be sick."

"Yeah," said Abigail. "It's in a first aid kit. First cupboard on the left. Next to the ..." Her face blanched. "Oh shit, next to the flasks."

Will was the first to catch on. "Flasks—" he gasped. "Pete Burrows! Jesus, is he still out there?"

All three made for the front door and rushed into the pre-dawn light part-running, part-sliding down the icy garden path towards where the detective's SUV was still parked. Will yanked open the driver's door, activating the inside light to illuminate the pale, still form of Weston's sergeant.

"Pete! Pete! You okay, man?" Getting no response, he pressed the detective's neck, checking for a pulse.

His head lolled to one side.

"Is he alive?" wailed Gabby, who, like Abigail, was peering anxiously over Will's shoulder.

"Yes. Yes, he is, thank God. His pulse is very weak, though. Hang on, what's this—" Will moved Pete's head so the side of it faced the light. "Oh, shit! He's bleeding from his ear! Gently, he moved his head the other way. "Both ears. He needs an ambulance. *NOW*! And get me something warm to cover him with."

Abigail flew inside to find her phone. Gabby followed as best she could along the icy path. "I'll get some blankets," she cried after making it to the door.

Minutes later they were back at Pete's car. "We're not to move him under any circumstances," panted Abigail. "The dispatcher said we should keep him as warm as possible."

"Take this, William," Gabby said, handing him a duvet. Will tucked it gently but firmly around Pete.

Burrows' keys were dangling from the ignition. Once he'd finished with the duvet Will twisted round and fired up the engine. As gently as he could, he shut the door on the detective and moved around the car to the passenger side. "You two get inside the cottage. Close the door, stoke the fire. I'm staying with Pete until the ambulance arrives. The car will soon warm up."

"What about Emma?" said Abigail.

"One crisis at a time," said Gabby. "We don't know where she is or what to do. At least not yet. But this man needs us now."

"Okay."

Inside the house, they followed Will's instructions. Both frozen to the bone, they lingered in front of the fire hugging themselves as the logs caught. "I'll get us something hot to drink," said Gabby. "It's been a long night and it's nowhere near over yet."

Abigail nodded. "I'll take one out to Will. I'm going to call Donna, too. She and Pete are close."

While Gabby scurried off to the kitchen, Abigail made the call. She kept it strictly to how they'd found him. No point in raving on about witches. Who the hell would understand that? Though it was glaringly obvious to them that Burrows had encountered Margaret, it was more than possible his situation might at least be medically explicable. She could only hope.

It took fifteen minutes for the ambulance to arrive. The two women went upstairs and watched in silence from Emma's bedroom window as Will met the paramedics, gesticulating and shrugging and shaking his head as if he had no idea what had happened to the poor man. The medics opened the car's front doors and leant inside. Seconds later they upped the pace, one scurrying away to the ambulance to return with what looked like a big wide collar while the other fetched a gurney. Five minutes later, lights flashing, they sped away.

"Pete's in a bad way," Will said, as he came in and made

for the hearth. "It won't be long before one of us gets a phone call from Westen. I have no idea what to tell him about what happened to his sergeant. Or where Emma is."

"About that. I rang Donna," said Abigail. "She knew why Pete was here. I told her you were up early and went outside to see if he wanted anything and you found him collapsed in the car." She shrugged. "Seems like these days, I'm doing nothing but making up stories. Anyway, she said she'll tell Westen. And of course, she asked about Emma. I told her the hospital gave her sleeping tablets. Said we thought it best to let her sleep and not upset her until we had to."

Will regarded her miserably. "Telling a lie usually entails telling another. I think you've just managed about four." He let out an audible breath. "It won't make any difference. Westen's bound to want to talk to her. He won't be fobbed off that easily!"

Gabby hovered at the door. "Well, if Donna said she'll deal with Westen, that's enough for now. Probably best not to answer your phones. To *anyone.* He might use someone else's if he thinks you're not picking up when you see his name on your screens." She moved to the fire next to Will. "We've a bit of time. If he's in London, it'll be well into the evening before he gets back, and he'll probably go straight to the hospital if Donna's told him Emma's alright."

"Yes," said Will. "But after that, we all know where his next call's going to be. And we don't even know if Emma's ..."

"Alive?" said Gabby. She turned to Abigail. "What do you think?"

Abigail gave a quick smile, acknowledging Gabby's faith in her Sight. "She's alive, and I think she's safe, at least for now. I don't feel her with me or anything like that, it doesn't work that way. I'd know it if she was... gone, though. I don't think she's been harmed, so at least that's something."

The three hung about the living room, rag-tag and defeated.

"We need to think," said Will. "It's been a long night and it's going to be an even longer day."

One by one they sat down, tried to glean as much comfort as they could from the roaring fire. Will said, "Pete got caught in the crossfire, didn't he? Received the full blast of what we were treated to."

"I'm afraid so," Gabby replied. "Oh, I do hope he's going to be alright. I've never met him but going from what you've all said he seems a nice lad."

"Good police, as the American's say," said Abigail. "He's lovely—though a bit more than a lad. Brighter than he makes out."

"What's our next move do you think, Gabby?" Will asked.

Despite everything, a smile lit up her face.

"What?" Will quizzed. "What have I said?"

"Nothing. Nothing at all. It's just that you asked me for advice. Which means I'm on the road to forgiveness. Thank you, William."

Will gave a weak smile. "Now, come on, enough of that. Where do we go from here?"

"Well …I don't think searching the village will get us anywhere," Gabby replied. "There's not enough of us. We could try the Orb?"

Abigail's heart lurched. "Yes. Yes, if you think it would do any good."

"Would you be up to it?" asked Will. "Seems to me it's put you through enough for now."

Her eyes welled. "Emma matters more." She stirred in her seat, ready to get her things.

Will shook his head. "No. Stay where you are. We can't ask that of you again, not if you think it's too soon. Emma wouldn't want it." Almost to himself he muttered. "We're all a bit broken. We need to look after each other as much as we can."

They fell into an uneasy silence. Then Will said, "I don't know enough about how Margaret operates. I mean, is she *generally* at large?"

"To an extent," Gabby replied. "But there have been no sightings of her. Apart from Sandra's of course. She can come and go as she pleases now the Devil Door's been opened."

"But I shut it when we were in the undercroft," said Will, "and I managed to move one of the bolts. It was rusted to hell but I shifted it enough to catch."

Gabby chortled. "Oh, that wouldn't make any difference. Don't forget, though it's been opened from the inside, it still lies beneath layers of earth outside. It's not about *physical* entry or exit. We're not talking about a fully corporeal entity here. She'll have her own way of using it, shut or not."

"Her body kind of … changes," said Abigail. "It's made of leaves and stuff. But they become, I dunno, solid when she wants them to be. I think she can fall apart and come together again. Except I'm not sure how that works with her head. It looks like a proper skull, though it's got branches growing out of it." She shuddered.

"Lovely," said Will.

"Though the village will be very unfamiliar to her now," mused Gabby, "Margaret knows the terrain. She could be absolutely anywhere. She'll have taken Emma somewhere where they can be *together*. The more I think about it, the more I believe that's what Margaret wants. I don't think she means to kill her. She can't know that keeping Emma is impossible. She isn't thinking as we would."

"I agree," said Abigail. "Even after she'd … looked inside me, you know, at the church … I knew she didn't mean me any harm. Emma's really important to her. She said so when she came for her."

"She *spoke* to you?" said Will.

"Yeah." Her face clouded over.

"What?" said Gabby.

"She said she'd be coming for me too."

"That settles it," said Will, getting up. Grabbing his coat he said, "We're wasting time we don't have. Margaret may not mean to hurt either of you, but the murders tell us she isn't sane. Jesus, who would be after what she's been through? She might have very little sense of who—or *what*—she really is." He shrugged on his coat and put the collar up. "As Gabby said, we do have a bit of leeway. If she'd wanted Emma dead she'd have killed her the night of the miscarriage. So ... we're not going to look for her. She's going to come to us. It's..." he looked at his watch, "seven o'clock. Get some sleep if you can. I have some reading to do. Meet me at the church at midday. I'm going to get her to tell us where Emma is. Then I'm doing the exorcism."

37
LIMBO

A breeze. A soft, gentle breeze. Wafting over her.

As in summer.

Emma breathed it in, this unseasonable change in the weather. It wasn't right; she knew it wasn't right, but she lay there anyway, savouring it, letting it flow over her … before her brain would force her to leap into a reality she was not yet ready to confront.

She didn't have long. Couldn't sustain her denial of not being at Clearview, or in her bed, or that it was the wrong time of year. And there was a smell she couldn't quite place. Unpleasant, dissonant, acidic. Nothing for it but to open her eyes.

And in so doing hope died. There were bars right in front of her face.

Instant terror. Eyes flitting up and down, eyes side to side, eyes prying her cage, she tried to move—managed a few inches, but not much more. She opened her mouth to scream, to yell, to bring the bloody heavens down; but something, some tiny thing in the back of her mind made her close it again. For she sensed she was alone. She needed to keep it that way for as long as possible. She'd been taken by that creature and would need time to marshall all her wits. Starting with being quiet.

So Emma breathed down the panic; and shoved to the back of her mind the dread she bore at having to face the witch again.

And assessed her situation.

Not bars. At least, not iron bars. They were brown and gnarly. So … made of wood, spaced about six inches apart and criss-crossed. Within the very limited range of her vision and movement she realised she'd been put in some kind of woven capsule. Like a human-sized lobster trap. Her heart lurched.

Or a casket.

She could lift her arms—not by much—but enough to bend her elbows to grab the struts and rattle them. They wouldn't shift. Wouldn't shift a millimetre.

It seemed she was not lying completely flat. She arched her neck and back and could just discern that the cage seemed to be slightly angled against the trunk of a huge tree, its deeply ridged bark riddled with knots and furrows. It supported part of a massive, elaborately woven but open structure, completely at the mercy of the elements. It had a shape: four walls, a wide opening that seemed to serve as an entrance, and a vast open-weave canopy which allowed the beams of the sun to ripple through. And it seemed to be … decorated?!

Mobiles of twigs and dried berries, twisted branches and roots dangled down from above. Some were beaded with the skulls of tiny animals, shrews probably, all swaying or spinning in the breath of the gentle breeze. Lining the walls, dozens of carved wooden plaques hung, black with age and carefully curated. They looked down on even more artefacts that rested on the floor and out through the wide, open entrance: hundreds—*thousands*—of them, large and small; a cornucopia of sculptured woodland creatures—bird and squirrel and owl—hewn out of wood and clay, lining a wide beaten-earth path that meandered as far as her eye could see.

Margaret was an artist.

The trail was edged with banks of tree roots covered with ivy and mosses. Above, their vast gnarled trunks loomed wide and impossibly high before breaking into branch to spread their shade. It seemed a place more *under* the woods than *in* them. Secret. Subterranean.

A grotto.

Despite her desperate situation, Emma couldn't help but drink it in. So unexpected, so overwhelmingly beautiful, it took her breath away. Perhaps this was why her capsule had been angled again the tree instead of laid flat.

Did the witch want her to take in the damned view?

Thinking of her made Emma suddenly realise the path would be the way she would come, and her chest tightened at the prospect. Lovely though this place might be, she had to bloody-well get out of it.

Get out of it fast.

She set herself at the wooden bars again. Pushing, pulling —grunting—she tried all her strength to prise them apart. But the weave held. Didn't budge. It was as if it had been welded together.

She thought again of crying for help, screaming out her lungs. But she knew it to be as useless as it was risky. This place was *other*. Unreal—*surreal* even. Jesus, even the air felt different. No one would, no one *could* come to save her. Her din would only bring the witch, and she'd put that off forever if she could.

No matter how bloody creative Margaret was.

If she couldn't prise open the bars, maybe she could move

the whole thing off the tree it leant against. Maybe that might loosen something or break the cage open.

She started rocking. Sure enough, it moved! Only slightly, but it was a start. She grabbed the bars again and swung herself side to side, the capsule rocking more wildly as she gained momentum. With one last, enormous push, she felt the whole thing come away from the trunk and tumble onto the earthen floor. Her back to the entrance-way, she now faced the tree.

Nothing had changed. She was still held fast.

Issuing a throaty groan of impotent fury she beat her palms against the weave and almost silently raged. She raged against her capture, raged against the witch, raged against Westen and Will and Animus and Ben and all the fucking Blackstones.

And she raged for her baby.

For its loss.

No. No. She wouldn't go there. She was *not* going to lose it. Not after everything she'd been through—had *come* through. She wouldn't give up. *Wouldn't.*

Setting her jaw, she breathed it all down. Then, chin up, arching her back for leverage, she grasped the bars, took a gulp of air and—

And that's when Emma saw her.

Suspended from a lower branch of the supporting tree, encased within her own woven casket, the body of Sandra Davis hung. Like an exhibit.

Like a trophy.

Like a sarcophagus.

She had died in captivity, blue-grey hands encircling the wooden bars of her casket in much the same way as Emma's were now. Her milky eyes looked down on her sightlessly—accusatively—her mouth set in rictus horror that looked almost like a smile.

And she was the source of that smell. That sulphurous acidic stench Emma caught when she first came round.

Stale urine. She could see the stain on Sandra's jeans. The poor woman had ended her days in terror. And had been turned into a bauble.

It was like finding Peter all over again.

Emma puked. She threw up over and through her bars, her stomach spasming so much she thought she'd injured herself. Her arms pinned, she couldn't hold herself or wipe her nose or her mouth, so she just lay there until the lurches stopped.

She was too spent to scream. Too defeated to escape.

Caged and silent, Emma lay inert and impotent, staring back at the dead priest.

Awaiting the inevitable.

And it made her womb ache.

38
THE RIGHT EXORCIST

Twelve o'clock.

Gabby had gone ahead to the church an hour earlier to go through the order of service with Will leaving Abigail to go to the church alone. When she got there, she found the great oak door was slightly ajar, a notice pinned upon it.

Due to unforeseen circumstances there will be no services until further notice.
(Albert Reed, Church warden)

As she stepped over the threshold, Gabby emerged from the door to the undercroft. "Hope this changes soon," said Abigail, jerking her head towards the sign.

"So do I," Gabby scowled. "And I hope I don't, in your vernacular—blow it today."

"You won't."

"Won't I? I'm still upset about burning that twig-wreath. Seems I'm always blowing it. And William still hasn't forgiven me for Peter, you know. Not really."

"Maybe. But he will eventually. He couldn't do otherwise; it's not in his nature."

"I suppose you're right."

"Do we know how Pete Burrows is? I was going to ring the hospital but wasn't sure they'd tell me anything."

"Will rang Robbie. He says the sergeant has come round and is stable. He's talking, but it's not good. His eardrums were ruptured. They're not sure what caused it—working on the theory it was some kind of viral infection. Robbie says they were very badly damaged."

"Oh, poor Pete! Is he completely deaf then? Will he get his hearing back?"

Gabby shrugged. "I've no idea. I suppose we'll have to wait and see. Apparently, Westen's been in touch and is planning on taking the train back as soon as he's met with his superior, some time this morning, I think." She grimaced. "He wants Will to ring him. He can't seem to understand why everyone's ignoring his calls."

"No pressure, then," said Abigail. "Let's hope Will really is ready."

They walked through to the nave. Abigail shivered, and it wasn't just from the cold.

"It feels kind of abandoned," she said.

"Yes, it does. We'll have to do something about that—when this is all over."

The grim January light hardly made an impact but Will had come armed against it. Boxes of candles and matches rested on the rack of hymnals just inside the church. Despite everything that weighed against them, Abigail felt an overwhelming wave of relief flood in; a confidence that they were in the sensible and secure hands of someone who really knew what they were about. And something else. Something wonderfully familiar.

Incense. Will must have set some going somewhere.

They found him on his knees in the sanctuary and before the altar, his head held high as he faced the polished silver cross gleaming in the light of the two candles he'd lit either side. The scene lifted Abigail's spirits even further. And this was where the incense was coming from; a smoking thurible lay on the floor near the wall emitting clouds so thick, it made her cough.

He must have heard them come in, for he bowed his head for two seconds then stood up. Actually smiled.

He looked resplendent, literally awesome in his priestly garb, his thick mop of black hair tumbling to the edge of his red sash and plain white surplice. The sight of him suddenly made Abigail's pulse race and she felt herself blush, shocked at her own reaction to a split-second of attraction. For Will? For God's sake, get a grip! Not possible. Not appropriate. Not in any circumstances.

"You look ... good, Will, considering you've had no sleep," said Abigail, shyly.

He grinned. "Yes, well, after I left you both, I let myself into the vicarage. Crime scene or not, I needed to get to my library and hit the books. I thought Sandra might have got rid of them, but everything was as I left it. She mustn't have used the library at all. Had to nick her surplice and a stole, though I doubt she'll mind."

Abigail's eyes rested on the small white flower he'd pinned to the sash.

He noticed. "We aren't supposed to add decoration of any sort. But I don't care. Peter is going to be with me everywhere I am." He raised a stubborn chin. "End of." Turning to Gabby, he said, "I didn't know what colour stole to wear. The Church doesn't have the exorcism of witches in its calendar. I could have used white I suppose...You know, for funerals."

"Red is fine, William," said Gabby. "Margaret will rest once the Holy Spirit finds her, no matter what colour you wear." Her voice grew hesitant. "Did you … did you manage to talk to—"

"God?" Will gave a half-smile. "I did. First time in a long while. Whether he heard me is anyone's guess."

"Oh, he'll have heard you," said Gabby. "Or one of my lot —ex-lot, I should say."

"Angels *listen in?*" Abigail exclaimed, "So, there's privacy issues up there, too!" She pointed upwards, grinning. "Huh!"

Will ignored her. "Thanks for this, Gabby," he said, holding up the same book she'd given Sandra. "Current Anglican liturgy doesn't have a prayer that remotely serves our purpose."

"It's old, very old, but it'll do. God will hear it."

"If some nosy angel doesn't get there first," muttered Abigail.

Will tutted and shook his head at her. Changing the subject he said, "I put a box of candles near the door. Can you fire them up? We need more light, and I think it should be the kind of illumination Margaret will understand." He smiled, sheepishly. "It's not only that, to be honest. We could turn the lecky on, but I really don't want her to blow the fuse box."

Abigail grinned at the release of tension. Will was so good at this. *So* good!

"I'm glad you're both here," he said. "Truth be told, I'm scared to death. If this doesn't work, Emma—"

"Of course, it'll work, William," Gabby interrupted. "It has to. Besides, you're no Sandra Davis. You might have fallen out with God, but your faith is still strong. Even I can see that, even after everything that's happened."

"Peter's here, too" he said, quietly. "I can feel him. He's watching."

Gabby smiled. "Yes. I feel him too. It's what he does now."

Will took a deep breath then let out a thready sigh. "Right. I think I'm ready. Light those candles, if you wouldn't mind, then come back here."

It took a little longer than Abigail expected. For some reason her hands shook, and she struggled to strike the matches, but she got through her share and once they were all lit, she and Gabby returned to the sanctuary.

"Is there anything else you're expecting us to do?" she asked, "You know, when Margaret arrives?"

"No, I don't think so. Gabby went through what you did during Sandra's ceremony. As before, your roles are to be witnesses. If I need you to join in at any point, I'll indicate it in the liturgy. Just ... listen for it. Don't let Margaret distract you. She may have tricks up her sleeve. Oh, and I don't want you behind me. Take a position to my right. I want her to feel we are all supplicants—in it together, if you like. I want her to feel our fellowship and to trust me. From everything you've told me about her, I think it's the only way she'll ever tell us where Em is, for I do not believe this creature is beyond reason."

"Right," said Gabby. She picked up the cushions they'd left behind the altar and indicated to Abigail where she thought they should kneel. As they took their positions, Gabby gave a little chuckle. "D'you know, I think I'm actually looking forward to this. Will's decided to start with a shriving, you know."

"Come again?" said Abigail.

"Shriving? It's an old word for when a priest offers absolution for the confession of a sin. If he's to restore Margaret's soul, William thinks she'll have to be shrived first."

"Why didn't we do all this the first time?"

"I've attended thousands of services down the years, but I've never come across a liturgical expert quite like William. Prayer isn't—or shouldn't be—a fixed and static thing. It should respect tradition, for sure, but it should also respond to the moment. Sandra had no grounding in prayer. None whatsoever, as far as I could see. She was completely out of her depth, and we relied far too much on the fact of her ordination. It was nowhere near enough. My instincts weren't up to it either." She smiled. "I was built for protection, not ministry. Will, on the other hand ... well, he's an adept."

They took to their knees. "Remember, Margaret is essentially a lost soul, a soul that's been driven to madness. She will feel every minute of this exorcism. William and I talked about it. He thinks we'll only be able to banish her from this world if her soul is laid to rest properly. But she won't go easily. It will be visceral—for all of us."

Rustling.

The witch.

Heart sickening with every beat, Emma endured the all-to-familiar snapping and cracking of leaves and twigs that augured her approach. Her back to the entrance, she could see them in her mind's eye, forming and reforming, propelling the creature inexorably towards her, as it had the night it took her baby away.

Baulking at the reek of her own breath and vomit and the growing stench of rotting vegetation, Emma closed her eyes fast shut. She didn't want to see as she heard Margaret enter the space and stop between her capsule and the hanging ornament she'd made out of Sandra.

Yet she couldn't keep them shut for long. She couldn't help but face her captor. She simply had no choice.

As Emma's eyelids opened, Margaret's lower limbs ceased their churn. In a cascade of debris, they fell completely away so that it seemed that she knelt. Right in front of her.

Was she going to touch her? Was she going to stretch out that hand… ? Please God, please God, no.

She did not reach out. Oh, would that she had! Instead and much, much worse, the witch leant towards her, the gorgon head she'd seen in the moonlight now inches away, antlered with branches—top-heavy—tipping to one side as her pinlight eyes pierced her.

Then words. In her head.

You are safe with me here, sister. I will not hurt you.

A conversation? Did the bloody thing want a *conversation?*

Emma swallowed. Alright then. She could do that. She could have a chat with a monster.

She'd done that before.

"Why have you brought me here? Get me out of this … thing. Take me back. I want to go home."

Then you will be in danger. You will be forced to go back. To him.

"Who?"

Faider.

"Oswald? Oswald is dead, Margaret. He's been dead for a long, long while."

The witch's head tilted once this way, once that.

You lie. Faider is everywhere. I can feel him. I have always … felt him.

"I promise you he is gone. He cannot hurt you anymore. What you're feeling is … trauma. Men like him are monsters. They make you fear them long after they're dead."

That head-tilt again.

He will hurt my sisters. I must protect.

"By killing them? By burying them? As you were?"

The earth hid us for a while, until my spirit found me. It was gentle.

Us? *Us?* Oh, oh sweet Jesus! Despite the vomit, despite the cage, despite Sandra, a wave of compassion surged within her. "You were … *with child* when he buried you?"

The head bowed, and great globules of dark crept from the corners of her eyes.

"Oswald?" Emma cried. "The baby was Oswald's?"

The witch solidified an arm again. And with it *that*. That hand. Emma flinched. But Margaret didn't touch her. She touched herself. Where her belly must once have been.

We can never be free of him.

Christ! Was she still ... carrying it? Was it still somehow part of her? Emma had no words, none that could possibly speak to the indescribable horror of bearing a child that could never be born; not even for an eternity. So she spoke for herself.

"Please, Margaret, please. Will you let me go?"

I do not want you to trick me. As she did.

Margaret turned her pinlights on Sandra.

"Tricked you? How did she trick you?"

She released me.

Suddenly it dawned. "Because she opened the door? In the church—the undercroft?"

Margaret dipped her head again.

She gave me hope in my return. But it was not me for me she opened the door. She would betray our family. She sought only to profit. I sent her a message.

"Through her window?"

Dip.

Then she summoned me and I had to show myself. But she was an empty priest. I felt the hate in her heart. Hate for everyone. I brought her here as a punishment.

"And you killed her."

No. She died.

Emma listened. Truly listened and suddenly her fear began to subside. Not just because of a cynical realisation that perhaps she could work the witch—work Margaret. She couldn't help but recall what she'd lost before Gabby burnt the twig-wreath.

Kinship.

Despite everything, Margaret belonged to her. The bond she'd felt was filial, and she had missed it.

The priest brought to the chapel another true sister. She is … beautiful.

"Her name is Abigail. And yes, she is very beautiful."

She will be strong against faider. I feel it. As will you, now. I released your daughter so he could not have her. Now there are three of us. When A-bi-gail joins us, we will stop him forever. And I will not be alone.

Emma had no reply. What could she say? How could she answer to what this creature had been through, and for centuries! She tried to hang on to the hatred and repugnance she'd held for the witch, for all the loss and suffering she'd bestowed on her. But suddenly she found she couldn't think of her in those terms any more.

The ravaged, deluded wreck that communed with her now would forever be simply … Margaret.

But it didn't change the fact that Emma had to get out of this place—wherever this place was. She started to understand. It should be winter, but it felt like summer. The mix of trees was right for Seely Woods, but they seemed wilder—and had clearly never seen a coppicer's axe. It could be a world of Margaret's own creation, or some different dimension she couldn't even conceive. So how the hell was she to get back to her own space; her own time?

She hadn't a bloody clue, but getting out of this damned cage would be a start. She'd talked the curse out of Ben. Could she talk herself free?

"Yes. We're family aren't we? You, Abigail and I? I'm not sure how we can be together but we will work it out. I promise, promise I won't trick you. Please, just get me out of this thing."

I know you will not trick me, for I will not allow it. My work is not finished, and I cannot have you hide from me while I am away. Dangers lurk in this place. I will find our sister. Bring her to us. When we are together, you will be freed.

Suddenly Margaret's head jerked upwards, her pinlights glowing bright and angry. Emma's head filled with a static hiss which sucked the air out of her ears, making her want to pop them and swallow.

The pinlights flew back in furious regard as with a leafy surge Margaret rose to tower over. Something had angered her—Emma hadn't a clue what—and she became as witch again: full of threat, deadly and incandescent with rage.

The agony in Emma's head increased tenfold, every bone in her body screaming a futile plea for her to thrust her hands against her ears. But the cage wouldn't let her and all she could do was scream against the pain, terrified for her eardrums.

Yet despite it all the witch's words cut through.

I trusted you!

~

Margaret Blackstone, we summon thee. We summon thee before God and before these witnesses and in the sins we have committed. Join us in our confession…Almighty God, our heavenly Father, we have sinned against thee and against our fellow men, in thought and word and deed, through negligence, through weakness, through our own deliberate fault. We are truly sorry and repent of all our sins. For the sake of thy Son, Jesus Christ, forgive us all that is past; and grant that we may serve you in newness of life to the glory of thy name. Hear us, Lord, Amen.

"Amen," returned Gabby, clear, forthright—full of

certainty. Abigail, kneeling next to her, whispered the response, unsure of the word. She felt awkward saying it.

Will pushed on.

Heavenly Father, we are gathered here to pray for the soul of Margaret Blackstone.

The candles flickered. The air moved. Gabby slowly smiled.

Lost in the wilderness, deprived of thy light, she lives in darkness most terrible. We summon her, that she might confess her sins as we have confessed ours, trusting in thine infinite mercy that we may be forgiven. In the name of the Father and of the Son, Amen.

The two women responded again, Abigail a little more confidently as she took her cue from the prayer. Will paused the liturgy for a heartbeat.

This time there'd been no draft. The candles were still.

Raising his eyebrows a jot, he carried on.

Margaret Blackstone, we know thee. We name thee. We command thee in the name of the Lord our Father to come upon us now.

Suddenly, Abigail's ears felt weird. Not like the last time she was here, or yesterday when Emma had been taken. Similar, for sure, but not as extreme—she could hear through it. She saw Gabby swallowing down the pressure and Will too, was cracking his jaw and wincing. No doubt, now. The witch was definitely paying attention. Slowly, Abigail stretched out a trembling hand towards her friend, and Gabby took it in hers. It felt warm and … stalwart.

The pressure increased in the church, too, and the candles suddenly flickered. They blew out as a violent blast of air hit, their flames restoring immediately. A vastly stronger response than Sandra had received, for sure. Maybe the witch sensed Will meant business.

In the name of Our Father and of all that is holy, I command thee, Margaret Blackstone, to show thyself. Come into the light and confess thy sins.

SINSSSS!

The air had pulled into itself somehow and created ... what? ... a soundwave?

Loud it came. Clear. Echoing around the sanctuary. Not the inside voice Abigail had been treated to during the first ceremony.

And it was angry. Very angry.

She shuddered and squeezed Gabby's hand more tightly. A torrent of woodland litter spewed in, a rustling avalanche of stinking, reeking compost. Blending with the smoke from the thurible, it swirled and eddied around and around the walls, making tiny starbursts where a leaf caught a candle flame.

Abandoning his script, Will lifted his chin and in a voice much deeper and sonorous than Abigail had ever heard him use, cried, "You are reaping your own whirlwind, Margaret Blackstone, but the whirlwind of the Lord goes forth with greater fury. A continuing whirlwind, it will fall violently on the head of the wicked!"

"Oooh, Jeremiah," whispered Gabby excitedly and with considerable awe. "William's quoting Jeremiah! My boy's back!"

The vortex honed-in and closed over Will, circling above his head. But still he continued, eyes on his text, as if it wasn't there.

Heavenly Father, I repent of my sins and ask forgiveness for the opening of the door that allowed a witch to enter thy sanctuary. In thy name, I shackle the source and power of Margaret's wickedness and close all gates and exits that there be no escape from thy holy reckoning.

After his words came the sound of a door banged shut and the whirling, earthy detritus lost its momentum and floated down upon Will, sullying his white surplice and burying him knee-deep in crap.

He shook his head and swiped at his hair but didn't bat an eyelid as he continued on:

For it is only through our Father and his Son Jesus Christ, that forgiveness can be wrought, that Margaret may be brought into the light of thy—

The words seem to catch in the back of Will's throat as the stinking air looped in on itself again, the pressure far stronger this time. Then Abigail heard the sickeningly familiar brushing sound coming from the nave. She would not look, she could not look, so she fixed on Will instead.

To his credit he only stopped speaking for a few seconds as his eyes widened and his jaw dropped just a little, as, for the very first time, he beheld the witch in all her antlered glory. Furiously she ambulated into the sanctuary and came to a stop before him. Every leaf and every twig that comprised her body cycled and coursed through it, causing her figure to pulse and undulate as she stood.

It was as if she breathed rage.

Abigail's resolve not to look deserted her and she could not but help gaze. There was kind of splendour about Margaret. A magnificence. And in a weird way she felt … *close* to her in a way she had never known before. Is that what sisterhood felt like?

Whatever it was, as the witch faced her nemesis, in a flash of the Sight, Abigail suddenly understood her for the troubled entity she truly was. Gabby had called her demented, Will said she was insane but Margaret was no such thing! Vengeful, perhaps, and definitely confused by the world she now found herself in, but out of her mind?

No. No more than Will.

It was a meeting of equals, and he would have a chance with her. This was not a remake of Sandra's exorcism, but a fighting chance to reason with the creature Margaret had become so that she might give up their friend.

Margaret tilted her head in that way Abigail remembered, weighing up the priest before her, the pencil-beams of her eyes glowing a furious stark white, never leaving his face.

The air folded around them.

You call me here for this? For these words? They are nothing! You call me to talk about my sins, preacher? What of those who sinned against me? What had you to say about Faider? Where were you then?

The atmosphere felt charged. Electric.

Will raised his eyes from the little book, brown pools of calm. "I am not the preacher you think I am, Margaret. I stand before you many centuries from your time. I cannot speak for my brother in Christ then, for I was not there."

Chrisssst! Do not talk to me of your Chrisssst! He cares not for me.

"You are wrong, Margaret. He cares very much for all his children. Even you."

Margaret threw back her branchlets and made the air shriek, a long angry wail that ricocheted from wall to wall. Abigail shook herself from Gabby's grasp to slap her hands to her temples. Her friend did the same.

Will balled his fists, stretching their skin so tight his knuckles blanched. But he kept them on the altar table, his gaze unwavering.

He shouted over the din. "I too, know about suffering. We are a vicious species, Margaret. At times we prey upon each other, as your father preyed upon you."

This is what Gabby must have meant by responding to the moment. Abigail had expected the prayers—thought they'd be Latin, actually—and grand hands-on exhortations, but she hadn't for one moment thought Will would actually *talk* to Margaret.

The shrieking stopped and the creature angled her head again, as if the man before her was a problem she had to solve.

Preyed upon me. Yes, he preyed upon me. Then he buried us.

Abigail's stomach clenched. *Us?*

Omigod.

Will got it too, and his face paled as he softened his posture. He hesitated, then lifted a foot to kick away the litter and waded through the rest. He stepped down from the dais and stood before the witch. No. No. Not a witch. Abigail didn't want to call her that anymore. Margaret was a victim of the Blackstone curse as she and Emma had been. But more so. Infinitely, infinitely more so.

Facing her on one level now, Will held out his hand. A display of trust that asked for trust. "Margaret," he said. "I am truly sorry."

That tilt of the head again as she regarded it. It had been nigh on seven hundred years since she'd experienced any semblance of compassion—possibly not even then. Did she even knew what Will was offering?

But the words must have hit home because part of her torso stopped its churn and shaped itself into the hand of Abigail's nightmares.

And placed it in Will's.

He didn't flinch.

Abigail's eyes welled at the sight. At the extent of Will's courage. At the extent of Margaret's suffering.

The air leaned into itself again.

It is important he does this to no other child.

"He cannot, Margaret. Oswald is dead. He died a long, long time ago."

I protected them.

"By killing them, as you were killed? No, Margaret, you weren't protecting them. They were innocents as their parents were innocents. You are the cause of great terror and harm to our village."

The air fell silent as she turned her pinlights—ultimately lifeless—first on Gabby, then on Abigail.

We are sisters.

The girl held her breath. Nodded.

I have made our other sister suffer.

Abigail did not know whether this was a question or an observation. Margaret dipped her head anyway.

I am wicked.

No," said Will. She turned back to face him. "What you did was wicked. But you can atone."

How?

"Tell us where Emma is. Tell us where your sister is."

Then I will be alone.

"You can never be alone, Margaret. God will be with you."

As he was when I died? As he has been, since then?

Abigail nearly cried out at the timbre the air had taken on. The cavernous black sockets which housed those febrile, dead eyes, seemed not so much horrific, now, as sad. Mournful. Desperately, desperately mournful.

Will must have felt it too, for with his other hand he sought the place where Peter's flower rested. Had he not told them that he too thought his God had deserted him?

"Where is she, Margaret?" murmured Will. "Where is Emma?"

I don't want to be alone.

"Bearing the sin of what you have committed makes you alone, Margaret, no matter who is with you."

Faider is not alone.

"Your father will have reaped his own whirlwind. You are my concern and only you. Let me help you find peace."

How?

"Tell me where your sister is."

I know what I am. I know what I've become. I'm an … abomination.

"No, Margaret. You are a child. A child who has been very, very wronged."

Pray for me, preacher? Let me confess?

Will seemed to freeze a moment, then gave back her hand. Breaking what had been an unflinching gaze at her, he turned—agonised—to the women. "I have to do this. I *have* to accept her confession. She has asked me to."

Abigail cried out—she couldn't help it. "Wait! Won't that mean she'll be forgiven? And won't *that* mean she can leave? *Go?* You, can't do it, Will! Not until she tells us where Emma is."

"He has to, child," murmured Gabby, calming her. "William cannot refuse."

For a moment it looked as if Will was about to ask Margaret one more time to give up Emma's whereabouts, but the words never came; she had solidified another bone-thin arm and in a gesture that surely must break all their hearts, brought both her skeletal hands together.

In prayer.

What else could Will do but walk back to his place behind the altar? About to resume his declamatory stance, he hesitated, finally saying the words they all wanted to hear. "Margaret, we *will* hear your confession, but you must agree to tell us where you have taken our friend. Do you agree?"

She bowed her head.

But would she? Could they trust her?

With an almost imperceptible shrug, Will slowly blew out his cheeks and raised his hands, palms to the ceiling, and restarted the prayer of Confession.

For if there was glory in the ministry of condemnation, the ministry of righteousness must far exceed it in glory. Margaret Blackstone, do you confess your sins?

The air bent.

I confess my sins.

- Do you repent of your sins?

I repent of my sins.

- Do you renounce evil?

I renounce evil.

- I am the door: by me if any man enter in, he shall be saved, and shall go in and out, and find pasture. Margaret Blackstone, I command thee in the name of our Lord Jesus Christ that all thy sins be forgiven and that all thy father's sins will be forgiven.

Lord God, cleanse this soul of its wrongdoings, break its ties with the hidden realm and release its hold on this thy servant.

He slumped slightly. Eyes conflicted, he threw his friends a silent apology before uttering the word that, for good or ill, would seal Emma's fate forever.

- Amen.

"Amen," Gabby responded.

Abigail said nothing. She couldn't process it. Couldn't come to terms with the horror of Margaret, the horror she'd been through ... and the horror that they might lose Emma.

But Will waited. Simply ... waited. She knew he wouldn't continue the liturgy until she had agreed. No choice, then.

"Amen," she mumbled.

What had they just done? What if Margaret wouldn't tell them where Emma was? Would they ever be able to find her? Could they forgive themselves if she was lost? She certainly wouldn't, no. Not ever.

As Will finished his closing prayer, the atmosphere folded in a long, long sigh that whispered and echoed around them.

Then Margaret collapsed.

Her body suddenly losing all integrity, fell apart in a cascade of leaves and twigs and fragments that scattered everywhere about the stone floor. Left with no means of support, her antlered skull also fell to the ground, its thin, chalky skin parting and curling...

... before the whole thing turned to dust.

39
WHAT NOW?

"Nooooo!" screamed Abigail, rooted to the spot she knelt on.

Gabby gaped as Margaret disintegrated. She turned to Will in disbelief. "I thought you had her, William. I was sure she would tell us where she'd taken Emma!"

Surrounded by all that was left of their witch, Will stood transfixed, his arms still raised. Then, as the shock of it all receded, he brought them down and slumped, visibly defeated. Devastated. "I had no choice but to save her. As a priest, I can't turn down any soul that asks for confession. Even if it meant losing Emma... I thought Margaret genuinely repented and would honour our agreement."

Abigail suddenly realised the toll this was going to take on him. Losing Peter and now Emma—how the hell was he going to cope? How were they all going to cope?

"I ... I have to call Westen. Now," he said. "Tell him she's missing and hope to God his team can find her."

"They won't, William. I'm sure of it," Gabby said, unhelpfully. "Margaret's been ahead of us every step of the way. She could be anywhere. Worse still, she could be nowhere."

It was Abigail who voiced their worst fears. "The Devil's Door. It doesn't lead to anywhere in our world, does it?"

No one answered.

No one wanted to move, either. It seemed a sacrilege to walk over Margaret's remains, no matter how thoroughly she'd screwed them.

"You had no choice, William," said Gabby. "Even if you'd known she wouldn't tell us where Emma was, you'd still have had to go ahead."

Will didn't reply. Eventually, he straightened. He unpinned the flower on his priest's stole which he tore off together with his surplice, flinging them at the floor.

"Have we really lost her?" whispered Abigail at Gabby, getting off her knees. "Lost Emma?"

Gabby was trying to clamber to her feet, too. "Give me your hand Abigail. My mortal joints don't seem to want to cooperate."

Abigail held both of her elbows and helped her up to stand with her, both aghast at the detritus that lay everywhere. Only then did she reply.

"It's a catastrophe, Abigail. A complete catastrophe."

The suddenly, Gabby cocked her head. Leaving the girl's side, she picked her way around the litter careful not to disturb the tiniest piece of it. Abigail assumed she was making for the door and began to follow, but Gabby stuck out her hand. "No. Wait there. Don't move."

Having tip-toed to the altar dais, Gabby stepped up to join Will who was busy pinning Peter's flower onto his shirt. As she surveyed the scene from this different viewpoint, a quivering smile began to form at the edges of her lips. She dug Will in the ribs with her elbow.

"Ow. *Ow*," Will cried, rubbing his ribs. "What the—"

"Look. Look, William!" She gestured around the floor and

then to Abigail. "You come too, child, but be careful. Don't tread on anything."

Abigail did as she asked, making elegant jumps from gap to gap whenever she found one.

"What do you see?" said Gabby. "Squint your eyes a bit. Jiggle them."

Then Will gasped. "Oh. Oh, my living Lord!"

It took Abigail a while longer before it all came together. Then her heart took a sudden leap. Margaret Blackstone had kept her promise.

"Oh!!!" Abigail cried, too. "It's a map! A map of Seely Woods! See ... That's Wither Road skirting it." Eye's dancing, she scanned the schematic all over, then stopped and leant forward, peering at a particular spot.

"There! See? Something's glinting. I can't make it out, it's not like the rest of this stuff." Excitedly, she turned to the others. "It's the witch's circle. She made herself into this map and marked the place where she took Emma!!" She spun back, peering at the spot in wonder. "Of course! It all makes sense. Emma's at the circle!"

"I'm not even going to ask you what you're on about, Abs," said Will. "No one told me about any such thing. But if you say it's there and the map points to it—and you think it's significant—then that's good enough for me." Eyes suddenly shining, his expression the epitome of relief, he cried, "Let's go. Let's go, *now*. You can fill me in on the way!"

Will and Abigail made for the door, but not in a straight line. Despite the urgency, they trod carefully, edging around Margaret's remains before speeding down the nave.

Gabby held back for some reason, but soon caught up, legging it through the chancel as best as her mortal joints would allow. Will grabbed his coat and led the way through the door, not even bothering to lock up. Once into his old Beetle, he fired up the engine.

It gave a sickening whirr and then fell quiet. "No. No. Don't you bloody-well dare," he said as he yanked the ignition for a second time. The engine sparked into life, and after a collective sigh of relief they headed out to Wither Road, getting there in record time. Abigail, nose glued to the window, watched out for the entrance.

"There! It's there," she pointed. "On the left."

"Is it wide enough for a car to get down?"

"Maybe," she replied. "Yes, I think so. At least for some of the way. And it doesn't look like there's any police, thank God."

"There wouldn't be. Westen has, sorry … *had* a suspect in custody. I expect he thought they'd got their man after the murders stopped."

He slowed as spotted the gap, but he overshot; the angle was too tight. "Damn," he cried. "Hang on." He parked for a few seconds to wait for a gap in the traffic so he could reverse before trying again.

Fifty yards in, the trees thickened. Another fifty and the path forked into three, each winding their way further into the woods.

"That's it," he said, bringing the car to a stop. "This is as far as we can go."

They climbed out. Abigail took a second to get her bearings than started down the left-hand path.

"Are you sure this is right?" said Gabby. "From here it looks like it loops round. Doesn't this take us back to where we came from?"

"Of course I'm sure," the girl snapped. "Come on, let's get on. It's really windy. Emma will be freezing!"

They reached the clearing. "This is it!" exclaimed Abigail. "Look, there's the circle!"

The faces of the others suddenly suffused with wonder as they caught sight of it for the first time, but there was no time to waste. They split up, calling and shouting and scouting around. Emma didn't reply.

"She's not here," cried Abigail, hardly able to bear the disappointment as they came together before the weave.

Gabby walked around it, tentatively touching it then pushing and prodding. "I think there's a possibility that she *is* here ... but at the same time I'm wondering that maybe she ... isn't."

Will rolled his eyes. "Schrödinger, Gabby? Seriously, *now?*"

"Don't be silly, William. The man was an absolute horror, what with everything he did to those poor children. And I was never convinced by his silly theories. No. The Devil's Door isn't the only portal we're dealing with. I think this is one, too."

"Right," said Will. "I've had enough of pussyfooting. If this is a portal, I'm bloody well going to use it." And with that he leapt through the middle.

Only to land in plain sight at the other side.

"Damn," said Abigail. She frowned; started feeling around the circle as Gabby had just done, pressing random twigs or woody knots as if she might come upon some kind of open sesame. "Aaagh! If this is a portal, why on earth did Margaret make it in the first place? Don't you Christians believe in purgatory? If that's where she ended up, why would she construct something that would only take her back there?"

"Haven't a clue," said Will. "But her map was clear. She did what she promised. If she told us Emma was here, then she must be. So, I think Gabby's right, though that in itself doesn't take us any further forward. It's going to be more complicated than simply walking through it. Any random dogwalker could do the same!"

"I'm surprised she left it so unprotected." said Abigail.

"I am, too," Gabby replied. "Maybe it isn't. Maybe she put

a glamour on it so that anyone who comes across it doesn't really notice it, if you see what I mean."

"The police did. That's why Westen asked me and Emma to come with him to see what it was."

"Yes," said Gabby. "Interesting, that. I don't know, then." Then a thought struck. "What if she was *using* it when the police found it? The glamour—if it was one—wouldn't work then, And, of course, once seen it couldn't be unseen. A glamour is the slightest of illusions. It wouldn't fool anyone with the Sight. You, Abigail. Emma too, possibly. Thing is—"

"Too much blathering and not enough thinking," Will exclaimed. "Come *on*, how do we use it? Is there some kind of ... I dunno, key? Doorways need keys, right?"

Abigail nodded, the idea growing on her. "Yeah. Yeah, they do. But whatever it is, Margaret..." Her eyes widened with excitement as she worked it out. "would have it on her! Oh! It's that thing I saw glinting on the map! It marked the spot!" She grabbed at Will. "We've got to go back. Got to go and get it. It's the key!"

"Erm. No need," said Gabby, digging into her pocket to take out the shiny object Abigail was talking about. "Something told me we might need it, so I picked it up on my way out. And guess what ..."

She held it up. A matt black pendant in a fancy setting, blowing in the wind as it dangled from its glittering gold chain.

Abigail took in a breath as she touched it. Wondered at the relief inside. A tiny blackbird! "It can't be. It *can't*! It's Emma's pendant!"

"No, it isn't," Gabby replied. "As I keep on saying, that's long gone. I promise you. There must have been more than one made. Margaret left it on the map not only to mark where Emma is but—"

"To work the portal," said Will. He shook his head. "You

should have told us about it straight away, Gabby. We've wasted time."

Gabby's smiled faded on her lips as he snatched away the chain. He put it over his wrist and wound it round his watch, tucking the pendant beneath its base. "Okay, how are we going to do this?"

"We should make a line and hold hands," Gabby said, chastened by Will's tone. "You lead us through, William but no one let go. We don't want to get stuck."

Will held out his hand to Abigail. Lean, strong. Capable. Hesitantly—shyly—Abigail took it, and instantly felt a frisson; a tiny charge of energy. That weird attraction again. She knew she was heading for the embarrassment of a lifetime but now was not the time to think about it. She held out her own hand to Gabby.

"When we get to the other side," Gabby said, "we must stay close to each other—and don't lose the pendant, William. We've no idea what's waiting for us when we step through, and it could be terrible. Without it, we'll be trapped there for the rest of our lives. There'll be no coming back."

Will looked at her, nodding his reply. "Are we ready?" he asked.

"No," they replied.

~

The frequency of the world changed.

Once through the circle, the three friends couldn't help but stand and gape—and feel—gripping each other tight after transitioning the portal.

It wasn't cold anymore; summer warmth pervaded the atmosphere and Abigail couldn't help but drink-in its purity in huge, great breaths. Looking at the others she found they were doing the same.

The path beneath her feet lay verdant with green and gold mosses, giant trees in full leaf massed on either side, their arched branches swaying sky high in the gentlest of breezes.

Awestruck, Will exclaimed, "It's ... it's absolutely not what I expected. It's ... it's wonderful! And a bit alien, I suppose. Like a landscape painted by an old master."

"We're still in Seely Woods," said Abigail, slowly spinning around. "I'm sure of it. But maybe in Margaret's time. A time she never left." She sighed. "On her own for seven hundred years. *Seven. Hundred. Years*. It's ... inconceivable."

"Yes, it is," Will replied. "And beautiful though this place is, I bet she felt every minute. Look what it turned her into. She'd have been desperate to leave!"

His face clouded over.

"What is it, William?" asked Gabby.

"The circle was her portal into our world. She could have returned here after her repentance."

"So?" said Abigail.

"So ... she chose to die instead. It ... it's desperately sad. I know she killed all those poor children but, I can't help but feel sorry for her." He blew out his cheeks and shook his head in the wonder of it all. Then he collected himself and briskly took off his jacket. "Emma! Emma!" he yelled. "Call out, we're here! We're coming for you!"

The two women shuffled out of their heavy coats too and followed suit, screaming and shouting until they were hoarse, following the path for what must have been at least twenty minutes.

"How far does this go?" Abigail said as they paused to take stock. "If this place mirrors ours, she could be as far as Sandmarsh—or Witherington."

"I don't think so," said Gabby. "Remember, witches are tethered to their territory. Even here, I doubt she would have been able to wander far beyond the bounds of the parish."

"Emma could still be almost anywhere!" Abigail replied, looking at the vast landscape ahead. "Did Margaret leave any further clues for us?"

"No, only the pendant," Gabby replied. "But she didn't leave us that for nothing. She said she would tell us where she'd hidden Emma and she did. If it had been any more complicated than sticking to this path, she'd have told us. Keep the faith, dear."

"Are there others here?" said Abigail. "You know, like Margaret? Witches ... Spirits?"

Gabby shook her head. "I doubt it. I think this is a void of her own conjuring, with a population of precisely one. I told you she was a powerful witch. Though, ultimately, she might not have had total control over her creation. Emulating her world would have entailed the inclusion of some of the creatures in it, and a wild fox or boar can turn into something really nasty when given seven hundred years to evolve."

"Oh, oh!" cried Abigail, suddenly excited. "It's an alternative universe!"

Gabby rolled her eyes and tutted. "Best not to get into all that. It's hard enough to keep track of our universe, let alone—"

"Shh," said Will, putting out an arm. "Did you hear that?"

He called out again. Back came a faint cry.

They picked up the pace, shouting louder and more frequently.

"Here!" they heard. "I'm here!"

"It's Emma!" Will yelled.

They broke into a run, calling and listening, until the path broke and they turned into the sudden shade of a grove whose beauty surpassed everything they'd seen on their journey so far. And there were signs of civilised life. Hundreds upon hundreds of carvings and sculptures lined the trail surprising all of them.

But there was no time to linger. "Look!" shouted Abigail. "Under that tree. Emma's got to be in there!"

Right at the end of the grove attached to the wide trunk of an enormous oak, stood a massive open structure, weirdly woven into the rough shape of a house. There were four walls and even a porticoed entrance. Though no door. A wondrous thing, Abigail thought, as she ran up to it with the others. Wondrous and moving. A piteous attempt to replicate the style of part of a life once remembered.

They rushed inside.

"Oh, thank, thank you, thank you, God," said Will, spotting Emma's capsule straight away. Crying, laughing then crying again she'd managed to poke a hand through one of the gaps in her cage. He knelt down and grabbed it. "It's alright, Em, it's all going to be alright." He glanced up and down the cage. "What the hell did she put you in? Are you okay? Are you hurt?"

"No. I'm okay, just so, so relieved to see you! I'm not in any pain, just ... oh, get me out, Will. Just get me out."

Gabby and Abigail looked on, grins all over their faces. But they were soon wiped off. Gabby gripped Will's shoulder.

"William, look."

He glanced to where Gabby pointed.

"I know. Sandra," said Emma. "Margaret ..." She couldn't finish. Her body started to convulse and great, choking sobs overcame her.

Will tore his eyes away from Sandra's gaping stare and angrily set about prising open the weave of Emma's prison. "Bloody thing. How the hell did she make it this strong? It's only made of sticks! Oh, and you've been sick. Emma I'm so sorry."

"She said she was going to let me go, Sh-she wanted to get you, too, Abigail. Then we would s-spend the rest of eternity here together, p-playing happy families."

Gabby sighed as she too joined Will's efforts to open the cage. "I'm not sure that would have worked. I don't think simply being here would make you both mortal. You'd have had to—"

"Shut up, Gabby!" Will was getting near to the end of his tether trying to gain more traction on the weave. Gabby flushed and went quiet.

Abigail tried to rescue the situation. "I think I saw something move. On the side."

Will saw what she was getting at: a thick seam of twigs and whips ran down the edge of the casket, containing a series of woven-in pins that closed it. After finding the knack to take out the first, it took no more than a minute to liberate the rest and for Will to hold out his hand to Emma.

"Thank God for that," she cried, clinging onto him as he hauled her up.

"It's okay, Em. It's okay. You're safe now. We've got you."

They stood like that for a minute or so. It was a reunion no one was in a hurry to break up. Then suddenly, Will gave a loud, deliberate sniff. "Come on, you. We need to get you home. You need a shower!"

The comment did the trick. A tiny laugh broke through her tears as she drew away.

Suddenly, she winced. "Abigail, I need the loo. Can you help me outside?"

"Of course I will! We obviously came in the nick of time."

"Don't be too long," said Will. "I'm a bit nervous about staying here. Now Margaret's no longer with us—"

"She's *what*?" exclaimed Emma, as she arched her stiff back ready to hobble outside. "Margaret's *gone*?"

"Yes," Gabby said. "William went through with the exorcism. Well, it turned out to be more of a confession, really. Simply put, he laid her soul to rest. Then she showed us where you were and that we had to come through the witch's circle."

"She told you all this *after* she passed?" said Emma.

"It's complicated, Em," said Will. "We'll explain everything later, but getting to the nub of it, now she's truly dead, I'm not sure what might happen to her world. Things could go awry any minute."

"That's my thinking, too," said Gabby. "And any glamour she might have placed on the circle will be gone too!"

"Jesus, Gabby, why didn't you say so earlier?"

"I-I was going to. But you said we were blathering too much and then I forgot."

Will's face reddened with fury. "You *forgot?*" Had Abigail not known him better, she thought Will dangerously close to losing it altogether. Then he closed his eyes; breathed, as if some kind of technique was at play. A few moments later he opened them again. As if to himself—and without looking at Gabby—he said, "Never mind. Emma, go and do … whatever you need to do outside. I'll get poor Sandra down. We're going to have to take her with us. I won't leave her here. It isn't right. It's not where she belongs."

On their return, it became clear Will had had to suspend hostilities with Gabby for both of them were still trying to unhook Sandra's cage. It took even longer to get her out of it. All of them knelt and gathered round, trying to release the locking pins since the weight of Sandra's body had deformed the weave. They eventually managed it but then came the really hard part. Lifting her out.

"How long has she been here?" said Will screwing up his nose as he placed her gently down. "It's a lot warmer here than back home. She's starting to decompose."

"She was here when I woke up," said Emma, "but I don't really know. If she's started to smell it will be about three or four days. Don't tell me how I know. I must have picked it up from Robbie. Or Westen."

"That means her abduction happened soon after we got her home from her exorcism, then," said Gabby, "Albert didn't say anything about her going missing, which isn't like him at all. I'll call on him when we get back. See what I can piece together."

"I expect Margaret did to her what she did to Emma," said Abigail. "Got in her head and put her in a trance."

"*That's* how I got here?" cried Emma.

"Yep. Proper zombie you were! I saw you leave the cottage, but she wouldn't let me move. Margaret turned up the volume on that din of hers and minutes later we were all passed out."

Everyone ready for evacuation, Will took a moment to gaze around the witch's lair for the first—and last—time, sombrely taking in the artefacts she'd surrounded herself with. "Poor, Margaret. There are so many, many beautiful things here. Even so, not enough to fill seven hundred years."

"What are we going tom say?" Abigail pondered. "When we get back. How are we going to explain Sandra?"

"Well, no one's going to believe we found her inside a witch's circle, that's for sure," said Will. "More to the point, we can't take her through straight away. There's no room in the Beetle for a body and I'm sure as hell not going to stuff the poor woman in the boot!"

"We'll take her as far as the entrance," said Gabby. "If that's alright with you William? Then you and I can come back for her. She'll be safe there. The circle's been up for weeks, I think it'll stand for another few hours till we can get her back."

"That's a plan, I suppose," said Will. "It also gives us time to decide how we explain what happened to her."

Will screwed up his nose again and crouched to heave the

dead woman over his shoulder. Abigail hadn't realised how strong he was until now. She found herself smiling at him.

Oh, stop it. *Stop* it! What the hell was wrong with her!

They set off. Abigail lent an arm to Emma, who still hadn't found her legs properly yet. She wondered at her friend's forbearance; her capacity for dealing with catastrophe. Not a day had she spent at home after coming out of heavy sedation—and that after a witch made her miscarry. Add Animus and then *Ben* to the mix… !

With Emma leaning on her more and more heavily, and Sandra's dead weight making Will grunt with practically every step, the return journey took way longer. By the time they reached the circle all four of them were drooping with exhaustion.

Emma and Abigail plopped themselves down on a nearby bank and Gabby joined them. With a groan of relief, Will gently laid down Sandra's body and arched the stiffness out of his back.

"We should have used one of the caskets, William," said Gabby. "I'm sorry I didn't think about it earlier. Two of us could have carried her and it would have lightened your load."

"Yeah, maybe. I had thought about it but is seemed wrong, somehow. All the things she made … they're all together now in that house of hers. Seemed more, I dunno, fitting." He turned to the others. "Catch your breaths, everyone, but let's not take too long. If Gabby was right about this glamour thing, the circle's in full view of any casual passer-by. It makes us vulnerable. It's freezing on the other side and I doubt there'll be many about. But you never know."

"Do we just … go through? Like we did on the other side?" said Abigail.

Gabby shrugged. "I suppose so." With a sudden urgency, said, "Tell me you've still got the pendant, William!"

He lifted up his wrist and flashed them his watch with the chain still wrapped around it.

"What pendant?" asked Emma from the bank.

They froze.

"Oh, Lord," muttered Will, whipping his hand in his pocket, wincing at his blunder. "Em, I need you to trust me on this. Can I tell you once we've got you home? I think you'll need some time to process it."

Emma held his eyes for a moment before giving a weary nod. "More crap?"

"I'm afraid so, yes. More crap."

Despite the urgency, they lingered just a little longer. It was almost as if they were reluctant to leave. The beauty, the *verdancy* of Margaret's world had captivated them—though perhaps not Emma. It gave Abigail a great deal of comfort to realise that Margaret's purgatory had not been as hellish as she'd imagined; she'd visions of it being full of fire and, for some reason, tons of doors to choose from. Hellish enough, though, to be stuck here through the centuries without any hope of leaving. As Will said, Margaret had preferred to die rather than come back. Or maybe she just couldn't live with the fact she'd killed all those girls.

Breather over, they clambered up. Emma stepped up to the circle first. "Strange to think we're on the other side of this," she said. "I hope one day I'll be able to come to terms with Margaret. With what she did to those girls and what she did to me."

Abigail went up to her and gave her a hug. "You will. But it'll take time, Ems"

Will too wasn't quite ready to leave. He was leaning over Sandra's body. He hadn't been able to close her tortured, milky-glazed eyes, but he moved her jaw so that she looked a bit more peaceful. With his finger he drew a cross on her forehead and muttered a prayer. He found his coat and placed it over her.

"I won't be gone long," he said to her. "I promise." He turned to the others. "Okay, I'm ready. But once we've got Emma settled back at the cottage, I'm coming back. Sandra isn't staying here a minute longer than necessary."

The others nodded their agreement.

"Please can we go now?" said Emma. "I thought we were all supposed to be in a hurry!"

They lined up before the giant weave and held hands, then one-by-one stepped through the circle.

Witnessing their entrance back to their own dimension—holding an axe—stood a lone, dark figure. Dishevelled. Stooped.

Pete Burrows.

40
IT'S NOT OVER 'TILL IT'S OVER

He was standing about twenty feet away from where they'd emerged. "I had an idea you lot might turn up," Burrows said, loudly—almost shouting. "What does the Guv call you all?" His words came out like a sneer. "The Scooby Gang?"

Emma stared aghast at the detective—and the axe. "Pete?" she asked, a bewildered half-smile playing on her face. "W-what are you doing here?" She looked past him and around. "Is … is Westen with you?"

Abigail, squeezing her arm, said quietly, "Pete was in the car last night, guarding the house, remember? When Margaret came? None of us could move because of the sonic stuff she did. You weren't affected 'cos you were in your trance thing, but …"

Emma spun back to Pete who was glaring at them all with murder in his eyes. Almost shouting he said, "I can hardly hear a bloody thing," he exclaimed. "Doctors said I've burst both eardrums. They don't know if I'll ever get back to normal."

"Pete—" Will said. Then shouted. "Pete, you should be in the hospital. I'm surprised they discharged you."

"They didn't. I came-to in the night. Couldn't sleep. Couldn't come to terms with," his voice hardened, "... with what I saw."

"You saw!" exclaimed Gabby. "What did you see?"

Pete's lips curled, and he tightened his grip on the axe. "Don't you patronise me. You're this Gabby woman, right? The Guv has a lot to say about you. About how you lead Emma on, making her hide things from him." Suddenly his face screwed up and he cried out; tried to rub his ear against his shoulder while still gripping the axe. The pain must have been excruciating. "I don't know what the bloody hell I saw, but I know it wasn't anything from this world."

"But ... how did you know to come here?" asked Abigail.

"When that fucking bedlam started in my ears last night, I turned my lights on. Full beam. There it was—some ... *thing* —coming hell for leather at the cottage." He shuddered. "I clocked the way it moved, its face. The crap on top of its head reminded me of that thing you just came out of. Something about it spooked the Guv, too. The more I thought about it, the more it made a weird kind of sense." He stopped. Took a breath. "I'm not wrong, am I?"

"Give me the axe, Pete," said Emma, taking a halting step forward. "You can barely stand."

"I'll live. But that thing's going. I'm smashing it."

"No!" said Emma. "You can't ... there's—"

"There's what?" Burrows said.

She couldn't reply.

His lips curled again. "The Guv always said you kept stuff from him. That you knew more than you let on. And all four of you always in the middle of everything that goes down in Flammark."

"No Pete, you're wrong," Emma said. She glanced at Will

and inwardly winced at the desperation on his face, knowing full well that if Burrows got past them and did anything to the circle, Sandra's body would be lost to them forever.

Pete tightened his grip on the axe. Stepped forward.

Will put an arm out and took a step back, instinctively guarding the circle.

"I might not be up to much," Burrows jeered, "but I can still easily take you, Turner. Get out of my way."

"You can't take all of us, though, can you?" Abigail intervened, coming to Will's side. Gabby followed. Emma, heart filled with dread and exhaustion, reluctantly followed suit.

Burrows wavered. Tried another tack.

"So ... what's in there? What will I find if step through?"

The friends exchanged glances knowing full well what he would find. They couldn't let him pass. *Couldn't!"*

"Let me drive you back to the hospital." Will called. "Abigail, can you sort out a taxi? I'll meet you all back at Clearview." Burrows swayed slightly, the pain obviously taking its toll. "Seriously, Pete, you're in a terrible state. Let's go."

Burrows stared at him. Shut his eyes then opened them again, as if clearing fuzz from his brain. He lowered the axe and swayed some more, then seemingly defeated, started to back off.

Emma let out a long, breath as he made for the path out of the clearing. Throwing each other relieved glances, the friends left their positions and began following. At the edge of the clearing Burrows suddenly stiffened. He turned to face them once more.

"I want it. I want to see what's on the other side."

Variously, all four returned, "No! ... Not a good idea! ... Don't! ... Pete, give it up!"

"It's not as if I'll be able to tell the Guv, is it, now? He'll think I've gone bonkers." He winced and scrunched up his face again, lifting his other shoulder to his ear. "It's why you kept things from him, Emma. This bloody village ... it's full of woo shit, isn't it?"

"Not going to lie to you, Pete," said Emma. "Yes. And yes, we've been involved. I'm glad you understand why Westen had to be kept out of it."

"Oh, I do. It'd bloody finish him. Take the floor out from under him." The detective started on his way again. "Okay. You win."

They'd just relaxed into following him once more when Pete suddenly spun round and flung the axe at Will who, by a miracle dodged it. But he recovered too late to prevent Pete from swerving round the others and running to the circle.

They all gave chase except for Emma, who was still too wobbly to run. But Pete's surprise move gave him the advantage and he reached the weave before anyone could stop him. He was already pulling apart one of its struts. By the time they'd caught up to him he'd managed to collapse most of one side and was setting about the other. Will grabbed Pete's arm, but not in time to save the second strut.

The top arch toppled. The circle broke.

Will slumped as parts of the weave swayed and fell. No point in holding him, he let Pete go. But the man was so fragile—everything he had, spent on this act of destruction—he nearly fell over, so Will clung on to him again, and put his other arm around his shoulder to prop him up. But Pete would have none of it. He shrugged him off and broke away.

"Look!" he sneered as he staggered over the bottom lip of the wrecked structure. He turned and held up a hand. Waved. "Can you see me?" Even though it wasn't how the circle worked, his point wasn't lost on them. "You can, can't you? Whatever was on the other side, it's gone."

Emma saw the way Will stared at the man. She'd seen

that look before. The loss of the circle meant that Sandra was lost, and there was no way he could get her back.

And Pete. In his own way, he was lost too.

She stepped over the broken twigs. Taking one of his hands, she drew him towards her and this time he let himself be embraced. "It's alright. It's alright. I've got you."

The detective put his head on her shoulder and … wept. Shock, trauma; it was all there, in every sob.

When the worst of it was over, she said, "Come on, Pete. Let's get you back to the hospital."

41
CIRCULARITY

It was nine o'clock that evening before Westen knocked on Emma's door. Interesting that he'd decided not to use his key.

When she opened up, his expression told her all she needed to know about the day he'd had—or, to be more accurate, the two days he'd had. Haggard didn't cut it. Simply put, Westen looked destroyed.

And she knew she was going to destroy him some more.

She smiled awkwardly and stepped back, letting the door hang open so he could follow her in. His face fell. He must have been expecting at least a hug—and he had every right to—but she couldn't give him one. It felt … dishonest.

"At last!" she said. "I'll get you a drink. A proper one. You look as if you need it."

They stepped through into the kitchen. Emma reached into a cupboard for the whisky bottle. She poured some in a tumbler, then thought twice and poured a little more. "How's Pete?"

He didn't answer straight away. Just regarded her evenly. He took the glass, started to raise it, then put it down again.

"Fucking terrible, is how Pete is. But I'm not here for him. What's going on, Emma? I thought I'd receive a welcome at least a bit warmer than I've had so far."

"You tell me. You weren't there when I woke up in the hospital and you haven't been anywhere near. I understand you've been up against it, still..."

"I know. I know, and I'm sorry. I told you what happened to my suspect. But ... I *was* there, at the hospital. All the time. After I found you I never left your side, except when Mason forced the issue and told me to get some sleep. Jesus, Emma I was out of my fucking mind! I was there when you woke too but so was Turner." He hung his head. "I didn't want to interrupt."

She wanted to go to him then and there; understood his jealousy, unfounded though both of them knew it was. But she didn't. Though not much of a drinker, she poured herself a shot, her hand trembling slightly. She was going to need it.

"How are you, love?" He asked her, so gently she knew her heart would break.

She downed the shot. "Oh, tired, obviously. I've spent most of the afternoon sleeping." No word of a lie. After what happened in the woods, she could barely drag herself upstairs. Will had wanted to stay with her but that would have been all manner of a bad idea.

"What happened to you, Emma?"

"You know what happened. I had a miscarriage. Thank God you found me when you did. Robbie told me I nearly died."

"There's something you're not telling me, isn't there? When you came out of the anaesthetic you were raving. That's not a usual reaction to a miscarriage. You were traumatised, for Christ's sake!"

"Miscarriages *are* traumatic. I'm sorry you think I overreacted."

His eyes widened as a sudden flash of anger hit. "*What?* What the fuck's that supposed to mean? Look, I'm sorry I didn't join in with your reunion with Turner. I'm sorry I didn't answer your texts. I'm sorry I didn't bring you home. I wanted to *but I couldn't get away.*" Then his face softened. "I love you, Emma. I thought I'd lost you. You deserve more. You—" He moved towards her, obviously craving the closeness she craved too. She desperately wanted to be in his arms, but equally desperately...

...didn't.

He must have sensed her quandary. Resumed his position behind his glass, he took a sip from it. "Well, I'm glad you're better. How's Turner? Is he all better too?"

"Thank you for finding him, Westen. I ... you know how much I—"

"Missed him? Of course. I saw it with my own eyes, remember?"

"You're jealous," she said, trying a half-smile. "I get it. But you can't possibly think there's there's anything romantic between us. You don't do you?"

"No. I'm not stupid. After we—you—discovered Martin's body last year it was clear the man swings only one way."

"So ... what's the problem?"

"You know the problem."

"Do I?"

"Stop it! Stop, it, Emma. You're fucking breaking my heart. Five days. *Five days* you were out of it. Staring into space. Two minutes of William Turner in the room, and you're chatting away as if nothing had happened. Why him? Why not *me?*"

"I ... I can't say. I don't know. He means—"

"More to you than I do."

She fell silent. At least she might be spared one thing: maybe it would be him that ended it.

Instead of her.

"It was my baby too," he said quietly.

To her horror, Westen's eyes moistened. Glittered in the harsh light of the kitchen's halogens. And suddenly her heart melted as it suddenly and stupidly dawned on her that she hadn't really thought about the impact losing the baby had on him! How could she have been so selfish?

She couldn't help but move towards him now, despite her resolve not to. But he looked away, gulped at his drink. Her turn to be rebuffed. "It was too early on to know whether it was boy or a girl. I'd have wanted a girl. She'd have been like you."

He drained his glass as if drowning a sorrow "I'm so, so, sorry, Emma. For it all. The miscarriage, the trauma. It's all my fault. I should have had someone on your doorstep from the moment those fucking gouges appeared on the door."

"Of course, it wasn't your fault! I wouldn't let you, remember? And you were stretched. All those murders."

"Yes, well, at least we got the fucker. Though he had the final word."

"What do you mean?"

"My meeting with the ACC. It didn't go well. This first major case since I was promoted and it ended in a suicide. He says I need more time. He's more or less desked me. Put me on cold-cases. I'll be working out of Oakmarsh from now on. I'm hoping Pete might follow me there after he's recovered. It'll be less full-on. Poor bloke looks lost."

"Oh, Westen, I'm so sorry."

"Could've been worse. There was an opening in the Met. But London's not for me. A man can lose himself there," He took a long breath. "The ACC's left the door open. He's given me a year then maybe I can stage a comeback. Can't say I blame him. A death in custody is a big problem. Plus, we had the review team in. The evidence against Sweeting—that was the suspect—was circumstantial at best. We might not have got a conviction. They weren't happy."

Emma tried a grin. "A clusterfuck, then!"

He smiled back. "A fucking clusterfuck. Yeah."

They fell silent. She was waiting for more. He must have been, too. But it was as if they'd exhausted everything they had to say to each other.

"It's over, isn't it?" said Westen.

Eyes brimming, all Emma could manage was a little, tight nod.

He smiled. Reached out and took her hand. He cupped its palm against his lips and kissed it so tenderly it hurt.

Then left.

A few days later Emma was out of her cottage, on a walk through the village down to Wither Road. She was still reeling from Westen's visit. She could still feel his kiss—would always feel his kiss burning in her hand. She yearned for him to be back in her life but it would never work. Soured by lies, the relationship would never have lasted. And that wasn't fair to him. Wasn't fair to either of them.

He hadn't been in touch since he left. She hadn't expected him to be.

It was all made so much worse because Robbie had insisted she should take another week off work. It gave her far too much time to dwell, a situation made worse by the fact there'd been scant sign of Will. He'd told her a meeting with the bishop was imminent and that he intended to return to the retreat house to talk to Abbot John first.

Not sure what that was all about. He'd told her he'd pretty much made up his mind to stay in Flammark—thank God! But he'd seemed strangely reluctant to discuss getting back to his heritage work. She also wondered if Sandra's plans for the vicarage would go ahead. Abigail had told her Will hadn't thought it a wholly disastrous idea.

Sandra.

She was the real reason behind her walk. Emma had decided to return to the spot where the circle had stood. To pay her respects. She'd never liked the woman—and Sandra certainly returned the compliment—but she didn't deserve what happened to her. She had no idea how her disappearance had been explained. Will and Gabby had cut her completely out of the loop, saying she had to take Robbie's advice and heal.

She'd worked up quite a sweat, even more so as it was a mild, quite sunny day. February now. How she'd got through the last month, she'd never know!

Undoing the toggles on her duffel, Emma made her way through the now familiar gap in the trees and down the path that led to the clearing. As the way opened, she gasped in surprise to see snowdrops had burgeoned everywhere, swaying in the gentlest of breezes. Just then, a break in the cloud let through a ray of weak sunshine flooding the clearing with early Spring light. Such beauty! A total contrast to the barren landscape of only a week ago.

Breathing in the scene, she spied a kneeling figure at the far end of the clearing where Margaret's circle had been.

Will. Who else?

"Something must have told me you were going to be here," said Emma, as she came up behind him, noisily picking her way through the snowdrops so as not to startle him.

He got up. Blew out a huge sigh. "I can't get her out of my mind, Em." She's here and yet she isn't. Lost in a time and a space we can neither fathom or ever access. Hard to get your head round it."

"I know. I've been thinking about that too. So, what happened? How did you explain her disappearance?"

"Didn't have to. After we dropped you back at Clearview —you know, after Pete..." He dropped his eyes to the ground and kicked at the grass. "Anyway... Gabby called on Albert. Very distressed, poor bloke. He thought Sandra had simply just decided to up sticks and go without telling anyone. Didn't know what to do, whether to call the police, or what. So, Gabby told him to talk to Bish about it and see what he thought. I saw him today, actually. Albert did go to see him and told him how she'd gone out and returned one night in a hell of a state. She had a bad dose of the shakes, apparently, looking out of the window, jumping at nothing, that sort of thing. He wondered if she was having a nervous breakdown. She'd already refused point-blank return to the vicarage."

"Was that the night of her exorcism?"

"Yes, it would have been. Bish advised reporting her missing to the police, so the two of them did it there and then. Problem was, neither he or Albert could in all honesty deny she might have left of her own free will."

"So, the police did nothing." Emma grimaced. "Poor Sandra. Good for us, though."

"I know. Actually, it got a bit worse. Bish said her previous parish has no record of any family and since she started in Flammark she broke all contact with the clergy team there. Then it came out that she'd been unhappy there for quite some time. Apparently, they'd recommended her in the hope she might thrive better somewhere else but, to be honest, I'm not sure that's true. It sounded to me like ..."

"...they wanted get rid of her."

"Quite so."

"I don't think she'd made any friends here, either," said Emma. "Though she did make quite a few enemies."

"So I gathered." He kicked at a sod of earth. "I never met

her in life and it upsets me that I'm as much saddened with the tragedy of her passing as I am guilty about its convenience. We've been let off the hook. No one's going to know except us, and no one's going to ask awkward questions. It isn't right, Em. It isn't right."

He hitched his breath. "When Wyland comes back from the States, I'm going to ask him to lay another stone. Like ... like the one he laid for Peter."

Emma put her arms around him and rested her head on his shoulder. "You are a wonderful man, Will Turner. I'm so glad I have you back." She lifted her head. "You are staying, aren't you? How else did it go with the bishop?"

"Okay," he said. "At least, I think it went well." He took a breath. "I'll be coming back as priest-in-charge of St Jude's."

"That's great news! You decided then!"

"I have. But I won't be back full-time. I had a long chat with Solomon Barnes, you know, the chap that took over the heritage stuff? He's got a mind like a steel trap. I've always liked him. His archaeology is world-famous, you know."

"Yes," Emma chuckled. "I've been told." She took Will's arm and led him to a huge log. "Let's sit. Tell me everything."

Once settled, Will continued, fired with enthusiasm. "Solomon's to take over all the heritage work of the parish permanently—he's also going to help develop the conference facilities at the vicarage. I want to take back the residential retreats and Bish is more than happy to let me. Seems their absence has been noticed. Though not just yet. He says I still need more time, and I think he's right. No point in rushing things. I'm still not over what happened to Peter." He bowed his head and fingered the pin on his coat. "Never will be, I expect."

"Okay. Good. So, no youth ministry?"

"Not on your life. It's wonderful work, don't get me

wrong. But I'm just not cut out for it. To be honest, I don't really think Sandra was, either."

Emma stared at the spot between the two oaks. "No. I'm not sure Sandra was cut out even to be a priest and certainly not a vicar." She gave her head a quick shake, "So the plans for the vicarage won't be going ahead, then?"

"No, they're not. Solomon will need somewhere to stay during the conference season and rooms need to be available for when the residentials start up again. And … I have news!'"

"*More* news? I can hardly bear it!" she chortled.

"Bish has given me leave to study. There's a Masters course at Lanchester Uni I'm interested in. Two evenings a week plus the odd day here and there."

"Study! Will, I had no idea that's what you wanted!"

"Nor did I until I talked with Solomon—and Abbot John, of course. I'm telling you, Em, there's no end to what Solomon knows. We spent an entire day looking over his work—it's archived and available to the public in the cathedral library. Then it all sort of came together. I'm going to study Celto-Christian history." He pulled a face at the mouthful. "Solomon's putting in a word for me. He's sure I'll get offered a place even though it's been an age since I've done any serious study. Bish thinks it an excellent idea. I'm self-funding—I've got quite a bit put away, so there'd be no cost to the church. But there is a catch…"

"Uh-oh."

"I'm to have a curate."

"Okay… Why is that a catch? Sounds like a good idea to me."

"I've worked with a curate before and it didn't go well. Long story—I'll tell you it some time, but not now. Suffice it to say, I've never wanted a repeat performance. But, I can't be a full-time vicar as well as being a student and there's the residentials and the mentoring of course, so ..."

"So we'll have someone new to hide everything from."

"Absolutely! Great, isn't it!?"

They laughed and Will shivered. "Is it me or is it getting chillier?"

The temperature had definitely dropped. Though the clouds had pretty much cleared, the breeze had strengthened.

They got up and by common consent, strolled back to where the circle had been.

"She'll be okay, won't she, Em?" whispered Will.

"I'm sure she will. You can perform some kind of ceremony when Wyland lays the stone. Put her to rest properly. Seems he's done of lot of that lately."

"Sure has. But, yes. A ceremony is a splendid idea. But I'll always feel guilty about her. That we never brought her back through."

"Yes. I feel it too."

"I went to see Pete Burrows, you know."

"You did? I planned to pay him a visit but I didn't know what to say or how to act. And since breaking up with Westen—"

"—you didn't want to bump into him?"

"Sounds a bit shallow, but yes. How is Pete?"

"Well, the good news is his hearing is much improved. Still not perfect but it's a start. He may get it all back, in time."

"Good. That's a relief."

"It is," Will shivered. "Come on. Let's walk back. I didn't bring my car, and I'm starving. I'll treat you to lunch at the Flammark Arms."

"Okay, deal."

They set off, arm in arm. "So, you were saying about

Pete…" Emma said. "Did he mention anything else about, you know, about seeing Margaret."

"Yes. It was one of the reasons why I visited. It's the kind of thing that can affect a man."

"Of course. And it's completely the reason why Westen and I couldn't carry on. If he knew about the real Flammark, it would change everything. Change him."

Will thrust his hands deeper into his jacket pockets. "We should talk about that one day, Em. I'm not sure that's right. You and Westen were perfect together. But it certainly all went wrong for Pete. He's not going back, you know."

Emma stopped in her tracks. "Not going back? What, to his job?"

"He's giving it all up. Says he hasn't the heart. Seeing that 'thing' as he called it, changed everything. He's already resigned from the force."

"Oh, no! Poor Pete! Westen'll be really upset to lose him! He was hoping he'd follow him to Oakmarsh." They started walking again. "No. Strike that. He'll be furious to lose him."

"Yes. He put his fist to the wall, apparently. Pete said he'd never seen him so angry. I expect it wasn't just because his sergeant was leaving him, though." Will gave her a sideways glance. "Was it?"

"Probably not." She gave a deep sigh. "Thinking about it now, I didn't really give Westen the time to talk it all through. You know, what happened to me and all that. He felt the miscarriage badly. I … I hadn't realised."

"Give him time, Em, he'll come round. You both will."

"Will we? I don't think so. What happened hit us both too badly. Anyway, I couldn't bear the lies and having to keep things from him. Gabby said it would be our undoing in the end and she was right."

He gave her arm a squeeze. "So, no Westen and no

Burrows, eh? We're doubly bereft. Pete's a good man. They worked well with each other. I'll miss them both."

"So will I. I still love Westen and I think I always will. I only hope I've done the right thing."

"Well, he's only in Oakmarsh. Plenty of opportunity to see him again should you have a change of heart."

Emma shrugged. Didn't reply.

"And you? You're staying, then? For sure?" asked Will. "I know you've had your doubts."

"I can never leave this place, Will. I don't know why, but I can't."

"I don't think I'd let you, if I'm honest," he replied. "And I don't think we've seen the last of what Flammark has in store. It was a quiet parish before you came, except for the curse, of course, but even that was linked to you. Then the business with that monster and … Peter." His hand found the white daisy again. "And now Margaret."

"What is it about me? Am I attracting all this in some way?"

"Dunno, but it's an intriguing question. I don't know what it is about you Blackstones, but there's a circularity about all this which is undeniable." He stopped. Digging into his pocket, he took out Margaret's pendant. "Talking of circularity, I wanted to give you time to recover before I gave you this."

Eyes widening, she took it from him. "*This* is what made the circle work? A *second* pendant?"

"Yep. We told you that Margaret scattered her remains on the floor of the sanctuary after the exorcism. She marked where she'd left you with this. And it was also the key that let us through. Gabby worked that last bit out."

Emma held it in her hand. Couldn't keep her eyes off it; an exact replica of another key, the one she used to open the box to capture the spirit that had possessed Ben. Taking off a glove she ran a finger over its familiar lines—and its setting, of course, that had fitted so exactly into the little black box that trapped Ben's tormentor.

"What are you going to do with it? Sling it?" asked Will.

"No. I'm a Blackstone. Abigail told me what Margaret said to her ... you know ... that she won't be able to have children. Poor Abigail. She's trying to come to terms with it though I think she's finding it hard. But it does mean we are the end of our line. Completely. It's ... it's a big weight to bear, actually."

Emma gave the necklace back to Will and turned so could he fix it around her neck. "Besides," she said. "This is the second time a pendant like this has proved useful. I don't expect it will be the last." She reached up and patted it. "Funny, it feels good to have it back. Sort of."

She gave a wan smile and they started walking again. As they made the turn onto Wither road, she slipped her arm through his once more.

"D'you know," she said. "I'm really starving too. Fancy some fish and chips?"

ACKNOWLEDGMENTS

Thanks as ever to Noel, my grammarian friend and now sole editor of my books. (The only person I trust to guide me through my very odd sentence structures.)

To *Pamela is Dead,* the fabulous Instagram account that became my inspiration for Margaret.

To my girls for their endless support through some pretty tough times this year and also to the growing number of series fans and followers who've given me so much amazing encouragement in bringing The Witch home.

What a monster! (Or was she???)

WHAT NEXT FOR THE CHARACTERS?

The good news is, there *will* be another installment! A second (and final) three-book season is planned which will at last get to the bottom of what really troubles the village of Flammark. So, new adventures—new horrors—and, of course, some different characters to get to know!

In the coming weeks, an omnibus edition of the series will be published and also a Kickstarter campaign is planned to raise funds for a quality audio-book narrator.

My Newsletter contains progress updates and release dates, as well as other stories, character info and village background. I'd love it if you'd head over to my website to sign up!

https://pjmordant.co.uk

Alternatively, ebook readers can click my Linktree.

I also have a very active author page on Facebook (Author Polly Mordant) and another page dedicated to the series (search for Friends of Flammark.)

Thank you SO MUCH for reading The Witch. To have got here means you read both *When Angels Fear* and *Animus* too - so great that you kept with me! Please consider leaving a review on Goodreads and/or Amazon.

Supporting authors in this way really gives us the social proof we need to help spread the word about the quality of our work.

MORE GOTHIC HORROR FROM SIGILHOUSE

If you're enjoying the Flammark Series you might like to try this standalone supernatural thriller by Guy Cross.

A stormy night; a hit and run and Stephen Porter unleashes a train of

events that delivers him—and his family—into the clutches of a terrifying dark magician.

Gregory Rook ...

... whose magic works through the medium of blood - and the innocence of children.

Stealer of souls, shapeshifter devil, how can he be defeated?

The answer lies in the memories of a teenage boy who has no idea they form the key to getting rid of Rook forever.

The question is, will he realize in time?

The Memories In Blood is available from Amazon.

ISBN: 9781838199920

Printed in Great Britain
by Amazon

37205624R00205